STUNTS

Charles L. Grant

STUNTS

TOR
HORROR

A TOM DOHERTY ASSOCIATES BOOK
NEW YORK

STUNTS
Copyright © 1990 by Charles L. Grant
All rights reserved, including the right to reproduce this book, or portions thereof, in any form.

A Tor Book
Published by Tom Doherty Associates, Inc.
49 West 24th Street
New York, N.Y. 10010

Printed in the United States of America

Library of Congress Cataloging-in-Publication Data

Grant, Charles L.
    Stunts / Charles L. Grant.
        p.   cm.
    ISBN 0-312-85013-1
    I. Title.
    PS3557.R265S7   1990
    813'.54—dc20
                                      90-38890
                                        CIP

First edition: November 1990

0 9 8 7 6 5 4 3 2 1

For Nancy H., the San Diego Dudette.
Thanks aren't enough, Bim;
maybe this will, in a small way, acknowledge the debts.

|

BETTIN

WELLS

One

Bettin Wells on the Plain, too large to be a true village, too small to be a small town. Its High Street, whose cobblestones had long since been paved over and forgotten, became at both ends a narrow road that twisted through hedgerow and woodland, low hills and farmland before linking itself to the motorway that soon crept into Salisbury. The shops and offices were Georgian stone and Tudor half-timber and a few dark-glass faces set in contemporary concrete; three pubs, a handful of restaurants, newsagents, a bookmaker, one small hotel that had catered to lost or wandering travelers since the time of Queen Anne, and another that had been struggling since the end of the Great War, patiently waiting for either the explosion or the end. There were no trains, a three-times-a-day bus, and in season a few high-riding coaches that brought in bewildered tourists who wanted to see something no regular tour provided.

Bettin Wells; which the vicar believed was a corruption of vulgar Latin, basing his loud pompous claim on the occasional coins and bones uncovered in pastures and basements, and on the fenced-around-segment of crumbling mossy Roman wall that backed the churchyard; the librarian, who thought the vicar a proper ass and not to be trusted, was positive that "Bettin" was a corruption of "betting" somehow; and no one had a clue where the "wells" could have been.

It didn't matter; no one cared; it was just something to talk about when all the talking was done and there was nothing left to listen to but the wind that coasted the hills and grass of the Plain.

There was always the wind.

Bettin Wells.

In October.

A low and weeping slate sky.

Two

1

Momma, don't let your babies grow up to be dreamers, Evan sang silently; don't let 'em get pissed when their bosses get . . . when their bosses get . . . something.

"Oh lord," he said with a crooked grin, "it's getting thick in here, pal. You're losing your touch."

He stood at the living-room window, briar pipe in his mouth, hands in his pockets. The late afternoon light was grey, the narrow panes stippled with droplets, and with half-closed eyes he could sense the way shadows played over his face as the clouds played with the sun.

It was a pose, he knew it, the pipe wasn't even lit, but there was little chance of anyone passing the cottage and seeing him standing there. A shame. With the open-necked white shirt and dark sweater, long wavy hair and rather prominent chin, he suspected he made a fairly decent, fairly recognizable Heathcliff-like figure. Too bad he wasn't on the moors; it would have played better.

He also would have been so embarrassed at being caught, he probably would have shrunk to the size of a pea. And a pretty puny one at that.

"Oh, you're a brave man, Evan Kendal," he said to the faint, wavering reflection superimposed over the front yard. "Especially when you're alone, and isn't that a fact."

He laughed at himself. A frustrated actor-turned-teacher who took to amateur theatrics in the privacy of his home. After thirty minutes of Tennessee Williams or William Shakespeare, with a dash of Marlowe thrown in to spice the evening's entertainment, applause filled the hallways, rained down from the upper story, had him taking modest bows, grandiose bows, terribly correct bows wherever he stood.

Not quite a sham, not quite the truth.

It was no worse, or sillier, he supposed, than those who pulled down the shades, cranked up the stereo, and proceeded to conduct Beethoven or Tchaikovsky with more vigor and passion than they ever showed in their daily employment. Or rode at top speed in their cars, slid a cassette into the deck, and bellowed country laments at the top of their voices to the ten thousand female fans eager to shed their tears and clothes. He had done it himself, many times, and more often than not ended up giggling hysterically on the floor or pulling over to the shoulder until his control returned.

Acting, on the other hand, though often essential in the classroom, was something he knew he came dangerously close to bringing to the outside world.

The world he had to live in when he wasn't living alone.

momma, don't let your babies

"Oh for god's sake, Evan," he whispered, "let's not start that again."

He took the pipe from his lips and peered into the empty bowl, laid it carefully on the table in front of the window and turned to cross the room, heading for the

6

kitchen entrance and the kettle that had started a sputtering shrill whistling while he'd stumbled over a rhyme for "pissed." By the time he reached it, he was once again amazed at the size of the place.

The living room was at least fifteen feet square, with a modest stone fireplace, two couches and two wing chairs arranged about the raised hearth, a walnut-framed oil of a stag on a hill over the mantel. On the left-hand wall, between the arched entrance to the front hall and the smaller one to the kitchen there was a carved oak sideboard and glass-fronted long bookcase. The ceiling beams were exposed, and on the tables by the couches and flanking the large rear window were brass lamps with shades he suspected Queen Victoria would have loved.

On the other side of the entry was the dining room, not quite as large; and upstairs were two large bedrooms, each with its own bath.

A cottage indeed. At home in Port Richmond, New Jersey, or almost anywhere else in the States, for that matter, a cottage would have meant a building half this size and nine times the rent; but it was just one more thing he supposed he'd never really get used to on this side of the pond.

Five months in Bettin Wells, on the Salisbury Plain, and he still sometimes felt as if he were a stranger. Not because of the way the villagers treated him—which wasn't badly at all, all things considered—or the way his mind would wander at odd moments and give him unexpected trouble with the coinage. It was the language. A common ground of English that, discounting the local vernacular, sometimes felt as if it were shifting beneath his feet, like tides of dry sand. The words were the same, but the delivery altered them in ways he didn't think he'd ever understand.

"Comin' down to the Hart for a pint then, Evan?"

7

wasn't a question, it was an invitation that had to be examined forty ways from Sunday before he said either yea or nay, hoping that his answer wouldn't bring offense.

It was tricky.

He'd embarrassed himself a hundred times over since he'd stepped off the plane, but he was determined to get it all right before he had to leave.

Acting; it was, in the end, all acting.

The tea was too hot; he burned his tongue sipping, and cursed loudly, strongly, until he began to chuckle. Then he sat at the kitchen table and held the cup in both hands, looking out the back door to the small yard cluttered with shrubs and vines, and the ancient brick wall at the back beyond which he could see the hillocks and rises, the silhouettes of the Plain.

Dampness seeped under the door. The wind gusted now and then to rattle the panes. The beech on the far side of the Tudor-style cottage scratched earnestly at the roof, sending echoes through the rooms, making the fire seem too small.

A look at his watch, and his fingers drummed on the table.

momma, don't

Another look at his watch.

Paul and Addie were late. Again. It was getting to be a habit, one he couldn't understand.

He sipped.

The wind blew.

And suddenly, in less time than a blink, the world fell dark.

"Hey," he said.

Heavy clouds took away the last light and turned the windows black; rain shotgunned against the panes and made him jump, then lower his cup slowly; the power failed, dousing the lamp and the fire and leaving him blind until his vision adjusted and all he could see were shapes and shadows and something moving outside.

The cold deepened to winter.

His teeth began to chatter until he was able to clench his jaws.

"Hey," he whispered and pushed back his chair. Stood. Stared at the door and watched the knob begin to turn.

A thump on the back stoop.

Gliding his hand against the table to guide him, he backed toward the living room. Straining through the gloom, trying to see through the patterned curtains that covered the back door's top half.

Whoever was out there pushed then, and the hinges creaked, pushed again and turned the knob quickly side to side.

"Who is it?" he called out.

What had happened to the electricity?

The tap, a gentle tap, of a knuckle against the glass.

"Who is it?" he demanded. "Whatever it is, I don't want any."

Tap.

Rain sluicing out of the gutters to splash against the outer walls.

Tap.

The wind found a voice in the throat of the chimney.

Dark; something dark.

Then he sagged against the refrigerator and called himself ten times the fool. Paul, or Addie, or both, that's who it is. He'd been daydreaming, and they hadn't been able to rouse him at the front door, so had come around the back and were getting him back for leaving them out in the storm.

"All-right," he said.

Tap.

9

"All right, give me a break, okay? It's dark in here."

He knocked against the table and turned away with a start, his elbows sweeping a glass from the counter into the sink. It didn't break, but he jumped as if it had and cursed loudly enough for his friends to hear him.

Tap.

The cold.

He rubbed his palms together and took hold of the knob. Said, "Jesus Christ!" when the cold nearly burned his fingers.

Someone knocked on the front door.

The wind.

A dark figure standing on the other side of the curtain.

"Well, let go, for crying out loud," he called when the knob wouldn't turn. "C'mon, Paul, let go and I'll let you in."

Someone knocked on the front door.

"Oh, for Christ's . . ."

The dark figure, waiting, and the knob wouldn't turn.

"The hell with you then," he muttered, and hurried out of the room, banged his shoulder against the jamb and rolled his eyes toward the ceiling. This was not going to be a good day, he decided, stumbling through the front room, nearly tripping over a footstool and grabbing at the sideboard to keep from falling, yanking his hands away when the glasses there trembled and threatened to fall.

A pounding on the door, and he could hear someone calling.

"All right, all right!"

Tap.

As clear as if he were still standing in the kitchen.

He yanked open the door and stood back against the rain that pushed Addie Burwin inside and caused her to stumble into his arms.

"My *god*," she exclaimed, looking up into his face. "Where the hell were you? I would have drowned out there in another minute."

The lights snapped on.

Evan blinked and shaded his eyes, smiled tightly at the woman and ran back to the kitchen.

The knob turned.

The back stoop was empty.

"Nice to see you too," Addie called from the hallway. "Did you leave the kettle on? Or are you hiding the evidence?"

He heard her shake out her raincoat, heard her footsteps cross the bare flooring.

"Evan?"

He looked over his shoulder. "Sorry. I wanted to let Paul in."

"Paul? You mean husband Paul? Good heavens, he isn't here. Didn't you get the message on that ridiculous machine of yours? I've come alone." She hurried to his side and pushed the door shut. "That's the trouble with you Yanks, you know." She took his arm and brought him to the table. "You have all these marvelous little gadgets, and you never use them. It's a puzzle, really it is. I don't think I'll ever understand it. Here, that must be cold, let me heat the water again."

She took the cup from his hand before he even realized he'd taken it up, and he watched as she bustled about the kitchen, opening cupboards, finding saucers and a cup for herself, an open tin of shortbread biscuits, a handful of paper napkins she plopped in the table's center.

He said nothing.

The wind.

She wore a snug print dress under a worn green cardigan, and her hair, gently fine and sable, was lashed into a ponytail. Though she was considerably shorter than both he and her professor husband, he could think of several times when, for just a moment, he felt as if he were looking up at her instead of at the top of her head.

He glanced at the door.

The shower seemed to have ended though the clouds remained thick, and the light hadn't returned.

When her back was turned, he blew out softly, inexplicably puzzled because he couldn't see his breath.

Brother, he thought, and forced himself to shudder, hoping to drive away whatever he'd felt before.

Someone—

"There," she said, and took the chair opposite, pushing a saucer with refilled cup toward him. "Drink up, Evan, and put a fire in your gut. Doctor's orders." She winked broadly. "That's me, remember?"

He did, and didn't understand why she kept staring at him until he saw his hands—they were shaking.

"Sorry," he said, and set the cup down.

She pushed a wisp of hair from her temple. "Did I frighten you, Evan?"

"Lord, no," he protested, leaning back as he took what he hoped was an unseen deep breath. "There was someone at the back just as the electricity went out."

"And you thought it was Paul."

He nodded.

"Well, there's no one there now, is there?"

"No one that I could see. It must have been the wind or something. With the electric going out and all, I guess I must have . . ." A sheepish look. "You know."

It was her turn to nod, and she did it decisively. "It's

12

the Plain, you know." She looked into her cup, blew away a banner of steam. "It does that to some people."

He understood. He had seen it himself often enough among visitors, and even a few of the locals on occasion. The wind's constant soughing, the current of the grasses, the way the sky looked at dusk and winter's dawn; a sensation more than a feeling, a fleeting certain knowledge that, if you looked just the slightest bit sideways, you'd be able to see what a cat sees when he stares at the corner or up at the ceiling.

It had nothing to do with Stonehenge.

It was the Plain.

Suddenly he laughed and shook his head, and when Addie looked him a question, he shook it again. "Nothing," he said. "I was just thinking about . . . here, and what my Uncle John would say if he could hear me."

"Ah, the infamous Uncle John." She smiled, setting dimples to her cheeks that, as she aged, looked less and less cute, more and more seductive. "I really must meet this mythic figure someday."

"All you have to do is run away with me," he said with a wink. "I'm sure he'd love you."

"And what about Paul?"

"Why should I run away with Paul?"

She laughed, and he followed, and neither looked at the other for several seconds, until he asked her at last why her husband hadn't come.

"Well," she began, "if you'd listen to that damned thing in the living room, my dear, you'd—"

"You said that already," he reminded her.

"Right. So I did." From her sweater pocket she pulled a pack of cigarettes, lit one, and blew the smoke toward the ceiling light. "He's off on another one of his research jaunts, yes? I got a call just a bit ago, and he tells me he doesn't know when he'll be home, he's not feeling well."

He waited, trying not to watch her too carefully to see if it was only an excuse. But her wide eyes, normally steady, disconcertingly so, shifted side to side, up and down, as if she couldn't decide what to look at besides him.

"Is it bad?"

"No. That is . . . I don't know, Evan. That's why I came over. I need to ask you a favor."

"Ask away," he said expansively. "I owe you both one or two after all this time and all you've done."

She blew smoke again at the light, and ran a trembling hand around the back of her neck. He said nothing. He couldn't think of anything. But he had never seen her like this; generally, when she was worried or upset, she talked ten to the dozen and never let anyone get a word in edgewise. Sooner or later she'd come to the problem, but always in her own good time. It was frustrating, but he'd known them both long enough to at least have some patience.

This was different.

"Addie," he prompted softly.

She dropped the cigarette into her tea. "Evan, I think he's dying." Her hand fluttered. "Or rather, I think *he* thinks he is. I'm not sure which."

"What?"

"Oh, the fool doesn't say anything, but I know." She poked her chest with a finger. "I know. He's been down to London too many times in the past few months, more than he ever does. Now he's been gone for five days— no, nearly a week. And it isn't to work, I know that; he has no research to do no matter what he says, no candidate interviews, not now, this time of year. No; it's doctors, I'm sure of it. He won't come to me, I'm only his wife, he's never let me treat him for more than a bloody cold." A pause. "He's got something, Evan. He's got something."

14

He waited for the tears, but they didn't come. She only lit another cigarette and tried to blow smoke rings.

And he felt like an idiot because he didn't know what to say. He'd met Paul Burwin eight years ago, visiting a colleague in Port Richmond while he guest-lectured at NYU. Evan had been invited to a cocktail party, was introduced to Paul as a fellow history nut, and for a reason neither of them had been able to explain, they'd become virtually instant friends. When Paul married Addie three years after, Evan had flown over for the wedding, to be Paul's best man.

Now Addie claimed he was dying, and Paul hadn't said a word, hadn't dropped a hint.

It almost made him angry.

"Have you talked to him? I mean, actually asked him what was wrong?"

She laughed, blowing smoke. "Are you kidding? Talk to Paul?"

He shrugged without moving.

"He is, my husband, the original Sphinx. My god! On his deathbed, you know, if I asked him if something was the matter, he'd say, 'My dearest Adelaide, whatever makes you think I'm troubled by something?'" She crushed her cigarette out in a saucer ashtray. "The bastard."

He smiled. She smiled back, mirthlessly, helplessly, and he reached across the table to cover her hand.

"He's going to die," she said softly, "and he isn't going to tell me."

Three

Going to die? Paul?
Nonsense.
But he held her.

It was perfectly natural, nothing erotic or illicit; they stood beside the table and one hand stroked her back gently while she muttered into his chest and rubbed her forehead against his sweater.

And the moment they came together, he thought of a dozen other reasons why Paul, who had never behaved like this before to his knowledge, wasn't home—it really was work, he was researching one of his pet secret projects that would soon turn into another book, and she was worrying unnecessarily; the train had broken down; it was another woman, a mistress; wildcat strikes, traffic jams, weariness . . .

Dying?

Not Paul.

Surely not Paul. They were nearly the same age, and no one his age died, it wasn't done.

"Listen," he said to the top of her head, "tell you what we'll do—we'll get something to eat, okay? At the Cross and Sword. He's not home by the time we're done, we'll grab a late train in."

"In where?" she said, raising her face. "I don't know where he is."

He frowned. "A point." He closed one eye. "How about I take out an ad in the *Sun*?"

Her lips twitched. "Evan, I certainly hope he'll be back by then."

He tried to remain solemn. "Okay, then, suppose— it's like waiting for a taxi, you know what I mean? You've been waiting for hours, so you light the most expensive cigarette you have, and one comes along, the driver makes you put it out. Like taking a bath to make the telephone ring." He held her away. "So what we'll do is, we'll go into the front room, take off our clothes, and Paul, with my luck, will waltz through the front door."

He grinned.

She was skeptical. "What if he doesn't?"

"Then I freeze my ass off."

Immediately he said it, he knew it was wrong. He could see it in the way her eyes narrowed just a little, and in the set of her mouth, which had almost given him a smile.

It startled him.

My god, he thought, she wants to?

The telephone rang.

He let his hands slip away from her waist and down to his sides as he shrugged a *see what I mean?* and hurried to the living room. The telephone sat on an end table by the couch nearest the front window. He dropped onto a cushion, lifted the receiver, and listened for a moment.

"Addie! It's for you!" At her expression when she left the kitchen, he added, "Sorry, it's not Paul."

He stood then and walked to the window, watched the clouds tear themselves apart to let the last of the sun turn the last of the rain to diamonds. She didn't want to, you know, he told himself; she's Paul's wife, remember? You

17

read it wrong. You read her wrong. She didn't. She's Addie.

He turned when she rang off.

"There's been an accident," she explained, hastening to the foyer to grab her raincoat from the coat rack. "Drunken fool clipped a kid on a bike." She shook her head in anger. "Hit-and-run."

"You've no one covering for you?" he asked as he opened the door. The air was warm, sunbright, still.

"Evan," she said, "all I did was come out to have a quick talk. How was I to know the world would fall apart while I was gone?" At the threshold, she squinted up at the sky. "Besides, business isn't all that good anyway." An apologetic smile. "I'm off. That offer still good?"

He hesitated. "The meal."

She grinned, and slapped his shoulder. "The meal, you great idiot, yes. Seven. At the Cross and Sword. You can hold my hand while I stuff myself and curse my husband." A grateful kiss to his cheek. "Ta, Evan. Don't forget to put on that damned machine."

He leaned against the frame and watched her swing onto her bicycle, give a wave, and pedal off, almost instantly taken from him by the hedging that fronted the yard. The nearest house was a hundred yards down the lane, Bettin Wells itself another mile farther on. He took a quick step to the stoop then, thinking he should have offered her a lift, and scowling when he realized it was too late.

Something's up, man, he told himself; something's up there.

Although Paul was a professor loosely attached to London University, he had spent most of the last three years involved in more administrative functions. Which meant he was out of town quite a bit. Which meant that Addie was often too much alone. And Addie being Ad-

18

die, she refused to let that prevent her from enjoying both her practice and her life. So there were dinners, a movie or so every month—friends that happened to be a man and a woman.

The telephone rang.

He had never even considered the possibility that it might turn into something more.

"Ridiculous," he muttered.

The telephone rang.

He checked the sky again, took a long breath, and returned inside, leaving the door open to air the place out. He hoped the police would catch the man; he also hoped they wouldn't let Addie Burwin near the son of a bitch. Old age and birth, the usual run of childhood and adolescent ailments, the scraped knee, the bruised shin, the thumb whacked with a hammer—those things she could cope with. It was what she often called the "lightning bolt" that she hated most about her profession. The no-reason-at-all accident or death.

Like a hit-and-run driver.

The telephone rang.

He snatched up the receiver, said, "Two-nine-eight-eight," and grinned broadly at the fireplace as he slumped onto the couch. "Shirley m'dear, how the hell are you?" A check of the clock on the mantel. "Lord, it's only eleven back there. You on a break or what?"

Shirley Atkins, her voice as clear as if she were shouting at him from the staircase, laughingly told him she was indeed on break, they'd been hanging around the faculty lounge bitching and moaning and generally having a good time, thought about him, and decided to call and ruin his day.

"We've got tons of quarters," she said with a laugh. "What's new?"

"Same as always." He stretched his legs out, rested his

19

head on the couch's padded back. "Paul couldn't get me the position at London University, I told you about that, but he's scrounging me the occasional lecture now and then. I don't mind. I get to travel. Like, this Friday I'm off to Edinburgh, bore the little Scottish beggars to tears about one thing or another. To tell the truth, I think I'm a curiosity more than anything. But what the hell."

Right, he thought; what the hell.

"So, how's the prison?"

"Same as always," she echoed. A voice called something in the background. "They want to know if you'll come back and shoot the bastard. We're getting up a collection." A muttering, some laughter. "We can give you about four bucks. You pay your own airfare."

He grinned. "Would that I could. The fact is, I'd do it for nothing."

And he would. Given half the chance, and a gun, he believed he really would shoot Eric Linholm square between the eyes. The principal of Port Richmond High was the reason he was now living in England, talking to a woman once a history department companion, now a voice in the air.

The grin faded.

Part of the reason.

Laughter in his ear.

A glance at the *Evening Standard* lying on the cushion beside him reminded him: "What's the rumor mill say about stunts this year?"

Halloween stunts. Every class had an unofficial committee, every committee unofficially charged by several decades of tradition to be imaginative without being destructive. Trick without treating the school, or the teachers, or the principal, without hurting feelings. Unless you couldn't take a joke.

"Funny you should ask," she answered seriously,

"and you're not going to believe it. We had an assembly this morning. Command performance, don't you know. The principal you know and love gave a long speech about being true to your school, keeping them grades up, tote them bales, lift those barges, then officially banned them. The stunts, not the bales and barges."

He almost sat up. "Son of a bitch, no kidding?"

"That's it."

"But he can't do that, for god's sake. Good god, what's Halloween in the Port without stunts?"

"I think," she answered, "he's still ticked because of what they did to his precious car last year."

He picked up the folded newspaper and slapped his knee with it angrily. "For god's sake, soap comes off, doesn't he know that?"

"It was raining, Evan, remember?" But she giggled.

How could he forget? Two years ago, the senior class had wrapped his own car in orange and black crepe paper. It had been raining then, too. By the time he'd left the building, most of the crepe paper had turned to mush. It had been like peeling off papier-mâché, and he'd gotten thoroughly drenched in the process.

He smiled at the memory. "Well, I hope they pay no attention to him. I hope they stuff his office full of pumpkins. I hope they spray-paint his damned lawn in purple. I hope—"

"—his mistress gets the clap."

His eyes widened. "He has a mistress? Linholm has a mistress?"

"That's what I hear," she said.

"Who? Eva Braun?"

"Who knows? Who cares?" An unintelligible musical chorus broke out in the room, boisterous and off-key. By the time it ended, Shirley had the hiccups. She begged him a minute, covered the mouthpiece, and re-

21

turned with: "Lyanna wants to know if you're getting any."

Her tone was near to plaintive, near to warning: another part of the reason.

He ignored it.

"That woman is a disgrace to her profession. Tell her to clean up her act or I'll drop an anonymous note to your landlady about the orgies you guys are having on the second floor."

"Don't have to," Shirley said. "She caters them."

That too he believed. Neeba Oakland was an elderly woman who refused, on principle, to conform to expectations of age and propriety; contradiction, it seemed to Evan, was her religious foundation.

"How's John?"

A faint buzzing on the line forced him to repeat the question.

"Okay," Shirley answered at last. "I guess, anyway. I haven't seen him much lately. He's been kind of keeping to himself the past few days."

He frowned. "He's all right?"

"Sure. Neeba would have said otherwise."

"You sure?"

"Evan, c'mon."

Call, he reminded himself; it's been three weeks. Forget the letters, and call. John Naze was the only relative he had left. To lose him through inattention would be criminal, would be a damned sin.

They spoke for another five minutes, Shirley relaying messages and comments from his former colleagues, Evan responding as succinctly as he could so not to waste the time and their money. And when it was done, goodbyes and promises to call again made, he cradled the receiver and folded his hands across his stomach.

The power failure and adventure with the back door

were forgotten. Calls from his friends always did that to him—gave him a sentimental good feeling, which generally led to a brief bout of homesickness, then anger at his having been driven away from his home, then a little honesty that told him he hadn't been driven, he had run.

"Right," he whispered, tossed the newspaper aside, and stood up. Time he got ready for his date with Addie.

The door slammed shut.

"What the hell?" he said.

And the lights went out again.

Four

1

"Damned wind," he said, glad his voice didn't sound as shaky as he felt. An exasperated glance at the nearest lamp, a quickly composed letter of complaint about the Power Board to the local newspaper, and he felt his way toward the staircase, tugged at the door, and locked it without really knowing why.

Then, head cocked, he listened.

"Hello?"

No answer; he went to the kitchen where he grabbed the knob and turned it.

The door wouldn't open.

He yanked, and the door snapped sharply in, nearly knocking him off his feet. In the yard the trees were gaps bitten out of the sky.

That's what it was, he decided as he closed the door again, firmly; no one was out there, it was a tree shadow he'd seen, and the door had only stuck. Add a drop of imagination . . .

He locked it and returned to the stairs.

Halfway up, he paused.

"Hello?"

Nothing; he had heard nothing, no one had gotten into the cottage, no one was waiting in the shadows to lop his head off, and if he didn't get a move on, he was going to be late.

Dinner; nothing more.

It meant nothing more than that.

By candlelight he showered quickly, dressed quickly and clumsily, and the moment he took his close-to-frayed peacoat off the foyer rack, the lights buzzed back on. At the same time, the wind went on a tear around the house, severely testing the eaves, the walls, the panes, the roof. When it was done, the silence left behind almost as loud, he blew out a shuddering breath, snapped up his collar, and hurried out to his car, parked in a small garage around to the left.

The sky was dark, no stars but no rain; the scent of wet leaves and wet grass, mud and wet tarmac; the feel of midnight yet to come.

Though his imagination recommended he waste no time getting to the Cross and Sword, he nevertheless took the narrow lane cautiously. Sodden leaves and wind-blown twigs made the surface slick, and the high hedgerows on either side seemed more like brick walls. The engine whined, the steering was stiff, and by the time he broke onto the main road and was able to pick up speed, the promise of a headache had already been made behind his eyes.

Swell, he thought sourly, rubbing his temple hard with a thumb; you're going to be great company tonight, I can see that. And you'll probably have to park halfway to damn London.

Luck, however, found him a space in the narrow parking lot beside the High Street pub, and inside, Addie was already at a tiny corner table, a mug before her, and a plate of steaming cottage pie. She was tucked into the corner itself and she waved; he smiled as he threaded his way through the midweek crowd that had already begun to fill the small place up.

He sat opposite her with an exaggerated puff and grin, unbuttoned his coat, dropped his collar, and cheerfully blessed a no-nonsense waitress who set dinner—the same as Addie's—and a pint of bitter in front of him.

Addie had ordered for him, for which he was grateful, but as he picked up his fork and smacked his lips, he noted that she had already finished half her meal; he also saw the lines at the corners of her eyes. He ate, he drank, he ate again and said, "You lost him, huh?"

She nodded. "Before the poor devil got to hospital." Her hand slipped around the glass mug barely touched. "Jamie Lauder. You know him?"

"Ah damn." He did. Not well, and not for long. A heavily freckled stick of a boy who swept out the chemist's and ran errands for the greengrocer. He wasn't capable of much else. Lived with his parents on the far side of town. Sullen. Always squinting suspiciously at people who greeted him. As Evan did each day.

"And the guy who hit him?"

She did give him a smile then, but it wasn't a pleasant one. "They found him in Salisbury, ten sheets to the wind, trying to take down the cathedral."

"What'll happen to him?"

"He'll burn in hell, that's what," a fluted voice said cheerfully over his shoulder.

He didn't look up. The expression on Addie's face, and a breeze of potent mint aftershave that churned his stomach, identified the man instantly. "That's not what I meant, Vicar," he said, and took a mouthful of his dinner.

"Nevertheless, lad, nevertheless," the minister said, easing his way around to stand by the table without having to keep his back to the room. He was a short, paunchy man, with brushed-back, thick salt-and-pepper hair that gave him less distinction than age. There was no thumb on his right hand, two fingers were missing from the left. Evan had never found out why, and no longer had the inclination to ask.

"Vicar, please," Addie said politely, but wearily. "Not while we're eating, all right?"

The cleric, a brimming glass of sherry in one hand, the other tucked into his grey jacket's pocket, beamed at her. "You're not to worry, Dr. Burwin. If the courts, as usual, let this one slip, God, as usual, will not."

"It's not him I'm concerned about right now, Reverend Flaunter," she said tightly. "It's Jamie."

Rupert Flaunter looked at her over the top of his glass. "As much as we hate to acknowledge it, Doctor, it was clearly Jamie's time. He'll be taken care of by his Father in Heaven, have no fear."

"Time?" Addie said, her voice rising.

Flaunter cocked an eyebrow.

Keeping his head down, Evan took another bite, took another drink, studiously wiped his mouth several times with a napkin. He wasn't about to get into this one; he had heard it and a dozen versions of it a hundred times since he'd been allowed by the locals to comment and contribute to their evening conversations. He still hadn't decided whether the vicar deliberately baited his audience, or vice versa. Whichever it was, the result was always the same—a good deal of shouting, some laughter, and more quoted Scripture than he'd ever heard in his life.

"To everything there is a season, my dear," the reverend said.

"Bull—"

"Say," Evan interrupted, "I guess it's my round, yes?" He stood, grabbed her glass though it wasn't quite empty, and nodded to Flaunter. "Vicar?"

Reverend Flaunter held up his glass. "I'm quite all right, thank you, Mr. Kendal." Then he turned to Addie again. "Doctor, you're quite right." A modest bow of apology. "Neither the time nor, I suspect, the place." He bowed again and eased back into the crowd.

Evan sat.

The room warmed as the noise level grew.

Addie took her glass back and drained it. "That man," she said, wiping her mouth with a tattered napkin, "is so damned pious, so damned sure of himself, I could throttle him."

Evan said nothing. He knew that the vicar did not believe in coincidence, because God's hand was in everything, including the senseless killing of a slightly retarded boy by a drunken driver; Addie believed in the wrong-place-at-the-wrong-time theory, in which neither God nor Satan held a prominent place.

Though often pressed for comment during such debates, he didn't think about it much, and when he was forced to, he supposed he leaned more toward Addie's view than Flaunter's.

He supposed.

"'Twas Him, you know."

Damn.

He looked forlornly at his rapidly cooling dinner, well aware that the owner of the new voice wouldn't take points of etiquette, or even a blunt hint to get lost; he was equally aware that Addie was hastily dabbing at her mouth to hide a smile, perhaps cork a laugh.

He inhaled deeply and, slowly, looked to his right.

"Mrs. McNair," he said with grim courtesy, "I don't think he was driving that van."

Ida MacNair, a spectacularly large woman, spectacularly swathed in an open, vividly patched coat, scarves and mufflers of all colors, open-fingered pink gloves, a handful of sweaters, and not perspiring a bit for it all, bobbed her great head as if testing a rein, worked her wide mouth as if easing a bit. "Him is always driving, Mr. Kendal. Him is always around when you cannot see him." A chubby finger jabbed at the scarred table and rocked it. Addie grabbed her empty glass. "You know aught, Mr. Kendal, you deny Him."

"Will you have one with us, Ida?" Addie asked before he could muster the strength to respond.

Mrs. MacNair fussed extravagantly with a tattered muffler about her neck, red-veined nose wrinkling in concentration. At last, a rueful shake. "You're very kind, Doctor, but I'd best not. It's a'right for him and you, but not for me." She leaned forward slightly. "Him is about t'night. My wits, you know. My wits."

A finger to the side of her nose, a touch to her lips, and she turned to bellow at someone at the bar, demanding immediate retribution for the foul and disgusting language of a leather-jacketed youth not yet clear of his soiled nappies. Those nearest who heard, laughed.

The jukebox was turned on.

The door was propped open as the evening's patronage began to spill congenially into the courtyard.

Mrs. MacNair scolded again as she heaved toward the bar.

Evan leaned over and said, "Addie, for my sanity—who the hell is Him?"

She shook her head. "No one knows, I don't think. It's not the Devil, nothing like that." A one-shoulder shrug. "Not sure, tonight, I really care."

He knew then it wasn't the dead boy that bothered her; it was Paul. Obviously, he still hadn't returned. And just as obviously, she had begun a swing from fear to hurt anger. He reached over and touched her hand, watched her eyes as they finally, truly, focused on him, then picked up her glass and made his way to the bar. A few customers asked after his health, a few more about the cottage he was renting, and Reverend Flaunter, still holding his sherry, suggested through a very thin veil of pastorly concern, that being seen alone with a professor's wife so often and so intimately in a town so small did not always sit well with the older members of Bettin Wells society.

Evan, a glass in each hand, suggested through a veil of propriety just as thin that the vicar, and his collar, were both turning an unsocial shade of brown.

Approving, roaring laughter drowned out the vicar's red-faced reply.

Evan, feeling at the same time righteous and stupid, took his order back to the table.

Addie had stacked her empty plate beneath his; she cupped her refilled mug with both hands and turned it slowly, catching the light. "Am I being silly?"

A shake of his head and a laugh short and deep in his chest as he picked up the plates and thrust them at the waitress passing behind him.

"I assume," he said, "we're talking about Paul."

Addie nodded.

30

"Well . . . I think you're working yourself into a state, for one thing."

She wouldn't respond; she drank instead.

"I also think that I don't know any good jokes that will make you feel better."

A half-smile.

"Thirdly," he said as an elbow nudged his back, "I think some fresh air would do us both some good."

She was up before he had finished, and after a deep breath, he took their drinks, eased back, and let her lead the way into the courtyard.

There were a dozen villagers there, standing near the door, and Addie exchanged greetings with them all as she walked toward the low stone wall that fronted the road.

The Cross and Sword stood at the top of the High Street, all the shops and offices stringing down and away from it into the center proper. The only cars at the curbs were those of the pub's patrons; two hundred yards down, a small group of teenagers had parked themselves under the marquee of a cinema.

There were no pedestrians.

Traffic was intermittent.

They leaned side by side on the waist-high wall, elbows nearly touching.

"He's not dying," Addie said at last.

"Oh?"

"I mean, I'm a doctor, right? These are things I ought to know. He's not dying."

He sipped and listened as she ran deliberately through symptoms of diseases some of which he had never heard of, proving to him conclusively that Paul suffered from none, including various forms of exotic cancers. Then she emptied her mug in three swallows, set it on the wall, and turned around to look at the pub.

"It's a woman, wouldn't you say?"

"Addie, for heaven's sake, you've only been married for five years. As I get these things, you've hardly begun to know each other."

She laughed soundlessly. "As you say, you're not quite the expert." She turned her head. "Evan, I entertain myself with fifteen different moods a day. The dying, the research and his work, counterspy, gambling, hunting for birthday gifts, trouble with the underworld, secret projects for the government, and women." Her hand knocked hair away from her eyes. "It always comes back to women."

Evan had never considered his friend the adventurous type, much less an adulterer, and he told her so. For heaven's sake, the man didn't even swear and was offended when others did; how could he find the courage to get himself a mistress? She only shrugged as she leaned back against the wall, her left foot tapping the ground without rhythm. He didn't know what else to say, and so finished his drink, fetched them both another, and returned outside to find a fine drizzle sifting out of the dark, like the touch of a heavy fog. Addie had her back to him, and he handed her the mug, which she took with an absent nod.

Across the street, flanked by a shoe store and a realtor, was a newsagent, its display window dark and its green-striped awning still unrolled. In the recessed doorway a man stood. Or at least he thought it was a man; the figure was too indistinct to tell, a streetlamp not ten feet away casting the buildings opposite into dark shadow. He hoped the guy wasn't waiting for a bus, because the next stop was three blocks farther down.

A cyclist with a rider clinging to his back roared past, swerving sharply from lane to lane.

"Kill himself, that one," Addie said, watching the

black machine and black riders fling themselves out of town and into the dark beyond the last streetlamp.

"No," Evan contradicted, "that's the kind that gets others killed, you know what I mean?"

She nodded, swung suddenly around and gripped his free hand. "Evan, what am I to do?"

There were no tears in her searching eyes; they were all in her voice.

Well, he was tempted to say, you could always start an affair of your own, if you want revenge.

"London," he said.

She blinked.

The drizzle thickened, and an automobile backed out of the parking lot into the road, backfired, and crawled away.

"Tomorrow I can go into London for you. Look around. See what I can find."

Her smile was sad and grateful. "And where will you look, O intrepid one? In case you hadn't noticed, it's rather large for its size."

He was aware, too aware, of her fingers lightly coiled around his hand, but he didn't pull away. "I don't know. I'll start with the places we usually go, I guess."

"I see." Her head rocked back slightly. "And he'll be there with his mistress?"

He clicked his tongue against the roof of his mouth. "Dumb, huh?"

"I would think so."

The cyclist roared back, lifting onto his rear wheel, and Evan scowled at him, turning as if to shout something in his wake. The noise of the motorcycle amplified against the darkened buildings, and echoed.

The figure in the doorway was still there.

A heavy heel behind them. "If you intend to be indiscreet," Reverend Flaunter said, "at least have the courtesy to do it elsewhere."

Evan looked over his shoulder. "Don't you have any female friends, Vicar?" he snapped.

"I do," the cleric said. "But I don't hold their hands in broad daylight. As it were."

He felt Addie release him quickly; felt his own cheeks begin to flush. But before he could furnish a retort, the cyclist returned.

And a lightless sedan backed out of the parking lot without slowing.

3

Evan barely had time to shout a useless warning before the collision, before the cyclist somersaulted over the car, and his rider, arms flung back like a diver's, rammed headfirst into the driver's door. It was only then that he heard the brakes scream and metal give and glass shatter and shower; it wasn't until he raced into the street behind Addie that he saw the flames.

"Addie!" he yelled, and grabbed her shoulder, spun her around and gathered her to him.

The explosion deafened him.

Heat seared the back of his head and neck.

On the damp tarmac slow growing puddles steamed as bits of metal dropped into them. Someone in the courtyard screamed. Addie broke from him again and ran toward the wreckage, shouting at him to fetch her bag from her car. He did as he was bidden, returning just as a hooting fire truck and panda car reached the scene simultaneously. In the sudden confusion of

34

conflicting official instructions, gawkers pressing as close as they dared, and a fast-moving handful of those wanting to help wherever they could, he found her by the cyclist.

The man's helmet had cracked but not split. The visor was up, and blood seeped from one eye.

"Addie?"

She nodded her thanks brusquely, and he realized he would be no use to her here. He backed away with a weak smile, nearly tripped over a hose working on the burning car, gagged at the stench of burning rubber and flesh, and found himself a moment later in the middle of the street, watching with the others as rescuers pulled the rider away from the car, clothes steaming, one leg feebly kicking.

Someone called his name.

He glanced around, frowning, and the figure in the doorway stepped out from under the awning.

It was Paul.

He ran over, but Paul, face hidden by his hat, immediately held up two gloved hands.

"Don't touch me!" he warned hysterically. "God, Evan, stay where you are!"

Evan stopped, confused.

Paul looked at the accident, at the pub's courtyard, then looked at Evan and said, "Can you meet me tomorrow night? London? Eight o'clock at The Plough? You remember it?"

Without thinking, he nodded.

"Don't tell Addie."

"Jesus, Paul, she's—"

"Swear to me!" The voice was harsh, almost not Paul's at all. "Swear to me you won't tell her!"

Evan's mouth opened, closed as he nodded.

"New York, Ev," he said then. "Remember New York."

And before Evan could move, Paul sprinted away, coat flapping at his legs, his hat spinning off as the wind came up and the drizzle turned to rain. He vanished around the next corner.

"Evan?"

He spun, his mind not quite catching up with the sight of Addie hurrying toward him through the rain. Reverend Flaunter intercepted her before Evan could reach her, and he saw her yank her arm from his grip, heard her say above an ambulance's approaching cry, "Was it Priscilla's time, Vicar? Was this your daughter's goddamn time?"

Five

1

In spite of the month the evening was still warm when Evan finally reached London, and he almost regretted bringing the sleeveless sweater he wore under his denim jacket. Later, when the sun had been replaced by streetlamps and neon, the true chill would come and he would be thankful; for now, however, the slight discomfort, abetted by crowded traveling on the train and overheated Underground, was simply one more item to hold against Paul Burwin.

He stood at the top of James Street, a short straight block that took a gentle downhill slide to the market square in Covent Garden. The pavement was crowded, pedestrians spilling happily over the curb to the empty street itself, clearly taking advantage of the unseasonable weather while it lasted. There was, he noted, hands deep in his pockets, an equal mix of camera-slung tourists and well-dressed office workers, patiently lining up at the restaurants on the right, flowing down into the square to catch a bargain or a snack before the market and stalls closed, standing outside the pubs and corner café, drinks in hand, a post mortem for the day.

It was only just past six, yet on his left, the blinding white of the Royal Opera House had already begun to shade to grey as the light sifted away.

The strong smell of roasting chestnuts on a hooded portable brazier; the sharp stench of liquor from a shattered unmarked bottle in the gutter.

His stomach lurched when a man in studded black leather strolled by with a steaming hot dog and a mug of coffee. He laid a calming hand across his belt buckle and scowled; his stomach had been complaining since he'd left the rush hour chaos at Waterloo Station, another mark against Paul for the embarrassment it had caused.

Yet he hadn't been able to stay home any longer.

Sleep had played a diabolical game of hide-and-seek with him the night before. Whenever he had felt it close in, ready for the tag, he was confronted with an enraged Addie shrieking at the vicar, with the vicar puffing his chest and stalking away, tears polishing his cheeks; he saw flashing blue lights, heard people muttering, listened helplessly as Addie sobbed when he reached for her, shoved him aside, and climbed into an ambulance without looking back.

He had hoped she would call him once she had returned from the hospital.

When she hadn't, he had hoped Paul would somehow get in touch and reveal the macabre joke he was playing.

He had almost called Uncle John; only the time difference had stopped him.

And when the cottage became oppressive, when he couldn't pace another damn step or listen to the wind for one more second, he had left—fled, actually—counting on taking a meal in the city and finding something to keep him occupied before meeting Burwin at eight.

"You looking for a job as a bleedin' statue?" someone

muttered behind him, and he moved on without comment, without looking around, stopping at the bottom of the street where he leaned against one of the thick, brown wood railings that prevented automobiles from entering the market proper.

His stomach burbled.

A woman with two corgis on a single leash glared at him for his breech of etiquette; a blonde standing at a flower cart just ahead of him looked over her shoulder as if he'd made a comment about her wares.

Paul, he thought, you're a dead man.

The stone market building was high, its broad roof glass-paned, the filigree around it the color of aged copper, the columns that created a walkway along the north side stouter in growing shadow.

The sun lowered, creating a curious twilight in the square beneath a still, brittle, blue sky.

If I were smart, he thought, pushing away from the railing to head to his right across the paving stones, I would get back on the train and go home. Now. This is stupid. This is cloak-and-dagger stuff, and I should be shot for leaving the house in the first place.

You're dumb, Kendal.

don't touch me!

All the way into London for a meeting which, by right, should have taken place back in Bettin Wells, where Addie waited, going mad with confusion and fear.

for god's sake, stay where you are!

Son of a bitch! The anger was sudden and unexpected, and he decided that as soon as Paul had given him whatever fantastic excuse he had come up with for his bizarre behavior, Evan was going to haul off and deck him. Right there on the street. No question about it. And no one would think the worse of him. Certainly not Addie.

A good smack to the face, right on the button, Evan the cowboy rides again.

He almost laughed aloud at a slow-motion image of him swinging righteously away, at the taller and much heavier Paul sprawling on the pavement and rubbing his jaw in pain and astonishment.

Not quite, alas; and he exhaled twice sharply, realized he was growing nervous, and hurried on, swinging around the face of the market toward the entrance of the Punch and Judy pub. But the place was too crowded, too noisy, too many chattering men and women taking too much of the space in the downstairs bar and the eating area outside. He snarled without moving his lips, and wandered to the south end, where he found a place among the stalls to buy a lukewarm hot dog and a can of soda, which he took back outside.

At the head of the square was a wide plaza between the market building and the front of a plain, low church whose walls formed much of the square's western boundary. Its overhung roof was peaked, without ornament save for a large blue-faced clock, and supported by four massive marble pillars that permitted pedestrians to pass through without having to brave the sometimes slippery stones.

To the right of the church were several simple wood benches for foot-weary travelers and those who weren't eating in the restaurants. He found one unoccupied and sat with a silent groan, stretched out his legs, and unbuttoned his jacket, pulled the sweater away from his chest. Some thirty feet away, directly in front of the church, a string quartet played to an appreciative audience, the music resonating off the marble, off the market, creating a dome over the square that kept the city's voice from violating the moment.

A glance at his watch—an hour and a half to go.

Dumb, Evan; you should have told Addie.

As he ate and watched the people streaming through the square, he counted the days since he'd last seen his friend, and stopped in midchew when he realized that it had been at least three weeks, if not more.

No.

That couldn't be.

Paul had never let more than a few days go by before either visiting or calling.

Three weeks?

Impossible.

He drank, and lit a cigarette.

The quartet finished its last piece with a peaceful flourish, and the cellist passed a ragged cloth cap while spirited applause still held the city back.

Three weeks, without a word.

"All right," he whispered, and nodded. "Okay, so it's three weeks."

Don't tell Addie!

2

New York.

And what the hell was that all about?

New York?

He drank again and tried to replay the times he and Paul had spent in the city. There hadn't been that many. Four, if memory served—three of them when he had gone in to listen to Paul's lectures at one school or another, once when Paul had just wanted to blow off some steam after a stultifying conference and they had taken a midtown hotel room and launched into an American version of pub-crawling.

He smiled to himself.

Not much of a drinker in the first place, he had really done himself wrong that night, despite the food Paul insisted they keep eating.

"Roughage, my boy, roughage," the man had declared, shoving another burger into his hands. "And it soaks up the gin so you can gin yourself again."

As far as Evan had been concerned, it hadn't soaked up a damn thing; and the only roughage he got was the beating his head had taken the next morning.

So what the hell was the man talking about?

New York?

The woman with the corgis strolled by, glared at him, strolled on.

Evan stared at the two dogs.

Oh shit, he thought; god, he can't be serious.

3

It had rained that spring night.

The streets lay like sheets of black ice when there was no light to touch them, reflected and distorted the neon and streetlamps in puddles swirled with oil; taxis hissed, buses spat, delivery trucks swayed over the uneven blacktop; a cloud settled over the top of the Empire State Building like a cotton cap that trapped the glow inside; and in the air a mist that never quite became a decent fog.

They had been drinking, Paul and Evan, down in the Village, when Paul decided he wanted to see Times

Square. There were no cabs to be had, no rides from a friend, and he refused to take the subway. So they walked. At the time, it hadn't seemed too great a task. After all, they were men, they were in their prime, so what was a few dozen blocks, give or take?

And as they walked, they talked—about things only men talked about when they were drunk and drunkenly stupid. Things forgotten in the middle of a sentence, things picked up a hundred yards farther on.

Then the lights went out.

Evan remembered they had somehow managed to swing onto Sixth Avenue, were just abreast of Bryant Park when suddenly the world went dark. Paul had whooped and laughed, Evan had jumped much closer to sober, and they launched into several quiet choruses of songs the words to which they could barely remember. World War II songs; folk songs; college songs from both sides of the Atlantic; drinking songs that led them giggling to the "Star-Spangled Banner," after which it was only proper to give due to "God Save the Queen."

No one paid them any attention. The traffic had slowed to a timorous crawl. Pedestrians lit matches and lighters and held impromptu parties on street corners in front of bars. Lanterns and candles in the bars themselves. Police cars with flashing lights. Headlamps that dragged their cars behind them.

Into Times Square where the party became raucous, and Evan grew nervous. There were too many people here, trying to make light of no light at all, and he finally grabbed Paul's arm and made him stop.

"I think," he said, "my legs are falling off."

"The hell," Paul told him. "Don't stop now, son, the hotel's just ahead."

Then the taller man frowned, and stared over Evan's head. Evan turned and saw a tall fence behind him, glass

43

ovals cut into it at eye level every fifteen feet or so. Above it rose the skeleton of a new building, a generator keeping lit several dozen naked bulbs on the several dozen unfinished floors. Paul moved to one of the windows and looked in.

"Dark," he pronounced at last.

Evan shook himself and grinned. "A man died down there last week."

"Really?"

Evan stood beside him, peering around his shoulder. A single bulb down there in the construction site pit, too many shadows and not enough shapes. "Yes. Some boards dropped from the fifth or sixth floor. Caught the guy square on the head while he was eating lunch."

Paul belched loudly.

A siren in the distance, growing distant.

"In the valley of Loch Mairen," he began to sing softly, "where the stag and his kin keep us fed through the snow."

Evan smiled, closed one eye in order to think. "And the something or other walks up the slopes of Ben Karren, and looks down, and sees, and hunts something or something else."

Paul snorted. "You can't sing, you old fool."

"I'm not old."

"Well, then."

Evan looked back into the pit. "It came to us then in moonlight that season, taking food from our bairns and starving the women."

"Better," Paul said.

Evan shrugged.

An old song from the days when the clans meant more than an annual party. A lament. Almost a dirge. A wolf that stalks the secluded valley of Loch Mairen, killing the deer that kept the village alive during winter. When the killing became a slaughter, hunters were sent out, a

44

young man among them, to destroy the intruder and save them all from starvation. It was colder than usual, darker than usual, and they were puzzled, the hunters were, because the tracks and the carnage told them that the wolf hunted alone, and because it didn't seem to care which deer it attacked. The sick, the strong, the battle-tried, the old—it didn't seem to matter. It simply killed, and it didn't eat. The young man got lost in the forest, in the dark, and tripped over something hidden in the snow. He was stunned. He cried out. When his head finally cleared, he could hear the wolf killing the hunters. One by one. Screaming. He tried to get up, but the wolf found him first. Its eyes were green and slanted, its fur crusted with snow and blood. It stared at him; the young man stared back and prayed. Then the wolf snorted steam and moved on, a flash of red between the trees. It killed someone else. The young man finally ran away, back to the village, to report the horror. But they shunned him, even his beautiful young wife, because the shadow of the beast had fallen upon him; and when people began dying for no reason at all—a tree falling, a hole in the loch's ice, a sickness—they drove him into the wilderness. Where he died. And the wolf moved on.

There was more, the words slurred, the words too properly enunciated, and they finally ended with an arm-waving flourish and a suddenly self-conscious laugh.

Paul rapped the fence with his knuckles.

The lights came back on.

"A miracle!" Evan cried, laughing.

Paul looked into the pit. "The shadow of the wolf is in this place, Ev," he said. "That poor man won't be the last of his kind."

Evan grabbed his arm. "We're drunk," he said, dragging him up the street toward the hotel. "You're drunk."

45

Paul wrapped his arm around his shoulder. "I am," he admitted, "but that don't change the facts."

4

Evan shook his head to discard the memory, but a fragment remained, distant, an echo.

Did it matter?

He didn't care.

He checked his watch and blew out a breath. Still time to kill. But it looked as if there would be another performance soon, out there on the stones, so he might as well stick around; there was no place else to go. A finger rubbed at one eye. New York. Paul must have meant one of the other times; he couldn't be serious about that one. But it was funny, now that he thought about it. They hadn't forgotten the construction pit or the singing in spite of all the drinking. In fact, once Paul returned to England, he'd dug around a little and uncovered several other poems, other songs, other tales, among various European cultures, as had Evan among the Indians from Canada to Central America.

Attempts to explain why things happened.

The answer was as simple as it was horrid—they just did.

The shadow of the wolf, or the hawk, or a nameless god, or a curious cloud, passed over a region. And things happened. No rhyme, no reason.

They just did.

So what, he wondered, was Paul's point then?

He didn't know.

And trying to think about it threatened to birth a headache.

Especially when he remembered that another worker had indeed died at the site, and two women had been severely injured in a crash just around the corner.

Oh Christ, he thought; knock it off, boy, all will be revealed all in good time.

5

Several minutes later, a scrawny young man dressed in a wet suit decorated with garish occult symbols took the quartet's place. He announced himself loudly as the Incomparable Wizard of Anti-Gravity, took a long sweeping bow, and rummaged in a burlap sack he had dragged out with him. His enthusiastic patter was unintelligible, but his intent was clear, and a new crowd began to gather, most as young as he.

Evan caught himself smiling, but he didn't care.

Covent Garden, despite a number of misguided efforts to curtail the free entertainment, was still home to dozens of street performers in dozens of guises, and while many substituted fervor for talent, a good many more, like the string quartet, were genuinely worth the time.

Evan had his doubts about the Incomparable Wizard.

The young man opened his act by juggling four flaming tennis balls he managed to catch more often than not, the ones that he dropped rolling toward his audience, making the girls squeal and laugh, making the boys jump clear and blush.

Beneath the church's overhang, shadows merged with the stone; the face of the market building grew darker despite the hanging lamps inside and the streetlamps at the corners.

The flaming balls were replaced by flaming batons.

"He's not bad," a voice said, and Evan almost lost the can of soda. He looked to his right, into the white-whiskered face of a stout man wearing an expensive tweed jacket and club tie, a furled umbrella propped on the bench between his knees. His eyes were partially squinted in judgment.

"I'm sorry?" Evan said.

The man nodded to the juggler. "He's not bad, you know."

Evan shrugged. "Better than I can do."

The man smiled tolerantly. "It's the ointment, of course, you see."

"The what?"

"The ointment." The man held out his palms; they were scarred smooth to the heel and the base of the fingers. "The ointment keeps you from getting burned. The lad uses too much. That's why he fumbles." His lips pursed in judgment. "But he's not bad. Not bad at all."

The batons became Indian clubs, a half-dozen, all in flames, passing around his neck, under his legs, feinting toward the crowd that reacted with grins and scattered laughter.

"You're an American," the man said.

Evan nodded.

"Vacation?"

"Not really. I'm a guest lecturer of sorts. History and English. University."

"Ah." The man's hands folded over the grip of his umbrella. "Not in London, though?"

"Sometimes. It depends on where I'm wanted."

The man nodded polite understanding.

One of the Indian clubs struck the ground, and the Wizard said something that made the crowd applaud.

"The ointment," Evan said with a smile.

"Exactly! Splendid!"

They shook hands, exchanged names, and Wallace Trinton explained that, in his younger days, much younger, he had done a bit of juggling himself. To amuse himself on rainy days. Self-taught, eventually found the nerve to let others see what he could do, played a few local night spots in the Midlands, twice down in London, until he'd misjudged one evening and damn near set himself on fire.

"All for the best, though, I suppose. It made me concentrate on my work for a change. Had an annoying habit of bouncing stacks of money and pens in the air. Sometimes added a small stool. Very disconcerting to the paying customers, you can imagine. My superiors did not approve."

"Banker?" Evan guessed.

Trinton laughed without a sound and stroked his beard with one finger. "You might call it that, now and again, if I kept taking your money." He reached into his jacket and pulled out an embossed card he handed over. "Bookmaker, actually. I won a fortune on your last election. Nobody believed you'd actually elect that man again."

Evan didn't know what to say. Too many movies had forged a seedy stereotype of Trinton's profession, and despite the elaborate business card and tailored clothes, he was tempted to call the man's bluff.

With a shout that echoed, the Incomparable Wizard announced his grand finale, and at the jocular caution that followed, the crowd moved back several steps. Evan spotted a little girl clinging excitedly to her mother's hand, and for no reason at all he was reminded of Paul. A check of his watch; if he left now and walked slowly, he'd reach the Plough by just eight. His left hand

49

touched his shirt pocket; the return tickets, both Underground and train, were still there.

"Are you enjoying your stay?"

Evan nodded. "Very much so."

"Homesick?"

He admitted the possibility with raised eyebrows and a tilt of his head.

"Incredible."

"Sorry?" Evan said.

Trinton used his umbrella to point at the juggler.

The Incomparable Wizard had exchanged the regulation-size clubs for ones twice as large. There were four, two of them afire, the other pair dead black. The flames were bright and sharp, the sharp slap of thick wood against his hands the only sound now as he pretended to lose control, regain it, lose it again in an ever-widening circle that pushed the crowd farther back.

"Boy, I sure hope he knows what he's doing," Evan said, gauging the distance between him and the clubs and the gold of their fire.

"I would bet on it," the man assured him, standing with a wink and taking several steps toward the performance. "Amazing. The lad is strong in the wrists, I'll give him that."

The lad, Evan thought, is stupid to try such a stunt with so many people around.

Trinton half-turned and held out his hand. "A pleasure to meet you, Mr. Kendal."

Evan took the hand and rose himself, a similar sentiment offered and accepted.

The juggler slipped on a loose stone, recovered, and broke into a slow trot, his gap-toothed grin proving it was all part of the act.

Trinton scratched a temple and said, "I think the lad's over his head now, wouldn't you say?"

50

Evan didn't know, but he released the man's hand and edged away from the bench. It was time to leave. He had no idea what the Incomparable Wizard had in mind now except to scare the wits out of his audience, but he didn't think he wanted to be around when those clubs had to be caught, all at the same time.

Applause, louder as the juggler moved faster.

Whistles, cries of encouragement, one elderly woman waving a white scarf.

The Wizard slipped again as the arc of his circle neared the old man and Evan.

Laughter, and applause.

Fire brighter as the light died, high clouds drifting up and over from the south.

"Ah well," Trinton said as he turned to Evan and hooked the umbrella over his crooked arm. "Must run. Perhaps we'll meet again. A small wager on your next election?"

"Okay. Sure."

They shook one last time, eyes and lips smiling, just as a black club pinwheeled into the back of the old man's head. His grip tightened on Evan's hand as he fell, dragging Evan with him to his knees.

Someone screamed, the only sound.

Trinton toppled onto his face.

Evan saw the blood in the white hair, saw one leg kick, saw the back bend as Trinton tried to rise, lift his head.

"I seldom come here, Mr. Kendal," he said, his eyes wide in disbelief. "A whim. A whim."

He fell again.

And blood from his shattered nose splashed over Evan's coat.

II

THE
PLOUGH

Six

1

The Plough was a local pub, wrapped around a quiet corner in Bloomsbury, only a short block from the British Museum but seldom used by the tourists, who preferred for some reason the pub directly opposite the museum's tall iron gates. It was a long and narrow place, with a restaurant upstairs, the bar on the ground floor, the lower half of its wide windows masked by undistinguished print curtains. Outside, iron braces over the entrance and at the corner held a dozen hanging plants not yet brought in for the winter, and on the pavement were several tables and chairs, white iron and round, but none were in use when Evan finally arrived. He went inside immediately, ordered a scotch—a double, no ice—and brought it back out, where he sat alone, sipping. The side street was dark, deserted, with several automobiles parked with their offside wheels on the curbing, while down at the other end was a pizza parlor whose patrons came and went without much noise.

By the time the glass was empty, his hand had stopped shaking.

By the time he had fetched another, a foaming pint of bitter now in a faceted heavy mug, his shock had been replaced by a deliberate sullen rage.

Wallace Trinton had been taken away on a stretcher almost immediately after his second fall. Luckily, a constable had been on the fringe of the crowd, and an ambulance had been summoned without delay, first aid swiftly delivered on the spot by a nurse just off duty. The Incomparable Wizard had left with the police, tearfully protesting his innocence of malice; Evan had told the officer what had happened and had been sent to the men's room in the Punch and Judy to wash the blood from his jacket with what seemed like gallons of cold water.

"A whim," the bookmaker had said.

Evan drank.

A goddamn whim; and he uncharitably wondered what Reverend Flaunter would have said about that had he been pontificating in Covent Garden tonight.

He was beginning to feel like a jinx.

In his entire life, aside from the odd schoolyard battle with a bully, the rare temper explosion, he had somehow avoided major confrontations with violence. Now, within the space of two days, he had been flooded with it, smeared with it, and he jumped when he heard a backfire blocks away.

He lit a cigarette, looked up and saw nothing but black above the buildings. But he could tell that the clouds had taken over, no moon or stars tonight—the early evening breeze had grown steady, damp, and mean, and he suspected there'd be rain long before midnight.

A check of his watch.

Paul was late.

So what else is new? he thought, and crushed the unfinished cigarette beneath his heel.

He fetched a second pint.

The way things were going, it would probably make good sense to stay in London—finding a bed-and-breakfast would be easy in this part of the city—and return home in the morning, just in time to pack for his Friday trip. He had forgotten to check the time of the last train, but even if he made it to Salisbury, he didn't think he'd be able to catch a bus to Bettin Wells.

The curse, he thought, of not owning a car in Great Britain; on the other hand, those he had hired on an occasional fortnight contract for spur-of-the-moment transportation, like the one now growing dust in his garage, nearly sent him screaming into the nearest cathedral for sanctuary. Driving on the left usually proved too much for his conditioned reflexes, as Addie had laughingly noted whenever he closed his eyes when she drove.

"Evan."

A whisper from the shadows across the street.

"Evan. Here."

He looked up without raising his head, saw Paul move to the low curb and check the street in both directions. He had found another oversize hat, his topcoat gleamed with grime, and his hands were still gloved.

"No coppers," Evan said sourly. "It's clean, you son of a bitch."

In three strides Paul was at the table. "I could use one of those."

"Get it yourself."

"I can't."

Evan closed his eyes and drank.

"Ev, really, I can't."

Paul was a head taller, broader at the shoulders, and his face had once been pleasantly rounded and smooth. But now, in the muted light from the pub window, Evan could see that the man had grown gaunt, his complexion unhealthily close to jaundice. Christ, he thought with a brief surge of alarm, maybe he is ill after all.

Reluctantly, his anger not yet dismissed quite so easily, he waved his friend to a chair and went inside. The bar was lined with customers, every table and the wall-benches filled. It took him almost ten minutes to get the bartender's attention, and after throwing a bill onto the counter, he hurried out, half-fearing Paul had left.

He hadn't.

But he had taken the chair against the pub wall, to put the light and curious eyes behind him.

"I feel like I'm talking to Lamont Cranston," Evan complained lightly as he pushed the mug over, noting that Paul didn't touch it until his hand had withdrawn.

"I know what I look like, Ev," Paul said without rancor. "And to put some part of your no doubt curious mind at ease, I am not suffering some rare disease. Nor a common one, if it comes to that."

The breeze kicked; Evan snapped up his collar.

A black cap bumped down the street, amber roof light glowing while the driver whistled through his cranked-down window.

Up on Great Russell Street, in front of the museum fence, a gang of leather jackets began singing, more like shouting, and their voices echoed, were hollow. It didn't take them long to pass on, and when they had, the silence left behind was quickly pierced by a motorcycle's racing engine.

Evan held his mug in both hands. He had to. He was afraid, now that Paul had finally showed up, that his earlier daydream would become reality, that a single wrong word would have his fist in Burwin's shadowed face. And that bothered him. Upset him. It was as if the two accidents he had witnessed in the past twenty-four hours had somehow nudged to stirring a need to commit violence himself. Yet Paul clearly required help, from a friend if not a doctor.

"I take it back," he said when Paul didn't seem anxious to talk. "With that getup, it's like talking to Claude Rains in *The Invisible Man*." He smiled quickly, no humor. "So why don't you tell me what all this is about? But I warn you, Paul, it had better be good."

Burwin shrugged. He hadn't yet touched his drink, his hands remaining in his lap beneath the table.

Evan waited, corralling his impatience, every so often glancing up into the pub when someone walked by. It was either that or look at Paul, and he couldn't. With all the light behind him, the man had no face.

"In the beginning," Paul said at last, "I thought I was crazy."

Though the neighborhood was quiet, Evan still leaned forward in order to hear it all.

"Things pile up. Bills, obligations, debts. You don't even have to work at it, they just pile up, like dust balls beneath the bed. One minute they're not there, one minute there they are. Addie and I haven't been getting along all that well, either. Nothing to worry about there, I thought. A natural consequence. A rough spot." A hand finally reached out and poked at the brimming mug. "Just one more bit of pressure, you see. Do you know what a scrum is, in rugby, Ev? When all those blokes in muddy shorts gather round in the mud and the ball is dropped in the middle and they kick it all to hell? That's what I felt like."

Evan stared at his drink and frowned. There was something odd about Paul's voice, something not quite in tune.

"Funny thing is, I even remember when it started. I don't know why I do. I was in Windsor, that group of American high-school students come over to sop up culture at that magazine's expense—I forget the name, I just cashed the check, same as my colleagues—and I happened to be their illustrious leader for that week. Native-born and all that, get the real scoop, forget the books and stupid lectures. You know the routine. We were on the castle grounds, and they wanted to see where good old fat Henry number eight was buried, I wanted to take them up the tower so they could see the countryside. The fields of bloody Eton and all that." The hand curled around the mug, forefinger tapping the glass. "It wasn't so much that we had an argument, mind, just a difference of opinion. In my scholarly brilliance, I gave them a choice—the tomb or the tower. Then I hied off across the courtyard like an overweight Mr. Chips. I thought some would follow. None did.

"Have you ever been to Windsor Castle, Ev? Ever climbed that tower? It has a staircase barely wide enough for a fat man, and it goes round and round, round and round, and you never think you're going to reach the top. It's just too high. A mistake made and time to turn around before your heart gives out. But you do get there, you know. Just when your lungs are ready to pack it in, you come out this little doorway and you're there. You can see everything.

"You can see it all, Evan.

"My Lord, but you can see it all."

Evan drank and tasted nothing.

The man's voice was too high. Not high-pitched; just too high.

The breeze kicked again.

Inside the Plough, someone began a song.

Paul lifted his mug and drank slowly, deeply, until it was empty.

"Now listen, Paul, this is all very nice, but I don't understand why you don't tell Addie—"

"They let me climb up there alone, Ev. The little bastards let me climb up there by myself. Round and round. All the way up. But the funny thing is, I wasn't alone. Not when I got up there. I usually am, you know. Alone, that is. I've climbed that tower a hundred times, and just about every time, I've been by myself. I like it that way. Gives me a chance to think, you see. Gives me a moment to myself, up there above it all, people like ants, cars like toys on the High Street, clouds close enough to touch. I like that.

"But this time, by god, I wanted them with me! They didn't need to see a goddamn tyrant's tomb, for Christ's sake. What the hell did they need that for? They needed perspective, Ev. Perspective. That's what being up there would have given them. Bones they can get at a butcher's. Perspective they get from me."

The voice too high. And hoarse, as if he'd been shouting for hours.

Cold on Evan's cheek. He brushed it away, and it returned, and he looked up into a light mist.

"Paul, what do you say we go inside, okay? It's—"

"No!"

He raised his palms quickly. "All right, all right. But look, I really don't think you're—"

"I wasn't alone, Ev. The one time when I wanted someone with me, I wasn't alone, thanks to those idiots on the ground. Are you fucking my wife?"

2

Evan gaped. There had been no change in tone, no increase in volume.

Do you know what a scrum is? Are you fucking my wife?

The taxi returned, amber light extinguished.

Inside The Plough someone began to sing, a raucous tune by the sound of it that was soon shouted down, laughed into silence, and begun again by someone else. Shadows massed in the windows. Another song near the back in counterpoint. Bedlam for no more than half a minute before it unraveled, calmed, and the shadows dispersed.

"She never really loved me, you know."

Evan squeezed his eyes shut tightly, opened them when the sparks began to sting. "Jesus, Paul, what's—"

Paul's head tilted to one side; he still had no face.

"I simply asked a simple question, Ev. A civilized man would give me a simple answer. It's only right, you know. I wasn't alone, either. It was a clear day, you could see more horizon than you could stand, if that's what you wanted, and I could see the little beggars queueing at the chapel door like proper ladies and gentlemen. Have you ever seen it? The St. George Chapel? Hell, man, I've seen villages in the North smaller than that. They were all lined up, and I was looking down at them, and the next thing I knew, my friend, I wasn't alone. Strange, wouldn't you say?"

Evan said, "Get to the point," as flatly as he could.

"You're going to Edinburgh on what, Friday? Yes. A lovely town, their Edinburgh is. Castles and cannon. Lads and lassies. Loveliest city in that misbegotten country, though I'm no architect and don't really give a damn."

"Paul."

"Actually, you'll find them terribly interested in American history up there. I expect you'll give them the Wild West speech, yes? They'll love it. Hot-blooded Scots wha' hae and all that. And you won't be alone, Evan. I wasn't, you know. Alone. All that sky, all that grass, all those little beggars down there and I wasn't alone."

"The point, Paul."

Paul's other hand flopped heavily onto the table, the

dark leather glove soon glittering with beads of moisture as the mist became a drizzle.

"Jamie Lauder is dead," he said.

Evan gripped the edge of the table to keep the world from tumbling away. "That's right. Your wife was with him when he died. Which you would have known if you had been there, you sonof—"

"I was."

"The hell you were, Paul. Forgive me, but the hell you were. I was there. Addie was there. *You,* on the other bloody hand, were off on some mysterious goddamn adventure that none of us knew about." His chest was bound in iron; his mouth coated with grit. "You were gone. Gone! And your wife wanted to know if *I* knew where the hell you were." He felt himself rising, forced himself down. "Which I didn't, of course, because you hadn't the courtesy to let me, anyone, know what the hell was going on!"

Paul leaned back, the shadow that was his face shifting uncomfortably beneath the hat's floppy brim as his lips and jaw moved. "I see."

"I wish to hell I did."

A slight nod.

A shattering glass in the pub.

"Paul—"

A song begun and ended in a single note.

"You and I are quite alike, Evan, believe it or not. We are both keen students of history. We are grave robbers of the past. We are the Burke and bloody Hare of education. We study the cause of this global war and the effect of that local skirmish and the totality of universal misery as it relates to the fact that you are, no doubt, a great comfort to my wife, whose name you seem to have forgotten."

Evan stood so quickly, his chair scraped back over the

curb and fell on its side. "Will you *please* stop this bullshit and start making sense?"

"Sit down, please."

"Because if you don't, Paul, if you don't give me a straight answer right now, no more speeches, damn you, I am leaving. I have had it with all this crap. In three days, Paul, I have been in some way been touched by people dying and people getting grievously hurt. Including just a few hours ago. I was in Covent Garden and a man—" He waved it away abruptly. "Never mind. It's a little upsetting. It's damned upsetting! And frankly, I don't have the time to listen to you accuse me and Addie of adultery while you spin some idiotic story about—"

"Evan, do sit down or I'll kill you."

Seven

1

It wasn't the threat that had Evan reach down to right his chair and swing it back to the table; it was the sudden, incredible belief that Paul Burwin meant it.

Paul would kill him, no questions asked.

And it was at the same time ludicrous.

Almost laughable.

Not five feet away were a score or more people, drinking, telling jokes, perhaps planning who they would bed that night, or who they would dream about bedding when their plans didn't work out; at the other end of the block more people drank, and ate pizza, and told jokes, and who the hell knew what they were planning for tonight?

Paul was crazy.

One move, and Evan could yell, throw a chair through the window, and be halfway to the next street before anything could happen.

Paul was crazy.

"My wife," the man said, picking up his mug in both hands, holding it high like a Communion chalice for a second, then lowering it to rotate it before his face as though it were a precious gem, "is a lovely woman. I am, of course, not the best of husbands, and therefore do not blame her for seeking solace from a friend."

Say something, Evan told himself; for god's sake, man, say something!

"Ev, I'm going to kill myself tonight. I just wanted you to know why."

"Oh Jesus, Paul."

"Ah, no pity, my friend." The mug turned, caught the light. "I've thought this out quite thoroughly, as is my wont. Pros and cons, the usual procedure. As a result, there is nothing I can do."

"Paul, come on, you're talking . . . it's silly, and you know it," he said quietly. "You can come home with me, talk to Addie, get some help. Good God, surely you know how much she loves you?"

Paul laughed in rapid bursts that sounded more like wheezing. "The idea of me, perhaps."

Evan said, "Christ!" in undisguised disgust.

Paul slammed the mug down on the table; it cracked but didn't split.

Evan felt fear again.

People singing, telling jokes.

"You must not humor me, Ev. You must never humor me. I know things now that I had once prayed to God I would never know. I feel things now that I . . ." He shook his head; he began to giggle, cut it off with a wave of his hand. "Forgive me, old friend, I'm not myself." Another giggle. Another wave. "Not myself—classic understatement. The trouble is, you see, I was indeed myself until that afternoon in Windsor. But then, all of a sudden, I wasn't alone. It's all quite simple, really. Up that tower, those kids chattering below, and with all that wondrous countryside surrounding me, I learned what it is like to know what it's all about."

66

Dizziness forced Evan to close his eyes, see the sparks flare behind them. Fear, laughter, concern, distress, fear again as Paul began to rock in his chair, thumping the mug lightly on the table.

"New York, Evan."

"Yes. I remember."

"Do you now?"

Evan stared at the table, at the pits in the metal the white paint couldn't hide. "We were drunk."

"Indeed we were."

"We sang halfway across Manhattan."

"Indeed we did."

Evan's left hand clenched. "The construction site. You said something about . . ." He tried a smile. "Forty-some verses of that dumb Highland song."

Paul rocked.

The mug thumped.

"Not so dumb, Ev, not so dumb as you think."

He didn't know whether to scream or cry. "Paul, this is getting beyond me. I don't know what any of that has to do with what . . . why you're here."

Paul's head swiveled slowly left to right, his shadowed face darker. "If you truly remember that song, my friend, you know damn well I wasn't alone in that tower."

For Addie, Evan ordered himself; stay for Addie. There has to be a way out of this mess, a way to talk to him, a way to stop him.

"So. What are you?" he said with a quick laugh. "You telling me you're that killer wolf or something?"

"Oh lord, no," Paul answered behind a patient sigh. "I wouldn't be so presumptuous. I am, after all, only human. No, Evan, I'm the hunter."

He felt a laugh bubble in his throat, swallowed to kill it, swallowed again to kill the first hint of a tear. This was a cliché, it was madness, and the only thing he could do about it was feel a traitorous temper begin to fray while he prayed for someone to save his friend's mind.

"Paul, it's only a song, for god's sake. We were pissed out of our minds."

"Jamie Lauder is dead, Ev. I know. I did it."

Oh God, please.

"Priscilla Flaunter? That boyfriend of hers? The woman in that car? Do you remember, Ev?" A thumb pointed at his chest. "The hunter. Me. I did it."

"Paul, that's crazy."

The rocking stopped.

The thumping stopped.

Evan spread his hands, determined to be reasonable, uncertain now why he should. "Damnit, Paul, I was there, remember? Across the street with . . . with Addie. I saw it all. You were on the other side of the street. Unless you shot that guy or something, you didn't do a damn thing. You couldn't have."

Water dripping from the eaves, plopping onto the table, onto Paul's hat, the hollow sound of an old toy drum.

The voice higher, more hoarse.

"I didn't say I did it, Ev. I said I did it. There's a subtle distinction there that you are not yet aware of."

"Did it?" Evan asked, "Or caused it? Jesus, you're talking like a professor now. Paul, please—"

"You'll never know, my friend, if you don't stop interrupting."

The threat again.

Evan glanced side to side, praying for intervention—someone from the Plough, a policeman, a bum, anyone who might distract Burwin's attention long enough for him to get up and get away. But at this time of night, the narrow streets around the museum were deserted. The students staying in the cheap hotels and bed-and-breakfasts were all out drinking, the tourists were at the theater or dining.

"I actually considered assassinating the Prime Minister." A laugh short and brittle. "A foolish notion, one might even say a mad one. A test, you see. To see if I was right. A grand thing, really. The perfect murder, Evan, because I'd kill that pompous bitch and never touch her with a finger. But of course you wouldn't understand that, because you've been touching my wife for god knows how long without harm to either of you, and if I should do anyone in, I would imagine logic would point directly to you."

"Paul!"

"Or her." A shrug. "Makes no never mind to me."

As quietly and firmly as he could: "That's enough, Paul."

"That's enough, Paul," Burwin mimicked in a childlike voice.

Evan stood.

"Sit down, Ev."

He shook his head. "No."

"Evan. Sit. Down."

He leaned over stiffly, glaring into the shadow-face, a breath hard to come by. "Sorry, but I've been patient long enough. My friend. You wanted me to meet you. I did. You wanted to tell me something. I've been listening. And so far, all you've done is accuse me of screwing Addie, threaten to kill me, and ramble on about some stupid-ass folk song we could only remember because we were drunk, and god knows what—"

"I suspect He does," Paul said calmly.

Evan wiped a hand over his hair, his palm coming away wet, reminding him with a slight jolt that he'd been sitting in a light rain without feeling a thing. He dried the hand on his jacket, the hand bunching into the jacket's pocket.

"Sit down."

He sighed the end of tolerance and shook his head. "Paul, call me when you're ready to make sense, okay? Better yet . . ." Resolve shifted without weakening. "Jesus, Paul, come home, all right? Come home with me. Please. You need help, damnit, and I can't give it to you here."

Paul let his hands slide away from the mug. It fell apart cleanly, the halves rocking on the table.

Evan couldn't stop looking at them, fascinated by the glow buried in each of the facets, wasn't aware until Paul cleared his throat that the man had taken one of his gloves off.

The hand had no fat on it; the hand of a man forty years older.

"If I were to touch you with this," Burwin said, holding up his fingers and waggling them slowly, "you would know without question what the hell I've been talking about. You would know why the hunter was driven from his home. You would know what Hell is, my dear and trusted friend. You would know how I managed to see the vicar's slut for a daughter dead so that you would have proof that I am not . . . insane."

He stood, and Evan stepped back.

"But you won't listen, will you?"

So hoarse now, it pained Evan to listen.

"You just want to get back to Addie."

"I quit," Evan said unhappily. "I give up, I'm leaving. When you're ready for real help, Paul—"

Paul shrieked.

Evan froze.

Burwin raised his fists over his head and shrieked again—a man broken by fate, the tantrum of a thwarted willful child. His arms trembled, his body quaked, when he lifted his face toward the city's dark sky, saliva at his lips had bubbled to foam.

"Murder!" he screamed, and alarmed faces pressed to the Plough window.

"You shit!" he yelled at Evan. "You shit, goddamn fucking son of a bitch, I am going to make sure there's nothing left of you, you goddamn bastard, you cocksucking bastard, shit-eating fucking son of a bitch!"

He smiled, drooling.

"Oh Ev," he said quietly, "you're going to die."

2

Evan couldn't move.

Shapes and shadows milling at the window, hurrying footsteps on the pavement, Burwin's ragged breathing sounded almost like a laugh as he stretched the hand out.

Terrified, Evan took a half-step backward, then lunged forward, grabbing the edge of the table and shoving it into Paul's thighs. The man bellowed and fell against the pub wall, slipped and vanished under the table.

But Evan was already gone.

He sprinted around the corner, slapped his way through a small crowd of drinkers standing at the entrance, and raced across the street and up, rounded the next corner and ran toward the lights and traffic of Southampton Row three long blocks away. Under the trees that hissed at his passing, dodging a young couple huddling under an umbrella, veering around an old woman walking her small dog. The massive block of the

71

museum on his left across the road, lighted windows of Georgian rowhouses on his right. People inside. One looking out and frowning as he ran by. Distant shouts behind him.

He didn't look back.

Into the dark when the foliage buried the streetlamps, slowing a little, gasping for air.

He didn't look back.

He didn't think.

Across another street, nearly stopping when a car honked angrily as it turned, swerving around it and slapping its trunk as he leapt the curb and ran on.

Considering for a brief second hiding in the mud and rough walks of Bloomsbury Square park, changing his mind—it was too small, he was too frightened, he'd never be able to stay still if Paul should follow. The car park beneath it then, but it would be empty, no place for concealment, no corners to vanish in should Paul manage to find him.

Lights ahead. Cabs and buses and cars by the dozen; pedestrians, shopkeepers, police. Safest there, he could lose himself, slow down, find someplace to rest, to think, to hide.

Another street to cross, and he skidded on the wet tarmac, spun his way to the pavement. A row of motorcycles at the curb, a huge marble building on his right unlighted.

Far behind him: "Evan!"

He exploded onto Southampton Row and had to grab a lamppost to keep himself from running into the street. No one paid him heed.

A look back—a shadow loping past the park.

Traffic was heavy. Shops alit across the way, hotel marquees, late-night grocery, pubs, a man in front of a magic shop trying to hawk rubber masks. And hundreds of people moving in a hurry, the drizzle not quite heavy enough for all of them to use umbrellas. Horns. Brakes.

He caught a break in the flow and dodged, ran-skipped to the opposite sidewalk.

The Underground.

All he could think of now was getting a train out of London—speed for distance, it was the only way. But to his right, the Row grew dark as the shops ended, and the Underground entrance on High Holburn was too far away.

To the left then.

He trotted.

He could do no more, though something screamed at him to fly. His lungs had begun to burn, a flame blossomed in his side. He could feel his shirt drenched in perspiration, cold when his jacket pulled away from his waist; mouth dry and tongue seeming to swell, cheeks puffing, eyes blinking as the drizzle hardened to a light rain.

A glance over his shoulder; Paul wasn't there.

A glance across the street, and he saw Burwin through a break in the traffic, keeping pace without seeming to hurry.

Oh hell.

Hunter.

He couldn't move any faster. His only hope was finding a chance to duck off the main thoroughfare before Paul could chase him. He looked ahead, the block long and unbroken once he'd passed a bar- and restaurant-lined alley. Someplace; there had to be someplace.

He slipped sideways when a paving stone wobbled under his weight, nearly toppling him into a newspaper rack.

Another hotel, a newsagent, a chemist's, a clothing store.

A corner coming up, marked by a bank on this side, and a tall Victorian hotel on the other.

He looked left.

Paul stood a few yards ahead at the opposite curb, and waved gaily as he slapped at the side of a slow passing cab with a red stripe down its side.

Evan frowned—a trick, don't slow up, it's a trick, you idiot, keep going—and tried to swallow, concentrated on the traffic light ahead, on the hotel beyond, trying to decide the best way to the Underground. There was little time left. Straight ahead to the next corner where there were people around, or cut around this one and find the strength to sprint through darkness.

He looked across the Row again.

Paul grinned and waved, and pointed dramatically.

And Evan swiveled, still moving, as the agonizing squeal of hard-pressed brakes made him wince and hunch his shoulders. Others had already stopped and turned, whispered loudly, called out a warning. A bus slammed to a half-spin halt. A horn blared. A cab, red stripe on its side, skidded across both lanes of the Row, bumped over the low curb and knocked several people down, ran one over with its rear wheels, plowed into the front of a shoe store and back out again before it stopped. Smoking. Radiator hissing. Glass falling on its roof and shattering, falling again. A bare leg beneath the chassis, heel thumping spastically on the pavement.

Nothing moved.

A woman screamed.

Evan's eyes widened, and he searched frantically for Burwin, couldn't find him, didn't believe it, and ran, not caring about the protestations of his legs or the fire in his stomach or the acid in his throat or the way his feet found scant purchase on the ground.

He ran.

Grabbed the edge of the bank's recessed doorway and flung himself around the corner, into the street and down to the narrow road that backed the hotel. He ducked into it, not much wider than an alley, and crossed over, skidded and fell, slid on his knees until they slammed against the curb. A gasp, a moan, and he staggered forward, scrabbling for balance and not finding it until he reached the next corner and was forced to slow down to prevent a collision with a huddle of rags painfully climbing the street in a wheelchair.

Twenty feet away, the light of the Underground entrance.

A look back.

Paul up on the main street, turning slowly in obvious confusion.

Evan fumbled for his ticket as he made his way through the crowd leaving the station, stepped inside and looked to his right, toward the elevators. None of the three were at street level; his only chance were the steps, one hundred and seventy-five of them, a long spiral into the tunnels, a sign on the wall warning of the distance.

Outside, someone yelled an angry protest.

Evan grabbed the slick metal railing and started down.

He was alone.

The pale tiled walls caught his footsteps and flung them behind him; a stiff hot wind as a train pulled in with a screech and bellow, nearly a quarter of a mile below; his gaze only on the spiraling steps narrow at the core, on his feet, concentration to prevent himself from falling, counting for a while, grabbing the back of a thigh to knead it loose when it tightened.

Around.

Down.

Tiny bulbs in their rusted brackets flickering and dim.

Please, God, let there be a train.

Down.

Someone following.

Don't look; don't stop; don't look.

The squeal of brakes.

A violin playing somewhere deep in the tunnels.

Please, God.

Falling out of the stairwell at speed, tripping forward and striking his shoulder against a silver car so hard, one of the passengers inside leapt to his feet, briefcase at his chest like a leather-bound shield.

Evan half-ran, half-crawled inside and fell against the opposite door.

Watching the stairwell.

"You drunk, pal?"

Watching.

"You're drunk, I don't want to be thrown up on, do you hear me? You just get off. Get off now."

The stairwell.

"Hey!"

Evan looked at the man and said, "I'm not drunk."

The doors closed.

Paul fell the last two steps and sprawled onto the platform, arms outstretched, fingers into claws.

"You look drunk."

The train shuddered and moved.

Evan stared.

Paul pushed himself to his feet and saluted, kept walking pace with the car as long as he could and mouthed, *I'll see you later.*

Eight

1

By the time Evan reached Salisbury station it was already a few minutes past midnight.

Raining heavily.

The wind scouring the platform, the parking lot, the downward slant of the street that led to the main road.

All the pubs were closed, most of the shops dark, and he could only sense the spires of the cathedral that slammed into the low clouds.

Hands in his pockets, arms tucked close to his sides, he hurried along the empty street, keeping close to the buildings, not bothering to check behind or ahead, not bothering to duck away from the water pouring off rolled-up awnings, damning himself for not bringing the damned car. When he had reached Waterloo Station, disheveled and limping, he had just made the last train out, and had spent the first twenty minutes scouting the cars to be sure Paul hadn't arrived before him. Then he had dropped into a seat in a damp and chilled car and, against his will, had fallen into an exhausted sleep despite the aches, despite the burning.

Only the conductor had saved him from riding past his station.

"You all right, sir?"

"Yes."

"On your way, then, have some coffee."

His feet slapped the pavement. His knees stung, his right shoulder felt numb. Puddles shattered and regrouped, reflections too bright, too confusing to be stared at for very long. Streams of water from folded awnings. Gurgling water rushing toward the storm drains in the gutter. The tarmac a black mirror, awash with rain and oil, pocked with sodden islets of newsprint and crushed paper cups, a single overturned boot, a shard of cloth without color.

The wind thumped his back.

Water dripped down his neck and coursed in ice floes along his spine.

He staggered, paused to lean against a door and rub absently at his shoulder, his teeth chattering until he clenched them, his legs wobbly until he pushed off and walked again. Shying from a hissing tomcat on a pub's flower box, slipping off a curb hard onto his heels, stepping into a puddle deep enough to run over the tops of his shoes.

He didn't feel a thing.

He was soaked through, nothing left to get wet, and so numb there was only the inside of him left to react to the cold with a sudden tremor that shoved him a step right, a sudden stiffening that knocked him a step left, a knife in his spine that stopped him in his tracks.

He couldn't walk all the way home; he knew that. His knees burned and stung, he ached too damn much, but he kept walking anyway—to stop would be to fall asleep, as if he were trudging through a blizzard; and to fall asleep would mean he would never wake up. At the moment the idea was not all that unpleasant, but he kept walking anyway—to pause would tempt a look over his shoulder, would produce a tall shadow following his wake, drooling, grinning, a skeletal hand outstretched to grip his shoulder. The way he felt now, however, death or what would follow could not be any worse, but he kept walking anyway—to do anything but walk, to focus motion into his legs, would mean remembering what he had seen, what he had heard, and once that began, there would be no stopping the speculation, the claw for logic, the twisting of what he knew to be true into what he knew could not exist.

The fear.

He walked on.

And when he spied the glass-walled phone box on the next corner, he focused on that instead, on the sputtering light inside, on the telephone itself, on its shadow on the sidewalk when he stepped into the tiny booth and let the door swing shut, grating on its hinges.

Away from the wind, the rain, the illusion of warmth and safety gave him a violent chill, his body no longer forced to struggle, the elements no longer fueling tension and mindless protection.

His fingers couldn't grasp the coins.

His eyes closed and he made his jaw rigid.

He tried again and spilled what he had onto the shelf, poked the coins around until he could count, could figure. Then he blew on his hands and gasped at the needles that pricked his palms and the tips of his thumbs. The receiver was too heavy. It fell, whacked against the glass wall, swung out, and hit the wall a second time, a third until he snatched it up and pinned it between cheek and shoulder.

The booth trembled in a gust.

Someone rapped on the wall behind him.

"Jesus!" he yelled. Whirled. Dropped the receiver so

that it slammed against the wall. Scattered the coins with an elbow so that they spilled to the wet floor.

Pain in his arm and the small of his back.

Pain in his knees.

The wind gusted again.

A face at the door, dripping rain, smiling without teeth, a palm held up beseechingly while the other hand held a tattered topcoat closed.

"Go away!" Evan shouted, trying to find the way to breathe once more.

The beggar knocked again. Smiling. Palm up.

"Damnit, bugger off!" he shouted, and turned his back, groaned when a foot kicked a coin, and knelt to fetch them, cursing in frustration each time one skittered away from his reddened fingers.

The beggar knocked.

Please go away, Evan pleaded silently; Jesus God, please go away, leave me alone.

He straightened with the aid of one skinned hand pressed against the glass, retrieved the receiver, and took a long, deep breath.

Slowly, now, he thought; careful does it.

A coin slipped into its slot, the digital amount of his credit beeping into view on the screen over the push-button dial.

He smiled weakly.

A second coin.

He frowned.

How much? Does it matter? Who the hell cares?

Two more, and he punched Addie's number, heard the double-ring burr, and let his forehead come to rest on the top of metal phone.

The beggar knocked; it sounded almost polite.

When she answered, he glanced skyward and felt his mouth sag open.

"Addie? It's me."

"Oh god, Ev, what's the matter? You sound terrible."

Thank you, he thought; he wasn't sure it was a prayer.

"I'm in a phone booth. Salisbury. I have no money, no car, I can't get home, Jesus, Addie, can you come for me? It's . . . it's raining."

"Evan, where have you been? I've been trying to get you all day. What are you doing—"

"Addie, please!" He slumped against the door. "Addie." Softly now. "Addie, please, come get me. I'm catching pneumonia out here."

"Where's the box?"

"I don't know. Wait." He looked around for a street sign, a landmark, and gasped when he looked straight into the beggar's eyes.

The beggar knocked.

Evan stared at him. "I don't know where it is," he said, keeping his voice, as if the beggar were listening, taking it all down. "On the High Street, that's all I know. Near the cathedral, I think. Hell, you'll find me. I'm the only American in town, standing in a goddamn phone booth. In fact, I'm the only living thing on the goddamn street."

The beggar smiled.

"Evan, don't move. Do you hear me? Don't move a muscle, I'll be there in fifteen minutes."

"Addie?"

"Yes?"

Paul wants to kill me, Addie. He thinks—

"Hurry, okay? Just . . . hurry."

The line went dead.

The beggar walked away.

Evan watched him blend into the night, turned away and slowly replaced the receiver, hanging onto it for a moment to keep himself from falling. His lips moved soundlessly, his right foot began to tap against the floor, his left hand scooped up the remaining coins and dropped them into his pocket without losing one.

The booth trembled.

His feet turned to ice.

He pulled the door to him and stepped out into the rain.

And walked in the direction the beggar had taken, hands back in his pockets, collar up, head down.

Addie would find him.

And if she didn't, Paul would.

2

She made him strip off his coat, his sweater, his shirt and trousers, his shoes, his socks, curled him onto the front seat beside her and tucked a rough-woven car robe around him until only one bare foot and his head were visible. Then she grabbed another robe from the back seat and toweled off his hair as best she could, until he grunted a protest when the hair began to pull and the cloth scratched his forehead. Once behind the wheel, she turned the blower fan up as high as it would go. It was too hot, stifling, but he didn't care. Heat leeched the cold. The wind couldn't touch him. The rain sluiced down the windshield and was battered by the blades.

"You poor darling," was all she'd said when she'd pull up beside him.

Poor darling.

He closed his eyes.

The little car hissed away from the curb.

Poor darling.

The radio had been muttering; she switched it off. He shifted, and she reached over to tuck the blanket around him again.

"I'm okay," he whispered hoarsely. "Keep your eyes on the road."

In the dashboard light her smile was grotesque. "You're alive, then?"

"Barely."

"Are you hurt?"

"I don't think so."

"Did you have an accident?"

Black cab; red stripe; the jerk and twist of a body as heavy tires crushed it.

"No."

"Are you going to tell me what happened?"

He looked over.

Had there been a catch in her voice, the choking of a sob?

"It's a long story."

Her hands gripped the beveled wheel at ten and two, and they didn't look as if they could slide or move even if she wanted them to.

He held his breath as the compartment filled with harsh white, released it when a truck passed them and splashed them and vanished redly into the night. Then he sneezed, rubbed his nose with a corner of the blanket and vanished inside it. Not caring. Stripping off his T-shirt and flinging it over the seat, hearing it strike the rear window with a loud, wet smack.

"I hardly think you're in any shape," she said lightly when he resurfaced.

He sneezed again.

Salisbury dropped away, into the night, as she swung into a series of back roads marked by high hedgerows and narrow lanes, an infrequent streetlamp that outlined a stone wall, a canted signpost, the rusted remains of a bicycle on the verge. The black was accentuated by the twin glow from the headlamps, and nothing seemed to move despite the evidence of his ears—as if the car were on a treadmill, the same greying stretch of road drawn under them time and again. And inside the car, the green from the dashboard etched their ghosts onto the glass. No matter which way he turned, he could see himself. And her.

"You must tell me," she said.

"Oh God, Addie, I've had a nightmare."

Her right hand left the wheel again, touched his shoulder. "Good Lord, you're shivering! Are you warm enough?"

"Fine. Yes. Fine."

"All right. I'll take your word for it. For now." A sharp turn; rain blasted the passenger window. "Now tell me your nightmare, Evan."

He drew himself into a tighter curl, pulling the robe down to uncover his mouth. "I was in London. I saw . . . I saw Paul."

There was no reaction.

She drove on.

Green rain on the windshield, grey rain through the headlamps.

"And there was a man called Trinton. He—"

"Wallace Trinton?" she said, mildly surprised. "*The* Wallace Trinton? The bookie?"

"Well . . . yes, I guess so. He said he was a bookmaker, anyway."

"It was on the radio. He was hurt in . . . Covent Garden? He's in hospital now."

"I know, Addie. I was there when it happened."

"Your nightmare."

"Yes. Part of it, anyway."

touching my wife
"Yes," he said. "Part of it."

A wisp of fog snaked across the hood.

"Damn," she muttered. "We may be in for a long ride if this gets any worse."

Worse than what? he wondered; worse than . . . what?

"Talk to me, Evan. Talk to me before I scream."

He cleared his throat, which made him cough, choke, spit up phlegm he spat outside when he'd rolled down the window. Rain spattered on his face. The window caught halfway up, and he swore at it until it closed.

The rain.

A fist of wind that shoved the car into the other lane and made him hold his breath.

The blower softening when she turned the fan down a notch.

hunter

"Paul thinks we're having an affair."

She nodded, and kept on nodding.

"He . . . God Almighty . . . he believes we've been seeing each other for quite a while. This sort of came out when he was talking about the tower." He frowned. "No. Wait. This is wrong, I'm doing this wrong."

"You're doing fine," she said quietly.

"No, I'm not. Give me a second. I'll start from the beginning. From last night. When I saw him."

"Last night?" She stared at him. "You mean you saw him last night?"

"While you were with that bike rider. He was across the street. He made me promise not to tell you until he'd told me what he wanted."

"And you didn't say a word."

"Addie, you didn't see him."

"I know."

"I mean, you didn't see him the way he was."

85

"And how was he, Evan?"

He considered.

"Like death. He was like death."

3

He talked as the rain pummeled the car, the wind played with it, the fog fought the storm to try to bury it.

With his eyes closed, watching himself in a dimly lit film, he told her as much as he could remember. Dialogue as much as he could, word for word. Giving her a few spoken stanzas of the Highland saga, not caring about the words, only the sense. Doing his best to be objective, and failing whenever he saw the skeletal hand, the drool, the foam, the shadow for a face. In a monotone most of the time, while his mind sorted Paul's ravings into some sort of logical sequence—the infidelity first, the castle and tower at Windsor second, the song of the banished hunter somewhere else along the line. Somehow they were tied together, he was sure of it, but by the time he had finished, he still didn't know how.

The accusation he could understand, though he didn't know why Paul had kept such a belief to himself for so long a time; the person with him in the tower, if that person existed, he didn't get, couldn't find a clue for, wasn't at all sure he ever would, given the state of the man's mind; the goddamn hunter made no goddamn sense at all.

"Then he screamed."

"What?"

"He screamed, Addie. I had had enough, I was angry and, quite frankly, scared at the same time, and I told

86

him I'd had quite enough, thank you, he could contact me again when he wanted to talk." He shrugged. "So he screamed."

"My god, Evan."

"And I ran."

He could see the tear.

It bulged on the rise of her cheek, shimmered with the car's shimmering, and didn't fall.

It fascinated him; it repelled him.

He closed his eyes again and picked up the story. This time there was no attempt to be fair; no glossing of Paul's part in the chase. He faltered when he told her about the accident on the Row, the people injured and perhaps dead, the shop window smashed, the shop itself very likely destroyed; he faltered, but he told her. And grew breathless as he described the race to the Underground at Russell Square, weary after that. So terribly weary.

"He's going to come, Addie," he said when he'd finished. "I don't know when, but he's going to come after me. You."

She killed the tear with a finger. "I don't want you to say anything for a while, Evan."

"But Addie, you don't get—"

"Not for a while, all right, Evan? Just let me drive. I'll need all my concentration." A wavering smile. "You know how you love my driving. Let me get us home in one piece. All right? Right."

He obeyed.

He rested his head against the window and watched his breath fog on the glass; a finger poked out of the bundle and traced through it. The thrumming of the engine kept him from sleeping. The occasional glimpse of the roadside had him frowning to see more.

Paul believed . . . did Paul honestly believe he had caused that taxi to crash? Had he done something? No.

He'd only hit the side. But the cab had crashed. Cause and effect? It happened because Paul believed, or Paul believed because it had happened?

The vicar's daughter.

Jamie.

i am the hunter

Paul had been nearby when the accidents had occurred, and connections had been made. But the same logic would be true for him as well, with Priscilla Flaunter, the bookmaker, and even the cab. That was ridiculous.

He started.

Jesus, had it been Paul outside the cottage? Had it been him all the time?

He sat up.

Holy shit, had Paul seen him hold Addie?

"What?" she asked.

"I don't know. I'm not sure."

"He's obviously quite . . . mad."

He reached out to touch her arm. "Addie, why don't you let me drive the rest of the way?"

Tearstained, her face swiveled to him, and away.

The car sped up.

Trembling again he sank back into his corner and decided that thinking in his present condition wasn't going to get him anywhere. He would only create fancies where none existed, build bridges where there were none to build, nothing to cross. And all of it would only get him into trouble.

He laughed to himself.

So he wasn't in trouble anyway?

Aw hell, he thought; aw hell.

"We're here."

He blinked. "What?"

"We're here." She turned off the ignition, unstrapped

her seat belt, and squirmed until she was able to reach into the back and yank his trousers free of the sodden pile on the floor. "I need your keys," she explained, showed them to him when she found them. "You stay here until I tell you, understand?"

"Addie—"

"I'm the doctor, you're the idiot. You stay here until I call you."

Before he could protest again, she was outside and running to the front door. It opened, and she ducked inside. The foyer light snapped on. The living room. He shivered as the cold seeped in and killed the heat.

But he waited.

A single light in the hall window above the door flared on, giving form to the rain, streaks and slashes that merged into planes like falling mirrors.

He sneezed mightily.

She appeared at the door and beckoned.

I'd rather die, he thought, and opened the door, grunted as he stepped out into a riverbed of mud, and said, "Fuck it," when the car robe fell from his shoulders.

"You're wet," she scolded when he stumbled across the threshold.

"Big deal."

She herded him upstairs, into the bathroom, where the claw-footed tub was already filling with hot water.

"Jesus Christ, I'll scald to death in there," he said, batting away the steam.

She snapped the band of his underwear. "Then add some cold, you great clot, and get in. I'll put the kettle on, get something to eat." A shove. "Do it, or I'll just dump you in."

"Jesus, Addie—"

"Don't kid yourself, Yank," she said, vanishing into the hall. "I've seen better."

89

Don't kid myself?

Jesus.

It took a while for his fingers to grasp the tap without slipping off, but he finally added the cold water to take the fire from the tub, then stepped out of his underwear and into the bath. Sighed. Slid. Draped his arms over the sides to hold himself up. Felt the storm flee and confine itself to rattling the pebbled window overhead.

When Addie returned, she had a tray with teapot, two cups, a bowl of sugar, and a pile of biscuits. She set the load on the sink and used a bath towel to dry the floor. Then she dropped one to use as a rug, and sat, brought the tray with her and said, "One lump or two." A hand up. "Never mind. Two level spoons, but I'll be damned if I'll put in lemon."

"I like lemon," he said, his head against the hard curve of the tub, his eyes closed, nostrils testing the air for the strength of the tea. He liked his dark; she liked hers light.

"Screw the lemon."

The spout banged against the cup.

The cup nudged his hand until he opened his eyes and pushed himself up high enough to be able to hold it without drowning. After his first sip, which burned his tongue and he didn't care, he looked down at her.

"What are you doing there?"

"Because if I were there," and she nodded toward the toilet, "I could see you."

"Oh." He felt stupid. And suddenly very naked.

"Your knees," she said, and nodded.

"Huh?"

"Raise your knees."

He did, and bared his teeth at the raw red, the tiny dots of black, the scratches. "Swell."

"I'll get some tweezers to pull that tar and stones out."

"The hell." He lowered them back under the surface. "Later, maybe."

"Later, yes," she insisted gently. The cup to her lips; she looked over it at him. "Now tell me again about Paul."

"Addie, please."

"He said he was going to kill you, Evan. For god's sake!"

He drank. "Do you believe him?"

"Do I believe you?"

"He said it, Addie. I swear to God, he said it."

"I don't know." She turned until her back was against the tub. "Do you?"

He stared at the tea, at the steam, at the top of her head.

"Yeah," he said at last, damning himself, damning her. "No. Yeah. Hell, I don't know."

Nine

He awoke to the sound of tapping glass. Disoriented, fearful, he lay rigid beneath the blanket, refusing to open his eyes, trying instead to send another part of himself out there, into the room, the hall, the ground floor, the yard—a secret self that would be able to scout around for him, uncover the traps and identify the noises and return to him in safety, without his moving a muscle.

But all he could do was hear the rhythmic tapping.

Until a voice said, "I rather thought it would be better than an alarm or a bomb. If you had a heart attack, I'm not sure I could explain why you're naked, and I'm here."

Startled, he opened his eyes and stared at the plaster cracked above the bed, barely seen since the drapes were closed over the room's single window, creating a twilight that sharpened rather than softened all the edges. Then he shifted his gaze until he saw Addie sitting on a chair beside his dresser. On the dresser was a cup; in her hand was a spoon she rapped against the saucer.

So much, he thought as he wriggled to sit up against his pillow, for my extrasensory powers.

"Welcome back," she said, laying the spoon down. She wore a dark blouse and slacks, her hair was out of its habitual ponytail, falling over her shoulders, making her seem even smaller than she was.

He looked down at his bare chest, felt silly when he took the blanket as casually as he could and drew it up from his waist to the first rib.

Naked.

Then she . . .

"Have no fear, Master Kendal, your virtue is secure," she assured him wryly. She stood and brought him the cup. "I slept in the other room. That bed is too damn soft. It's a menace. Do me a favor and shoot it first chance you get." With a soft groan she placed her hands on her waist and twisted, stretched her spine, which drew his look to her breasts and quickly away. "I feel like I've been run over by a horse."

"That's why I'm in here," he said.

And remembered.

As good as her threatened word, she had deftly plucked the bits of tar and pebble from his knees, rubbed ointment into his shoulder, took his temperature and pulse, and hustled him off to bed. A pinch of medication in his tea, she had explained when he'd protested, yawned, glared accusingly at her; and Paul, she was sure, wouldn't try to drive all the way from London on a night like this.

He looked around for his clothes.

Addie, by the window, grinned over her shoulder as she thrust the drapes aside. "I'll get you something in a minute. Come awake first."

Outside it was near dark, the panes running rain.

"Christ, what time is it?"

"Seven, give or take."

"At night?"

"Morning. You've slept a good five hours."

"Nothing good about them," he muttered. He reached for his watch lying on the nightstand, and his shoulder threatened to explode into his neck. "Jesus!" A raging bruise gathered at the top of his arm. When he felt it, it was warm.

"You'll live," she said.

"Right. Tell me another." And, when she went to the wardrobe, "You don't need to do that. I can—"

Her look was a doctor's forebearing a stubborn patient, then she grabbed a folded pair of jeans from a shelf, and a dark brown shirt with mock epaulets. With an exaggerated grimace at his taste, she tossed them on the bed, then rooted through the dresser for socks and underwear, muttering to herself about bachelors who couldn't organize even simple things, like clothes.

"When you're ready," she told him, "come down. I'll have a proper breakfast for you."

Why the hell is she so calm, he wondered.

"Have you called the police?"

"Perhaps later," she answered calmly. "Get civilized first."

"You're the doctor." He swung around gingerly, keeping the blanket over his middle. Flab around his waist; his chest was too soft; the meat of his thighs no longer hard. He rubbed a palm from throat to stomach, imagining what he looked like, and wishing he had truly started that exercise program he'd been swearing he'd start every New Year's for a decade.

At the door she paused and put her hands on her hips. "Don't take all day. I . . . I need to know what to do. What we're going to do."

A one-shoulder shrug as he reached for his socks. Then he looked at her and groaned in false pain. "I don't think I can do this by myself."

Her lips parted in a silent laugh. "Then you'll have to come naked, won't you?"

She was gone.

He flexed his knees carefully, flinched before he could

94

even put a hand on his shoulder, and dressed. Amazed at how composed he was, after last night. Conventional wisdom and cinematic cliché should have had him pounding on the nearest police station door, demanding immediate protection, round-the-clock surveillance, a new identity, something, anything. But despite the story he had told last night, now, in daylight, such as it was, he still couldn't bring himself to believe that Paul would really kill him, much less do him real harm. It had been the madness talking, not his old friend; it had been whatever Paul had convinced himself had afflicted him that had brought on the prediction.

But if that was so, why had he run?

Easy—belief then had been based on proximity to Paul's madness; doubt now was based on distance and a sense of security within his own walls.

"Evan, did you fall asleep?"

"Coming," he called, and stopped in front of the mirror atop the dresser.

Oh Lord, Kendal, are you sure you're not dead?

Scrubbing his face dryly to return color to his cheeks, he picked up his shoes and hurried down the stairs, glanced at the front door and realized it was locked. Addie sat with her back to the window, patted the cushion beside her. On the coffee table between the couches were two plates of fried eggs, slices of toast in their holder, butter scooped onto a saucer, and coffee for her, a glass of milk for him.

He didn't accept her offer. He took the couch opposite so he could see around her to the outside, dropping the shoes to the floor.

"I don't think I'm very hungry," he said, looking down at the eggs.

"It doesn't matter," she told him. "You're going to eat anyway."

95

Which he did, astounded at the extent of his appetite, grinning around his food whenever she rolled her eyes in disgust at the way he shoveled the breakfast in. When he finished, she ordered him to stay put and carried the dishes into the kitchen.

He heard water running in the sink.

The panes lightened, shadows in the rain growing more distinct, becoming the hedge, the trees, the shrubs. He wanted to stand up, to make sure Paul wasn't out there, and scolded himself instead. The man wasn't there. Wouldn't be there. He was still in London.

Waiting.

Please God.

Addie returned and sat beside him, slumped back, bare feet propped on the table. She wiggled her toes.

"So," she said. The skin under her large eyes was taut, the lines at the corners of her mouth deeper than he remembered. "I think we ought to do something besides sit around and wait, don't you?"

"You want to try and find him?"

She waved toward the front yard. "It's not a big country, Evan, but it's a big country out there nonetheless." Her hand dropped to her leg. "No, obviously we can't go looking."

"Then—"

"First suggestion—there's a message on that machine I think you'd best hear."

"You've been snooping," he said.

"I needed to know if it was Paul," she replied without apology.

The answering machine was parked under the telephone. Grunting when his shoulder pulled on him, he reached over and ran the tape back, then stared at the fireplace.

"Mr. Kendal? Are you there, Mr. Kendal? It's Brian.

Brian Oakland. Boy, I call all the way across the world practically, and I get a machine. Neeba's gonna kill me when she sees the bill. Mr. Kendal, I know you're busy and all, but could you call me when you get a chance? It's not an emergency or anything, don't worry, but it's been a while and all, and we'd kind of like to talk to you. Can you call? We'll all be here, at my house this weekend, if you can. On Saturday? It's just after midnight now, my time. Thursday. Call, Mr. Kendal. If you're not busy, that is. You can make it collect, or whatever you call it over there. Okay? Thanks. I guess that's it. Goodbye."

Dial tone, too loud.

He switched it off and cupped a hand thoughtfully over his mouth, playing it again in his mind.

"What is it?" Addie asked.

He twisted around, pushed himself into the corner and pulled his legs up, grabbed his knees. "Beats the hell out of me. Brian—I've told you about him, I'm sure, he was one of my best students, not a genius, but he always wanted to learn—he was always a pretty steady kid. We write—him more than me, I'm lousy with letters—but he's never called before." He stared at her, looked away to the foyer. "Just what I need."

"He said 'we,' Ev. Is that his grandmother too?"

"Neeba?" He laughed, once. "Not that old lady. She's so independent, she'd die before admitting she ever needed anyone's help. No." A frown; a sniff. "I don't know. Maybe some of the other kids. His friends." His chin rested on a knee. "Rita Galiano, I would guess, and maybe Corky Ploughman, Greta Rourke, Blue Cross."

She chuckled. "You're kidding. Blue Cross?"

"Sadly, yeah." He stretched out his legs, his feet finding their way onto her lap. "His real name is Theodore. They used to call him Ted, naturally, until he busted himself up in a football game when he was in eighth grade.

97

Five weeks in the hospital. He came out Blue Cross. The poor sap."

Her hand lay gently on his instep. "You like those kids, don't you."

"Yeah, they're all right. For kids."

She squeezed, and a sharp pain shot into his calf.

"Okay, okay," he said, yanking the foot away. "They're nice kids, all right? I used to talk with them now and then. Sometimes they listened, sometimes they didn't." He looked up at the ceiling. "I have to admit, they made it nice to get up in the morning."

"Then I guess they're in trouble." She frowned briefly. "Don't they have parents?"

"Sure. But sometimes there are things you just can't tell your folks. At least they thought so." A quiet snap of his fingers. "Stunts," he said, grinning. "Damn. I'll bet it's the stunts." He explained what he meant, finished with a quick gentle laugh. "They're not in trouble at all. At least not yet. Five to one they're looking for Kendal dispensation. I give my blessing and they blow the town up."

"Father Evan?"

"The devil's more like it."

She grabbed his other foot before he could pull it away too, and he didn't resist. Her fingers worked an unconscious massage, one that had his eyes half-closed before he realized what was happening and sat up, placed his feet flat on the floor, and his hands flat on his knees.

Addie said nothing.

He stared at the window, seeing nothing outside.

Time.

The slow ticking of a clock.

"Evan?" No more than a whisper.

He wanted to throw up his hands in denial, shake his head and contradict loudly the traitorous, treacherous, partially formed but all too recognizable thoughts that fought with the concern in Brian's voice. Instead he sat stolidly, aware of his breathing, aware of her beside him, aware that if he looked at her now their friendship would be over, would become something else.

"Evan." Her professional tone.

He could have kissed her.

"What are we going to do now?"

He put his palms together, pressed his fingers under his chin. "The accident," he decided. And once he'd said it, he knew. "Who survived?" he could sense her puzzlement. "Come on, Addie, who survived?"

"The car's driver, Josie Vesage."

"Josie?" He looked at her. "Waitress, right? In the fish 'n' chips place?"

She nodded. "Yes. Banged up, but nothing serious. That is, nothing life-threatening."

"What about the guy on the bike?"

"Coma," she said flatly. "I could call in. He's not mine, but I can check if you want." She pulled a handful of hair from her shoulder. "Why?"

"You think I can talk to her? Josie?"

"Why, Ev?"

He couldn't lie; she wouldn't believe him. "It's something Paul said last night." Too many images, then; too many hours and too many words. "Did I tell you?"

She shook her head.

"He claimed he caused the accident." When her hand fell away, he took it back quickly. "He was there. I did tell you that. I could see him, Addie, from where we were standing. He couldn't have done it."

"But he said he did."

"Yes."

She rubbed her eyes with one finger and shook her head. "I don't know what's going on."

"Neither do I," he said. "I swear to god," he insisted when she looked at him oddly. "I really don't know what the hell he's up to."

"A mystery."

"A pain in the ass. But if we can, we can find out from Josie, at least, if Paul was sniffing around her car."

He pulled his hand free, but gently, slowly, and leaned over to put on his shoes. As he did, she leaned over as well and kissed his cheek.

"I'll call the hospital to see if she's able. I don't suppose you'll want to wait until she gets home."

"How long?"

"A few days. Three, perhaps four. I want to keep an eye on her. Just in case." She tucked her hair behind one ear. "It's not just the physical I'm worried about."

"You and me both. But if she's up to it, I'd like to see her soon. This afternoon maybe."

He watched her think.

Then she nodded. "You're a good friend, Evan," she said, and stood.

God, no I'm not, he thought; no way in hell.

THE HIGH STREET

Ten

1

To every thing, thought Rupert Flaunter, there is a season, isn't that right?

Isn't it?

Of course it is.

Otherwise, what would be the point?

He brushed a blade of dead grass away from the sagging grave and leaned back against the headstone. He wasn't afraid of it toppling; it had been here centuries before he had arrived at St. Agnes and would no doubt be here centuries after he had found his own place, here among his parishioners and those who had gone before.

The churchyard was small, no more than five or six dozen plots. Most of Bettin Wells had come to prefer the larger places north of the village, airy, sunlit, with maps and things, a handful with guides and booklets and photographs that made death look almost pleasant. Here there was nothing but ancient trees, ancient gloom, and a handful of faithful ancient crows that called the ghosts to rest each morning at dawn. He hated the damn birds. They were forever waking him up, worse than a damn alarm clock and a damnsight more accurate.

Everything has its season.

From here he could look across the well-kept grass, the encroaching weeds, the flowers and wreaths, to where Priscilla would lie tomorrow afternoon, at the base of the sturdy back wall between her mother and her aunt. Queer old duck, was his wife's elder sister. But then, so was his wife. Both of them, despite his calling, had put more faith in their gaudy fortune-telling cards and weekly horoscopes than in his Sunday Gospel. Neither had been able, unfortunately, to foretell or forestall their own passing. So much for crystal balls.

He shifted his buttocks on the damp ground, drew the flaps of his topcoat tidily over his legs.

Sitting here was a pleasure. Had been for years. In the solitude, the shade, the bothersome grumble of the village behind him, the sermons would come on the voice of the Plain, the advice, the working out of crises large and small, while the crows and the sparrows and the rooks and God knew what else prowled and pecked and fought and built their nests. Eggs. Chicks. Life among the dead, and glad he was for it. Had this been like the graveyards in the movies, all fog and creaking stone, he would have gone mad ages ago.

Everything.

Priscilla.

Pris my Pris.

He clamped a hand around his throat to trap a sob, but he wasn't quick enough to stop a tear from trembling in the wind. He let it fall. Blinked. Patted the ground beside him.

"Not to worry, Lemuel," he said to the ghost of the seafaring man he felt stirring beneath him, put down in 1650. "Just a tear, not to panic, I shan't lose control. God's will, you know."

The wind slipped over the Roman wall and touched his

face, moved the branches of the tree that overhung the grave. One branch in particular, low on the trunk, thick, without leaves, groaned a little, and Rupert glanced up at it.

"Now suppose, Lem," he said, pointing, "that were to fall. Crack me straight open, I've no doubt. Sooner or later they'd find me, fuss and bluster, and isn't it too bad about the vicar. A foot either way and he would have been spared. A horrid coincidence. Terrible. Who'll say grace at the next festival then?"

A crow settled in the grass beyond the soles of his rubber boots. It preened.

Rupert stared at it. "Will one of them even think that perhaps God is done with me? Will it never occur to them that God knows what He's doing?" A bitter snort for a laugh. "Lem, they'll never understand. I know that now. They'll never understand."

He sneezed.

Pris.

The crow flapped off.

For the first time in his life, Rupert was alone.

He heaved and twisted himself to his feet and dusted off his trousers, his coat, glanced down at the grave and said, "Lem, if I were to think that Pris was gone for no reason, I would lose my mind."

He wandered then, nodding to old friends, plucking a tall weed now and then, finally arriving at the front wall—new, brick, as high as his chest—and followed it to the iron gate that released him onto a stretch of lawn. On his right was the church, brownstone and small even with its spear belfry and soaring entrance; on his left past a high row of ragged evergreen shrubs was the rectory, brownstone and small even with its three chimneys and peaked slate roof. Straight ahead, the lawn only ten feet wide, the land dropped to the road, climbed again to a deserted field.

A car slowed, stopped, and as he watched, it pulled turtle slow into the driveway that disappeared on the far side of his house. A woman was at the wheel. She waggled white-gloved fingers at him.

I do not want visitors, he thought as he smiled back, but he knew Flo Winnry had seen him, he would have to walk over there and endure the condolences, the sympathies, the stories of relatives similarly erased in accidents and disasters. She meant well, God knew. They all meant well. They were killing him. He fingered the plain gold cross lying against his chest. They were killing him, but he would survive because he was their shepherd and he had to.

O Lord, he thought, if You would just tell me why.

2

The High Street was a gentle downward slope until it reached the intersection at Wellington Road. Flat then, more stores and offices, and on the corner the Queen's Lance, a restaurant and pub. In front, and raised above the sidewalk by a single stone step, was a patio on which were wood tables and benches for the good days and sunlight, and for the oldsters who liked to sit of an afternoon and watch the pedestrians, and the traffic.

An hour before noon, a woman in a black coat, black tam, white hair flying like a flock of startled geese, nodded further down the street, toward St. Agnes. "So I says to him, Reverend, you ever need anything you just call me. You was there for my Sid, rest his soul, it's the least I can do. That's just what I said to him this morning. Drove to the church, there he was just coming out of the churchyard. Picking a place, I expect. Next to her mother."

Her companion was similarly dressed, though her hair was fire-alarm red to match her cheeks, the tip of her nose, the point of her pointed chin. "And you're right, Flo, it is, isn't it? The least, I mean. After all the poor man's done for us. Nobody else gives a damn if we live or die, and that's the truth." A sour glance over her shoulder at the restaurant entrance, filling now with clerks on early lunch. "Old, that's what they think. No good for nothing. Baggage is what we are. Stick us in the closet, take us out when we're needed, and precious few times that is, I can tell you."

"Now, Dulcie, remember your heart."

Dulcie Dennis scowled and thumped her chest, proving it would take more than a temper to stop her these days.

On the table, aside from their cups of tea and cucumber sandwiches on stiff paper plates, were two small bags of birdseed. A half-dozen pigeons fluttered at the patio's edge, patient, watching them with one eye, heads up. Flo Winnry pushed one of the bags closer to her friend. "Here, take some, the bag is still full, those poor things haven't eaten forever, what with the rain. Come on, now, throw them a handful before they go for your ankles."

Dulcie sighed. "That poor man. Right in front of his very eyes. I shudder to think of it."

Flo agreed. "Worse yet, that doctor was there too. Right on the spot. Saw Pris was dead the minute she laid eyes on her. Must've been horrid. Can you imagine it?"

"I heard the American was there too, Flo."

"He was."

107

"Pretty chatty, wouldn't you say? With Doctor Burwin, I mean."

Flo tightened her lips, narrowed one eye. "I know exactly what you mean, Dulcie Dennis, and you get them ideas straight out of your head. He's a good man, that Mr. Kendal. Talked my Eric out of leaving school, didn't he? Made him see the light when he wouldn't take the time of day from me. Grandmothers don't count for much these days, but that Mr. Kendal, he knew just what to tell that boy without getting the dander up. Amazing, if you ask me."

"Amazing Eric understood him."

"Dulcie!"

"Well, I'm sorry, Flo, but your Eric's not one for listening, is he? Need a bullhorn, don't you, just to get his attention."

The tables began filling as weak sunlight began to filter through the overcast. Chatter, laughter, more than a few calling hello to the women who fed the birds.

A gust of wind.

Flo squinted at the cars, at the passersby who seemed decades younger than she. Then she glanced up at the sky and shuddered.

"Are you cold, dear?" Dulcie asked.

Flo shook her head. "No."

A pigeon hopped onto the table and Dulcie batted it away. "You feel it," she said, one hand burrowing into a bag, pulling out seed, tossing it on the ground.

Flo looked at her sideways. "Sorry?"

"You feel it."

"I don't know what you're talking about."

"Don't be playing daft, Flo. I'm not your doctor, am I. You feel it. Just like me."

Flo didn't have to nod. They were old, no arguing that, and being old had taken some things away, precious and irretrievable, drained them here and there, robbed them and left them. But there were also compensations. Like the knowing. She didn't believe it was anything unnatural, just an extension of things learned and things seen and things felt over the years, all of it come together, like some kind of sixth sense they're always talking about on the radio. It stood to reason, didn't it, that age had to leave you with something. Otherwise you might as well be dead. So she and Dulcie had the knowing. Sensing. Nothing to put a finger on, mind, but knowing just the same that things in Bettin Wells were somehow not right.

She was neither bothered by it, nor did she ignore it.

It was just something else to deal with today.

It might even prove just a little exciting.

"There!" she whispered, pointing at a dark car idling at the intersection.

Dulcie shaded her eyes; the sun had found a break. "Who?" She leaned forward, staring at the two policeman strolling past. "Two coppers? It's only Ludden and that new boy, I don't know his name. So what?"

"Not them, you goose," Flo answered impatiently, and stabbed her finger at the car again. "Doctor Burwin, silly. And Mr. Kendal."

"Oh. He doesn't work, does he? Must be rich."

"Eric says he lectures now and again down in London."

"Like I said," Dulcie answered, and took a bite of her sandwich.

Flo would have snapped at her but her attention shifted from the car pulling away now to a woman marching up Wellington, away from them. There were only a few shops up there, which soon gave way to cheek-by-jowl houses brick and wood and distinguished from one another only by their gardens. A few blocks later there were fields, woodland.

The Plain.

Ida MacNair didn't live up that way.

Flo wondered what the nutter was up to now.

3

"Him," Ida muttered.

She stared at the pavement, clothes fluttering and flopping, heels barely heard over the rasp of her breathing.

"Him."

The vicar, the poor soul meaning well, doing his best in a heathen world, talked too much of God and the devil, as if they had anything to do with living day by day. He never did understand her when she tried to explain about Him, as patient as she was, as many hours as she had taken. But that was all right. Few did. Like children they all were, thinking their mum was out of touch with the world, not knowing how right she was until they were older and, sometimes, it was too late to do anything about it except say I'm sorry. Mothers knew that sort of disbelief, that youthful skepticism was part of the agreement—raise the child, let him go, let him come back and exclaim how wondrous, and how dangerous, the life out there could be, and not once, not once did a mother say *I told you so.*

Nor would she.

Because there was no time to wait for Bettin Wells to grow up. Something had to be done now, before Him got in the way.

And to do that she would have to walk every street, every alley, every mews, every lane in the village.

She would do that.

She would find Him.

If she had to walk forever.

4

"Cycles is what I'm talking about," said Cable Ludden, for emphasis tapping his polished nightstick against the black iron railing that fronted the Royal John Hotel's lawn and gardens. "All things work out in cycles, you see. You study your history, laddie, you can't miss it. Nowt happens but it does in cycles. Mark my word. Quiet, riot, quiet again. You check your Romans, you see what I mean. Cycles. Round and round, just like a . . . a cycle."

Police Constable Garret Purdy nodded, even though he hadn't the faintest idea what the hell the idiot was talking about. Which, all in all, was all right with him. The day he began to understand the old crock was the day he marched into the station, turned in his badge, and went back to greasing and praying over dead engines in his dad's Birmingham garage. It wasn't that he disliked police work, though the accident the other day was the worst thing he'd ever seen in his life, had made him lose everything he'd eaten. God, that was a mess, gore and shit all over the street, Doc Burwin damn near taking the vicar's head off, and half the damn village crowding around shouting instructions to the fire brigade, which didn't know what to do first—wash off the blood or put

111

out the damn car. He had a hell of time that night, for damn sure.

"A fiver there's something else before sunset."

Purdy nodded again. Kept his own counsel. One of these days he was going to take one of Sergeant Ludden's bets, double it the next time, the time after—he'd probably be able to retire before he was thirty and move the hell out of this place. Sure as hell before he was in line to head the local force. Ludden wasn't all that old, though he acted it sometimes, and would probably be around even long after Charles took the crown. Not much room for advancement.

Which was fine, truth be told, by him.

"Not a car this time," the older policeman said, glaring at two schoolboys cutting across the High Street in the middle of the block. "Too coincidental. A fire." He grunted. "That's it. A fire."

"Right," Purdy said.

"Look sharp, lad," Ludden said then, a quiet smile in his voice. "We're famous again."

Purdy just managed not to grin as he tried not to make a show of expanding his chest, sucking in his stomach, looking official and British as all hell, while on the long brick path leading to the hotel entrance, a handful of whispering tourists had attached cameras to their eyes.

"Slow and steady," the sergeant said from the corner of his mouth. "Just like in the movies."

Purdy chuckled.

Ludden sniffed his displeasure.

Ah, bugger off, you old fart, the young man thought.

The hotel behind them, they followed the High Street as it swung gently to the right, a short block of offices giving way to a school playing field and, beyond, houses Purdy knew he'd never be able to afford unless he found a way to triple his wages and steal a little on several

112

sides. They crossed the street, paused, and headed back for the town center. Slowly. Making sure those in their gardens saw them, chatting now and again with a pedestrian, looking in on shops randomly, completely ignoring those offices that had, on benches just inside the door, security men who looked as if they'd spent half their life in the nick on breaking-and-entering. By the time they reached the station, his back was running sweat.

"Gawd, you smell!" Ludden exclaimed as they pushed inside. "You home too late last night to shower?"

A single large room, a long counter separating two desks and a dispatch radio from the front. Constable Eisley crouched at the radio, long snout, thin mustache, long fingers that caressed the microphone obscenely. They called him Ratty and kept him off the streets. He didn't mind; he knew no one else in the county could have kept the equipment running.

"It's damn hot," Purdy grumbled, sweeping off his hat and brushing his hair back. "October ain't supposed to be this damned hot."

Ludden sighed. Loudly. "Lad, maybe you'd best see Doc Burwin, get a pill."

"I'm not seeing no woman doctor."

The sergeant laughed.

Purdy slammed up the counter gate and stomped through, heading toward the day room to get himself a cuppa.

"Garret," Ludden called. "I'll call the lady for you, what do you say? A private consult? Maybe she'll be impressed."

He laughed again, raucously, and was joined by Ratty, stuck in the far corner.

Purdy looked over his shoulder.

A gun, he thought as he glared at the two men; please, God, let me have a gun. Just once.

113

5

"He's a faggot, y'know," Police Sergeant Ludden said to the dispatcher after the door had closed none too quietly. "Wants us to think he's having it on with that waitress what got bashed up the other day, but I know better. Faggot. Can tell 'em a hundred miles away."

"Bugger off, Cable," Eisley muttered.

"Exactly," Ludden said. "Exactly."

The front door opened.

Ida MacNair stomped in.

"Balls," Ludden whispered.

Eisley giggled.

"You!" Ida called. "Inspector! Come here this instant! I want to report a fire!"

Eleven

1

He had no idea how the argument had started.

"Are you still going to Edinburgh tomorrow?"

"How'd you know that?"

"Evan, I've known for ages."

"Christ."

"Is that wrong of me?"

"No, of course not. I just didn't realize you knew that much about me."

"Well, I'm sorry, I'm sure. But it is your job, you know."

"Jesus H, Addie, I know that."

"So?"

"Sew buttons."

"My, you are in a state, aren't you?"

"I'm not in a state, Addie, for god's sake! I'm just . . . hell, never mind."

"You'll have to pack."

"It's only until Sunday. A thing on Friday night, an early talk Saturday, be nice to the hosts, let them show me around, that sort of thing. Just a couple of things in a small bag, I'm not moving home, you know."

"Then you are going."

"I didn't say that."

"You meant it."

"Addie, just leave it, all right? Just leave it. Right now I'm not sure what I'm going to do. I'll decide later, if that's all right with you."

"Suit yourself."

"I will."

"Fine."

"Good."

And the drive out to the hospital was made in chilly silence, sunlight brighter as blue drove off the grey, windows reflecting, grass unnaturally vivid. It ought to be dead, he thought as he stared sullenly out the passenger window; it's October, for Christ's sake. It ought to be all dead. Jesus, don't they have winter over here?

His denim jacket was stiff from being draped over a radiator all night, and he kneaded the sleeves, yanked on the front, snapped the collar up and down, did everything but drop it on the floor and stomp it back into shape.

Addie giggled.

He glared at her.

She glanced at him, gave him a one-sided smile. "If I swear never, ever to pry into your private life again— which I wasn't, but just for the sake of this ridiculous argument—will you stop pouting and give me the time of day?"

After a long moment's deliberation, he made a show of pulling back a sleeve to expose his watch. "It is precisely two-fifteen." A sharp nod. "Precisely."

"Thank you."

"Don't mention it."

They had stopped outside of town, at an overly large pub that catered primarily to tours and tourists seeking

116

rustic England. The meal wasn't very good, but it filled him again. The argument had taken place there.

"And you're right, you weren't prying," he said as she swung off the main road, into a wide lane shaded by oaks as thick around as the car.

"No, I wasn't."

"So I guess I'm sorry."

"You are that."

"Man," he said, "you don't give a guy any slack, do you?"

"Trousers," she answered. "We call them trousers."

His sigh was an explosion.

Another turn, a second one, and they passed through the gateless entrance to Greenfield, more a brick-faced clinic than a hospital, on a low flat hill surrounded by gardens and a slow-browning lawn. An artificial pond to the left served as a staring point for several patients wrapped in coats and mufflers. A nurse stood by, chatting with an attendant. The parking lot was directly in front of the two-story building. Addie pulled into a space with her name on it.

"Very nice," he said, nodding to the hand-painted sign.

"Did it myself. Director keeps taking it down, I keep putting it back. He's going to disassociate me one of these days."

They walked into a small lobby, smelling, he thought, of universal hospital—age, disinfectant, fear, boredom. After a word with the receptionist, Addie led him down a long corridor, around a corner, and into a spacious sunlit ward with eight beds on either side. Most of them were empty. Greenfield dealt primarily with simple cases and emergencies that would, eventually, be passed on to facilities with larger plants and a larger staff.

Josie Vesage lay in the last bed on the right.

Evan almost changed his mind and left.

The walls were a soft white, framed and cheery paintings above each bed, fresh flowers on the bedstands, the mirrorlike floor a checkered cream and green. Pleasant, save for the circumstance, and it had nothing to do with the other night. There was no horror here, no lives in imminent jeopardy, just a middle-aged man in a brown dressing gown wearing earphones and conducting with one lazy finger, a younger man asleep, a woman sitting up, knitting, every so often holding her work to her chest as if fitting herself.

She smiled shyly.

Nothing to do with Paul.

He slowed.

Addie moved on, waving at Josie when the young woman saw her and called out her name.

I am going to feel like a jackass, he thought.

He stood at the foot of her bed and slipped his hands into his pockets.

A real, genuine, dyed-in-the-wood jackass.

Josie was in her indeterminate twenties, bobbed red hair, enough freckles to distract from her undistinguished blue eyes. Her head was wrapped in a bandage, and her left hand was swollen with gauze. A few scratches across a slightly swollen nose, a vicious bruise blotching her left cheek.

"Look like hell, don't I?" she said glumly as Addie perched on the edge of the mattress and fluffed the two pillows so the waitress could sit up. "I know I'm lucky, should've been dead, but lord!"

Addie leaned over and plucked the chart from its footboard hook, checked it and pursed her lips, raising her eyebrows before placing it on the bedstand. "Fever last night?"

"A bit. I'm alive, though, so I don't care, do I?"

A faint lisp; a high pitch that sounded like constant laughter.

She looked at Evan suspiciously, then grinned. "Hey, you're Mr. Kendal. The professor."

He smiled.

"He comes in to my place, that's how I know him," she confided to Addie. "Lots. Don't eat proper at all, the way I see it." She patted her stomach lightly, but Evan saw the wince she tried to hide. "Too many chips," she told him, "you'll end up like Ida."

"Hush," Addie told her.

Evan watched then as a pulse was taken, another temperature level recorded with an electronic thermometer, and a closer examination of the most visible injuries, which turned his head away from the sparks of pain so evident in the young woman's eyes. He guessed concussion, a broken rib or two. At the impact, Addie had told him on the way out, Josie had not been wearing her seatbelt and had been thrown across the length of her car's front seat. The door, not properly closed in the first place, had sprung open and she'd been dumped, stunned, onto the street. The explosion, though not great, had thrown her another ten feet. She'd hadn't known what had happened until she had seen a doctor staring down her.

"There," Addie said. "All done. You'll live, love."

"Oh god," the waitress said, "it hurts."

"I know."

"I want to go home."

"A day or so." Addie stood. "Just to be sure."

"But what about the job?"

"It'll be fine, dear, it'll still be there when you're better."

Josie fussed then about her cats, her budgies, the general state of her apartment, and Addie assured her that all would be taken care of, not to worry, just get well enough to manage on your own, there's a good girl.

Addie kissed her cheek.

Evan smiled and winked.

Josie frowned for a moment. "Damn."

"What?" he said mildly.

"There goes the sale, don't it?"

"What sale?" he asked.

"My car." She rolled her eyes in disgust. "Was going to sell it, get me something that wouldn't fall apart every morning when I was in a rush." A scowl made worse by the bruise and scratches. "No sale, no car, I'm going to have to walk. Damn, wouldn't you know."

Evan tried not to sound like a cop. "Who were you going to sell it to?"

She rolled her eyes again. "Not sure, I don't think. I mean, there was a couple of people interested, but no one wanted to give me my price. Says the old thing ain't worth it." She laughed once, no bitterness. "They're right, now." A look to Addie. "You tell your husband for me, okay? Nothing to think about now, that's for sure."

"Paul?"

Evan felt nothing.

"Yeah. Last week it was. Came around the shop. Didn't he tell you? Maybe it was going to be a surprise. Heard I was selling, took a look at it, said he had other places to look, but he'd call me. A real gentleman, that's for sure. Didn't have to tell me he was looking other places. But he did."

"Did . . ." Evan cleared his throat. "Did he drive it?"

"What? No. Was in a hurry, he was." She winked broadly at Addie. "You know men, Doctor. Thumped it, poked it, made all kinds of noises like he knew what he was doing. Maybe he did, I don't mean no offense, but—" She shrugged.

"So," Evan said, "he didn't . . . fuss with the engine or anything."

"Lord, no, Mr. Kendal. He wasn't there but a couple of minutes. While I was on my break. Nice man, but a little peaked, if you ask me. He been sick, Doctor Burwin?"

"No," Addie replied quickly. "A touch of the flu, that's all."

"Wish that's all I had. Lord."

Evan couldn't think of anything more to say, to ask, and walked toward the exit while Addie gave the waitress instructions about walking, eating, other things that were lost as he pushed through swinging double doors into the empty main corridor. He leaned against the wall. A soft double bell sounded somewhere in the building. A muffled voice on the public address system. It all sounded too hollow.

Jackass, he told himself.

Addie soon joined him, patted his arm to herd him toward the lobby. "Well, what do you think?"

"I don't know."

"Evan, please."

"All right, all right. He wasn't lying about that, okay?" Outside, on the steps, they stood for a minute. "But the accident wasn't caused by any mechanical failure, any electronic system's malfunction, right? Right." He started down the steps. "She backed out the car park and the motorcycle hit her." A squint at the sky. "An accident."

"That's exactly what I was thinking." She opened the car door and looked at him over the roof. "I've been thinking something else."

"Oh?"

"I've been thinking that Paul was jealous."

She ducked in before he could close his mouth.

2

Evan said nothing as she drove back to Bettin Wells. He knew that the wrong word, any word, would sooner or later lead him to ask if there was, in fact, anything for

Paul to be jealous about. It was a question that terrified him. But her attitude and her driving gave him no clue to what her answer might be. She swore at a sheep trying to cross the road in its own good time, rolled down the window and yelled a laughing greeting to a teenage cyclist trying hard to race her, and finally, once they were back on the High Street, she asked how long he'd be staying in Edinburgh. He told her again, just until Sunday morning. It was a quick lecture set, a quick fee, in and out before anyone had any time to wonder what had hit them. When she laughed, truly, he relaxed; when she poked a finger toward the police station and suggested they probably had no reason to go in, he agreed; when she pulled up in front of her office—on the ground floor of a narrow, two-story building, a vacant office above her—and asked if he wouldn't mind walking home, he shook his head. It wasn't that far. The exercise would do him good, the time alone would give him the opportunity to review the lecture for points of improvement. On the sidewalk they shook hands, and he felt like a fool. Then she thanked him, told him she'd call when her hours were over, and kissed him quickly. On the cheek. Turned him around by the shoulders and gave him a playful shove. He waved without looking back. Stopped in at a newsagent for the afternoon paper. On the sidewalk again he checked the sky, amazed there was no sign of rain, and nearly collided with the women he called the Gerry Twins. Gerry, for geriatric. Affectionately, because Miss Dennis and Miss Winnry never failed to ask about his health, his work, his adjustment to village life. They refused to believe he didn't come from a major city, because they all were in America, weren't they? They smiled, he smiled back, and began the uphill walk. Seeing Josie Vesage in her hospital bed, seeing Paul examining the car, seeing the motorcycle, seeing the fire, seeing the horror on Reverend Flaunter's face.

Was that all there was to it?

Was Paul simply jealous?

Was jealousy, combined with whatever illness the man suffered, corroding his mind?

Paul didn't, couldn't have, caused the accident and Pris Flaunter's death.

Paul touched a London taxi and it plowed through a shop window.

"Christ," he said as he unlocked his front door, "give it up, Kendal. Just give it up."

3

He packed a bag.

He packed his notes.

He stood in the backyard and listened to the wind. It told him that, if he was going to be absolutely reasonable about this, there was no sense taking any of Paul's threats or ramblings seriously because the man was ill. No question about it. All he and Addie could do was wait for his friend—her husband, damnit—to make the next move.

Or wait for someone to call, to tell them that Paul was at last in hospital.

Or, he thought as the wind grew chilly, they could, in fact, talk to Sergeant Ludden. It was crazy, just leaving Paul alone in London, wandering, growing less coherent by the minute. It was worse than crazy—it was criminal. Ludden would be able to contact the Metropolitan Police. Addie was a doctor; she could tell him that it was imperative that her husband be picked up and placed in a hospital's care at once. Then, when it happened, they would go down and see him. Let Addie hear the madness for herself. And, with luck, one of the doctors would be able to tell them what Paul had and how he would be cured.

As he closed the door behind him, he smiled. Relieved, and saddened.

That was exactly what they had to do.

Because Paul was a friend.

And he was Addie's husband.

"All right already," he muttered as he headed for the telephone. "You don't have to keep reminding me."

Oh really?

"Really."

No one answered at her office, no one answered at home, but he wasn't worried now that the problem was solved. He even allowed himself to feel a bit stupid at his reaction; one might even call it hysterical, understandable, illogical. But whatever it was, it was also just plain stupid. So stupid that, as he stood by the stove and waited for the kettle to boil, he laughed aloud when he recalled his fright at the beggar in Salisbury, and wished without much guilt that he had given the poor man something. A hell of a story that'll make. The kids will get a kick out of it.

He blinked.

The kids.

A quick check of his watch—it would be just half-past nine in Port Richmond—and he wondered if he ought to make Brian's call now. He smiled to himself. Somehow, making a transatlantic connection just to encourage the gang to do what they'd most likely do anyway seemed a bit of a waste. Yet it would be nice to hear them again, Brian was expecting it, and the call from Shirley had, if he were going to be honest, sparked a touch of homesickness. A little soothing from home, considering all that had happened lately, would be welcome. But there was nothing he could do. He'd have to call Monday, explain about the Edinburgh trip; if he called now, and Brian didn't answer, Neeba would think there was something wrong. Not to mention getting poor Brian in trouble before his time.

"Oh well."

The kettle whistled.

The telephone rang.

He reached for the kettle's handle without thinking, and yelled "Sonofa*bitch*!" when he burned himself. The kettle clattered back onto the burner, water spurted from the spout and hissed on the stove. A few drops landed on the back of his hand. He swore again and turned on the cold water, held his hand under it, and listened to the ringing.

"Coming," he whispered.

The kettle whistled again, and he reached over, switched off the gas, and nearly fell against the stove.

"Well . . . damn!"

Grabbing a towel from a small rack above the sink, he raced into the living room and snatched up the receiver.

"Two-nine-eight-eight."

His fingers stung. He tossed the towel aside so he could blow on them.

"Hello?"

The kettle shrieked. Christ, he'd turned the wrong goddamn knob.

"Hello!"

He flapped his injured hand, blew on it, and glared across the room. "Look, if this is a joke, I'm not laughing." He hung up. Hard. Hurried back to the kitchen where he shut off the stove and used another towel to plop the kettle into the sink. He didn't want tea now. He wanted something stronger.

The telephone rang.

Kill 'em, he thought as he strode out of the room; I'll goddamn kill 'em.

"Hello!" he barked.

"How nice to hear your voice," Addie said. "Are you in bed with a naked woman or something?"

He sagged against the sideboard. "No. Sorry. Someone just called and wouldn't answer me."

"It was me," she said. "I could hear you, but I guess you couldn't hear me." She paused. "You thought it was Paul, didn't you."

"No," he said truthfully. "He never crossed my mind." He told her then that he'd tried to contact her earlier, and explained why. When she didn't respond immediately, he wondered if he should have said anything at all. "Addie, it isn't like we're having him arrested."

"I know that. I'm just hitting myself because I didn't think of it before."

He smiled at the front window. "My fault. Hysterical men, don't you know."

"Yes. I do know."

He switched the receiver to his other hand, spat a curse.

"Are you all right, Ev?"

"An accident," he told her. "Burned my hand making tea."

"Wonderful. You do live an exciting life."

"Yes." He carried the telephone to the couch and sat heavily. "I am blessed."

"Are you packed?"

"All ready to go."

"Ah. Well. Will you call me when you get back?"

"I'll do better than that. Why don't you meet me at the station right now, we'll tell Ludden, and then you can buy me a farewell-until-Sunday meal."

He sensed a hesitation before she said, decisively, "Fine. Ten minutes?"

126

"Fifteen," he said. "Ludden isn't going anywhere and I have to use the—"

"Spare me," she interrupted with a laugh. "God, you Yanks are a crude lot. What makes you think you can run the world?"

"Because," he said, "nobody takes us seriously until it's too late. Crude, you see. Very effective."

"Yes. Yes, I know."

4

There was no problem with the sergeant. In fact, his concern for Addie was demonstrably greater than his concern for Paul; so much so, Evan was embarrassed. But his one attempt to make a humorous comment was received with a look that made him turn away from the counter and study the notices on a bulletin board nailed up by the door. When their business was completed twenty minutes later, and after a brief laughing discussion of Ida MacNair wanting to call out the fire brigade to extinguish a pile of leaves burning in someone's yard, he walked Addie across the street, to an Indian restaurant not much wider than a fair-sized closet.

She was grateful he'd been able to think clearly.

That's what she called it.

He called it almost too damn late, but she refused to hear it. And she looked as relieved as he felt. They hastily assured each other that they were not making light of Paul's condition, but it was, wasn't it, rather nice to know that something concrete was being done. Worrying would only make them paranoid. She admitted that she'd not been thinking straight all day and would, probably, have gone to London herself.

They had several drinks.

He walked her home.

On her doorstep she took his hand and covered it with hers. "You're a saint, Kendal, you know that."

Her hand was warm.

"I know nothing of the sort. I'm just helping out a friend."

"And Paul."

"Of course. That's who I meant."

Her hand was soft.

"I know that, you oaf. I was teasing."

Her face, in the porchlight, was shadow and moth-wing.

"Paul," he said, cleared his throat, spoke the name again. "I wish I knew what was wrong with him. Physically, I mean." His tone was deliberately expectant.

"I couldn't begin to tell you," she said, half doctor, half wife. "I've been trying to think, remember, hunt for symptoms I may have missed. But I can't come up with a thing. And I can't even think about a true diagnosis unless I see him."

"I know, I know, believe me. It's just that he just looked so—" He stopped himself when he sensed her discomfort, when he saw Paul's face and had to shake it away. Speculation was a waste of time, futile, emotionally horrid, but he knew it wouldn't stop her. It hadn't stopped him.

The only thing he could tell himself for sure was that Paul Burwin was crazy. The why would have to come later.

"I'll call when I get back." When she nodded, he tapped a finger lightly against her brow. "And if you hear anything while I'm gone, you call me, yes?"

She nodded.

"You have the number?"

128

She nodded again, and made a performance of clutching her purse. "Right here. I'll make a hundred copies as soon as I get to work tomorrow."

"Very funny."

She looked up at him.

He couldn't see her eyes; it made him nervous.

"Thank you, Evan."

"Like I said."

She glanced up and down the quiet street, then kissed him quickly, and softly. On the lips.

He walked back to the car, left around the corner from the restaurant, and drove slowly home. By the time he was in bed, tracing the cracks in the ceiling, he was glad he was on his way to Edinburgh in the morning. It would be a good time to consider what the hell he was going to do next.

While waiting for the police to find his friend.

While wondering if she knew that Paul, the bastard, had every right to be jealous.

IV

WEEKEND IN PORT RICHMOND

Twelve

Port Richmond on the Hudson, sprawling westward from the lip of a boulder-bound, tree-dotted cliff whose shadow in the water was barren and dark gray. Its north end was tucked into a U-shaped extension of dense state forest that merged with the woodland across the state line, south and west boundaries simply other towns that touched other towns that snaked-danced south to the George Washington Bridge; shops and garages and offices and restaurants and one twenty-unit motel and two movie theaters and two parks and a truck-laden highway that slipped out of New York State; Palisade Row and Forest Road and Tyler Avenue and Hemlock Terrace and no streets with numbers to give visitors and newcomers a hint of where they were, where they had to go, where they could turn to get to Oak Street or Raven Road; one bus line, one taxi, and a train station that few had been to since the day it had closed.

Port Richmond with a name that lied about its function, though not about its origin, when gunrunners and smugglers used the fifty-yard rock flatland at the base of the cliff to avoid British frigates and British patrols; a secret name among rebels, made public when gunrunners and smugglers and Tories decided to stay.

Port Richmond at night, from the air, a sprawl of lights winked out by shifting leaves.

Port Richmond, in autumn.

High and deep October sky.

Thirteen

1

High and deep October sky.

"Admit it, Brian," the blonde said, voice low and husky. "This is something you've wanted to do practically since we met."

No clouds; a flock of Canada geese, ragged, heading south and calling.

"C'mon, be honest."

The morning's light frost replaced by a startling reprise of Indian summer.

"Well?"

He couldn't deny it; he had. Desperately. Foolishly. To the point of dreaming of it constantly—night dreams and daydreams and doodling dreams of it in class—wishing for it from the moment the weather had turned warm enough to temporarily shed overcoats and gloves and make the shade almost welcome again. From the moment he had stepped out onto Mickie Farwood's patio for the first time he had wanted to, and had never found the nerve to ask her if they could.

His grandmother would shoot him if she knew what he was thinking.

"Bri-an." Coyly. Teasing. Sing-song and low. One dark-nailed hand flat and warm against his chest, the other on the small of his back, pressing him to her without letting him touch.

"I guess," he admitted at last. The smell of her, sun-warmth and turning leaves and just a hint of wine on her breath. He grinned. "Yeah."

With a slow nod she moved away. Shorter by a head, slender, her hair cut high above her shoulders while his, three shades darker but still clearly blond, curled neatly an inch longer. To celebrate the break in weather, she wore a bumblebee-striped tube top and stone-washed denim cutoffs, her skin still lightly tanned from a sailing summer in the Caribbean. Her feet were bare; her legs gleamed gold.

When she looked at him over her shoulder, chin tucked, eyes narrow, he almost sagged against the wall.

She did that to him.

She knew it.

Every stride, every look; the flutter of her eyelashes when she was pleased, the moue of dark lips when she wanted something he wasn't sure he could give her, the way she touched her right ear with her left forefinger, stroking it and tugging it, her arm crooked across her chest whenever she was planning her next move.

Everything snared him, as she knew it would, as he knew it would. And didn't give a damn. In the real world, rich girls didn't much care about boys who lived in boarding houses with their grandmothers; in the real world, boys who lived in boarding houses seldom spoke to rich girls because they seldom had a reason.

Only in his dreams.

"Okay then," she said.

The hot tub took up most of the patio's southern edge, redwood sides and turquoise interior, three shallow wooden steps to climb in, tiled shelf wide enough for glasses, plates, bottles. It seemed near the size of a modest swimming pool, and was already filled, the water's surface rippling as a chilled breeze coasted across the backyard.

He looked nervously side to side.

"Bri?"

No one could see.

The two-acre yard, like all the others on the east side of Palisade Row, ended at a hundred-foot rocky drop to the sun-caught Hudson River. It was marked by an outer stockade fence and closely spaced trees—autumn-touched maples and hickory at cliffside, two rows of evergreens on the flanks—and an inner boundary of flowering shrubs trained to grow high and wide and tangled. The flagstone patio itself, dead leaves huddled in one corner, had a wall of its own, knee-high and brick, topped at intervals by potted plants Mrs. Farwood tended as if they were frail children.

No one could see.

Unlike home, where everyone saw everything whether he liked it or not.

He jumped at a sudden hissing, a bubbling, and saw Mickie bending over the control panel.

She looked back at him around one bare arm. The cut-offs rode high. She raised her right foot and kicked lightly at her rump. "You want everything, Mr. Oakland?"

"Huh?"

She chuckled, and pointed at an inset panel of buttons he couldn't see from where he stood. "Pay attention, boy. With this thing we got bottom jets, side jets, bubblers, shooters, a zillion combinations." She giggled, closed one eye, and licked her bare shoulder. "I got one

137

here, you could have an orgasm before you get your toes in."

Oh hell.

Not even in his dreams.

"Well?" Still looking over her shoulder, she rotated her hips. Once. "Want me to turn it all on?"

Her hips rotated again.

He blushed, and felt it—heat on his cheeks that had nothing to do with the sun, and a tight band around his chest that had nothing to do with the snug T-shirt he wore. He had no idea why she thought she had to talk that way; she must have read it in one of her magazines someplace. The now way to talk for sophisticated young women.

And she did it deliberately.

To confuse him. Excite him. Make him putty.

He had long since stopped asking *why me?*

Only last week, just as the English department monitor had passed out the quarterly final, she had leaned forward from her seat directly behind him and whispered, "You get an A on this, stud, and I'll fuck you bowlegged."

He had been so flustered, he'd barely finished half the questions.

Nevertheless: *why me?*

She stood slowly, stretched and groaned, then crossed her arms and slowly pulled off her top. Her bare back showed no white stripes. The tan was complete. She didn't turn around. "Brian, I'm not going in here alone. There might be sharks."

Nervously rubbing his palms over his thighs, he glanced through the sliding glass door into the house, his reflection jumping when a gust kicked past him.

"They're gone, Brian, remember? Golf, riding, something stupid. I don't know. Who cares?"

He checked the yard again.

"Damnit, Brian."

"Okay, okay."

He walked as steadily as he could toward the tub, stripping off his T-shirt, unsnapping his jeans. Casual; you do it all the time, stud, do it all the time. Flex the pecs, bulge the 'ceps. Hell, no sweat. Do it all the time.

Despite the temperature, he shivered. A kick took care of one of his sneakers. A second kick cost him his balance, and he banged into the tub's wall, his knee taking the brunt. He hissed and turned around, swore at himself and at Mickie, who laughed quietly.

"You all right?"

"Yeah."

Water splashed gently.

He turned back and saw her on the far side, sitting on a submerged ledge. The water boiled around her as she stretched her arms out along the shelf, froth and bubbles hiding all but her shoulders and the shining flat of her chest.

Don't stare.

She winked.

Jesus, don't stare.

She pursed her lips, kissed the air.

He checked the sky for a bolt of lightning, and decided, what the hell, I'm dead anyway. As quickly as he could, he stripped the rest of his clothes off and rushed in, backward. Catching his breath at the strike of water on his skin, sighing as he twisted awkwardly around and his buttocks found the ledge. He stretched out his legs and wriggled his toes. He closed his eyes.

"God," he said, "it must be great to be rich."

A feather-touch against his feet, sliding along his legs.

"It's much better," she whispered, "to be horny."

And sat on his lap.

Oh God, he thought, throat dry and neck taut; oh God, now what do I do?

After fluttering a bit, his hands finally lighted on her waist, touched silk and didn't dare move. She leaned forward, kissed him feather-light, leaned back and rested her hands on his shoulders. His own hands sank beneath the water, to the hard curve of her buttocks, where they froze for a second when they discovered the bottom half of a bikini.

It was time to drown himself.

Time to slip under the surface and let the cops find him naked; no way he could tell them he'd thought she was naked too.

I don't believe it, he thought; I do not believe it.

"Brian."

Okay. No problem. She's mostly naked, right?, that's gotta count for something, so just be cool, that's all, just be cool.

He grunted to prove he'd heard her, and let his hands drift up again, floating across her waist, not risking too strong a hold. At the same time, he was careful to avoid a direct stare at her breasts; it wouldn't be cool, it wouldn't be right, it would trap him the way her legs had trapped his thighs and her groin barely brushed his and moved away. And moved back. As if she were floating on the tide, unaware that she was moving at all.

"Bri?"

He focused on the diamond beads of water clinging to the hollow of her throat, quivering with the pulse he saw throbbing there. He didn't dare look at her eyes; he knew they'd be laughing.

"Bri?"

He grunted again. Speaking would be the end of him.

"I want to do a stunt."

He blinked, and looked up. "You what?"

140

Slightly forward.

"I want to do a stunt. I want to get in the school Halloween night."

I knew it, he thought, close to anger, closer still to disappointment. Rich girls and boarding-house boys. Who the hell were you kidding anyway, Oakland?

He almost pushed her away.

Sounding like a jerk instead: "We're not supposed to."

Slightly back.

A lopsided sneer. "That's the whole point, dope," she said, giving his shoulders a shove. "Linholm says we can't, so we do." Her head tilted back and she laughed. "My god, we pull it off and he'll shit a brick!"

Slightly forward.

"I don't know," he said reluctantly. "If he finds out—"

She leaned into him, and he closed his eyes, felt the give of her breasts against his cheeks, smelled her; she was warm. Her head came forward, her lips against his ear.

"He won't," she whispered. Her tongue on his lobe, circling. "But I will, if you will." Her tongue again, nudging. "Brian?"

Loudly he mumbled deliberate nonsense into her skin, and she giggled, arched her back to free his mouth.

"C'mon, Bri, please?" Her hand left his shoulder and a finger scratched down the center of his chest, poked at his navel, trailed downward, and up; he squeezed his legs together.

"If we're caught—"

She giggled. "Coward."

"No," he protested. "I just want—"

A car door slammed—gunshot in the sharp air.

She was away from him just as suddenly as she'd been on him. "Well, damn," she said without a trace of emotion. "I thought they'd be another hour."

141

A voice called her name.

He reddened and choked, flung himself out of the tub, slid and fell on his rump. He was going to die. He grabbed his jeans and yanked them on. He was going to be hanged. Socks. Sneakers. He was going to be frog-marched in front of his grandmother, who would lock him in the basement and throw away the key. T-shirt. No; she would scalp him first, cut off his arms, then lock him in the basement and throw away the key.

He turned.

Mickie was still in the tub.

"Hey," he whispered loudly, a frantic look at the doors. "Jesus, you'd—"

She pointed at the lawn. "If you hurry, you can make the trees before they get here." She stretched, lifted her breasts not quite free of the water and looked down at them, looked up at him without raising her head. "You're a little wet, you know. They just might suspect."

He wanted to kiss her; wanted to hit her; groaned and vaulted the wall, nearly tripped over his shadow and sprinted across the grass, angling left and batting through rose bushes and lilac, keeping low until he breeched the boundary of the yard next door. His lungs were cold when he paused, his legs trembling. When he heard Mickie call a cheery hello, he was off again, squeezing through a gap between the Farwoods' stockade fence and their neighbor's green-painted hurricane chain, keeping as close to the cliff-edge as he dared, not looking at the river below, or at the mountains across the way that walked to the horizon.

He didn't stop until he reached the safety of the woods, where he collapsed against a tree and sagged to the ground, holding his side, panting, blinking dancing black motes and sweat from his eyes.

I'm crazy, he thought; god, I'm crazy.

Over and over until the shaded chill reached him and his teeth began to chatter. A loud martyred sigh, a forearm dragged over his face, and he pushed himself up, checked his bearings, and trotted toward the road. He'd have to change before he caught pneumonia, but first he had to get into the house without anyone seeing him.

Dead, he told himself miserably; you're dead, you're doomed.

Two blocks, and he was forced to walk, one hand in his pocket, the other plucking the clammy T-shirt away from his chest. If his grandmother was there, he'd have to come up with a good one, but right now all he could think of was Mickie. Nude. Sitting on his lap. He had actually felt her breasts on his face, for god's sake! He had actually been *that close* to finally getting what she'd been promising since they'd met in September.

That close!

He'd also been that close to getting caught by her parents.

He punched his thigh.

Idiot!

He punched the thigh again and nearly gave himself a cramp.

2

At the next corner, Brian turned left, paying no attention to the pick-up games of football on front lawns and in the streets, the smell of leaves burning at the curb or in hole-punched trash cans, the sight of more than one man on a ladder, painting the trim, cleaning the gutters, taking advantage of the break in weather before the weather broke. On an ordinary day, he would have noticed; on an ordinary day, he'd have been at the football game, this week down in Ashford. But Mickie had asked him to stay home, she had something important she wanted to talk to him about.

He wiped his mouth with the back of one hand.

Something important—it looked like she wanted to get them both kicked out of school.

He paused in front of a green Cape Cod, for a moment puzzled by an unfamiliar automobile parked in the driveway. Then he shrugged without moving his shoulders and moved on. Mr. Kendal wasn't home, his place rented out to some family from Atlanta. Mr. Kendal was in England, teaching classes and, he had said in his last letter, "still trying to get used to the fact that I'm the one with the accent here."

At the time, it had made Brian smile; now it only made him resentful that the history teacher wasn't here. Mr. Kendal had almost always had time to talk, about whatever anyone wanted. He didn't know everything, but what he did know sure helped.

Sometimes it was even like having his dad back.

Sometimes.

He scowled at the sudden burning in his eyes, glared at the sidewalk until the burning left him. He walked faster. He trotted, arms heavy at his sides. He swung onto Forest Road, and grinned when he realized that he could tell his grandmother he'd been jogging, that's why he was so wet.

"Keeping in shape, Neeba," he'd say.

Neeba—because he'd never been able to say her real name, Anita.

"Just keeping in shape."

God, you're a liar. Not bad, but what a liar.

But it was a hell of a lot better than telling her that he'd been with Mickie after claiming he was going to the Luncheria to meet his friends. She liked most of them; she disapproved of Mickie. A lot. She had never actually said it to his face, but he knew it. He figured it was some kind of chemistry thing—hate at first sight, something like that. Mickie had only met her once, and Neeba had instantly gone all formal and polite, just the way she had when she'd met Mr. Linholm on Parents' Night last year and had barely touched his hand when it was offered.

Now *that* he could understand.

Linholm made a lot of people's skin crawl.

Why she didn't like Mickie, though . . .

He stopped at the foot of the driveway and glanced at the dark trees across the street, an arm of the state forest that always made his grandmother uneasy. Then he checked the house, a blue-shuttered white Dutch Colonial, small front porch flanked by evergreen shrubs and shaded by two willows, with a matching garage at the end of the drive. The place was empty. He could tell. There was something about it that sagged a little when she was gone. She was probably out shopping, or out for a drive.

Pure luck.

He was saved.

He grinned. And sneezed.

And a hard hand thumped his shoulder.

3

"Looks like you've been swimming, boy," an old and deep voice said, spinning him around, breath locked in his throat. "You're making a puddle here, you know that?"

Brian took a step back, waiting for his stomach to settle

back where it belonged. The voice belonged to John Naze, Mr. Kendal's uncle, who rented the small apartment above the garage. He was tall and bent, gaunt and rail-thin, wearing as he always did a worn brown topcoat and wide-brimmed brown hat. His hands were jammed deep in his pockets.

The old man smiled briefly. "You figure double pneumonia going to get you a couple of days off from school?"

"No sir," he said, smiling back. "I've been jogging." A vague wave toward the house. "Just got home."

Naze squinted up the drive. A hawk too old to hunt anymore, but not too old to remember how. He sucked at his teeth. "Thought maybe you busted a boiler at work."

Two or three days a week, thanks to Mr. Kendal, Brian had a job after school with the janitorial staff, polishing floors, washing windows, mowing the grounds. It wasn't making him rich; it kept him in spending money while Neeba saved for college.

"Nope," he said. "Just jogging." And he ran in place a few steps, grinning stupidly when his feet squished in his sneakers.

"Ah."

Another look away; another look back.

"Tell you what," the old man said after checking the sky, "you don't tell your grandmother I've been at the train station today, I won't ask you not to lie to me again." And he raised a thick eyebrow.

Automatic denial was as close as a shake of his head that instantly became a sheepish nod, a quick shrug. He almost held out a hand, but checked that as well. Mr. Naze never shook hands; they were so damaged by arthritis they reminded him of a shillelagh he'd once seen in a television show—all hardwood and crusty knobs.

"Deal," he said instead.

"Good boy." Naze winked and started up the drive, Brian shivering alongside him, from the chill breeze and relief. "She thinks I'm nuts, of course. Thinks I'm a loon, going out to a station house that don't have trains anymore. She told me once, a bear was going to grab me one of these days, tear me to shreds and then I'd be sorry."

Brian laughed. "A bear?"

"Swear to god, that's what she said."

Brian glanced over his shoulders. "It's the woods. She doesn't like them."

"They're not that bad," Naze said, angling toward the staircase at the side of the garage as Brian moved left, toward the narrow back porch and the curtained kitchen door. He turned his head, and Brian would have sworn he heard it creaking. "Don't forget, your grandmother is a city girl, Brian. Been here I don't know how long, she's still a city girl, always will be. Think I'm gonna give her bear steak for Christmas, tell her I shot it myself."

His laugh was canyon deep when Brian rolled his eyes.

"Well, maybe not," he said. "I'd have to eat my own cooking."

Brian turned away as the old man's left hand took precarious hold of the railing. Hardwood. Knuckles swollen into crusty knobs. Brian had no idea how the man was able to dress, feed himself, even turn on the TV. As he shuddered and reached for the doorknob, Naze called him.

"You gonna dress up for Halloween, boy?"

"Too far away," he called back. "Hadn't thought of it yet."

"Think of it," the old man told him, fumbling open his door. "You can borrow my hat and coat. Kids think it's me, you'll scare them to death."

The laugh.

The door closed.

Brian tried to smile, sneezed, and went in to change. Decided to shower to warm up and, as he lathered, cocked his head and said, "Hey, why not?" Though Mr. Kendal's uncle was sort of all right, not always friendly but not an old geek either, the little kids around here thought he was some kind of monster.

Because of his hands.

He grinned.

Jeez.

Jesus, why not?

It sure as hell would beat whatever off-the-wall stunt Mickie was planning. That, he knew, would bring him nothing but grief. No matter what it was, it would only bring him grief, and the wrath of Neeba on his head.

Fourteen

1

With a groan of disgust, Corky Ploughman pushed deep into the corner of the cracked leather booth, one knee drawn to his chest, worn denim jacket buttoned to his chin. His left hand circled but didn't touch a tall beveled glass that held a thick shake, dark chocolate. His right hand grasped the booth's scalloped top above his head. It was his usual pose, the usual back booth at Gilder's Luncheria, and the vague scowl on his face his usual thoughtful expression.

"The minute I am free," he declared with a sharp nod, "and my diploma is in my hand, I am going to burn that goddamn place down. Kiss that sewer and this town goodbye, all at the same time."

"Dumb," said Blue. He folded a long french fry into his mouth with a freckled hand and shook his head. Red hair so dark it was almost brown; brown eyes so dark they were almost black. His friends called him beefy; a failed football player gone to seed.

"The hell it is," Corky said.

Blue raised his eyebrows in a sigh. "Ain't gonna do any good if there ain't anyone in it. What kind of fun is

149

that?" He squirted catsup from a squeeze bottle onto his plate, took up another fry and poked at the thick mound until a space was cleared in the center. "What you have to do, see, is bide your time. Scope the place out. Pick the moment. Then mine the foundations, the ventilation shafts, stuff like that. Wait until the new kids show up in September, then . . ." He grinned. "Boom," he said softly. The catsup around his mouth looked like blood.

"You guys are sick." June glared across the table at them, thin lips curled in disgust. "You ought to be just glad you're on your way out."

"There was never any doubt I would be, Spinner," Corky told her smugly.

"Bullshit," Rita muttered and took a sip of her own drink. Corky was definitely not one of her favorite people. Too full of plans and not enough brains. All talk, no action. All hands and eyes. Thank god she had to be at work in an hour. Listening to him mouth off all afternoon would be enough to turn her into a nun, like her aunt.

"No, really," he insisted.

She turned to June, one eye partly closed, a finger tapping against her temple. "Think of it—the only male in the history of the illustrious Port Richmond Ploughmans to flunk physical education. Jesus. Now I ask you—how the hell do you flunk gym?"

June sighed loudly, dramatically. "I suppose you could start by cutting every other week."

"I did not!"

"Then you make wiseass remarks at the teacher," she continued, ticking off the points on her fingers. "Who used to be a Marine. In Vietnam. Green Beret. Volunteer."

"Who the hell said that?"

Blue ate another fry.

"Sad," Rita agreed. "Truly sad. You think Princeton will take back that early admission?"

"Entirely possible," June told her after due consideration. "Certainly not without precedent. I heard just yesterday that Shane Bishop's Stanford scholarship is on conditional just because he pulled a C in trig first quarter. And that's just a C, mind you. Who knows what'll happen when a true asshole *flunks* gym."

"Knock it off," Corky warned.

Rita ignored him and readjusted her pleated white blouse with an upright starched collar that kept digging into her jaw. It was bad enough she had to wear a stupid uniform at work, but yesterday her mother, in one of her helpful moods, had hand-washed it, screwed it up, and now it was too tight. Gaps kept opening between the buttons between her breasts. Too damned tight. And she was too damned big. She hated big. She hated everything about big. She wanted to be normal, like June Spinner, like Greta Rourke. Too big meant jerks like Corky would never be able to tell her the color of her eyes.

At the counter, someone asked loudly if anyone knew if the Redcoats had won their game yet; from a booth near the front, someone called back a "Who cares?"

A plate shattered on the floor, and half the customers cheered, the other half laughed.

"Y'know," Rita said to June, voice low in conspiratorial gossip, "on the way to school yesterday, I saw Mrs. Ploughman. She was at the funeral parlor. No kidding. Guess she figures it's all over now."

Corky lowered his arm. "Now look, Galiano—"

Blue slapped and gripped Corky's knee. "There is such a thing as cool, old son. Be it, and ignore them."

"What if I don't?" He glared at Rita. "What if I blow her up instead?"

You wish, she thought.

Her hands fluttered to her face and she rocked her head side to side. "Oh my. Oh me. Assault, assault. I am

151

trembling. I am afraid. Save me, June, save me." She stuck out her tongue. "One hand on me, creep, and my father'll rake you bare in court without even opening his briefcase."

Blue grinned around another fry. "Now we're talking sense, chums. Bare. Rake. But is it safe sex? And speaking of which, where the hell is Brian?"

Rather than answer, Rita picked up her soda glass and drank. Corky watched her chest, Blue watched her face, but she felt June turn away, pretending to check the half-dozen people at the counter. This, she thought sourly, is not going to be one of history's great semesters.

Then Blue picked up a fry and pointed it at her. "So, what do you think?"

"About what?" She checked her watch, looked to the ceiling, and grabbed the cardigan she'd dropped on the seat beside her. "I gotta go, guys."

"The stunt, jerk."

She nudged June to move along. "You're absolutely right, Cross. It's jerky."

June slid out of the booth.

"For Christ's sake, Galiano," Corky complained.

Rita followed, and waited until her friend had retaken her seat before caping the sweater around her shoulders and leaning against the table. "Corky, in case you hadn't noticed, some of us cannot afford to piss off the powers that be. There are too many other ways to screw up between now and graduation. Thank you, I'll pass."

"God," he said and fell back into his corner.

"C'mon, Rita, Linholm won't know," Blue promised her earnestly. "Give it a chance. If we plan it right, he won't know what hit him."

She pointed at Corky. "He does the planning?"

Blue nodded.

She shook her head. "Forget it. I'm late, I'm gone, and I'll write to you all in prison."

She didn't bother to ask what June thought of the idea. She already knew. The torch the girl carried for Brian Oakland was large enough to crush her, then burn half the state down. It would be laughable if it wasn't so sad. She hung around Blue because Blue was Brian's best friend. Better yet, Blue was Brian's neighbor.

"You got no guts," Corky muttered.

She tapped a finger against her temple. "But I got brains, Ploughman. I didn't flunk gym."

Without waiting for a response, she made her way through the sparse luncheonette crowd to the sidewalk, adjusted her sweater more snugly, and turned left. She didn't bother to hurry. The King's Castle restaurant was only four blocks away, and from the looks of Tyler Avenue, there weren't going to be many customers to take care of until much later.

That wasn't surprising. It always happened when the Redcoats were away—busloads of shrieking rah-rahs from school, and half the adult population, charged in a convoy to whatever stadium held the game. It wasn't that she didn't like high-school football. She did. She generally went to every home game when she could get off work. But she couldn't see following a team called the Redcoats from one end of the state to the other. Not even after they'd finally learned how to win.

Which meant, on days like today, hanging around at work, trying to look busy so she wouldn't get canned; which meant lousy tips, if she got any tips at all; which meant too much time to think.

A car honked at her.

She didn't look.

She kept her attention on the shop windows, trying to see past the Halloween decorations to the displays inside. But all she saw was her reflection—a hunched-over, slender, moderately attractive if she did say so herself Italian girl in stark white and black with her arms folded under her breasts, looking as if she wished fervently to be somewhere else. The moment she recognized the posture, she lowered her arms and straightened her spine. It was automatic. All she needed now was for her mother to drive by and yell at her in front of the whole town.

Don't slouch, Rita, keep your back straight! Hold your head up. Don't bend over like that, you look like you're in agony. Keep your arms down. Why do you part your hair in the middle all the time? It makes you look like a hippie. For god's sake, Rita, straighten up!

Easy for her to say. When her mother stood properly, her breasts didn't reach all the way to France.

Good grief, don't exaggerate, Rita. You're always exaggerating. Didn't you ever hear about the boy who cried wolf?

The boy who cried wolf had nothing to do with anything, and certainly not her bra size, as far as she could tell, but her mother always believed her point had been made, that Rita never needed any kind of explanation.

She burped, tasted onion and catsup, and smothered a giggle with her palm. Her mother had things to say about that, too. Her mother had things to say about *every*thing, for crying out loud. Even without asking, which was usually the case, she would tell you how to clean litter off the streets, how to get into college, how to get and keep the right man, how to elect the next president so he doesn't screw you with new taxes.

One spring afternoon after school, after her mother had tried to fix her up with Patrick the Prick Reynolds and Rita had rebelled strongly enough to cause a battle royal, she had sat in Mr. Kendal's classroom and tear-

154

fully wanted to know what right mothers had to think they knew it all—including the best boys for their daughters.

The first thing he had told her was that, believe it or not, love had a lot to do with it, no matter how poor the judgment or ugly the boy; there was, however, also a secret book maternity nurses slipped to all new mothers. It was all in there—every saying, every prediction, every remedy for everything from a cold to a triple bypass, every qualification and bank account size for every male that even breathes near the house.

Rita had laughed, and had only partly doubted.

Someone called to her from a passing car.

She didn't look.

Raucous laughter echoed behind her, but she didn't turn around. It had sounded like Brian, but it couldn't have been. Brian, word had it, was at Mickie Farwood's, in that part of town her mother would kill to live in.

June knew it too.

God, what a mess.

Mickie has Brian, June had had Brian once, and Rita, if she ever got the chance, would probably lock him in her bedroom until he swore on his grandmother's famous temper never to leave her side or look at another woman.

Oh sure; and tomorrow the Führer is moving to Canada.

What a mess.

A slap of wind hurried her on, and she didn't look up until she saw the mock-Tudor beams of the King's Castle on the next corner. At night, the amber carriage lamps flanking the entrance, the amber bulbs under the overhanging eaves, made it look special, the place to be for a good meal, and to be seen. In daylight, however, the sun made it look drab. A colorless photograph of a run-down dive in a run-down section of some run-down town.

"Hey!"

Hey yourself, she thought glumly, and stepped off the curb.

"Hey, Rita! Wait up!"

She looked around.

It was Brian.

2

Play this right, she thought as he trotted up, red-faced and grinning, and you'll only get yourself moderately killed.

"Going to work, huh?" he said.

She nodded and crossed over, acutely aware of him as he strolled beside her. Too aware.

"Hey, uh, you have to go in right away?"

She checked her watch. "Yeah, pretty soon."

"Oh."

His hands were buried in a denim jacket, his chin tucked close to his chest. A quick breeze slapped his hair over his eyes, and he snapped his head back.

"Problem?" she asked.

The sun was still warm.

A single cloud ghosted pale below it.

"Yeah, I think so."

She wasn't sure she wanted to know what it was; trouble, no matter what she did. A wave toward Gilder's. "So why don't you talk to Blue? I thought you guys—"

"Can't," he said. "I already looked." His shoulders lifted helplessly. "June."

Enough said, of course. The moment he walked in and was noticed, June would start one of two stock perfor-

156

mances, depending on her mood: she'd either be all over him as if nothing had happened, pretending they were still lovebirds and embarrassing the hell out of everyone in sight, or she'd freeze him out, ignore him, and bitterly cut him down to the others as if he weren't there, embarrassing the hell out of everyone in sight.

The old June, the before-last-summer June, had been almost a mouse, almost too shy to fall publicly for anything but a puppy. Then Brian had taken a liking to her, and she had fallen after all, fast enough and hard enough to crack concrete. When they broke up . . . Jekyll and Hyde, she thought. Mouse turned into a vengeful shrew.

Hurt, she knew, sometimes did that to nice people.

Brian sighed, and his miserable expression made her want to hug him.

"Y'know," he said, leaning a shoulder against the wall, "it wasn't all my fault. I mean . . . hell."

"I know," she said truthfully. "That your problem?"

"Yeah, I wish. No, it's Mickie."

Rita made sure her smile was rigidly polite. "Oh?"

He didn't seem to notice. "You're not going to believe this, Rita, but she wants to do a stunt."

"What?"

"Yeah." He looked at the pavement, kicked at it toe and heel. "I don't know what she's got in mind, but . . ." He looked up the street, squinting. "I don't get her sometimes, you know? I just don't get her."

I do, Rita told him silently; half the school does.

Then she realized he was mad. No; he was hurt. Something the bitch had said or done had hurt him, and she was ready, right then, to march over to Palisade Row and claw the goddamn bitch's eyes out.

And the abrupt rage startled her, frightened her, made her stammer until he stared at her and began to chuckle. When she grinned back, he looked away, and she stole

157

the moment to take a slow calming breath. This was crazy. She and Brian had been friends since he'd moved here after his parents had died; pals who had never before been jealous of a boyfriend, a girlfriend. Her fantasies about locking him up had been, she'd always thought, just one buddy looking after another, that's all, nothing more.

But this . . . this was worse than she thought.

This was getting too close to real.

"So," she said at last, forcing her voice steady, "you don't want to do it, or what?"

"I don't know what it is."

"So? You want to do it?"

He shrugged. He shook his head. He shrugged again. "Hell. Tell you the truth, she wants to get into the school for . . . whatever."

"Then don't do it," she said flatly.

"Yeah, but . . ."

Right, she thought, and wanted to grab his lapels, shake his teeth loose, and explain what taking advantage meant.

But he straightened before she found the nerve, reached out and squeezed her arm lightly before letting the hand fall away. "This is nuts," he said. "I shouldn't be putting this on you." He took a step away. Another. "See you later, okay?"

"Sure."

He half-waved, turned, and walked off.

She watched him until an elderly couple excused themselves past her and went inside the restaurant. Then she realized the time and grabbed the heavy door before it closed, glanced back up the street and saw June in the middle of the next block. Standing there. Staring.

Swell, she thought as she ducked hurriedly inside; swell, Galiano, just . . . swell.

3

That night, shortly after she got home from work, she called June.

When her friend answered, and heard who it was, she hung up.

Damn, Rita thought, staring glumly at the telephone; so what do I do now?

Her prediction seemed right—this definitely was not going to be one of life's great semesters.

Fifteen

1

Patrick lined up his shot and said, "It's not that I'm opposed to guns per se, Dominic, but what the hell do they have to do with the price of apples?" He closed one eye. The cue stick pumped once, shot forward, and the cue ball kissed the eight ball, which in turn rattled into the pocket.

Dom rolled his eyes heavenward and dropped his stick onto the table. "With guns, you don't care about the price of apples, you jerk. You just take them."

"You know what I mean. Rack 'em up?"

"You crazy? I owe you every dime I'm going to make until I'm ninety-six."

Patrick grinned, buffed his nails on his cashmere sweater, and walked behind the large wet bar. The basement room was long and narrow. The pool table sat at one end, a wall television screen dominated the other. The bar was in the middle, next to the staircase. "Drink?"

"Too early."

Patrick grimaced. "Don't be deviate, Pastori. It's never too early. Especially on Sunday."

Dom waved the remark off and dropped onto the

leather couch against the paneled wall opposite. He liked it on the couch. Here he could sprawl and not be so aware of how much taller Reynolds was; here he could make sure Reynolds noticed how broad his chest was, how flat his stomach, how round and hard his muscled arms.

Patrick—never Pat; that was his old man—never worked out, but was swift and quick of hand; Dom always worked out, and didn't need to be quick once he'd grabbed that quick hand.

Above his head was the room's only window, brown curtains drawn; the only light was above the pool table's slate felt.

He made a fist and put it against his forehead as if staving off a headache. "Just pay attention, Reynolds, okay?"

"Okay, okay," said Patrick. "I'm listening."

Dom nodded. "What I'm talking, see, is something these assholes will really remember us by, know what I mean?"

"Do I care?"

Dom showed him a middle finger, wearily. "I mean, what's so special about stealing a goddamn trophy and putting a pumpkin in its place, or painting the windows black, shit like that? That's not a stunt, man, that's games. I don't want games."

Patrick pulled a bottle of imported beer from under the bar, twisted off the cap, poured it into a frosted tall glass he held at eye level. "Dominic, when will you learn that it is all a game?" He drank, licked his lips. "The point is, it's a game the old farts expect us to play."

"So you don't want to play."

"Hell no. That's the point too. Linholm says we're too mature for kiddie stuff, right? Stunts demean the good name of the school, they cheapen the celebration." He drank again, smiled. "So he outlaws stunts officially. But he isn't stupid, Dominic. He knows someone's going to try it anyway. He expects it; we don't give it to him. And we make sure nobody else does, either." He spread his hands. "Voilà, the ultimate stunt."

"Bullshit." Dom cradled his hands behind his rough-shaven head. "The point is, Reynolds, that we don't play. We do it for real."

"You already had a drink, right?"

"What?"

Patrick held up his empty glass. "You've already been at it, haven't you, creep? You're drunk." Then he smiled slyly. "No. You're not drunk, you're floating." He leaned over the bar. "Let me see your eyes, wop. I dare you. Let me see your eyes."

Dom closed his eyes in disgust. "I ain't drunk, I ain't floating, you know better than that. Christ, you sound like that asshole, Kendal." He deepened his voice, lifted his eyebrows. "Mr. Pastori, there are better ways to screw up your life than drugs. Don't be an ass. Give yourself a break." He spat dryly. "Jesus Christ, that man was a shit."

"You are on something," Patrick insisted, grinning.

Dom glared at him. "Man, aren't you listening to me? Clean out your fucking ears. What I'm saying is, we could do something here that would kill this asshole crap off for damn ever." His eyes opened slowly. "And believe me, there won't be a damned thing they can do about it."

Patrick stared at him thoughtfully.

Dom leaned over and plucked a remote-control device from the table by his legs. He aimed it at the far wall; a pro football game flickered on, sound from speakers hidden behind the paneling. He was going to be there, one of these days. Pounding. Hitting. And getting paid for it,

162

too. He had the grades, and he had the skills, and sooner or later he was going to have the chance.

Patrick opened another bottle. "What do you want to do, kidnap the Führer?"

"Man," Dom said in admiration, "look at that nigger run." He looked at Patrick. "Something like that."

"You *are* crazy."

"Nope. I just hate Halloween."

Patiently he waited as Reynolds fussed behind the bar. That was the guy's trouble—always fussing. Everything had to be perfect, everything had to be just right, before he even thought about starting to make a decision. It drove Dom nuts. It drove him to his feet and across the room, where he reached over the bar and grabbed Patrick's arm.

"Come with me," he said.

"What?"

"Don't argue, dickhead. Just come with me. I want to show you something."

Patrick winced, nodded, and Dom led him upstairs, through the kitchen larger than his grandfather's apartment in Queens, and out the back door. The yard was immense, but Dom wasn't jealous. His own yard was at least as big, even if it was all the way down at the end of the Row, right at the invisible boundary between the Port Richmond Somebodies and the Port Richmond drones. No; what he envied was the house immediately to the left. Mickie Farwood lived there, and Mickie Farwood seldom bothered to wear all her clothes when she climbed into that pool she called a hot tub.

Her patio was deserted.

He grunted, and hurried to the driveway, jumped over the driver's door of his 1957 black Chevrolet convertible, and dug the keys out of his jeans. Patrick opened the passenger door to get in, and Dom laughed.

"What?" Patrick said.

"Nothing."

"Right."

The power muffler coughed, roared, settled to a menacing grumble, and Dom drove west, to the highway. He said nothing; the wind was too loud. He ignored Patrick's questioning looks. He only thought about his car, and the surprise in its trunk.

A grin. Carefully timed, to pique his friend's interest; a lazy hand to punch on the radio, FM, heavy metal, twice as loud as the wind; a check of the digital gauges he had installed in the dashboard, speed just high enough above the limit to make Patrick nervous, low enough to keep the local cops from making a federal case out of it if they saw him.

Two figures about to cross the street just up ahead.

Dom narrowed his eyes.

Patrick said, "Oh for god's sake, Dom, it's only Oakland and that old shit that lives with him. Don't waste your time."

2

On afternoons like this, John Naze liked to get out of the apartment and walk. It didn't matter where, just as long as he moved. He didn't get around as fast as he used to, naturally enough, but at least he was able to take almost a full youthful stride, unlike some of his peers who were barely able to make it to the park, where they spent every halfway decent day arguing over checkers and talking to the squirrels and greedy pigeons.

He couldn't sit like that.

He had to move.

And today, for a change, his hands didn't hurt.

A squint at the sky from under his hat—blue, but sharper now, a little darker than the last few days. The air just shy of brittle. A little touch of haze in the trees.

"Snow soon," he said. "Colder tomorrow."

Brian followed his gaze. "How do you know?"

John patted his chest. "Something an old man learns after a while. Stick in one place long enough, you'll be able to tell the temperature just by looking at the grass."

Brian hunched his shoulders. "No offense, Mr. Naze, but I sure hope I won't be around here that long."

"None taken," he said, and walked on.

He didn't know what the street name was, and it didn't matter. Port Richmond, while it stretched far enough in several directions to be able to call itself a town, wasn't all that big when it came to getting from one place to another. He knew all the shortcuts, most of the landmarks; getting lost was something he hadn't done since he was a kid.

He didn't bother with names.

He just knew where he was.

Which was more, he thought, than he could say for the boy. It had been damn near a shock when Brian had asked if John minded company for a while. Though he'd agreed, it made him uneasy. Suspicious. Kids who tagged along after old men were either after something, or hiding from something. After all, he wasn't the boy's grandfather, uncle, or even a close friend. They were, despite the shared meals, only neighbors. So he hadn't the vaguest idea what the boy wanted.

And the boy wasn't talking.

"Got a letter from Evan the other day," he said after a brush with a playful cocker spaniel.

"No kidding?"

"Says the lecture business has kind of dried up on him."

A glance and away; the boy was near to smiling.

"Yep. Seems his friend, that Burwin fella, the one that talked him into moving?, seems he doesn't have as many strings to pull as Evan thought." He kicked aside a fallen branch with his foot, aiming for the gutter. "I told him he was foolish, going all the way over there. Could've found a new job right around here, didn't have to leave his house to strangers."

"He wanted to go, Mr. Naze. He likes it over there."

"I suppose."

Another half block.

"Did he say when he was coming home?"

"Didn't say he was. Just said the lecture business had kind of dried up. I suppose he means temporarily."

"Oh."

At the next corner, an old black Chevy barreled past them, suddenly swerving too close to the curb. John had to stagger back to keep from being struck, was kept from falling by Brian's arm, which dropped away as soon as he was steady.

"Bastard," John muttered at the car's vanishing bumper.

"Dom Pastori's the driver," Brian said tonelessly, not looking. "That's Patrick Reynolds with him."

John glowered. "A friend?"

"Hell, no."

Good, he thought, and decided to head home. That had been a close call. Too close. Deliberate. Not a killing move; a scaring one.

And the sonofabitch had done it well.

3

"Love it!" Dom cried over the voice of the engine.

Patrick said nothing.

North on the wide, two-lane highway. Soon enough into the state forest, the top quarter of Port Richmond still on his right but hidden by several hundred yards of trees and sparse underbrush; in winter the houses there would be visible, barely. Not, he thought, that anyone would care; you come this far north in New Jersey, all you want to do is get the hell out.

Half a mile later he slowed down, checked the rearview mirror for cops, and swung abruptly left across the empty, southbound lane into a narrow dirt road. He switched off the radio.

"Found this last week," he said, pointing with his left hand. "Don't know what it is. Fire trail, hiking trail, something like that, I guess."

Patrick only nodded.

The road climbed as the car lurched side to side in the ruts, fell again as the road darted sharply left.

He smelled the leaves, the pine, and closed his eyes to enjoy it, opened them just in time to break at a seemingly roof-high boulder that marked the end of the line.

"Very nice," said Patrick dryly. "You play house out here, or what?"

Dom laughed once without parting his lips, made a swift, practiced K-turn so that they faced back the way they had come, then switched off the engine and jumped out of the car.

Patrick opened his door.

It was quiet. Not a breeze, not a bird. Just the sound of his soles on the hardening ground.

He opened the trunk and pulled out a rifle, scope, and metal ammunition box that gleamed as if it had been polished.

"Holy shit," Patrick said quietly, eyes wide. "What the hell are you—"

Waggling his eyebrows, Dom put a finger to his lips, shook his head, and led him around the boulder. One

167

hundred and ten measured paces along a trail that began on the far side of the rock; he had counted them eight times, once a day, since the idea came to him in a half-dream. He could do it in his sleep. He could do it blind-folded.

He could do it at night, when the only light was the stars.

He stopped at a thatch of fast-browning ferns and pushed through to a flat-topped mossy boulder that reached to his waist.

"Here," he said.

"Better and better," Patrick said, and leaned over the rock, looked down the gentle slope. Then he looked at Dom. "I think I have a feeling."

With practiced efficiency, Dom snapped on the scope, opened the metal box and picked out a single shell, popped it into the rifle, and covered the bolt with his hand. "What you figure is, see," he explained, setting a hip against the rock, the rifle aimed at the trail behind him, "is that there's maybe a couple of thousand cars a day go by this place between, say, noon and sunset. During the week, I mean."

A glance downward. A fifteen-foot-wide swath of new growth that provided a clear view of the highway. A fire had cleared it; there were still patches of black here and there on the ground.

"So the odds of you hitting someone you know are pretty damned slim."

Patrick's eyes widened.

Dom hauled the rifle to port arms, worked the bolt, and sent the shell into the chamber.

"Unless, of course, you know exactly when they'll go by, and what car they'll be in."

He braced his elbows on the rock, put the stock to his shoulder.

Patrick stepped away. "Dom, look, you aren't going to shoot anybody, right?"

"Bang," whispered Dom as a motor home sped past. If he had actually fired, the driver would have swerved, probably figuring he had a flat, though he probably wouldn't have figured that there'd be a hole in his wall, back by the john. Would have, if he stopped once he realized it wasn't a flat at all, most likely shit a brick when he realized he'd been shot at.

And hit.

And it could have been him instead of his vehicle.

Patrick's finger touched Dom's back.

"Dom, listen, this isn't a stunt. This is—"

"A stunt, if you work it right," he answered quietly, setting his eye against the scope. "Which I will."

Cross hairs. Automobiles and trucks and one motorcycle, one van, up close and damned personal.

The finger poked him again. "How can you work it right?"

Dom smiled, the wood of the oiled stock pleasantly cool against his cheek. He didn't raise or turn his head; his cheek hard now against the stock. "Pat?"

"What?"

"How fast can you run?"

"What!"

Dom stretched his neck, sniffed, kicked his toe lightly against the boulder. "I said, how fast can you run?"

Patrick made a noise that sounded like a squeal, and slapped his shoulder, hard. "Goddamnit, Pastori, what the hell are you talking about? C'mon, let's get—"

The nose of a van.

Dom giggled, and pulled the trigger.

"Jesus!" Patrick yelled, and was already running before Dom turned around, listening to the echo of the retort as

169

he snatched up the spent shell, the metal box, and sprinted after him toward the car.

He laughed as he jumped in.

He laughed as Patrick screamed at him.

And he wondered, joyful tears on his cheeks, a breath wonderfully hard to catch, how long he could make it last before he told the stupid prick that the bullet had been a blank.

Sixteen

1

Shortly before the sun, turning red, hit the trees, the fog began to move.

In strips and puffs it drifted across the streets, across the highway, splitting as cars pierced it, reforming and growing in their wake; twisting slowly in depressions, spilling slowly under shrubs, trailing along gutters and ruts and trenches and ditches; lifting toward windows and doors and faces that grimaced with the invisible touch of autumn damp; falling in slow motion off the cliff toward the fog that had already leeched color from the shoreline, took form from the river.

On Tyler Avenue it blurred the neon; streetlamps grew halos and shadows grew indistinct; footsteps lost their crack, tires lost their hum, and the bells in the steeple of the First Baptist Church sounded less like a hymn than they did buoys on empty water.

And on the fifty-yard line, the stands empty, no one else on the field, the stadium looked immense as the fog turned light to haze. So much so that Greta Rourke sank to the grass and pulled her knees to her chest. Ski sweater for the chill, shorts for the hell of it, tennis shoes and no socks, and a silver ribbon that loosely tied her hair.

Small.

She was so small.

And everything else was so big.

Even the sky had no clouds, and when she looked up she saw nothing but deep blue through gaps in the fog. Always blue. Sometimes so vast that she felt as if she were falling; sometimes so close she knew that if she let go of her legs, she'd be able to reach up and touch it, put her fingers through it, to the universe on the other side.

It made her dizzy.

She closed her eyes.

Her forehead drifted down to her knees, and she felt the heat there, the bone, and she opened one eye to see between her legs the grass. Like the tops of hundred-foot trees in an Amazon jungle. If she were in a plane, she'd be able to fly down, find a clearing, make a daring landing, and discover the only tribe in the world that knew how to live forever without once knowing how big everything was beyond the deadlands where the jungle and the river and the mountains ended.

Slowly her head rose, her focus shifting to the concrete stands beyond the track that circled the gridiron. They weren't very high. And behind them rose the brick and tinted glass school, which wasn't very high either. A single story. Roof flat, broken only by goosenecked air-conditioning ducts, toadstool heating vents, a pair of satellite dishes, a twenty-foot radio antenna.

Big.

Actually two squared U's joined by breezeways through their centers. In the two courtyards, trees and grass and benches; to the left, beyond the attached auditorium, a parking lot; to the right two smaller brick structures that housed groundskeeping equipment, sports equipment, arcane electrical and technical equipment she'd didn't for the life of her understand.

Big.

Enough rooms for four classes of three hundred students each, give or take, no crowding, the auditorium seated seven hundred. Teachers. Guidance counselors. Administration. Fifteen hundred people at any one time? Did that make sense?

Big.

And in no time, too quickly, her parents would be sending her someplace else. Someplace bigger.

When they knew damned well that small was all she wanted.

I don't want to be a lawyer, she had told them often enough.

Everyone, they said, expects you to study law, like your father.

Name three, she'd answered.

One of them had almost slapped her for her impertinence; the other had advised calm and control, that perhaps Greta, as a top-ranked senior in her class, might well be old enough to make up her own mind.

Good cop and bad cop.

One day one of them would threaten and the other would see reason; the next day, the roles were reversed.

It had begun last June and hadn't let up.

It would end in June, if she lived that long, if she didn't blow her brains out just to keep them quiet, just to keep them from squabbling over her future like hyenas over a meal.

Not that she'd really do it.

For one thing, it was dumb; for another, Mr. Kendal would probably follow her to wherever you go when you're dead and drag her back, give her a piece of his mind, then give her a spanking.

173

In his last letter, he had told her that despite her parental problems, she was lucky. He had one student who, unable to choose his vocation and under pressure from his folks to make up his mind, had opted for dropping out and roaming and had been shot in Italy, by the police.

She wasn't sure exactly what the point was, but she thought he was telling her, the way he always did, to hang in there, get to college, and then do what she wanted anyway. Parents, he had once said, look to their children to atone for their own failures. The kids who are ultimately successful refuse to accept even a taste of that guilt.

She wasn't sure, but she thought that dropping out sounded pretty good right about now.

Quiet footsteps on the dampening grass. She stiffened until her nostrils flared at the soft scent of lavender. Then she relaxed, let her hands drift down to grip her ankles, let her head turn to the right as a girl in denim from jacket to old jeans sat beside her, mimicked her pose.

"Taking one last look at the old place?" Sarra Marlow asked, blowing black bangs away from her eyes, a finger wiping the fog's touch from her glistening cheeks.

"Yeah, right. One last look. You wish and I pray. We still have a few months, y'know."

"Six months, one week, one day," Sarra corrected primly, the wet finger raised. "That's only life plus fifty without parole for us subhumans."

Greta looked back at the school. "Have you ever wanted to just blow the damned place up?"

"Every day of my life," Sarra answered. "No college in the world could be worse than this."

"My father says that's what he always said about his high school."

"Mine too."

174

They watched a dark bird hover over the building.
The fog shifted, settled.

Greta looked back at the grass. "He's full of shit."

"Right."

"I think," Greta said after a minute had passed, "I want to pull a stunt."

Sarra giggled. "You can't do that, Rourke. There's a committee for it, remember? And I don't remember either of us being asked to be on it."

Greta looked at her friend, cheek on her knee. "Fuck the committee," she said flatly.

A minute later Sarra nodded. Then she frowned, and scratched under one eye with her thumb. "So what about Linholm? He says we're not—"

"Fuck Linholm too." She grinned.

Sarra giggled. Sobered. "I was over at Gilder's yesterday. I think Corky wants to do something too."

Greta sniffed loudly, wiped her nose with a finger, touched the grass and felt the cold. Felt the fog. "Corky's a jackass."

"Yeah."

"Corky will screw it up."

"Yeah."

"Fuck Corky."

"I already have," Sarra said. "He screwed it up."

Greta's laughter bubbled, burst, rolled her onto her back and made her kick her legs in the air. She ignored the wet grass, the feel of it on the back of her neck, the smell of it in the air. "I saw Shane today," she said after she'd calmed down.

Sarra's eyes widened. "No kidding?"

"No kidding."

"He talk to you?"

Greta shook her head. Shane wasn't talking to anyone these days, not since his college acceptance had been put on hold. Before, he was a talker, a yakker, burn your ears off with all the stuff he said, half of which didn't make sense; now he was ghost, walking around the halls, muttering to himself.

It was spooky.

Everybody knew it wasn't his fault, though. The word was, Linholm had refused to submit a decent recommendation, something that had always been automatically done. The word also was, it had nothing to do with Shane's grades, which weren't spectacular, but they weren't a disaster either. But the Führer was always on his case about something. It didn't make any difference what, the principal was there, busting the poor guy's ass for practically just breathing.

And Mrs. Bishop wasn't helping things, not by a long shot—she had been pushing him since the day his father had walked out, and Greta had the feeling that Shane had finally opened his eyes and realized that his life wasn't his own anymore. It belonged to his mother.

Greta understood that all too well.

"You know," Sarra said, one hand waving ribbons over her head, "if anyone could come up with a good stunt, Shane could."

"The old Shane," Greta corrected.

"Yeah. I guess you're right."

Yeah, Greta thought; shit.

"Corky thinks he's queer."

"I think," Greta said solemnly, pinching the bridge of her nose, "Corky is queer."

Sarra shook her head. "Nope. Pat Reynolds is queer. Corky's just stupid."

True enough, Greta said with her nod, and watched the sky, saw a cloud, felt the settling cold on her spine and wished she had brought a jacket. She could freeze to death here, which may or may not serve everyone right. She snorted. Now that's stupid.

Besides, what if everything was big on the other side?

Sarra laid down beside her. "Okay," she said, "so what do we do?"

"I don't know yet," Greta answered carefully. "I don't know. But I will."

2

On the way home, batting at the fog and pretending they were in London, hiding from the Ripper, they caught up with Rita Galiano carrying a brown paper bag under one arm. The greetings were loud enough to bring one woman onto her porch, a small terrier yapping at her side.

"Gonna get arrested," Greta said in mock fear. "Disturbing the peace. My college career, forever ruined. My mother would just love a felon in the family."

The door slammed; they could still hear the dog barking.

"So kill yourself," Rita told her. "I'll come to the funeral."

"Thanks."

"I won't," said Sarra. "I'm busy."

Greta swung for her arm and missed. "Now how do you know that?"

"Whenever it is, I'm busy."

They walked on in silence.

Greta looked at Rita and sighed. Big. Now, she's big where it counts. Why the hell can't I be big, where it counts, and keep everything else the way it's supposed to be?

Sarra poked at the bag. "The food that good you bring it home?"

"Rolls," Rita explained. "My mother likes them. She tells my father she made them."

Greta couldn't help a whoop. "And he believes it?"

"My father," she said, "is Superman in the courtroom. At home, he's just another man."

They laughed, pushed at each other, fell back into silence.

Until Greta, with a wink at Sarra, said, "Is Brian a man?"

Rita glared at her quickly.

"Oh, whoa," Greta said, hands up in surrender. "Ms. Marlow, I think I've made a faux pas here."

"What's that?" Sarra asked.

"It means," Rita said without inflection, "she's just stepped in more shit than she thought."

"Hey, Rita," Greta said quickly, abruptly aware that her friend was only partly kidding, "hey, look, I didn't mean—"

"Speak of the devil," Sarra whispered loudly.

She pointed across the street, to two figures walking away from them into the fog. One of them was clearly Brian Oakland; the other was an old man.

"Who's the guy?" Sarra said.

"Mr. Naze," Rita answered. "Mr. Kendal's uncle."

"Oh."

They kept moving, and they kept watching, until watching had become too obvious. Then they faced front and said nothing more until Sarra peeled off with a hasty "Later," and ran up her street. The silence this time felt more like a weight, and Greta wondered if she ought to say something then, try another form of apology. She didn't want Rita ticked at her; things were lousy enough as it was.

"Brian," Rita said, "told me yesterday that Mickie wants to do a stunt."

Greta almost stopped, tripped herself instead and grabbed onto Rita's arm to keep from smacking into a tree. "You're kidding, right? Farwood?"

Rita nodded. "Fairy tales."

Greta pulled at her silver ribbon. "Has to be. That girl couldn't think her way out of a kindergarten class if she had a year's head start." The ribbon came undone, and she wrapped it around her wrist. "Stunt," she said disdainfully. "What the hell does she know about stunts?"

Rita shifted the bag to her other arm. "Y'know, if I knew what it was, I'd write an anonymous letter to the Führer, maybe he'd kick her tight little ass to Colorado or something."

Greta felt the fog settle on her legs. "So what's Brian going to do?"

"He doesn't know."

"Then he's crazy," she declared without thinking. "Dumb shit's being hauled around by his personal gonads and he doesn't even know it."

Rita nodded.

And Greta searched for a hole large enough for her to jump in. It would save Galiano the trouble of slitting her throat.

A block later she was alone.

The smell of damp leaves, oil on the street, and the sweet roll she held in one hand, that Rita had given her with a half-smile and a wink.

Truce.

Greta had almost wept.

And by the time she reached her house, the roll was gone, and she had figured out a stunt that would, if it worked, blow this town away.

It wasn't big.

It didn't have to be.

V

IN THE WOODS

Seventeen

The station house was small, of dark brick and peaked roof and an age that had already marked more than a century of waiting. There were no lights in the high windows arched and pointed at the top, no lights in the parking lot that stood empty behind it; the slanted roof over the platform shifted, sometimes groaned, and the handful of naked bulbs burning alongside the beams scarcely cast a shadow, barely lit the air beneath them. It was the moon that dimmed them, large and bright and full; and the air that hinted of a hard frost by dawn set them in fragile globes that seemed to shimmer when the wind hissed out of the trees.

The doors to the waiting room were locked.

Shutters had been closed over the barred ticket window, secured by a hook and eye that rattled on occasion.

Over the main platform, under the roof and hanging by two thin chains long since rusted to dark blood, was a sign that tried forever to twist away from the wind, succeeded only in swinging, creaking, short bursts of harsh sound that were brittle and without echo.

Port Richmond

And a cat, long and low and a deep rippling grey, slipped out of the trees to stalk shadows on the tracks. Caught for a moment by the dead glow of the moon, it blinked and arched its back, blinked again and began moving—slower than the night wind that hissed in the branches, slower still than the dark that filled the spaces between the worn and gleaming iron. Its tail twitched slowly, its paws ghosted over the gravel that lay loose between the splintered ties, and every few moments its head lifted, and it searched, and when it spotted the man sitting on the platform it twitched its tail and it stopped.

And listened.

And narrowed its eyes.

While John Naze stared back from under the wide brim of his hat, his own puffed eyes narrowed to further narrow his face.

He didn't like the cat. Never had. Never would. It didn't belong to anyone. It was wild, living in the woods, killing birds and chipmunks and god knows what all else, and watching him now the way it would watch helpless prey. Waiting. Patiently. For the best time to attack.

It reminded him of the gangs he had seen prowling in New York. Just as feral. Just as cold.

It reminded him of some of the kids he saw back in town.

Like the sonofabitch in that black car today, the one that nearly ran him down. Brian had told him, but he couldn't remember the kid's name. That's all right. If it came, it came; but he'd remember that car.

He shifted on the old chair, the creak of it loud and filled with comfort. The lower part of his worn overcoat fell open, and with an effort he folded it back across his legs. Not looking down. Not looking at his hands—contorted and swollen, arthritis distending the knuckles and rendering most of his fingers useless. There was pain, god *damn* the pain, but so much a part of him these last twenty years that he seldom felt it unless there was rain

184

for a day or the mornings were damp, or when he was in bed, staring at the ceiling, waiting to die.

The cat moved.

John followed it by jerking turns of his head until it vanished into the platform's shadow. Then all he could do was wait.

A grunt as he pushed himself back, another as he crossed his legs knee over knee.

An owl shadowed over the tracks, and five minutes later a nighthawk cried softly.

A gust of wind made him shudder and turn his face away. It was cold for the moment, and the snap of it against his drawn cheeks made him clench his teeth. A sniff; there'd be snow soon, perhaps in a day or two, perhaps nothing more than a pre-Halloween dusting to warn the town behind him that winter was on its way and October its herald.

A sudden inhalation when the wind blew again, and the cat darted into the open and raced across the tracks to the dark on the other side. A snap around of his head when he heard a twig snap in the woods.

This won't do, John, he thought; this won't do at all.

A flash of dark red back there in the trees. Too quick to focus on, there and gone, without a sound.

Now you're seeing things, you bloody old fool. Next thing you know, you'll be seeing the damn train.

Something red? Couldn't be. It wasn't the cat, wasn't a bird, wasn't some fool kid—even they had more sense than being out here in the damn cold. Seeing things is what it is. Hearing things. This won't do, not at all.

He was making himself nervous, sitting here all alone, though he'd sat here on hundreds of nights since the last day of his job. It was something to do. He didn't like television, and there was nothing on the radio anymore, not the music he liked, and his eyes were too dim and milky for him to be able to read even a newspaper with any satisfaction. Sitting here, however, drifted him into the past, when Port Richmond was seven decades younger, not so filled, not so loud; when he could walk with a straight back, when he could shoot pool with the best, when later he could take his wife in his arms and squeeze her until she squealed.

The platform, like the trains, took him away.

And he had every intention of a train taking him away for the last time, when it was time, and the pain didn't die when the night died with the sun.

Another twig snapped.

Another gust of wind.

He pulled back a sleeve and brought his watch to his eyes; just gone midnight, and he smiled to himself. Mrs. Oakland would finally be going to bed about now, flowery bathrobe clutched to her throat, all that hair in curlers, tiny feet in tiny slippers, leaving on the back porch's yellow light to show the way to his rooms, three of them, all to himself, nobody else. Just the way he liked it.

He shifted.

A flash of red, down there, at the edge of the platform.

Nope. Couldn't be.

He shifted again.

A curious one she was, Neeba Oakland, a city woman, just like he had told Brian on their walk this afternoon. City woman, city ideas. But he wasn't fooled a bit by her endless fussing or her kindness or her sly and coy glances whenever he left the house for one of his walks. Didn't fool him at all. Too old for that. She was after him. Had been, he supposed, since the day he'd watched his wife into the ground, even though he still had the old house then. Renting him the garage rooms at a rate that would make a young man weep, making his bed, cooking his meals when he bothered to eat; she never gave up, and he guessed he had to give her credit—she never pushed herself, letting devotion to his comfort do her speaking for her.

But now she was in bed, and he figured it safe to go back. The one thing he didn't need tonight was a brace of the present when he was so filled with the past.

Gravel crunched.

He looked quickly to his right, thinking there was someone walking along the tracks.

Kids.

Track iron dark under the moon; trees hissing.

Most of the time they left him alone.

Most of the time.

Except for that sonofabitch in the old black car, radio screaming, laughing like a jackass.

Using the heels of his hands he pushed himself to his feet, groaned when his legs failed, and cursed when he swayed and fell back again.

The time was coming.

He could feel it.

Any day now, any day, maybe even before his nephew finally came to his senses and came home. And that, he thought, would be tragic. He had always hoped Evan would be at his bedside when it happened, or standing with him on the platform when he finally gave up the fight. A good boy Evan was, even if he did travel too much and didn't spend enough time with his poor ailing uncle all alone in this cruel world.

He laughed and liked the sound of it, laughed again and shook his head.

Cranky; oh yes. A bit stiff in the joints and damn these damned hands, definitely. But not poor. And not quite ailing. Just . . . old, and getting older.

The wind.

All right, get up, you old fart, he ordered himself; get up before they find your skinny ass frozen to the chair.

His hands braced again, his shoulders stiffened, and he leaned forward, prepared to rise, and felt his mouth open when the lights flared out, one by one. The light walking away from him, until there was nothing left but the dead moon, and the dark beneath the roof.

I give up, he thought; the hell with it, I'm going home.

Then he saw something standing there, down the platform a few yards.

"Who. . . ?" he asked, voice rusty with silence.

It was too dark to distinguish shape and form, and when he rubbed a forearm over his eyes, all he could see was a flare of fleeting red.

"Brian, boy, that you?"

Probably. Neeba the city woman probably got worried and sent her grandson to fetch him. He shook his head, feeling for the boy.

"You could help me up if you stop standing there and move your feet a little," he said.

It moved, whatever was down there.

It moved swiftly, without a breeze, without a whisper, and for the briefest, longest, second something touched his hands, covered them, and pressed down, and he felt the pain in the knuckles, in his palms as the flesh was forced against the hard wood. He swallowed to cry out, thrusting himself back and feebly kicking out one leg.

Then the pressure was gone, the shadow gone, and he felt the perspiration running down his cheeks, matting his hair beneath the hat, laying ice along his spine.

He thought he had seen a flash of red across the tracks. Flickering into the woods. Vanished. Not a sound.

"Sonofabitch!" he shouted, though he couldn't see the man anymore. "Who the hell d'you think you are?"

When the lights suddenly popped on, all of them, one

by one, he stood quickly, heels cracking on the boards, and had taken several angry steps before he realized he wasn't shambling, that his hands were tight fists.

The wind.

Autumn wind.

Twisting sign.

He moved under the nearest bulb, took a deep breath, and raised his arms.

Then he looked at his hands, turned them over, and began to scream.

Eighteen

Neeba Oakland sat in the front parlor and listened to the wind as it slammed out of the trees across Forest Road. She didn't like it. It sounded like an army marching toward her porch, the blown twigs and dead leaves gunshots against the roof. Every time there was a clatter, she jumped; every time there was a lull, she tensed and waited for more.

It was days like this when she thought she'd made a mistake, moving here. Fifty-one years in the Bronx, thirty years of it living in the shade of Woodlawn Cemetery, and then her husband had died. Left her alone. Left her to cope with all she hadn't known, the simple things everyone else took for granted—writing checks, paying bills, getting the car serviced, walking alone to the shops through those packs of animals that stared at her, made noises at her, sometimes followed her, laughing. It had been terrifying, nearly overwhelming, more than once had sent her to bed weeping, shaking, praying for someone to take her away and take care of her again.

He had known all along she couldn't manage herself; *he* had coddled and protected her. Sheltered her. Deliberately, she was sure now. Kept her in her place, *his* place. No ideas of her own. Supper, sewing, and sex. But at the end she had fooled him; and when her son, rest his soul, told her about an available, affordable house he had heard about across the river, someplace in New Jersey, when he drove her out one brilliant Sunday afternoon and showed her the neighborhoods and the stores and the schools and the train station, she fell in love.

He, the son of a bitch, rest his soul, had sworn that prices in the suburbs were too high for simple people. The cost of living, buying groceries, paying the electric, astronomical. They could never afford to live there. The Bronx was their home. All their friends were there; they'd be there forever.

A lie. All her friends had moved out, all the buildings suddenly too old and too large.

She hadn't needed a realtor's convincing. The moment she saw the place, the Bronx was a memory. A few stocks *he* had left her, some of her savings *he* hadn't known about, and she had bought the first house she had lived in since she was a child.

"Ma," her son had said, standing with her on the front lawn just before the signing, "this thing is huge! I didn't realize how big it is."

"I like it," she'd answered.

"But Jesus, Ma, you could put an army in here."

"When I was two," she had told him, grinning at the house, "I was moved to the Bronx. I have lived in, under, and above apartments ever since." She threw out her hands. "Now I'm fifty-nine, and by god, I want room!"

He had laughed and hugged her, and it was eleven years ago that he, God bless him, and her grandson helped her move.

She just wished they had told her that the forest would still be right there, across the street. They hadn't told her plans to clear it and give her something to look at besides the waiting trees had been abandoned. Oh, the people on the block were friendly enough, never sneering because she was from the city, never whispering, but it was unnerving to look out the front window every day, every night, and not see anything but dark trees gathered in untidy ranks and taking out the western sky. The others, those who weren't from the city and had no other reference, they exclaimed over the positively bucolic view.

They didn't understand.

They had never seen the shadows.

The wind punched the house again.

She wished Brian were home, and immediately took it back. Her grandson—fatherless, motherless, because of a faulty airplane valve—had better things to do than fuss over an old woman.

He did, though. All the time.

"Neeba," he said hundreds of times, "I don't mind, honest. I'll go when I'm done, okay? Jeez. No big deal."

Neeba. Even *he* had called her that.

There were days, though, when she nearly had to take a broom and a shotgun to get the boy out of the house, out to his friends.

She wanted him to go.

Sometimes, though she loved him dearly, his energy and that so-called music he played up in his room rubbed her nerves raw.

But, a few years ago, when he was out at night, gone for a Saturday from breakfast to past sunset, even when he was only playing in the street with his friends, it had begun to get lonely.

It had been a godsend, then, that she had been granted permission to rent rooms in the huge place, and fix an apartment over the garage. She hadn't expected it. She thought the neighbors would complain, that Brian would think her crazy. They hadn't; neither had he.

192

"Neeba, for pete's sake, what are you worried about? You could use the company, right? You think I think you're gonna have orgies or something?"

"Watch your mouth!" she'd told him.

He had laughed, kissed her forehead, and, Jesus save him!, had pinched her waist on the way out.

So two of the four large rooms in the made-over attic had been taken by Shirley Atkins, a teacher at the high school, the other two by her friend and colleague, Lyanna Gough. And over the attached garage, her first boarder, John Naze.

Her John.

If only he knew it, if only he would stop thinking about the wife he had buried more than a decade ago.

The wind blew.

She sighed.

She glanced around the room, crowded and clean and today looking as old as she felt. She tried not to stare at the telephone by the couch. If she didn't watch it, it wouldn't ring; and if it didn't ring, it wouldn't tell her that John had been found. Dead somewhere, all alone in the cold.

Another sigh.

Her hands bunched in her lap, pulling at her slacks, one of them fluttering now to the collar of her blouse, plain but tasteful, suiting the narrow face, the age there, the black hair waist long, now caught in a bun at her nape, not pulled too tightly, not making her severe.

She watched the telephone.

It was silent.

Mrs. Oakland, it had said that morning, *I understand your concern, but Mr. Naze hasn't been gone all that long.*

Long enough, she had answered stiffly; he's an old man, with arthritis, and he could have fallen somewhere. Maybe in a ditch.

193

He could have gone to his nephew's.

How? she'd wanted to know, finally feeling the tears; he doesn't drive, he doesn't even have a car. Besides, the nephew is in England someplace. You think John flew to England?

Okay, tell you what I'll do. I'll make sure the patrols know he's been away all night. They'll keep an eye out. And don't worry, I'll give you a call as soon as I know.

She'd hung up without thanking him.

They were humoring her. Mrs. Oakland, city woman, sees muggers and murderers in every alley.

A glance at the heart-shaped watch pinned by her shoulder, and she pushed herself stiffly out of the chair. Brian would be home from school soon, no doubt needing to fill the bottomless pit he called a stomach. She would tell him he'd spoil his supper; he would grin and tell her that everything she cooked would find room in him someplace.

Just like his father.

Thank God, neither of them were like *him*.

A passing cloud darkened the hallway as she made her way to the kitchen.

She stood at the back door and stared at the yard.

The front door opened.

"Neeba?"

"In here, Brian!" she called.

God damn you, John, she thought to the wind; it had suddenly occurred to her that he might have another woman.

Brian called again, he was going up to change; and the telephone rang.

As she hurried to it, fixed on the wall by the kitchen table, she knew she was being silly; John had no other woman but the woman he had buried.

"Neeba?"

194

Her eyes closed briefly. It was Mrs. Galiano, mother of one of Brian's friends—Rita, who was sweet, kind of pretty, just the sort of girl Brian should be seeing, though he wouldn't listen to Neeba because she was, after all, only his grandmother and didn't know anything about love and women. And sex.

"Tressa, it's good to hear from you."

"Neeba, I got a problem. Suddenly I've got company coming, hardly anything in the house, and the car's on the fritz. I think it must be a law—things always have to screw up on Mondays after a good weekend. Anyway, Rita just reminded me about that marvelous sauce you make for pasta, and I was wondering . . . I hate to ask, it's such short notice, but do you think you could whip me up a pot? I know it's a lot to ask, but I'm in a bind, Hal's gonna kill me I don't have something decent to put on the table. I could send Rita over. What do you think?"

Neeba thought she ought to be staked out on an anthill and covered with maple syrup. Whip up a pot? Jesus and Mary, save me.

"I'll do what I can," she promised.

"Neeba, you're a saint. How long do you think? Fifteen, twenty minutes?"

She looked at the wall clock. "It's three-thirty. I'll send Brian over at six-thirty."

A pause.

The wind pushed the cloud away.

"That long?"

Neeba smiled grimly at the back door. "It needs to cook, Tressa. I don't get it from a packet."

"No, of course you don't," the woman said quickly. "I'm sorry. I'm just in such a frazzle. Hal's gonna kill me. Six-thirty's fine. I'll reimburse you. Ciao."

Neeba replaced the receiver without standing up,

rubbed a finger under her nose, tapped a finger on the table.

"Ciao," she said to the brass rooster on the wall beside the refrigerator. "Jesus, forgive me, but the damn woman's a pain in the ass."

A deep laugh from the doorway; she didn't turn around.

"Neeba, why do you do that all the time?"

"I like to swear, Brian. It keeps me young."

"No, Neeba. You know what I mean."

A shrug. "Because she's a neighbor. You help neighbors. That's what neighbors are for."

He gave her a deliberate, barely tolerant, prolonged loud sigh. "This isn't the Bronx, you know. This is Port Richmond. Neighbors don't give a shit around here. You should know that by now."

She almost snapped at him for the language, said instead, "You'll bring it over, yes? Save my poor old legs. Maybe Rita will invite you to stay."

The sigh this time was impatient.

"Neeba, I already have a girlfriend."

She shrugged shoulders and eyebrows. He didn't have a girlfriend. What he had was a tramp. A rich tramp. The body of a woman and the brain of a snake. Lord, she couldn't wait for him to grow up and learn what being a man is really like.

But experience advised she say nothing. She only asked him, since he wasn't working at the school, to make the afternoon rounds for her, while she started the sauce—fresh linens, fresh towels, fresh soap, for their boarders, and don't forget to open a window a little from the bottom, air the rooms out.

He told her later John's apartment was still empty.

She returned to the back door.

196

Evening had slipped in while she'd been working—trees and flowers cast dark against dark, and the streetlamps too white, too brittle. The sharp slam of a car door. The cry of a cat.

The stars were chips of ice.

The night would be cold.

Nineteen

Lost.

Dear god, how could he be lost?

There had been a time, and damnit it wasn't all that long ago, when he had known every tree in the woods, when all he had to do was stand still for a moment and look around, take a breath, and he'd know where he was, which direction he had to take to get him where he was going.

Exhaustion propped him against a bole, his legs stiff, his arms dangling.

He was on fire.

Everything inside burned.

How could he be lost?

He had grown up here, damnit! He had taken Evan through these woods and showed him the animals and the birds that had hidden from the town slowly growing, slowly taking the trees and fashioning houses from them, slowly pushing the wildlife deeper into the state, higher into New York.

He had camped out, alone and with friends.

He had made love here the first time, and dozens of times since.

How could he be lost?

Once he had stopped screaming, he had run from the station platform into the moon's pale night. He had thought he was running home. He had run into the woods.

Light followed dark.

Had he fallen?

A tender lump in the hair above his left temple suggested he had; a nasty bruise on his left hip confirmed it. But he didn't remember it. He didn't remember falling. And he didn't remember waking.

Dark followed light.

Dried blood on the backs of his hands; dried blood on his chin; dirt and slices of dead leaves and broken twigs clung to his overcoat, burrowed against his scalp.

Had he eaten?

His stomach argued against it; dizziness that closed his eyes and sagged him to his rump on a protruding root he didn't feel confirmed it. But he must have eaten. How could he have gone this long without it?

How long was it?

He lifted his left arm to check his watch, had to grab his wrist with his right hand to keep it steady. The watch was gone, a strip of angry red where it had been strapped. He stared at it for several seconds and couldn't remember what the timepiece looked like. He couldn't remember the time the last time he had checked.

Then he saw his hands again, but he couldn't scream anymore. The simple pass of breath through his throat made him whimper, so he kept the screaming inside, where it deafened him, and terrified him, because he couldn't remember why his hands were that way. He hadn't been to a doctor; he hadn't been taking medication. Yet his fingers were straight, slightly spotted with age, nothing out of the ordinary about either knuckles or flesh.

They were the normal hands of an old man.

They hadn't been—that much he could remember.

199

They hadn't been.

A slip of saliva escaped the corner of his mouth.

The shifting dark beneath the dying leaves began to strengthen; what few shafts of sunlight he could see began to narrow; the day's warmth rolled over and began to chill him, made him draw his coat close about his neck.

He wanted to move, but he didn't know where to go; he wanted to go home, but he couldn't remember how; he wanted to leave the woods and find civilization, but he was lost.

And he had never been lost before in his life.

That's what frightened him.

Not the dark, not the pain in his abdomen nor the pain in his head nor the scrapes on his arms and cheeks and brow. That was to be expected when you run blindly through a forest. That's the price paid for being a fool.

Lost, though. Lost in a place you used to know as well as you knew the block where you lived and the room where you slept and the place where you worked. He rubbed his face, pressed his fingers to his eyes. It was like meeting a stranger who called herself his wife.

The wind found him.

Palms close to his face, he checked his hands again. He cracked the knuckles. He pulled the loose skin. He traced a bulging vein from thumb to wrist.

The kids.

It had to have been those goddamned kids. A trick. They didn't like him. Scare him to death, why not, it's close to Halloween. Scare the old bastard to death. Fix him up when all he wanted was dying. The kids. It didn't make any difference how. It was the kids. They took advantage; they always took advantage when they sensed a weakness. He was weak. They took advantage.

Lost. Dear Lord, help me, I'm lost.

The kids.

Evan, for god's sake, why aren't you here?

I'm lost!

Dried blood on his hands; and when the cold sent them into his coat pockets, he found something there. He pulled it out and didn't scream. A small rabbit with its neck broken.

Had he caught it himself?

Did it matter? It was here.

His stomach lurched.

His breath steamed over the body, ruffling the fur.

With his brand new hands he tore the body in half as if it were paper; with his brand new hands he tore the meat from its bones as if it were candy; with his gaze on the tree directly ahead, barely seen now, moonlight not yet bright enough to show him the bark, he thought *the kids* and he ate.

VI

IN THE STORM

Twenty

1

"**R**abbit stew."

Evan looked dubiously at his plate, then up over the glass-hooded food display at the landlord of the Cross and Sword.

Bill Sholton smiled genially back. "You look a little under, Mr. Kendal. The weather and such, since you asked for what's good tonight, I thought this'd warm you up, take care of the insides. A good stew will do that."

"I've never had rabbit."

"Tastes like chicken." He laughed loudly.

Evan managed a half-smile and dropped a crumpled ten-pound note on the counter. Sholton appropriated it with a swipe of his reddened hand, nodded, and directed his attention to the next customer in line. The change from the tenner would be used for drinks, though Evan suspected he would need a lot more than that before this night was done. Considerably more, if he was going to wash the weekend's finale from his mouth—this was the first decent meal he'd had since Saturday night. God help me. Rabbit stew. He almost groaned aloud. But he made his way to a back corner table and sat facing the entrance.

When he had arranged silverware, plate, and glass of bitter to his liking, his eyes closed for a moment.

He inhaled.

A silent resigned sigh.

Rabbit for god's sake stew.

He tried to ignore the rain that lashed the windows, the thunder that grumbled just beyond the village, reminding himself that it wasn't London, it was only Bettin Wells, and all he wanted to do was eat.

Which he did, amazed at how good the stew was, and how it did indeed warm his insides. It eased his mood considerably, and by the time he was halfway finished, he thought he might even be up for Ida MacNair's half-baked Cassandra.

Luckily she wasn't there. The Cross and Sword in fact was not terribly crowded, about average for a miserable Monday evening—a few of the suppertime regulars, a few new faces, most of them congregated on the chairs and bench seats at the front, as if they were bound to flee as soon as their meals were over. Stranded strangers who never took off their coats, and flinched each time lightning whitened the windows.

He knew how they felt.

But it didn't stop him from cleaning his plate, after which he took up his glass and eased back into the corner. Watched the others. Eavesdropped without really listening. Felt his jaw tighten when a particularly emphatic explosion of thunder made his fork dance on the plate.

All right, Addie, he thought, where the hell are you?

The distance Edinburgh had put between him and Paul Burwin had not lessened his concern for his friend, but it had somehow further eroded the jagged edge of the episode in London. By the time he had completed his Saturday afternoon lecture—quickly added when the crowded morning session had been so unexpectedly, and enormously, popular—he had seriously considered taking a few extra days to really see the old city, be the tourist, visit the Walter Scott Memorial, the castle on the cliff, maybe even become emboldened enough to hire a car and ride into the country. He had glowed. He had felt useful. And he had felt so guilty about Addie being home alone that he'd twice come close to calling her Saturday night. But by the time his hosts had allowed him to return to his room, somewhat the worse for wear, it had been too late.

On Sunday morning he decided a trip wouldn't be fair to her, not until she knew more about Paul and his condition.

A puzzling urgency had him packed and gone before he had time to think, and, as though on a signal, he managed to ride straight into disaster.

The homebound train had come unglued just across the border, in the middle of hilly fields just the far side of nowhere, something, a conductor said, about the engine burning out. When it had become evident no quick repairs would get them moving for quite a while, British Rail had offered out-of-service buses to those whose destinations were nearby; the rest, like him, would have to wait.

Stiff upper lip.

The rain hadn't helped.

A light shower in the beginning, somehow adding a spring green to the fields that flanked the tracks; but the clouds had thickened, the wind strengthened, and before long he could no longer see through the window by his seat. The carriage's heating system failed. Two children at the front, racing up and down the aisle, threw up. A drunk across the aisle added scotch to the mixture. The rain prevented windows from being opened wide enough to clear the air.

He had stood at the door, the top pane pushed down, for over half an hour, not caring about the storm or the temperature, just staring at the fog-thick rain that turned the green to grey and erased all traces of the clouds and the sky.

Seeing Paul.

Grinning at him from the weed-covered embankment.

Sport, Burwin said, teeth exposed, hat blocking his eyes, *just think what I could do if the train had derailed*.

He hadn't reached home until long after midnight.

Images of Paul racing at him across a heath woke him at dawn.

For the next several minutes he had punched, molded, strangled his pillow, rearranged the bedclothes, opened and shut the window, and fell back to sleep on top of the blanket, not dreaming at all.

The storm caught up with him at midafternoon.

The Cross and Sword was his hastily planned escape, but Addie wasn't there, nor had she answered his calls, answered the knock on her home and office doors.

All right, Addie. All right, enough's enough.

He looked up expectantly when the door opened, slumped again when rain followed the Gerry Twins inside. Someone yelled at them to close the damnable thing before they all drowned, and Miss Dennis slammed the door so hard the landlord yelped in pain from behind the bar.

The smell of hot butter and wet wool.

Ten minutes, he decided, and I'll try her again.

He picked up a rumpled *Standard* from the seat beside him and flipped through it.

A three-car pileup at Heathrow.

Paul.

A sniper picking off children in a Dublin schoolyard. *Paul.*

A man falls from a second-story window in a Canterbury apartment block. He lands on a bush and suffers no more than a few scratches. But the child playing under the branches has her neck broken.

Christ almighty, he thought before he thought Paul's name again; you keep this up, you'll be as batty as he is.

Then someone maneuvered awkwardly onto the bench beside him, thumped a glass onto the table, and whispered, "That stuff'll kill you, you know."

Evan choked, coughed, felt his eyes tear and run. A hand slapped his back, a voice blurred conciliation, apology, and by the time he was able to breathe properly again, a fresh mug of bitter had been set before him, foaming. He leaned back. A few of the customers eyed him in sympathy, raised eyebrows in questions he nodded *I'm all right, thanks* to. Then he blew his nose, wiped his eyes.

"Gawd, sorry, Kendal."

Evan waved a hand. "No problem. I thought you were—you caught me by surprise."

Sergeant Ludden shrugged. "It happens." He grasped his glass in one hand, used the back of the other to smooth his narrow black mustache to either side. His uniform had been replaced by a rain-soaked mackintosh and a vivid red deerstalker cap. "Saw you here, thought you might want to know how we're progressing with Professor Burwin."

"What about him?" He already knew; Addie had left a dozen messages on his machine.

"We're not, if you want to know the cold truth," the policeman said, sounding as if it were an affront to his rank. "Not exactly high priority down to London, if you know what I mean, but still—" He drank deeply. "Still, you'd think there'd be something, wouldn't you."

"It's a big city, Sergeant," he said.

"Aye, that it is. But it ain't that big."

No sign, no word, no calls, no letters: that's what Addie had told him. On the machine.

"So what do you do now?"

"Nothing we can do, really," Ludden told him over the top of his glass. "The professor's a grown man."

"A *sick* man," Evan corrected.

"Yes, well . . ." Ludden emptied his glass, touched his lips with a finger, then swung himself nimbly around the table and to his feet. "There's only so much I can do up here, Mr. Kendal. Only so much."

"I understand that," Evan told him. "And I'm sure Mrs. Burwin's grateful for all you have done."

"Aye." The policeman stared. "So she said."

Evan smiled, no more than a flash, aware that Ludden watched him for several seconds before he made his way to the bar, muttered something to Sholton, and left with two other men.

The stew's balm deserted him.

He picked up the paper, tossed it aside, fetched another drink, and sagged back into the corner to watch Bettin Wells enter and leave, its voice an indistinct grumbling, its smell that of cigarettes and pipes and wet blacktop and beer. It occurred to him that perhaps Paul had been located and that's where Addie was; but if he had, Ludden was lying, which effectively killed that speculation. It occurred to him that Paul had returned, had taken her, or had murdered her; the thought stirred him for only a moment, just before he told himself not to be so goddamn melodramatic.

A flare of lightning made him squint.

The Gerry Twins hoisted their umbrellas and made their exit.

Police Constable Purdy, whom Evan thought would have been more comfortable in a Victorian novel, broke up a near-fight at the dart board. When the black leather combatants left, the constable nodded to all as though receiving applause and took a corner of the bar to himself, sipping a righteous glass of water.

Ten minutes later, just shy of seven, Reverend Flaunter made an entrance—black raincoat caped over his shoulders, floppy-brimmed hat dripping water on the floor, unfastened galoshes jingling as he stomped to the bar and picked up a glass of sherry the landlord had poured the moment the door opened.

Please, Evan thought.

The minister smiled in his direction, and moved.

Damn.

2

"Missed you at the funeral, Mr. Kendal," Flaunter said. His eyes were lightly bloodshot, his lower lip not quite still.

"I was in Edinburgh," he answered.

"Ah yes. I forgot. Speaking at some university function or other, as I recall."

Small towns in America had nothing on English villages, so Evan did nothing more than try to appear apologetic.

"I assume you were successful?"

"I guess. At least they didn't stone me."

The minister chuckled. Sobered. Inhaled slowly. "Still, I would have . . . a nonfussing friendly face would have been a boon."

Evan didn't know what to say. He had no idea the man

211

considered him other than a curiosity, and a temporary one at that.

Flaunter looked around, searching for a chair to drag over, saying as he did, "It was quite nice, actually. The weather cleared, the organ didn't stick. I didn't even— well, Pris would have approved."

"I'm sure."

Lightning again, and a face in the window by the door. Evan blinked.

"I did the best I could, naturally, but you can understand how difficult it was."

Ghostly, bleached of color, eyes narrowed against the rain, hair plastered like frozen black blood.

"Luckily there were—"

Evan shoved the table away, nearly toppling the minister, and ran for the exit. A voice called his name angrily. PC Purdy scowled.

Finally, the thunder—the storm was moving away.

He yanked the door open and threw himself out, swerved to the right and grabbed an arm.

"I . . ."

He couldn't speak.

Addie only shook her head, beads of water trembling on her forehead, slipping down her cheeks. A hand wiped her face; it did no good at all.

After a moment's hesitation, he guided her to the wall, and they stood there. In the rain. Backs to the pub and the faces in the window.

"He's dead," Addie said, clinging to his arm.

Shit, Evan thought; oh hell.

"Never woke up. The poor man never woke up."

She shifted her grip to hold his hand with both hers.

He looked down at her, so small in the near dark, and said, "Paul?"

"Oh god, no," she answered. "No. It was the driver.

Of the car. He died this morning without regaining . . ."
Her eyes widened briefly. "Dear lord, Ev, you didn't
think . . ."

A bus hissed down the High Street, lights on inside,
no one in the seats.

Evan swallowed, glanced over his shoulder, took his
hand from hers and said, "Let's walk."

"Evan, it's raining."

It wasn't a protest, so he took no notice, merely shifted
to the outside as they walked up the road. He felt no
wind, heard no thunder, and when they looked at each
other again, he knew she was the same.

Soap opera time, he thought a few silent minutes later:
This is wrong, Evan, so wrong.
Yes, I know.
It isn't right.
How well I know that, Adelaide. He is, after all, my friend.
Or was.
We will be damned for it.
Then let us be damned. I—

"Evan, what are you thinking?"

The village was behind them; he couldn't even see the
rain.

"I'm thinking that I must have a thing for pneumonia.
Maybe it's something I was supposed to have as a child."

Her laugh was almost, not quite, unstrained.

"I'm also thinking that I—" He looked ahead. Into the
dark. "That I was concerned about you when I couldn't
get in touch."

"I was at the hospital."

"So I gather."

"And you weren't concerned, you were worried."

"Sick."

"Afraid that Paul had somehow—"

"Yes."

213

Stop, Addie, he said without speaking; stop now, please.

They passed under a remote streetlamp, at the fork in the road where his lane branched off. At the fringe of the veil of light, she stopped and turned him around. Her face was in partial shadow.

"That's sweet."

"Yeah," he said. "That's me."

She kissed him.

She kissed him again, and he felt her arms slide around his back, felt her through the bulk of their coats, felt her lips at last and wondered why they were so cold.

When they separated, she said, "This is wrong, you know."

And he laughed.

It began as a blank gape, then a giggle, then a laugh that astonishingly invited her to join him, and she did. Not quite as loudly, not quite as long, but she had the grace to end up with the hiccups as they stumbled up the land, arms around waists, Evan praying that she was as terrified as he.

3

Her breasts were smaller than he'd imagined, than the glimpses he'd had; her hips were larger; her waist pleasantly extended by the soft and unapologetic bulge of her stomach.

And when they were done, rocked by fading thunder, she jumped off the bed and ran weeping into the bathroom.

Twenty-one

1

This, Brian thought glumly as he walked home from school, was not going to be such a fabulous week that he would remember it forever. He was sure of it. He would bet on it.

And he should have known it the moment he had opened his eyes this morning and heard Miss Atkins and Miss Gough arguing in the upstairs hall. Loudly. They didn't do it often, but when they did, he couldn't help thinking it was some kind of secret adult thing they had to do once in a while to get school out of their systems and their lives in gear. He didn't mind because most of the time they were funny, yelling about who borrowed what from whom, and who owed who which and what, at the top of their voices.

The problem was, they sometimes put Neeba in a rotten mood. Which meant that she would either spend all day driving around town adding to her collection of speeding and parking tickets, or make him go into the yard after classes and "make yourself useful, young man, it ain't Christmas yet."

Today, he had figured he would be lucky.

When he woke up, he could feel that the weather had finally changed back to true October—not too cold, not unseasonably warm, all the colors with a gold tinge that made the neighborhood look as if it had been painted on canvas.

Plus, tomorrow was what amounted to a Port Richmond holiday—the students were off because of parent-teacher conferences. After school yesterday, Gunnar Weldmar, the head janitor, had offered him some extra work: either report anyway and clean for a couple of hours, or come in today after practice and scrub the floors after the team had tramped dirt and spike marks all over them. Usually he didn't get a choice, so he grabbed the second option, figuring he'd be done in a couple of hours, get home to change and eat, then decide what to do with his midweek, no-homework Tuesday night.

So far so good, until he had gotten out of bed and the whole damn roof had fallen in.

To everyone's astonishment, the teachers' argument had really pissed his grandmother off, so much so that she'd actually yelled at them, said not a word to him at breakfast, and then didn't even say goodbye when he left for school.

He guessed part of it had to do with Mr. Naze not coming home last night. Or the night before that. He figured, and had tried to tell Neeba, that the old guy was probably just visiting friends or something. He did that once in a while, went off on his own for one reason or another.

But Neeba's concern had surprised him.

And if that hadn't been bad enough, it rained all morning, and the team hadn't just brought in dirt—it had trampled mud, grass, and god knew what else into every corner and crack of the gym and locker-room floors. A couple of easy hours with the broom and polisher became three dismal lifetimes; Mickie and her family had gone into the city; all the guys were gone by the time he had finished; and when he stopped by the Luncheria on the way home, he'd run into June.

She had snubbed him.

Cut him.

Froze him solid and left him standing on the sidewalk like a crud-crusted ice cube.

"Man," Blue had said in whispered awe, "you're so dead now, you're a zombie. Where do we send the flowers?"

Corky, oblivious as always, wanted to know if anyone was up for the movies tonight, and before Brian realized it, he'd agreed to meet them at the Galaxy for the eight o'clock show. Two blocks later, he couldn't remember the film; a block after that he ran into Rita, who told him, in passing, that she'd see him tonight.

Seeing her reminded him of Mickie, who, he figured with the way the day was going, would return unexpectedly from New York, show up at the theater, see him with Rita, and cut him just as dead as June had. Only worse. And although he supposed he did miss her after a fashion, he couldn't help feeling a curious sense of relief, which immediately switched to guilt, then to confusion.

By the time he reached Forest Road, he figured the best thing for all concerned would be if he just locked himself in the cellar and became a monk for a while.

Besides, he was tired. His arms ached, his head ached, and even some kids playing basketball in a driveway weren't able to make him smile. If Neeba was home, and still in her mood . . . he shuddered, blew out a slow breath, and hurried on up the street.

At the house, he slipped his hands into his jacket pockets and stopped, not wanting to go in.

A crow cried at him from the roof.

His stomach growled.

A single step up the drive, and a horn blared right behind him, making him jump and turn at the same time.

It was his grandmother, and she leaned over the front seat of her tiny car and yelled, "Get in."

"What's going on?" he asked, hastily squeezing himself into the front seat, glad he wasn't as bulky as Blue or he'd have his knees jammed under his chin, choking him half to death.

She drove off, didn't answer.

"Neeba?" He couldn't tell if she was still angry. She stared at the road, her hands rigid on the steering wheel. "Is it Mr. Naze?"

He saw her eyes move though her head didn't turn. "Yes and no," she answered. "Damn cops haven't found him yet. They must come from the Bronx. But I just remembered where he ought to be."

Fifteen minutes and several near-accidents later, she swung into the parking lot behind the old station. The cracked blacktop was littered with leaves that stirred as they drove through, dying animals in a pen reluctantly giving way. A large limb had fallen onto the roof, clung to the gutter with several smaller branches. A squirrel watched them from a window ledge.

When he stepped out, he shivered and hugged himself. "God, it's cold here."

She didn't answer. She wore a short coat and a scarf, her hands bunched in her pockets. He followed, not liking the way the light fractured through the trees; it was too dim for late afternoon. It was too much like twilight.

They climbed onto the platform.

The old man wasn't there, though the chair he'd probably used was over by the locked entrance. It had fallen on its side.

The wind rose.

The sign creaked.

She stood at platform's edge and scanned the tracks north and south. Her shoulders were up. The scarf fluttered over her hair.

Brian found a patch of sunlight and took it as his own, arms folded across his chest. He didn't like it here. It smelled different; it smelled old.

It smelled as if someone had died here.

Neeba said something.

"What?" he asked quietly. His voice sounded hollow.

"I said, this is wrong."

He waited for her to explain, but she only turned away from a darting breeze and stared down at the unused tracks. Muttering to herself.

Brian watched for a while, then looked away, toward the parking lot. She looked old out there, frail and lifeless, and he didn't like to see her that way.

But she looked old.

Too old.

And he thought, oh hell, she's going to die.

2

His inexplicable depression lasted until Neeba began swearing at the traffic, at the way the car coughed when she ground the gears, at the way Port Richmond had laid out its streets in curves and arcs instead of sensible grids. The extent of her stevedore vocabulary amazed him, sometimes shocked him, sometimes shocked him by pleasing him.

And after they reached home without killing anyone, she nearly drove through the garage door when he pointed out the faint light in Mr. Naze's window. He was glad the old man had finally found his way back; Neeba was so excited, she could barely wait to turn off the engine before scrambling out of the car and racing around to the side, to the narrow flight of stairs that led to the door.

Brian waited for a moment to catch his breath and wonder how old people could get so excited about other old people. Then he climbed out, stretched, and headed for the kitchen door, pausing at the corner when he heard her call Naze's name. When he looked, her finger was on the doorbell, her other hand was knocking, and she was calling. He wanted to yell at her, tell her to leave the guy alone, give him a chance to rest, when she suddenly stepped back, and the door opened.

She said something, her hands clasped, her head cocked.

Brian couldn't see inside.

She stepped over the threshold; the door closed behind her.

Maybe, he thought, the day had finally turned around and let him out of his hole, and he grinned when he imagined the scolding Mr. Naze would get for scaring her half to death. By the time she was done with him, he'd be joining Brian with the yardwork, just to get back on her good side.

A quick breeze wrinkled his nose—the unpleasant smell of polish and sweat that still clung to his clothes and his hands. Then he saw a bloated Siamese creep across the back of the yard. It belonged to the Rammons, three houses down. Despite the time and the need to clean up, he leaned against the porch post and watched it. Grinning. Rubbing the back of his neck. The Rammons called it Soldier, and the overfed cat thought it was a hunter, a tracker, a tiger in the jungle of rose bushes and laurel, lilac and ivy. It was also the loudest, dumbest cat he had ever met, and the neighborhood birds and chipmunks always had plenty of time to escape. But not before they tormented it, taunted it, sometimes made it falling-down dizzy by letting it chase them.

Neeba claimed Soldier was a disgrace to his species; Brian thought it was wonderful, and conducted a continuing campaign to get a cat of his own.

He didn't much like dogs; they weren't independent enough.

Another light gust made him squirm, and with a wave to the cat, he went inside to change out of his work clothes and take a shower to get warm and sluice off the stench. Thirty minutes later, when he went down to the kitchen to grab something to eat before heading for the show, Neeba was at the stove.

Mr. Naze, she told him, was home, he was all right, there was nothing to worry about.

That's all she said.

Flatly.

Without looking around.

"So where was he?" he asked, fixing himself a quick sandwich.

"You heard."

"Yeah, but—"

"Are you going out?"

"To the movies, if that's okay, Neeba."

"You be home before midnight?"

"No sweat. So, about Mr. Naze. Did he—"

She slammed a pot on a burner. "Brian, I told you."

Her reluctance and reaction puzzled him, but no amount of joking or sly provocation budged her into telling him more; he stopped when he sensed a *you're staying home, young man* in the way she held her back, the way her hands began to fuss with her hair.

221

She was sitting in the living room, magazine in her lap, when he kissed her forehead and left.

3

After the movie was over, Brian couldn't remember what he'd just seen except that it had something to do with a pair of rogue cops blowing the hell out of South American drug dealers with dumb-sounding names. Slow-motion blood and guts, rock music, and midway through it all, it had suddenly become little more than just a blur. Outside, standing under the marquee, he realized that the others were oddly quiet as well. Corky and Sarra, Blue, Greta, and Rita; none of them had seemed affected, none of them jabbered or replayed favorite scenes, quoted the best or the most stupid lines, or explained how, if they'd had the reins, they would have done it better.

It was a film Shane would have loved, given his love for special effects, and his oft-proclaimed vow to invite them all to Hollywood in ten years—after he had taken over the town and made his first ten million.

The usual pattern had been upset.

And when Corky, clapping his hands like a fussy tour guide, decided that the rest of this exciting night would best be passed at the Luncheria planning the ultimate stunt, which he had already devised, Brian shook off the invitation and said he had to get on home, his grandmother wasn't feeling well, he'd promised her he'd be in early.

No one objected.

He avoided Rita's eyes.

And once off the avenue, away from the late-night lights and traffic, he felt Blue come up beside him.

"Hey, you okay?"

"Yeah. Neeba, like I said."

"Right. Bullshit."

Hands in pockets, heads down; ignoring the leaves that husked overhead, ignoring the dogs that barked from dark porches.

"You got Mickie troubles, huh?"

"Don't start, Ted."

Blue held up a stiff palm, an indication that using his real name wasn't called for here.

Brian looked him an apology.

A pickup sputtered past, jouncing on springs that were springs in name only.

"Seems to me," said Blue, "that what we got here, see, is a failure to communicate. Not original, but apt, as my father always says. Forty times a week."

The night chill dampened.

The streetlamps were blurred.

"What I mean is, see, you and Mickie ain't saying to each other what you're really saying, know what I mean?"

Brian grunted.

Rich girls and boarding-house boys.

"Now I ain't saying she's jobbing you, man, okay? I ain't saying that. But forgive me if I got the impression these past few days that you two weren't exactly heading off to Vegas and the nearest wedding chapel."

"Yeah, well . . ."

Mickie had eaten lunch with him exactly once; she had talked on the phone with him exactly twice; she had sprung the New York trip on him last night.

They waited at the curb for a dust-streaked gold bus to belch past them.

223

"So, what do you think of Corky's idea?"

"Dumb."

"Sure it's dumb, man, that's a given. What I mean is, you think we can piss the Führer off a little?"

Reluctantly he grinned. "A little."

"See, I was thinking, we get some of my sister's stuff—panties and bras and shit like that—and hang them in his office window. Rita takes a picture or nine, and we send one to the newspaper. Otherwise, the creep's gonna clean things up, nobody's gonna see anything."

"Your sister will kill you."

"My sister," said Blue, "will do whatever I tell her."

Brian laughed. MaryBeth Cross was more in charge of that household than either of their parents. It had happened when Blue's mother had been months in NYU Medical Center, undergoing treatments for cancer. She'd survived, and the family had survived, only because MaryBeth had recovered from the shock first.

Brian looked at him sideways. "Y'know, as long as you guys don't expect me to get you into the school just because I could probably get the keys—"

"Who? Us?"

"—it'd be better to get at the trophy case in the front hall. That way, everybody sees it when they come in."

Blue rubbed the side of his nose. "Suppose the Führer gets there on time."

"Suppose the Führer has car trouble."

Blue slapped his cheek. "Oakland, I am appalled."

"You're Methodist."

"And proud of it." He thumped his chest. "Speaking of which, my dear fellow, you mayhap remember that Saturday, which coincidentally happens to be Halloween, is the night of the church party. May I expect you?"

An ambulance siren rose and fell.

Brian had no idea if Methodists were like this every-

224

where, but in Port Richmond, the minister had decided that raising a little money for the church, and keeping some of the kids off the streets at least part of the time was worth throwing a costume party for. It had begun ten years ago. Now it was the night few wanted to miss.

"I guess."

"Good. MaryBeth has just the thing for you to wear."

He laughed, shook his head, and Blue threatened to tear out his arms if he didn't play along.

"She needs the work, Oakland. Give her a break."

Another siren.

Brian shoved back his hair.

"Your grandmother really okay?" Blue asked quietly.

"Yeah."

"So . . . I'm gonna have to guess why you're cutting your throat tonight, or what?"

"I don't know," he answered truthfully. "It's been a shitty day from the minute I got out of bed, and I swear to god, I couldn't tell you why."

"The weather."

"Yeah?"

"A fact. I would not lie to you. We got our cold, see, then our warm, now it's getting cold again. You ought to listen up in science, man. Our leader explained last Wednesday that rapid and inconsistent swings in weather patterns adversely affect the psyches of many northern people, even if they've lived here all their lives. This, plus the fact that winter generally slows people down in the first place, gives you depressions, melancholy, and sometimes suicidal tendencies. Especially around the holiday season."

"Halloween?"

"Hey, I just call 'em as I see 'em, man. Like, for instance, you and Rita going to hook up any time soon?"

Brian glared at him.

225

Blue gave him unabashed innocence back.

Ten steps later: "I don't think so."

"Okay."

Five steps: "I mean, there's Mickie, right?"

"Right."

They rounded the corner onto Forest.

"Besides . . ."

Blue drop-kicked a pebble into the street.

"I mean, she's okay and all, but . . . you know."

"Sure."

The wind came up, hunching their shoulders, quickening their pace, snapping twigs from curbside trees and scattering them across the blacktop.

"God!" Blue exclaimed. "Christ, it's cold!"

Brian only looked up at the stars, and a moon that seemed flat and dead.

Twenty-two

Evan stayed away from the cottage most of the day. He stayed away from the village.

There was no destination—just lanes and sideroads, a sloping field where sheep were puffing out their winter coats, a portion of the Plain away from the Ringstones where he thought he saw a deer standing inside an oak grove. He wore a windbreaker over his sweater, jeans, boots for the mud, and the bite in the air made him think of fresh apples. He spoke to no one, though he was polite to those he met hiking along the way, and when he rested—against a tree, on a grassy embankment, once near railroad tracks that seemed to hum with a train long gone—he couldn't help wondering why the day was so lovely. Brilliant sky and sunlight weren't at all helping him to decide just how he ought to feel.

Addie had left without returning to the bedroom, picking up her clothes in the living room and closing the front door without a sound. No note, no cryptic message, just the scent of her left behind.

He had fallen asleep sometime during the small hours, listening to the rain.

Now he trudged along a narrow road more stone than tarmac, trees on the left and a fallow pasture on the right, heading back toward Bettin Wells. He was hungry. He was thirsty. And he was disgusted because he knew what he'd been doing since leaving the house. Acting. Tramping all over the hell and gone, arguing aloud with himself, arguing in silence, having dialogues, waving his arms, scowling, laughing, posing and posturing as if there were an audience up there in the blue, judging each emotion for honesty and truth.

What a crock.

He could have stayed home and done the same thing in comfort.

But Addie had been there last night, and she had still been there in the morning, whiffs and traces and corners-of-his-eyes of her. He hadn't been able to stand it, and hadn't the nerve to try to call her.

The problem had been between the "ought" and the "did."

By all rights and training, he *ought* to feel guilt, remorse, as much as shame for cuckolding his best friend, especially when that friend was seriously ill, evidently in all ways imaginable.

Yet he *did* feel a kind of adolescent elation, half-drunk giddiness, a certain chilling relief that he didn't have to lie to himself any longer. No excuses about loneliness, a man's supposed needs, a woman's supposed desires. No excuses left. Perhaps none to begin with.

He stopped and cocked his head at a blackbird pecking at something dead on the verge.

"Big deal. So now what do I do?"

The blackbird ignored him, a string of flesh in its beak.

"Thanks."

He moved on.

The temperature warmed slightly though the sun had begun to set, twilight less than an hour away.

He came to a stone bridge barely wide enough for a car, and at the top of the arch leaned against the wall and looked down at the stream. Leafy weeds lined the banks, water rolled over submerged rocks, a branch caught in the reeds built an island for itself as leaves and other debris were caught by it in turn.

Home was only twenty minutes away, just over a small rise spiked by trees he couldn't name. His reflection, distorted by the stream's motion, suggested a sour stomach and a hint of apprehension.

What if Addie was there?

Pretending all was as it used to be was out of the question, and there were no roles he could think of that suited the occasion of meeting a woman he'd made love to, and probably loved, and was lost to him as long as Paul remained alive.

The reflection showed fear.

A flash of light, fish leaving the shallows.

There were too many options: make her face her own part in the affair, play noble and leave town before he hurt her any more, play martyr, play jester, play the idiot and carry on.

Christ.

John would tell him that he'd been a jackass, taking advantage, and no man takes advantage; or he'd say that Evan had more of an obligation now than ever, to see to it that if harm were on the horizon, none would come to her even if nothing came of it. For him.

The old saying: you can run, but you can't hide.

Another old saying: no problem is big enough that you can't run away from it.

He grinned.

He decided *what the hell* and snapped a pebble from the wall into the water. His reflection fragmented. Dying sky and a small cloud losing its white as the day rapidly lost its light. When his face returned, disembodied above the shadow of the wall, he couldn't tell the expression, which, he supposed, was just as well.

Sighing, he flexed his legs, they were beginning to complain, and moved off the bridge, kicking at leaves and stones, stepping around a dead branch, looking up the slope as if it were a mountain he wasn't prepared to climb.

Paul stood at the top.

Evan grunted as if he'd taken an elbow in the stomach.

Though the man was at least one hundred yards away in shifting shade, a streak of crimson sky behind, it was clearly him—the hat, the coat, the horrid sickly smile.

First thought: *he knows.*

Second thought: *he's alive.*

He took a step, and Paul waved and began to run, a shambling awkward trot with his arms at his sides. Evan didn't know what to do, wait and talk, run for his life, and so he called Paul's name and the man slowed, finally stopped. The sun gulped by trees, dim light shimmering on a face that seemed ravaged by plague.

"God, we've been looking all over for you." Evan said.

Paul looked side to side. "Out here?"

"In London, you ass," he snapped. "We had the police out for you, Addie's near death with worry."

The smile—yellow teeth, canines rotting.

"Damnit, Paul!"

Burwin took off his hat and flakes and clots of hair fluttered to his shoulders. He flicked them off with one finger. "I was going to kill myself, actually. Remember? Something dramatic—off the Elephant and Castle and into the Thames with the tide." A shrug. "Changed my mind after you left. I was mad at you, my friend. Still am, if you must know. Decided I had things to do before it was over."

Evan started for him, stopped when a hand rose to stop him. "Paul, please."

230

"Ah? Please what?"

"Please stop and think for a minute, all right? You're sick, very sick, and if you'll let me, I'll ride you over to Greenfield right away. There's—"

Paul laughed. A quick, sharp sound that took Evan back a halting step.

"All right, then we'll go to Addie's office, let her decide what we need to do—"

"What we need to do," Paul said solemnly, black ghost in twilight, "is decide what I am going to do with you, old son. A predicament, wouldn't you say? Old friends and all that, it's a puzzle I've been trying to work out for days. Did you enjoy Edinburgh? Did you thrill them? Did you sing them our song?"

Evan sidestepped to the right. "Look—"

"Well, Ev, I wish I could. See things your way, see it from your point of view, perhaps even put myself in your shoes and what would I do then, poor thing." The smile did not falter. But the eyes, set deep, widened. "To tell the truth, I know precisely what I'd do. Poor thing. I would kill myself. But I've changed my mind. It was that afternoon in Windsor, you see, that—"

Evan ran.

It had almost been forgotten—the fear in London, the threat, the terror—replaced by concern for his friend's welfare. Gone now at the sight of him. The insanity so clear it was almost an extra limb.

He ran.

Paul laughed and ran after him.

Off the road and into the weeds. Brittle, stiff, they slashed at his hands, forced his hands up to protect his face as he followed the bank for several clumsy yards before suddenly swinging to his left and breaking into the clear.

Paul was behind him, stumbling, flailing, but not losing ground.

231

Up the slope, still slick with last night's rain, patches of bare earth turned to glassy mud. Twice he fell and shoved himself back up without stopping; once, he looked back and saw Paul standing there, dusting off his hat, slapping it on, and shaking a finger—*naughty boy mustn't run from poppa*—and charging.

Into the trees at the top, darker than he'd thought, sparse underbrush though the pine needles and fallen leaves made the ground as slippery as the mud. He slowed so he wouldn't fall, confident that Paul couldn't move any faster, wondering if he ought to pick up something to use as a weapon, breaking clear on the other side and down the far side, angling to his left, toward the lane, Bettin Wells down there and spread out in autumn haze.

"Evan!"

In spite of a screaming that called him a fool, he paused and looked back.

Paul midway down the slope, fifty yards or so back, waving his hat, his scalp mottled and red.

"Yoicks, the fox!" and Burwin doubled over with laughter.

Evan ran.

Reached the lane and ran harder, wishing the hedgerows weren't so high. Too thick to barge through easily in case he had to. And branches here and there overtopping the hedges, bare, trembling in the breeze. The sun gone now, shadow stretching from one side of the lane to the other, a pale moon on the rise, running through night while day watched and mocked.

He looked back; Paul wasn't there.

Pacing him, probably; on one side or the other, hidden, pacing him.

To conserve, preserve, he slowed to a steady trot, braced for a sprint in case it was needed.

A break on the left, a short gravel driveway that led to an empty house, peeling shutters at angles, the front door bashed in, half the roof sagging, the other half collapsed.

Another fifty yards, and a longer break on the right for a fence and a gate. His own place not much farther. He didn't know if he should go there. Paul might have taken a shortcut. Might be waiting. Alone, he didn't think he could take it. It would mean he would have to fight him, and he didn't want to have to make that choice. In town there'd be people. He didn't think Paul would show himself.

But neither did he think he could run that far without dropping dead.

His laugh was a gasp.

Listening, then, and hearing nothing but himself, and the dead leaves husking, the distant call of a bus horn, the overhead cry of a late hunting bird. No sound of pursuit.

Hedgerows higher as the land rose, dropping the lane deeper into shadow, falling away when he rounded a bend and saw the cottage, and the car parked on the verge. He nearly stopped; he had left the vehicle at the Cross and Sword last night, hadn't yet gone to fetch it.

Addie.

He fell against the rear fender and folded his arms across his stomach to forestall a cramp, to smother the need to retch.

"Evan?"

The turn came in painful jerks, his vision clearing and blurring as Addie in a light topcoat came hesitantly down the walk.

"Paul," he said weakly, and pointed back toward the stream. Sweat dripped from the finger.

"Paul?" She grasped the neck of her coat.

He nodded, coughed and swallowed, pulled himself up and said, "You've got the keys?"

"Yes."

"Get in."

He pulled and hauled himself around the car, fell into the driver's seat and waited. She hadn't moved.

"Addie, for god's sake!"

After a moment, waking from a dream, she came to the door, bent over to look through the open window. "He needs help, Evan. He needs—"

"He wants murder," he answered sharply. "There's no help for him now, believe me."

She reached in and he grabbed the key ring, fumbled for the right key and started the engine. Switched on the headlamps. Pounded the steering wheel and said, "Addie, get in!"

He could see her torso, nothing more, arm positioned as if her hand were on the handle, but he knew she was looking for her husband. She needed to see him. Nothing Evan could say would convince her she couldn't help.

"Addie."

He twisted to look over the back of the seat and saw something move back there, up the lane.

"Addie!"

He leaned over and pushed the door open, forcing her to move away, her face freckled with dusk, biting on her lower lip.

"Addie, for god's sake, he's going to kill you."

Straightening, gunning the engine, checking the rearview mirror and seeing Paul in the middle of the lane, at the bend. The rising moon turning his flesh to bone, his red scalp to blood, his coat and hat to tatters.

Addie gasped.

Paul waved.

She scrambled into the car and Evan pulled away before she'd closed the door, fishtailing, thumping onto the verge before he found control.

"Where?" she asked quietly.

"I don't know. The police."

"They'll do nothing."

"He's here now. They can catch him, force him to get help."

Rearview mirror—dark, nothing more.

He manhandled the car onto the road that became the High Street. "We'll stay in view. A pub, someplace. He won't do anything then."

"And wait?"

He glanced over; she wasn't looking at him.

"And wait."

"Until?"

"For god's sake, Addie, how the hell should I know?"

Twenty-three

The moon, flat and dead.

A leaf caught by the wind and teased over the street like a broken-wing bat.

No lights in the room, the flowered curtains parted, John in a rocking chair nearly as old as he, listening to the dresser clock in the bedroom chime an hour before midnight. He stared out at Forest Road, and knew he could destroy it all—fire, flood, earthquake, pestilence.

He could do it.

Goddamn kids.

He wore his hat, his topcoat, speckled with dead grass and dark stains.

He stared at the way the streetlamp dropped pale white to the blacktop, filled in the lawn's gaps with shadows to make it lush, made the willows seem solid.

He could destroy it all.

A creak of wood, and he pushed himself easily to his feet, buttoned his coat, adjusted his hat, a youthful swipe to the brim. A single step took him to the window where he placed his hands on the broad sill and stared at them. Looked up without raising his head and saw Brian and that chunky redhead, Cross, standing on the sidewalk, talking quietly, slapping shoulders, parting, Brian unzipping his jacket as he hurried up the driveway and slipped out of sight.

Kids.

Bile rose in his throat. He turned his head and spat, heard the splatter on the floor and didn't care. Let the old bitch clean it up, that's what he paid her for, though god knows she seemed to think the rent gave her something more, rights to his life she had no business expecting.

The old witch.

A sneer, spitting again and chuckling; he pulled away from the window and hunched his shoulders, tucked his hands into his pockets and left. He took the stairs easily, frowning only once—when he reached the ground and looked over his shoulder, trying to remember how he'd done that, how it used to be going up, grunting while his hands flared and cursing every step until he'd practically fall into his room.

A door slammed.

He walked.

Something . . .

A tingling in his hands, and he flexed them in their pockets, curled them into fists.

A dark car sped past; the guttering of a bus.

He walked.

The moon followed.

A group of kids on a corner beneath a streetlamp, laughing quietly, quieting abruptly when he passed them, and laughing again.

He glared back at them.

They were gone.

Tingling.

He knew it then, and nearly cried out in pain, in terror, in joy—he could destroy them.

He could destroy them all.

You're crazy.

He stopped. Blinked. Found himself back on Forest Road, standing just inside the trees across from his house. His home. No lights on anywhere.

You're crazy.

Of course he was crazy. Of course he was. He couldn't kill anybody. He was John Naze, born and raised and probably dying in this town. How the hell could he kill anybody?

He began to tremble. First his arms, then his shoulders; his head twitched, his hat threatened to fall; his left knee buckled and he grabbed the nearest trunk, felt the rough bark against his palm; his right leg jumped, and he stamped it several times. Stamped his left leg until the knee locked.

A tear unexpectedly popped from one eye and ran cold down his cheek. It was followed by another. He had no idea why he was weeping, only a vague sensation that something . . . a tingling . . . something had been lost.

A Siamese cat, fat and rolling, slinked from the shadows into the street, stopped at the white line and looked side to side before peering into the trees.

John stared back.

The trembling, the quivering, the tears stopped.

Behind him, in the dark, the hunting cry of an owl.

The cat puffed its dark brown tail, arched its back, as it backed away slowly, fangs exposed and dead white in the dead light of the moon.

Dear God, John thought, how could I kill anybody?

Easy.

Oh god, it would be so easy.

He stepped out of the trees.

Twenty-four

In the middle of the night, in the middle of a nightmare, Brian sat up, sweating, and heard a cat scream.

Soldier? he thought, and listened; Soldier, that you?

When the cry wasn't repeated, he lay back and inhaled slowly, deeply, and blew the breath out sharply as he wiped a forearm across his eyes. A dream; just a dream.

Moonlight slipped around the edges of the window shade, a lighter shade of black on the wall opposite his bed. Around it, objects began to assume slow definition as his vision adjusted so that the hole to the window's right became the outline of a poster, the gashes on the left a series of baseball pennants. The footboard was still invisible. The door not seen at all. Tall chest of drawers, drafting table for a desk, Salvation Army armchair, the glass cabinet stereo, none of it real yet, yet all of it there. Sensed. Waiting.

He rolled onto his stomach and punched his pillow, crushed his cheek into it, and closed his eyes. He wanted to sleep. He yawned mightily each time he thought about how long he had lain there, trying. He needed to sleep. Neeba had declared that his day off would be yard day— he had to finish wrapping all the shrubs in burlap, raking leaves, scattering wood chips where they were needed in Neeba's garden. That last was less for the plants than it

239

was for Soldier, who his grandmother had decided needed something to dig in when the ground had finally frozen. But cat or no cat, damnit, he needed to sleep. If he didn't, even for an hour, he would be a zombie before noon.

The furnace rumbled on.

Who the hell did Blue think he was, trying to start trouble by hooking him with Galiano, talking about Mickie that way, trying to . . .

Damn.

He flopped onto his back and stared at the ceiling, tried to imagine what Miss Atkins looked like, in her bed, upstairs. He couldn't. So he tried picturing Miss Gough without her artist's smock, without the red crayon forever tucked behind one ear, and the smear of paint that somehow always managed to find the tip of her broad nose. He couldn't.

He shifted to his right side.

Nothing.

Cheek back to the pillow, arms under his head.

Nuts.

Okay, count sheep, think of Mickie, write a letter in your head to Mr. Kendal and ask him why he hadn't called; fifteen ways to make love, twelve ways to strike a batter out, three ways to get out of raking the yard; nine ways to take care of Mr. Linholm, the son of a bitch, starting with a frozen needle slowly driven into each eye, fire-hot pliers applied to each ear, hands tied and thrust into beehives, large magnifying lenses taped to his naked chest after he had been staked out in the mid-July sun, acid dripping onto his knees through a narrow glass tube, splinters coated with salt shoved under his nails, a claw hammer—

"Jesus!"

He sat up and swallowed, put his palms to his cheeks and blew out several breaths.

240

"Jesus."

He felt as if he'd just sprinted from one end of town to the other, and had finished by skidding to a nerve-racking halt at the edge of the river cliff, toes hanging over, rocks and water waiting to take him. Cold puckered his skin; the shade snapped as a gust slipped under the sash. He drew the blanket to his chest and held it there, shifted his legs, leaned back against the headboard.

Jesus.

He must have fallen asleep at last. But god, he'd never had nightmares like that before. Usually, when he had them at all, they were about his parents; usually, they were about his failure to keep the airplane from taking off, soaring, crashing. He woke from them screaming, or trying to, or whimpering.

This one was worse.

In this one there was no terror; in this one there was excitement.

An image: Linholm in his office, his head in a clear plastic bag in which someone . . . in which Brian had placed several dozen scorpions.

His stomach lurched violently and he threw the bedclothes aside, staggered to his door and leaned against it, gripped it, gasping and licking his lips and swallowing the bile that bubbled toward his mouth. Deep breaths to hold it down, calm him down, smelling sour, tasting sour.

An image: Linholm shackled to the weight-room wall at school, and Brian at the opposite end, casually tossing Indian clubs at his already bloodied head.

He yanked the door open and ran down the hall, lunged into the bathroom, and just managed to get the toilet seat up before he vomited, letting the tears come as his throat became raw, letting his sobs come as he scrabbled for the handle, flushed, and threw up again. Until the water turned to blood, and his mouth tasted like copper, and when he looked into the bowl, Mr. Linholm looked back, grinning.

He screamed.

He sat up.

He leapt from the bed and raced into the bathroom, banged up the toilet lid, and threw up, and tried to scream.

He had liked it.

Oh Jesus oh god, he had liked everything he had done.

Twenty-five

1

"If we sit here long enough," said Addie, "people will talk."

What can he do, Evan thought; what can Paul really do to them? He's falling apart. He's literally falling apart. I don't believe it. Jesus, I don't believe it.

"Of course, there's always the chance Paul will walk in with a shotgun and blast us both to heaven."

He drank, and felt his bladder complain.

A part of him insisted stubbornly, almost whining, that they ought to be running, not sitting in a pub making sure people were with them, could see them, could, if necessary, protect them; or they ought to be out looking for Paul, driving up and down all the streets, shining lights into alleys, knocking on doors.

They ought to be doing something.

Anything.

Not just sitting.

"Evan, I swear to God right now that if you don't talk to me, I'm going to walk out. I will, you know. I'll walk out."

"Back in a sec," he told her with an unsteady smile

and unsteadily made his way to the men's room. No one was there. He made sure the small window high over the stall was closed and locked, the stall itself empty, before he stood at the urinal and counted the wall tiles, made shapes of faint stains.

What can he do?

Addie was gone when he returned, and in a panic he fled outside, saw her leaning against the wall, watching a red bus trying to make a U-turn.

"Fool," she said when he joined her. "Don't know what the hell he's up to."

"Addie."

The driver gave up and continued down the High Street, blaring his horn.

She turned to him. "Do you understand the phrase 'scared shitless,' Ev? It's universal, I gather." A deep breath. "If he really wants to kill us, do you think we ought to be standing out here?"

The lights went out behind them.

"Time, gentlemen," he muttered.

The police had duly noted their report of Paul's return, though the sleepy-eyed sergeant on night duty had been openly skeptical of Evan's claims of impending murder.

"Let us be the judge of that, sir, if you don't mind."

All patrols would be notified, eyes peeled, a few discreet inquiries made, don't you worry. There wasn't much else they could do. Bettin Wells was small, but the night made it large. Go home, then, and wait for us to call, Mrs. Burwin, there's nothing you can do here. The implication in tone and expression was clear: *Professor Burwin may be ill, ma'am, but he's no killer, you're just upset.*

For an hour they had driven, in slow silence, along the High Street, up and down Wellington Road, out as far as the hospital. Evan worried aloud about Josie, but Addie told him the waitress was already home. Back again, shop lights dimming, the hotels luring back their guests, the cinema closing down. The police were right; no sense in this, but nothing would send them home. Where Paul might be. Or might be watching. They decided to stay in public, and split the rest of the next few hours between the Queen's Garter and the Cross and Sword, and Evan hadn't been very good about nursing his drinks.

"Will he use a gun, do you think?"

"Addie, for Christ's sake!"

"Oh, for Christ's sake yourself," she retorted, grabbed his arm and pulled him close. Her expression alternated between anger and uneasiness. "I'm doing this on faith, you know. What you told me, about Paul, this is all on faith, on your say-so. For all I know all he wants is a good hot bath and a soft place to lie down." She snatched her hand away, shoving him back in the process.

"You saw him," he said.

After a moment, she nodded.

"I told you what he said."

She nodded again, then slipped her arms around his waist and laid her head on his chest. Briefly. Long enough. Pulled back and gestured that they should walk down the street.

Light and dark, streetlamp and space between, slowing at each corner, hurrying across to the other side. Stopping at a late-night fish 'n' chips for a plastic cup of coffee then only half-finished before tossing in the trash.

A cat prowling a trash can in an alley yowled at them to keep their distance.

The night wind grew colder.

Their footsteps sounded like thin cracking ice.

What can he do?

Evan knew, and shuddered.

"If I just knew why," Addie said once, more perplexed than worried. "If I could only see *why*."

"He said he was the hunter, remember."

She made a disgusted noise. "And what the hell does that mean, Ev? Some obscure reference to some ridiculously obscure song. It doesn't make sense."

"Tell me about it."

"Whatever he has," she said firmly, "it's madness that makes him talk like that. Hunter. Jesus, Evan."

Indeed, he thought. Forget the damn song, just pray he's caught. Then, and only then, would they know what was wrong.

"We'll go back to the police," Addie decided ten minutes later. "We've been looking, haven't found him, I'll be the dutifully distraught wife who just can't sit at home and wait." She sighed. "They won't kick us out for a while, I shouldn't think. These days, I can almost cry on command."

He took her hand and held it, knowing there would probably never be a right time. "Listen. About last night."

"Evan, if you say anything that sounds like 'I'm sorry,' I'll have your head."

A glance.

Passing a newsagent's whose lights snapped out with a muffled buzzing.

"No, actually I was going to say that while it's true there's some guilt here, I'd be in coma if there wasn't, I do not regret it." More than a glance. An inhalation. "What I'm trying to say is—if Paul is jealous, he has reason to be."

She lowered her head. If she answered, he couldn't hear her. But at least she didn't cry again, or slap him, or deny what they had done.

It could have meant anything; it served to make him feel better.

246

He brushed a hand over her arm. "You—"

"Cried, yes." She gathered her hair in one hand, pulled it over her shoulder, threw it back and shook her head. "Ask me about it someday. Not now. I'll tell you why."

"On the other hand, you did run away." He grinned. "Wham, bam, thank you, sir."

"It doesn't rhyme," she scolded flatly without meeting his gaze.

"It makes me feel cheap."

"Bastard." She smiled, head up. "It was nice though, wasn't it."

"Very."

"Oh yes. Very." The smile faded. "Do you have any idea, Evan Kendal, how godawful stage British we sound just now?"

"Yep."

Without stopping, she yanked him down, kissed his cheek. Released his hand as they approached the station. Ran fingers through her hair. Rubbed her cheeks vigorously with her palms. They stepped inside, and PC Purdy rose from his desk, tunic unbuttoned halfway down. He told them before they could ask that there was no word of Professor Burwin though the patrols were still looking.

"I want to stay," Addie told him, taking a stiff chair by the door. "He'll need a doctor."

"Dr. Burwin, I'm not . . . it's quite late."

"I'm staying," she said, a smile without showing a hint of her teeth. "I can't bear to be home alone."

"Of course," the policeman said, a sidelong glance at Evan. "Tea? Coffee?"

"Yes, thank you, coffee will do fine. And some for Mr. Kendal as well."

Purdy nodded curtly and disappeared into the back.

Prig, Evan thought, and stood at the window, not lik-

247

ing to see the High Street so dark. So many shadows, so much wind moving things he couldn't focus on, too much of the night's chill seeping through the glass. He started when he heard a scream, back in the cells, heard Purdy cursing, heard a heavy door slam. The screams soon became sobs that soon faded, soon died.

"Trouble?" he asked when the constable returned.

"Oh aye," Purdy said glumly, setting the cups on the counter for Evan to fetch. "Ida MacNair again." He shook his head in supreme disapproval. "Drunk, drugs, I don't know. Do you know, she actually wanted me to lock her up? Couldn't do it, of course."

"But she is," Addie pointed out.

"Sure, after she conked me with a cane. Had to then, didn't I?"

Evan smiled as he handed Addie her drink. "What's her problem."

"Who cares?" Purdy shrugged as he buttoned his tunic. "What the hell. She says somebody called 'Him' is out there and we're all going to die."

2

The radio spat static and Purdy excused himself.

Evan looked out the window again, scratching his head, the side of his neck. He wondered if the police had checked the lane beyond his house, or the bridge. He wondered how Paul could keep warm on a night like this. He tilted his head and looked up at the sky, seeing nothing, there were too many lights, and stepped back when a car swung around in a U-turn, headlamps glaring, blinding him for a moment.

He sipped his coffee—grimaced, it was too black—and set the plastic cup down on the sill. Then he rubbed his palms together, amazed he wasn't sweating, and thought again that keeping still shouldn't be the thing to do in a case like this. They ought to be running, fleeing in a car or galloping over a pasture or racing down a dark alley where no one heard their screams.

You're acting again, Kendal.

He didn't care.

Anything was better than just waiting.

"Come home with me, Addie," he whispered.

She shook her head, but he had seen the hesitation.

Ida MacNair screamed and sobbed.

Evan watched the street.

VII

TARGETS

Twenty-six

1

On Wednesday morning, Eric Linholm pushed away from his desk with a satisfied sigh. There had been a moment, just a moment there, when he had felt like shouting, and the sensation made his heels tap once on the floor, his fingers snap once, his tongue click against the roof of his mouth. No question about it, he was on the crest and there wasn't anyone around to challenge him now.

Nobody worth mentioning.

Lovingly, he passed a hand over the thick manila folders closed on the leather-trim blotter.

"Damn," he whispered. "Damn, you're good."

Six years ago, he had taken over Port Richmond High School at a time when even its most ardent supporters called it "Rich and Bitch High." Grades had been abysmal, attendance haphazard and virtually willful, college acceptances nearly at a state low for a school of its position and size; morale nonexistent; the sports program a joke; and at least once a week a story in the local and county newspapers about shortcomings, drug arrests, burgeoning anarchy in the halls.

The Board of Education, liberal to the core, finally panicked when several of its children had flunked out of the Ivy League before they had finished their freshman year, and an increasing number of the most affluent townspeople made it abundantly clear that filet mignon prep schools were infinitely preferable to the hash they served up here.

Enter Eric Staines Linholm, with a guaranteed contract, a free hand, and a mandate that read, in private, more like a death threat.

Linholm had come through.

Rebels among the staff were coldly driven out, parents were contacted and scolded and made to understand that this man wasn't vulnerable to any of their economic or status threats.

And the stupid bastards ate it up.

They licked it up.

They groveled as only the rich can when they haven't had money long enough to know what it meant; and the rest of them, the middle-class wimps wallowing in despair while they tried to aspire to higher things, they crowed and puffed their chests and behaved as if they had known all along that all it took was a firm hand, a strong belief in the system, and a canny way with figures that proved that their Janes and Johnnies weren't as stupid as they seemed.

Christ!

It hadn't been easy.

But it worked.

In six years the university acceptance rate had risen to well over 75% among those who applied. The others were either not good enough or hadn't the means even with scholarship monies, and even they had a Port Richmond diploma, which once again meant something in the job market they invaded.

The secret was easy: if you like kids, try to be their

adult buddy, you're doomed to endless sympathy and excuses; hate the little pricks, and you can get away with murder as you drive them harder than they drove their goddamn sport cars and pickups and whatever else they could steal from the pockets of their parents.

The fact that they learned to hate you in the bargain didn't mean a damned thing. When they saw what doors opened for them, when they heard the praise from admissions officers all over the country, they also learned damned fast how to be grateful with the best.

And this year's class—he applauded himself softly.

This year's class was going to be the final hook, the lure, the bait to draw more families to town—not because of the jobs, but because of the school. Why the hell spend all that money on a fancy-named prep school when, for a year's worth of property tax, you can get the same results, and keep the little prick home where you can watch him, to boot?

Being mayor, being governor, couldn't be sweeter.

Port Richmond had become his kingdom in less than a decade, and if he raped half the senior class tonight, they'd throw every bitch in jail for soliciting, if not worse.

God, he thought, life is good!

And if that moron, Bishop, had transferred last fall, life would be perfect.

Oh well. What the hell. Perfect would be next year.

He swiveled his chair around and stared out at the school's first impression to visitors—a well-tended, grass and garden oval centered by a white flagpole. From the bottom of the oval to Coolidge Street, a stretch of lawn that ended at a waist-high fieldstone wall, on the other side of which were bronze letters proclaiming the school's name. Stretching away from the drive in both directions, fifty yards each way, another wall—this one of low evergreen shrubs that ended at a hurricane fence.

Like a mansion.

His mansion.

Even the driveway that outlined the middle grass—entrance on one side of the wall, exit on the other, and narrow enough to discourage parking except in the designated lot far to his left, with its own entrance. His idea. Otherwise, the place looked like a factory.

The perfect setting.

One hell of a mansion.

Across the street, another vast lawn, this one dotted with flowering apple trees. The Methodist Church on the left, its parish hall in the center, both set well back from the road.

A car pulled in from the street.

He watched it without moving his head.

The lot was already half full. Parents who had arrived early, to get the conferences over with so they could get back to their Rich and Bitch games.

The sorry bastards.

But they came, didn't they, Eric? Of course they did. He had instituted Conference Day, and like sheep they obeyed.

A muted ringing.

He checked his watch: the first period just begun. Within three minutes, a secretary in the outer office would read the day's schedule over the public address system, telling the parents where to find the teachers they wanted. He grinned and steepled his fingers beneath his chin. Some of those fools might even read the large sheet of red construction paper he'd taped over the face of the trophy case, reminding the school that there would be no games this year, that irresponsibility and criminal acts had no place in Port Richmond's society.

Ergo, you little shits, the first son of a bitch that tries to pull a Halloween stunt this year is going to find his or her ass out on the grass. Forever looking in because, you fuckers, you ain't getting back in.

He applauded himself softly.

A knock.

"Come in!"

A tall, thin, black-haired boy stood at the threshold. Open-necked white shirt, pressed trousers, polished shoes.

"Bishop," he said dryly, "you look like hell."

Shane Bishop's lips tightened, but he said nothing, only stepped into the office and carefully placed a green binder on Linholm's desk. "The report, sir." Voice flat; no respect, no defiance.

Linholm pushed it away from him as if it were distasteful, then folded his hands on the blotter. "Mr. Bishop, do you have any idea why I asked you to do this little history exercise?"

The boy looked over his head to the window. "Yes sir."

"And why is that, Mr. Bishop?"

"To get my history grade back where it belongs."

Spineless little parrot, Linholm thought.

"That is correct. And because it's quite clear to me that what you lack is a sense of discipline, a sense of purpose. Any student of mine who wants to succeed in life must have discipline, must have purpose. It is the only way."

"Yes sir."

"It is, Mr. Bishop, the only way you're going to get into college."

"Yes sir."

He said nothing. He only watched the boy with eyes half-closed, not bothering to question the source of his animosity toward the creep, it just happened. There was always one. Every year, it seemed, there was always one

257

who pressed all the wrong buttons simply by existing. And this wimp had less backbone than some. Than most. He hadn't even had the nerve to demand an explanation for the lousy recommendation Linholm had given him.

The answer would have been easy: there wasn't one. Linholm just didn't like him.

"Get out of here, Bishop. Go home. Get out of my school."

"Yes sir."

The boy left.

Linholm smiled, felt slightly nostalgic for the days when principals were allowed a little corporal punishment, then swiveled the chair around and frowned when he saw someone loitering down by the wall. Not a parent, the clothes were too common. He stood and leaned on the narrow sill, peered through the tinted glass. He could see out; they couldn't see in unless their noses were pressed to the glass. His idea. *Uncle Eric is watching.*

A hesitant knock on his door.

Jesus Christ, can't they leave me alone?

A snapped, "Come in!", and when a woman half his age came in, he pointed and said, "Miss McCarthy, who the hell is that?"

She stood beside him. He could smell perfume, bath powder, hair spray, makeup. His right hand itched. He didn't look at her; she didn't look at him.

"I don't know, sir."

"Keep an eye on him. If he's not gone in five minutes, call the police."

There was no argument.

His arm brushed hers as he dropped back into his chair and kicked himself around to face his desk again. He glanced at the folders she'd placed on his blotter. Burying Bishop's report, which he would never read. "So, now what?"

"Finals results, sir."

He grinned in anticipation. "How're we doing?"

"Better than last year, by ten percent, give or take three."

His eyes closed in thanks. The best he had hoped for was a five percent increase. More proof that his methods were working; more evidence for those assholes on the faculty who still thought he was driving these kids too hard. Hell, he'd drive them into the goddamn river if he thought it would do any good.

He set the folders aside.

Another check of his watch—his first pair of simpering parents weren't due for a while—and he closed his eyes, leaned back, pushed away from the desk.

"Lock the door, Betty," he whispered urgently. "We've got fifteen minutes."

2

Just past noon, Rita slipped out of the house before her mother could check the set and cut of her uniform again, her hair, her fingernails, her for-crying-out-loud posture. It was like the army, for god's sake; not even her boss did more than glance to be sure she had all her clothes on.

Although she was close to being late, and a hell of a way to spend a day off, she tried not to run. The afternoon had turned chilly, the sun too weak to do anything but make promises. And the wind drove her in spurts, racing down driveways to shove her, then racing ahead to wait at the next block. Running would only make it worse, make her nose drip, stiffen her cheeks with red, make her lungs burn. No need to run. She'd make it, no problem.

Brian hadn't said much to her last night.

Corky wanted to know what they thought of painting the school orange. After all, he complained, they only had until Saturday and nobody was taking this stunt thing seriously, for pete's sake.

How true, she thought; Corky, you ass.

The wind again, more steady now.

Somewhere along the line somebody had mentioned Shane Bishop, but he hadn't been at the show. That surprised her. Cops and guns and buildings blowing up was his favorite mix; often enough, when they were in study hall together or stuck in line someplace, he would tell her about the screenplay he wanted to write, the ultimate explosion, total cataclysm, special effects that would tear the screen in half.

Poor Shane, she thought, and as she crossed Tyler Avenue, she reminded herself to give him a call if nothing else, see how he was doing, maybe hint that they could use him for Corky's dumbass stunt.

She saw him on the corner.

Fate, she decided, and waved cheerily as she approached. He wasn't wearing a jacket, the wind had thrown his hair over his eyes.

"Hey," she said.

He looked at her, and sniffed. "Hi."

"You hanging out or what?"

He shrugged. "Had to go in this morning."

"What?" She poked his arm, but he wouldn't look at her. "Who made you do that?"

"Linholm."

"The bastard." Her eyes widened briefly. "Oh, that stupid report, right?"

He nodded. "He won't read it, y'know. He won't even give it to Miss Atkins." He stepped off the curb, checked the traffic. "He isn't going to read it."

"Shane, wait."

A wave of a hand over his shoulder and he ran the rest of the way across, headed south. His back was straight, his head up, but Rita could feel from over here the anguished bewilderment, could hear the *why me?* over the sough of the wind.

God, she thought; god.

3

The house was small—three bedrooms, a living room, not much else, on a single white clapboard level. All the houses in this neighborhood were small compared to the monsters that lined Palisade Row. Shane had seldom thought of it that way before. Small. Large. Rich. Not so rich. Three years ago it hadn't made a difference; in eight months it would make all the difference in the world.

He sat on the back stoop.

He listened to his mother in the kitchen, talking with Mrs. Galiano. No doubt, he thought sourly, trying to fix him up with Rita. What a joke.

His head lowered; he stared at the step between his feet.

"Shane?"

A glance over his shoulder, a moment of tension until he realized his mother was only peering through the screen door; she wasn't planning to come out.

"I'm going to the store. Want anything?"

"No."

"See you later."

And gone.

Shane, he thought then; oh Shane, come back, Shane!

Christ, as if things weren't bad enough, his mother had to be a goddamn western fan. What the hell kind of a name was Shane anyway? Who gave a damn?

Shane. Come back, Shane.

He looked at the yard without really seeing it. He sensed it, rather, and the road beyond the trees. The highway that led past Port Richmond. Trucks this time of day, eighteen wheels shaking the ground; women on their way to a mall; salesmen; strangers; all of them passing by, maybe one in fifty catching a glimpse of him through and, perhaps, wondering who he was, or envying him for where he lived.

Perhaps wondering why he wasn't in school, like all high school kids are supposed to be on Wednesday afternoons.

He grunted.

He supposed the guys would be at the Luncheria, Corky mouthing off about doing something on Sunday. There was no sense in his going.

Why should he? All they'd do is ask him how the college thing was going, had he picked up his grade, had he appealed the suspension, had he stopped acting like a jerk and gotten his ass back in gear; all they'd do is make him wonder why he bothered to bother in the first place.

People riding by.

Not knowing about the nightmares he'd had the night before, black ones, seeing his goddamn barely remembered father and wasn't that a laugh running away from the house, shrieking with joy, while his mother sat at the telephone and tried to set him up with one girl after another.

People riding by.

But he knew they couldn't see him clearly.

They couldn't see how stiff his face had become, how vividly his cheeks had flushed with rage, with shame, how he swallowed dryly several times a minute.

262

Get out of my school.

Two years he had gone without the Führer noticing him, without the sonofabitch giving a damn. Then, late last April, he'd been standing in the hall, waiting for June and Brian, when Linholm marched up and said, "Mr. Bishop, is that right?"

Startled, Shane could only nod.

The principal had looked him over as if he were examining something filthy on the wall. "Jesus," he had said, "you are one sorry baby."

His mother hadn't believed him.

His friends had been too shocked.

But no one, not a single one of them, had done anything to protect him when the harassment continued—looks, whispered comments, sneers, suddenly showing up in his classes and staring at him from the back.

His mother didn't believe him.

The kids thought he was just being paranoid.

Then the Stanford acceptance conditionally withdrawn, but how the hell could he study with a vulture sitting on his shoulder all day, every day, just waiting for him to make a mistake. It would be *get out of my school* again, but this time forever.

A trailer truck backfired.

He stuck out his tongue.

He knew they couldn't see him.

And he knew they couldn't see the gun in his hand that dangled between his legs.

When he woke this morning, the first thing he'd done after breakfast was rummage through his mother's bedroom until he'd found it. He hadn't thought of the gun in years. It had been his father's, in case of burglars, and his mother had stored it in the attic because she couldn't stand to have it in the house, and she was too afraid to throw it away. She had taken it down when a house two doors up had been burglarized last month, the second one since May.

He hadn't thought of it in years.

He remembered it now.

He touched the mouth of the barrel to his chin.

Shane.

Cold.

Softly cold.

He curled a finger around the trigger.

Shane.

Oh hell.

Come back, Shane!

4

The King's Castle.

Rita grinned sourly at it, checked the street and saw no cars parked at the curb. She wondered where all the big spenders were, where were they having lunch if not in the Castle? If they were smart, anyplace but here.

She ducked inside, laughing to herself, and stopped as soon as the door hissed shut behind her.

It was dim.

The wind slipped under the door and kissed her ankles.

For god's sake, she thought as she let her vision adjust, why doesn't the jerk turn on some lights?

The centerpiece table candles were untouched, heavy wood furniture and dark walls, wrought-iron scrollwork panels that divided the dining room into five sections, separated the dining room from the even darker Royal Lounge where the furniture was small and dark, the booths draped in shadow. The only light sifted through the stained glass, oval front windows, the colors slumped on tables and chairs wan, nearly grey.

It was quiet.

A familiar quiet that told her that she had been right, there were no customers yet to worry about, and the others on her shift were probably back in the kitchen, sneaking a smoke and gossiping with the cook, that the owner wasn't here yet to crack the whip and get them to cleaning whatever had been cleaned already.

It was chilly. Unaccountably so. She lifted a hand to a grill in the wall above her head, wondering if some dope had turned the air-conditioning on. There was nothing, however, and she rubbed her arms briskly as she moved across the carpet toward the back.

She wasn't alone.

The thought made her stop and blink.

She wasn't alone.

A glance behind her showed her the shadows of the reception area, nothing more; but to her right, through diamond-shaped gaps in the ceiling-high divider, she saw someone sitting at the bar. His back was to her. He was dressed darkly, wore a hat pulled low, his right hand slowly shredding a cocktail napkin; he was no more than a shadow against the bottles ranged before him. The bartender was gone.

That shouldn't have been. No one was to be left at the bar alone; that was a house rule. Unless the man had just come in, and no one knew he was there. She looked quickly to the back, wondering if she ought to take his order herself or fetch the bartender.

His fingers began work on another napkin. A pile of white paper flakes tipped over the edge and floated to the floor.

He must be mad, not getting any attention. Bad for business. Worse for her.

Putting on her serving smile was automatic and easy; taking those steps forward somehow was not. But when she did, she was able to look over his shoulder to the bar's mirror framed by silver, and when she cleared her throat gently, he straightened sharply, as if startled.

It was cold.

She barely held back a gasp.

The man in the mirror had no face beneath the hat.

Just black.

Nothing but black.

Something rapped against the outer wall; something creaked in a far corner.

The man began to turn.

My god, run! she ordered, but in the dim light she could barely walk. Her knees weren't strong enough, her legs weren't quick enough, and she could hear his top-coat hiss as he slid off the barstool, could hear his shoes hiss as he shuffled in her direction.

Run!

Circles of light in the pair of swinging kitchen doors, too bright for her to look at, casting no light into the room, unblinking eyes that watched her collide with a serving table, collide with a chair. Voices back there, laughing.

She felt like a jerk, but she couldn't stop, couldn't turn, finally slammed through the doors and stood there, panting, while the others gaped at her, startled.

"A man," she finally said, and sat heavily on the floor.

Twenty-seven

1

Dom coiled the strap around his arm, put the stock to his shoulder. The boulder was cold beneath his elbow.

Pow.

A shame this highway sniping bit wasn't going to work, but it was too goddamn bad. Headlines would've been his, no sweat, no goddamn problem. But win some, lose some. There was still the stunt he'd been working on all week. Patrick had been drunk with excitement when he heard what was up, and if Mickie came through, they were gold. Solid gold.

And there was, after all, still the gun.

That part, if he had anything to say about it, Patrick wouldn't know about until it was too late. If the little shithead even suspected anything, even this close to Saturday, he'd find forty-two reasons for wimping out, and another forty-two for getting drunk to celebrate.

Pow.

A yellow convertible on the highway below.

Dom blew the driver's face off.

Didn't he wish.

Pow.

It was going to be perfect. Every detail. Every second of time it would take. Perfect. Stunt Night. Patrick shitting his pants because Dom had been in Gilder's this afternoon, alone in a booth with a hamburger and shake, listening to Ploughman shoot off his big mouth about their own gig on Saturday. Dom hadn't cared, had been disdainful, until, suddenly looking up and seeing nothing but light, he had figured out a way to bring his baby along.

Pow.

Patrick wanted the ultimate stunt.

Pow.

And if Mickie's ass was in gear, the way she promised . . .

Pow pow.

He smiled, whirled, shot the head off a squirrel.

Ejected the spent shell, chambered another, and turned back to the highway. Hey, he called to the cars passing by; holy shit, I am awesome, no frigging question.

Pow.

Trick or treat.

2

Panic and a curious rush of exaltation forced John into a stumble as he rounded the corner, one hand against the restaurant's outer wall to keep him from falling, his hat yanked down, lips working soundlessly, eyes squinting in the bright light. Too bright. Too much a contrast to the nonlight of the bar. Mica glittered in the concrete pavement, darts aimed to blind him; windows of side-street shops glared; his shadow cut ahead instead of flowing.

Too bright; nearly black.

He had almost touched her.

His eyes watered until he jabbed at them with his thumb.

Almost touched her.

A hand up to shade his eyes in spite of the hat.

Two blocks, and the shops were replaced by old brick houses behind hedges and picket fences. A few of them offices, most of them homes. Shedding trees at the curb. Browning lawns. Stalks of dead flowers. The river only four blocks farther on. He vacillated at a corner, confused at his reaction, unsure of his destination until he decided he had best go home. If he didn't, the old biddy would have half the damn police force out searching for him. He wouldn't put it past her to call the television and radio stations too, call the newspaper editor, even call his goddamn nephew in England, who obviously didn't give a damn about him or he'd be here. Now. Watching out for him. Taking care.

The bastard.

The hand shading his eyes dropped to hold the neck of his topcoat closed.

God, it was bright.

His eyes teared again until he slapped the tears away.

Too bright.

He had to go home.

blurred trees and falling leaves and some small animal pinned and mewling beneath his shoe.

His stomach growled.

He swallowed sour saliva.

Go home, old man, and get something to eat, go to bed. After sunset, he would sit at the window in his rocking chair and figure things out. He couldn't manage it now; he was too tired. Not weary, not exhausted, but pleasantly tired, as he used to be after working around the house, around the yard, creating things and repairing things and setting things right. A good tired. A righteous tired.

He smiled.

A post-office truck swung around the next corner, and the driver waved at him. John waved back and nodded.

He was hungry.

Maybe he should have had something to eat in the restaurant, a decent meal for a change; goddamn Mrs. Oakland couldn't cook her way out of a wet paper bag. Maybe he should have had something to drink. The bartender had stayed only long enough to tell him they weren't open quite yet, and had disappeared into the kitchen. John hadn't complained, though he knew the man had been lying. He didn't want a drink anyway. He wanted . . .

He wasn't sure.

Wasn't sure now.

He only knew it was important that he try to make contact with someone, that something would, or might, happen when he did.

Something different.

So he had followed that girl, that *kid*, when he had spotted her reflection over the bar.

For some reason, she hadn't run, though it was clear she dearly wanted to.

And he had been close.

So close he really could have touched her if he had only reached out; so close he could smell the sweet sweat on her back, the acrid sun on her blouse, the tang of slow-burning leaves that clung to her hair.

He could have touched her.

He could have.

And that, for now, was enough. That he could walk right up to someone and touch her, touch him. He didn't look any different, so they wouldn't be afraid. She had been afraid because he had been stupid. He had tried to sneak up on her, and she had heard him. In a dark place like that, who wouldn't be afraid of a man dressed in black. She'd probably thought he was a pervert; no wonder she ran.

But he could have touched her.

He could have.

Next time he would.

Then he would learn why he had to.

He looked at his hands, flexed his fingers, turned them back to palm.

Kids, he thought; goddamn kids won't bother me now.

Twenty-eight

Wednesday night.

High and black October sky.

The telephone rang.

Brian answered, and Blue said, "Hey, buddy, look out your front window."

Brian raised an eyebrow at the king-size sandwich he'd made for himself and hoped Cross wasn't pulling a gag. He was hungry. Too hungry for games. "Why?"

"Just look, you dope."

He made sure Blue heard the *okay, but just for you* sigh, then let the receiver thump against the kitchen wall and walked up the hall into the living room. Neeba was on the sofa, watching television, an open book in her lap. She glanced up and smiled as he walked to the window, pulled aside the filmy white curtain, and stared outside.

Okay, he thought; it's fog. Big deal.

A flickering to his right, then, and he frowned, pressed his cheek against the pane, and saw a faint glow above the houses and trees near the end of the block. Angry, diffused by the fog, pulsing.

"Wow," he said softly.

"What is it, dear?"

"I don't know. I think it's a fire."

He ran back to the kitchen and grabbed up the receiver. "What is it?"

272

"Don't know, Sherlock. You want to investigate?"

"I'm already there."

He hung up, grabbed a fleece-lined denim jacket from the hall closet and punched into it as he opened the front door. "Looks like a fire, Neeba," he said. "Blue and I are going downtown, okay?"

"You be careful," she warned. "Stay clear."

"I will."

She half-turned on the sofa. "I mean it, Brian. You be careful."

He was startled by her expression—as angry as the sky, and he nodded several times to prove he'd taken her point, slipped onto the porch and hunched his shoulders at the fog's caress. Blue was already on the pavement, beckoning, the size of him multiplied by the hazed air and the bulk of his red jacket. Brian, though taller, always felt smaller when beside him, but never threatened.

"Onward," Cross said. "Maybe it's the school."

"No such luck," Brian muttered. Trotted. Kept to the pavement because the street could barely be seen. House lights floated; streetlamps without form; in the headlights of a passing car, the fog looked like suspended rain.

"Saw Shane before," Blue said, lumbering easily beside him.

"Uh-huh."

"Said he wanted to kill himself with his old man's gun, but he couldn't find any bullets."

"Right."

"Jerk doesn't have any luck at all."

Brian kept his peace. He had sympathy for Bishop, but not much else. He figured it was the guy's own fault for slacking off, and he wasn't worried. Shane was smart when he had to be; he'd pull his grades up.

"What do you hear from Mickie?"

Again, Brian said nothing. Blue was another one who didn't much care for the Farwoods, but unlike Neeba,

273

Blue had told him so several times. The caution of a pal not to get involved with a known tigress. Brian had taken no offense. When he'd first moved to Port Richmond, Blue had been the first to show up on Neeba's doorstep and volunteer to show the new kid around. Neeba had taken to him immediately; it had taken Brian much longer, until he realized that Blue's fireplug size was a deliberate reconstruction of a frame more like Corky's— from medium height and slender to medium height and power. If there wasn't safety in actual strength, there was at least safety in its illusion.

They rounded corners in tandem.

They heard the sirens.

"You sure it's not the school?"

Brian grinned. "Wrong direction. It's on Tyler."

"Jesus, I hope it ain't the Galaxy."

The Galaxy: the only single-stage-with-balcony theater left in the county, a monster of a screen, where monsters were truly huge and explosions made you lean back and the women were large enough to give you fantasies for life. All summer there had been rumors that the owner had sold it to a medical group and it was about to close down; most of the town preferred the multiplexes at the malls and on the highway.

Brian and Blue preferred the Galaxy.

Illusions of size.

"If it is," Brian said, hurdling a wagon, "we'll buy it up and run it ourselves."

"Damn right."

"Reynolds pays triple."

Blue giggled.

"Unless we got naked ladies. Then we don't let him in."

Blue kicked aside a football, buried it in a hedge. "I get to be doorman."

"Okay."

"I want one of those coats those guys used to wear. I want to look like an admiral."

"You got it."

"I want to—holy shit!"

They slowed to a walk when they came out of the side street onto Tyler Avenue. The fog was gone, shoved back by the heat and the glare of the bellow of the fire that buried the King's Castle, a block down on the corner.

"God," Brian said.

He counted four fire trucks parked at various angles across the road. Police lines had already been set up. A crowd had formed behind orange sawhorses. Two ambulances. The firemen in dark slickers, dancing with hoses that sprayed into a wall of flame that in turn cast rolls of smoke into the dark above the light.

They didn't need to get any closer.

A pair of uniformed firemen yelled with megaphones at the growing crowd; puddles on the street set jigsaws of flame into the blacktop; shop windows reflected and doubled the glare; and the light wouldn't stand still, made the firemen and the policemen and the crowd seem as if they were jerking side to side, shrinking, growing, here and there melting into temporary shadow.

Someone stepped between them, took Brian's arm and held it tightly.

"Well," Rita said, "it looks like I need a new job."

He grinned at her. "You start it or what?"

She stuck out her tongue. "It wasn't that hot a job, but I wasn't turning down the money." A shudder; her grip tightened. "I only worked to six. God, a couple more hours . . ." She glanced at Blue. "You hear what happened?"

"We just got here ourselves."

Brian felt the trembling, saw the fire's autumn colors

275

flick over her wind-pink cheeks. When she looked back at him, he looked away quickly. He didn't want her to think he was staring. He didn't want her to think he was thinking more than he was. She was June's friend, and that was over. Long ago. June had kept talking about getting married after graduation, and all his kidding, then all his protests, then all his bitching, hadn't convinced her he wasn't about to trade college for an apartment and pumping gas.

"How the hell," Blue said, stepping off the curb and into the street, "can something burn so badly like that?"

"It's a law of thermodynamics," a voice said behind them.

Brian looked and rolled his eyes. "Corky, that hasn't got anything to do with anything, you jerk."

Corky, standing on a bus-stop bench, grinned down at them. "No shit. Sounds good, though."

A sudden gust, and sparks escaped the fire's column to shower onto the crowd. There were a few muffled screams, the megaphones blared again, and one of the hoses moved down the street, to join two others soaking adjacent buildings.

The stench made their noses wrinkle; Brian's eyes teared when another gust dropped a pocket of smoke into his face.

"You know what happened?" Blue asked without turning around.

"Arson."

Rita spun around, nearly taking off Brian's arm. "What?"

Corky, burrowed into a plaid hunting jacket, nodded. "I was over there before." He nodded toward the street this side of the dying restaurant. "Cop said someone's walking along, sees a sheet of fire suddenly shoot up the side wall. Next thing you know, the whole place is going. Gotta be arson."

"From the outside in?" Brian said, unable to look away.

Gaps in the fire now, nothing but black beyond.

Corky said, "Yep. Cop said must've been fifteen, twenty people inside."

"Oh Jesus," Rita said weakly and retook Brian's arm.

Two figures crossed the street toward them, shadows against the fire until Sarra Marlow broke into a run and leapt nimbly onto the bench beside Corky. Greta Rourke stood in front of them, her back to Blue.

"They found three women on the sidewalk right by the door," Sarra announced, up on her toes, neck craning. "They were just walking by and the door blew out or something. Cut to ribbons, I'll bet."

The roof collapsed; a sag in the flames, in the smoke, in the roaring so constant it had become nearly silent. Then it all exploded again, and the crowd fell back, several firemen darted for protection behind their engines, and one of the hoses abruptly shrank to a useless dribble.

"Too bad it's not the school," Greta said flatly.

Blue patted her on the head. "This kid," he said to the others, "is going places."

She set her heel lightly on his instep. "Touch me again, humanoid, you'll need hospitalization."

He laughed.

Sarra tried to convince Corky to walk her closer to the fire, so they could see stuff, maybe bodies. He was a Ploughman, who was going to stop them?

Greta stood on tiptoe and pointed across the street. "There's Shane. Taking notes, I'll bet." When no one said a word, she flicked her fingers along the underside of her chin and trotted over to him.

"The perfect couple," Blue muttered.

Rita said something Brian couldn't hear over the noise; he leaned down and asked her to repeat it, looking as he did toward someone who had broken from the crowd and headed toward them, slowly.

"There was a man there this afternoon," she said, rubbing a hand under her nose. "Weird. I thought he was going to rape me or something."

"No kidding."

"A bum, I think. I don't know. I ran into the kitchen, and the cook runs out, the guy is gone."

She turned her head, he turned his, and their faces were so close Brian could see the fire tiny and helpless in her eyes.

"C'mon," Sarra said to Corky. "Just a couple of minutes, okay?"

Then Blue said, "Uh-oh."

Brian glanced up, saw where he was staring, and turned his head just in time to see June stop in front of them, glare at Rita, and yank off her wool gloves.

"You bitch," June said, the fire's shadow taking most of her face. She glared at Brian, looked back to Rita. "I thought you were my friend."

"What?"

Brian eased a few inches away.

"You know he's mine," June said, and slapped her before Blue could grab her arm. "I'll kill you," she yelled, turned and ran into the crowd.

Nobody moved.

The fire sighed and settled under the artificial rain.

"Over there?" Corky said into the silence. He took Sarra's hand. "Sure, let's go."

Brian stared at his shoes. "Sorry," he whispered. "I'll talk to her or something."

"Don't worry about it," Rita said tightly. "She'll get over it."

Brian saw the red blotch on her cheek, and wished he could fly so he could be somewhere else.

Glass exploded dully; a child in the crowd began to cry.

"Changed," Blue muttered.

Brian frowned. "Huh?"

Blue pointed with his chin at the dark place where June had disappeared and shook his head in confusion. "She's changed, y'know? And it ain't just . . ." A glance at Brian, a look back to the fire. "I don't know. Maybe I'm just nuts."

Rita's hands slipped into her jacket pockets.

Brian watched the fire and said nothing; but he had heard that before. Different words, a different place, but he had heard that before.

It's wrong, his grandmother had said the other day, out there at the station; *it's wrong*.

He still didn't know exactly what she'd meant.

But he knew she was right.

June's changed.

Something's wrong.

VIII

HUNTING

Twenty-nine

1

In Bettin Wells, Wednesday's dawn was nothing more than a lightening of night. A high overcast provided shadows but no color, and a melancholy breeze only stirred the fringes of open shop awnings. A day for constantly checking the sky, the wind, gauging the minutes left before the clouds lowered, and darkened, and shredded to rain.

By noon, the dark had come but not the rain.

By two, there was more than one prayer to get it over with or bugger off.

Garret Purdy wanted the rain. It would give him the perfect excuse to return to the station, ostensibly for his rain gear, actually to have a cuppa and stall away the rest of his shift listening to Ratty bitch and moan about conditions and wages and the rest of the world's ills. Most times he didn't mind working doubles. The extra money came in handy, there were favors he could call in later when they were needed, and they gave him the chance to work at least some of the time on his own, without almighty bleedin' Ludden playing the grizzled sergeant teaching the raw young recruit.

Not today.

Today he wanted to get back to his flat, strip off his uniform, and fall into bed. Alone. Without dreams. Never again hearing sow MacNair's screams and wailing, never having to make small talk with that smug Yank everyone knew was plugging Doc Burwin. God, what a hell of a night.

He stopped in at the fish 'n' chips for some coffee, flirted with Josie's replacement for a few minutes, then stepped outside and looked up at the clouds.

"Depressing, isn't it?"

"You don't know the half of it, Mr. Sholton," he said, grinning at the landlord. Bill Sholton was on his afternoon stroll, a habit half the town set their lives by. To get his bar legs working normal again was how he put it whenever someone asked. "I feel like I've been clubbed and don't know it."

Sholton, in a fur-collared bombardier's flight jacket nearly worn through at the elbows and along the path of the zipper, sighed his sympathy. "Double shift?"

"Aye."

"You'll be dead before thirty, son, and what'll all that money do you then?"

"Pay for a decent funeral."

The landlord laughed, punched Purdy's arm lightly, and walked on, arms swinging, face turning side to side as if it were mechanically driven. A bus thumped its front tires over the curb at its stop at the corner, forcing Purdy back a step. He glowered at the driver, who only grinned and shrugged, mimed trouble with the steering, grinned again and drove on with a great show of clashing gears.

Bastard, Purdy thought.

An alley was his next stop, and he grimaced as he stepped into it, poking at the overflowing waste bins with his stick, doing his best to breathe shallowly so the stench wouldn't make him gag. It almost worked. This

284

was daft. No professor was going to hide in a place like this, for god's sake. In fact, he thought, as he hurriedly returned to the sidewalk, he doubted they'd ever find the man anyway. Not alive. That wife of his and her lover have already done the poor sod in, that much was as clear as your nose. All the noise, the demands, the staying at the station until dawn and ruining his evening—cover is what all that was. A show for the public. Soon as the body was found—carefully made to look like an accident, no doubt—she and that Yank would be off and running someplace. He knew it. Clear as your nose. A blind man could see it.

He passed the bus chuffing at a red light, crossed to the opposite curb and tried to decide which direction next. No rain yet, but he could smell the damp in the air and knew it wouldn't be long, so he didn't want to be too far from the station. Going as far as the Royal John Hotel was definitely out of the question.

The light changed.

He walked straight on, nightstick lightly to cap in an automatic salute to an overdressed pair of tourists greeting him and nodding, holding his breath again and checking a second alley.

One more block, he decided; one more block, no bodies found, and he'd turn around. Only an hour left anyway, no sense going halfway to bloody Cardiff.

An old woman scuttled by with her black umbrella already open, and he stepped nimbly away to keep his eyes and cheeks intact, smiling to himself, turning, looking up to look directly into the terror-wide eyes of the bus driver as the bus leapt the curb and pinned Purdy to a lamppost.

A little girl shrieked.

Purdy slapped feebly at the grill with his stick.

A taxi slammed into the back of the bus.

Rupert Flaunter stepped out of a men's clothing store just as Purdy's stick fell to the ground, clattered and rolled off the curb. The cleric was momentarily confused, not at all sure what he saw. Then he gaped and ran, shouting for the shopkeeper to call an ambulance. A quick look at the constable, and he dashed into the street, screaming at the cabbie to back up. Without waiting for a response, he threw himself onto the bus, ordering the driver to pull back, man, pull back, in God's name. But the driver only stared at him, blood on his chin.

"Damn you!" the vicar cried, reached over the barrier and grabbed his shoulder. "Pull back, you damned fool! Pull back! Reverse!"

The driver blinked stupidly, fumbled for the gear shift and yanked it into position. Flaunter watched him, lips moving in silent prayer, grabbing the dashboard as the bus lurched but didn't move.

"Again!"

The cry of an ambulance.

The bus roared.

Blood dripped into the driver's lap.

"Again!"

The bus moved a few inches and stalled.

Flaunter cursed and jumped back to the street, dodged a car trying to dodge around the scene, and stopped when he saw Purdy still upright, arms outstretched as if embracing his killer. A moment later the constable's knees began to sag, and he slid slowly down, as far as lamppost and grill would allow.

His arms didn't move.

Flaunter hurried around to the other side, elbowing aside a man in rags, until he was able to reach out and touch the side of the policeman's neck. The man's eyes were closed, his mouth hung open, and the minister pressed through seeping damp red and couldn't find a pulse.

286

The ambulance arrived.

Flaunter closed his eyes—*help him, Lord, bring him home*—and stepped back, hand trailing away reluctantly, gently, until it dangled at his side.

Sergeant Ludden raced up, and stopped so awkwardly he collided with the bus. "Jesus lord," he whispered.

Flaunter nodded. Walked away. Barely listened to the bellowed orders. Wiped his fingers across his new jacket, a fair grey blazer whose gold buttons gleamed. Wiped them again. Plucked at his matching new trousers. Paid no attention to the hasty questions flung at him as people passed on the run, barely avoided being hit himself by a car as he crossed to the other side of the High Street and kept walking.

No good to poor Garret, he'd been no good at all.

As he'd been no good to Pris my darling Pris.

A sour taste in his throat that rose swiftly to his mouth, and he spat into the street without thinking.

No one complained.

A siren cried.

By the time he reached the Queen's Lance his legs were heavy, his eyes moist. Wearily he climbed the steps to the dining patio and dropped onto a bench. Two couples sat behind him, speculating on the accident, there were faces in the windows of the restaurant and the pub. No one spoke to him. No one asked him about the blood streaked across his new blazer.

He stared at the High Street, hands limp on the table, not moving when a tear touched his cheek and fell. At least, he thought, I can still do that much for the man.

One of the couples left, hurrying down the steps while assuring the others that they'd be back with news as soon as they could.

To his right he could see the scene without obstruction, four blocks down—the red of the bus, the black hump of the cab, police at the intersection diverting traffic into the side streets by shouting angrily and thumping bonnets and pointing with caps and sticks. Pedestrians crossed over to join the fringe of the crowd, others left, crossing back. Autumn leaves caught in a black stream, pausing, moving on. Whistles shrill. A second ambulance sideslipping to a halt.

The minister's gaze drifted to his hands, heavy knuckles, fine dark hair, the stumps of his birth defects tinged with dried blood. They were steady. Not a tremble. He supposed he ought to clasp them and say a proper prayer, but the boy was an unrepentant Methodist who more than once had sneered at Flaunter's collar without appearing to do so.

Nevertheless, his conscience prodded; *nevertheless*.

His chest rose and fell.

His eyes closed.

He felt his head begin to drift toward the table and there was nothing he could do to stop it; he heard the double crash, the shattering of glass; and he heard a voice calling, "Here, call Doc Burwin," just before he blacked out.

2

Evan wrapped the bath towel around his waist and sneered at himself in the foggy mirror. The shower hadn't done him a whole hell of a lot of good. He still looked like death warmed over and felt as though he'd been bludgeoned by a rubber truncheon. He yawned. He scrubbed his teeth with one finger. He grabbed another towel and dried himself off, moved into the bedroom and dressed in fresh clothes that were too stiff for comfort, only marginally better than the clothes he'd worn through the night. No; that was wrong. The truth was, he couldn't tell because he was still so tired. Once out of the police station just after dawn, he and Addie had decided Paul wasn't going to be found if he didn't want to. And they weren't going to do each other any good by walking around like zombies. In movies they stayed up for days; in real life, lack of sleep made people stupid— so Addie told him, and so he believed. But she wouldn't come home with him, only squeezed his hand and promised she'd lock her doors and windows. He had done the same. And sleep, blessed or not, knocked him out before he could even pull up the blanket.

The telephone rang as he took a brush to his damp hair. He ignored it because he knew the news couldn't possibly be good.

It persisted.

"Oh hell."

He took his time hauling himself up the stairs with one hand, yawned again and lazily picked up the receiver.

"Were you dead?"

He couldn't help a smile. "Just about."

"Can you come to the Lance right away? I need you."

"Say no more."

He was still not quite awake, but neither had he been so asleep that he hadn't heard the siren in the background, fading but not quickly.

He grabbed his jacket and keys, locked the door behind him and was in his car and moving before he remembered that he hadn't taken the time to look around for Paul. The slip made him briefly cold. He blew on his hands one at a time, glanced in the rearview mirror, then suddenly leaned back and up and checked the rear floor. It was empty. He could have been killed. It was empty, but Paul could have been there, waiting with gun or knife.

Lord, he thought, and drove faster, skidded at the fork and ordered himself some calm. Driving like this was going to get him killed.

A jerk of his lips into a sour grin.

A way with words, Kendal; you've a hell of a way with words.

He passed the Cross and Sword at speed, slowing as he approached Wellington and saw the flashing lights, the people, and a bus oddly angled off the street just ahead. At the same time, he saw Addie standing at the near curb, semaphoring, then moving back as he pulled into the curb and let his right-side wheels jump over them before he stopped.

"What?" he asked as he slipped out.

When he reached her, she held up a *wait a minute* finger, took his arm and brought him to a near table, where Reverend Flaunter sat, an untouched glass of sherry in front of him and what looked like a wet handkerchief plastered across his brow. The jacket he wore was striped with blood, though it was clear the injury hadn't been to him.

There was no need for direction—Evan sat on the opposite bench, Addie beside the minister.

"He had a shock," she explained.

"I'm fine," Flaunter insisted gallantly.

"Of course," she said, and told Evan about Garret Purdy. He couldn't help looking over his shoulder. "When Rupert passed out, someone called me and the hospital, thinking he'd been hurt too."

"I told you I'm fine," Flaunter said, and picked up his glass.

Evan watched him drink, then looked to Addie, who wore a heavy green sweater, her hair loose, no makeup. She didn't seem tired. "What?" he asked again.

Her cheeks puffed and deflated, her hands lifted in a weak shrug. "I don't know, to tell you the truth. I saw the accident and I—"

He waved her silent; he understood.

Flaunter peeled the handkerchief away and folded it neatly on the table, evened the corners, touched the center with his thumb. His glass was empty. "I must be getting home," he said. "Thank you, Dr. Burwin."

"Do you have a ride?" Evan asked.

The minister rose stiffly, then dropped back onto the bench. "No, I don't suppose I have."

Evan pointed at his car. "My pleasure, then."

"No, please."

"Evan's right," Addie said. "You're in no shape to walk all that way. You're still in a bit of shock, you could get yourself killed. Come on, then, here you go," and she was on her feet, one hand on his arm. Flaunter made to resist, then gave Evan a grateful smile, allowed himself to be helped up, to be assisted to the car.

Addie bundled him into the back seat.

Evan apologized when they bumped off the curbing and back onto the tarmac, and drove slowly along the detour the police were still demanding. He said nothing.

Then the church appeared on the left, and Flaunter said, "God's will."

3

"You should have seen him," said Dulcie Dennis, both revolted and excited as she slipped the handle of the plastic shopping bag over her arm. "Like a bug, he was. It was horrid."

Flo Winnry nodded, though she hadn't seen a thing.

By the time she'd arrived at the scene of the accident, most everything had been cleared away but the glass scattered on the sidewalk. And even then, someone was already sweeping it all up.

They stood in front of the grocery, faces to the breeze.

Dulcie lowered her voice. "Was the reverend got there first, you know."

Flo's eyes widened. "You don't say!"

"I do, and that's the truth." The breeze strengthened, tugging her red hair in its wake. "He was in shock, Bill Sholton says. Walked away like nothing happened. Passed out at the Lance."

Flo frowned. "No."

"Yes."

They headed for the corner.

"Anyway, Dr. Burwin got there straightaway, then called Mr. Kendal and they took him right home. Nothing wrong. Shock. That's all it was, shock." She shook her head as they rounded the corner and headed up their street. "Poor man."

Flo picked up speed.

"Hey, what's this?"

She looked back. "We must go out there, mustn't we? He'll need us more than ever, this happening and all."

Dulcie wasn't sure, but Flo was already several yards ahead, and when something set her course, she wasn't to be moved. All the arguing in the world wouldn't change her mind. "I suppose you'll want me to come."

"I did say 'we,' didn't I?"

"Yes, but—"

"No buts, Dulcie. He's been good to us both. We'll drop our things and take my car."

Dulcie sighed as loudly as she dared. Flo driving in a state wasn't to be borne, nor, it seemed, was it to be denied this time. "All right," she agreed. "But you've got to promise no speeding. I don't want to be squashed like Garret Purdy."

Flo stopped at her gate, nearly buried by crawling hedging. "Just be here in five minutes, Dulcie, or I'll leave without you."

Dulcie watched her march up the walk to the newly painted brown door that marked her house from the others in the row. Then she hurried on, five doors down and white, knowing that Flo would not leave without her. That would have been too much to hope for.

Quickly, then, she let herself in, dumped her sack on the kitchen table and hurried into the ground-floor bathroom to straighten her hat and hair. She was a mess. All the rouge so carefully applied had gone from her cheeks, and now the makeup around her eyes made her look like a corpse.

A quick correction, a side-to-side check in the mirror, and she was outside again.

And there was Flo in her car, waiting at the curb.

A backfiring lorry lumbered into the street, blunt-nosed, its long open bed piled with discarded appliances corralled by thick rope.

Dulcie glared at the noise it made, then unlatched the gate and carefully latched it again behind her, turned and swore when her coat sleeve caught on a thick splinter at the top.

Flo honked the horn impatiently.

All right, all right, Dulcie thought as she worked the snagged cloth with near-trembling care; hold on to yourself, you old crow, I'm moving as fast as I can, can't you see that? That was, she thought, about Flo's only serious flaw—an impatience for action as soon as action had been decided. No delays were permitted.

The lorry backfired again, a belch of thick exhaust billowing briefly behind it.

Flo honked again.

Dulcie pointed at the snag and went to work again, not wanting to tear herself loose. This was the only winter coat she had left thick enough to keep the wind out. She was no hand at all with the needle and thread, so to ruin it now would mean wearing layers of sweaters. She had no money to buy a new one; she doubted she would have for a long time to come.

A cat ran into the road.

The lorry swerved to avoid it.

Flo raced the engine.

Dulcie freed herself and turned with a triumphant wave, took a single step, and caught her heel in a gap between the paving stones. She fell. Cried out more in fear than hurt as she landed on knees and outstretched hands, her hat flying off and the breeze became a wind that took it into the street where the lorry ran it flat.

Dulcie wept.

Flo scrambled from the car and ran to her side, crouched down and said, "Oh my god, dear, are you badly hurt?"

Dulcie, shifting on her hands and knees, looked up at her and said, "If I sued the council, do you think I could get a new coat?"

Flo smiled her relief and helped her friend to her feet. It was awkward, neither being strong enough or young enough to make the movement fluid, and when Dulcie was at last in her seat and blowing on her burning palms, the damp air turned to drizzle. Light. Barely enough to coat the windshield.

"You were lucky you didn't crack your head," Flo said as she started the engine.

"Yes."

"Could've had one of them concussions."

"Yes."

Flo patted her friend's knee. "You are the clumsy one, aren't you, Dulcie?"

"Yes," said Dulcie Dennis. "Yes, I expect I am."

4

"Oh, dear," Addie said as Evan pulled into a parking space in front of her office.

"What?"

She nodded to the car just in front of them. "That's Flo Winnry's. I hope nothing's wrong."

Evan joined her at the door, shoulders slightly hunched against the mist.

"You don't have to come in."

"Don't be a fool, Addie," he snapped without meaning to. "We were lucky last night. Let's not push it."

Her face paled, but she nodded, once, and pushed inside.

The reception room was small, its walls brightened by country oils done by her patients. The Gerry Twins sat on a couch beneath the front window, Dulcie Dennis weeping softly into a handkerchief.

Evan stood to one side.

"Your nurse said she had to post some letters," Mrs. Winnry told Addie, then nodded at Dulcie Dennis. "She fell. We was hurrying to see Reverend Flaunter, and she caught a heel. I say she ought to sue."

Addie knelt in front of the old woman. "Bad?"

Mrs. Dennis caught a breath and nodded.

"Well, then, if you've learned a lesson—men are not to be chased quite so boldly—let's go inside, all right? I'll see what I can do."

Mrs. Dennis tottered to her feet; Evan saw traces of running blood in the gap between her coat's hem and shoe tops. "Wasn't chasing no man."

"Then more's the pity," Addie told her, arm around her waist as she led the woman into the examination room. "What a waste of good pain."

Mrs. Dennis snorted a laugh.

Evan took a chair beside the door, crossed his legs, folded his hands. The normality of the scene unnerved him. Addie's pleasant chatter seemed too natural to be right. Yet he'd been unable to think straight enough, long enough, to decide what else to do. After they'd dropped Reverend Flaunter off and Addie was back in the car, he'd been tempted to keep on driving, leave Bettin Wells behind. Leave Paul behind. But Addie wouldn't let him. She had seen him, but she couldn't leave him, and he knew that she still didn't believe that he could do as he had claimed.

The threats of murder hadn't reached her yet, not where they counted.

"She tore her coat," said Mrs. Winnry.

He smiled vaguely. "I'm sorry?"

The old woman nodded toward the closed door beside the reception desk. "Tore her coat. Caught it on the gate. Was my fault, really, I was too in a hurry to get on." Her hands were tight in her lap. "Cut herself all up. Couldn't keep her from crying."

"Addie—Dr. Burwin's good for that," he said.

She nodded.

Shadow rain streaked the wall as the drizzle fell more quickly.

Evan asked about Eric, and Mrs. Winnry, her expression grateful for the diversion, chatted about his progress. School was hard for a lad like him, she said, but he'd make it soon enough, was already tinkering with some inventions he'd thought up and all he needed, she explained, was more schooling to help him understand what he was doing. A bright lad. Not a genius, mind, but bright.

"It'll work," Evan told her, "whatever he does."

"I know. Thanks to you."

He waved a hand.

Shadow rain.

And an explosion that rattled the glass in its frame.

Evan said, "What the. . . ?" and jumped to his feet.

Mrs. Winnry leapt away from the window, a hand to her mouth, eyes wide.

Silence.

Shadow rain.

The cry of a siren.

The back door opened, and Addie said, "What was that, for god's sake?"

Evan started for the door, but Mrs. Winnry beat him to it. "I'll just pop out for a minute and see," she said. And was gone.

"Evan?"

"Sounded like a gas main or something," he told her.

Mrs. Dennis called something and Addie disappeared.

He opened the door and looked right, saw nothing, looked left and saw a thick column of dark smoke rise above the village, somewhere toward its center. Cars had stopped dead in the street, drivers craning, a few standing by their doors and pointing. The blare of a fire truck. The wind took the smoke and tore it.

Brother, he thought, and was about to duck back inside before he got drenched when he saw Mrs. Winnry hurrying toward him. So out of breath she couldn't talk, she only grabbed his arm and pushed back into the of-fice.

"Fish 'n' chips," she managed once she'd dropped back onto the couch.

He frowned.

"One of the ovens exploded, they say. Don't know why yet. My Eric had just left. He said there were still three or four people inside." She began to tremble and looked up. "My Eric." She began to cry.

Immediately, he knelt in front of her and grabbed her hands. "It's all right, Mrs. Winnry. It's all right. He's fine."

"A minute sooner and he'd be . . ." Tears soaked the handkerchief he held to her cheeks. Her skin was cold. Her nose ran. "A minute—"

"But he's fine now," he said quietly, firmly, several times more until she leaned back and closed her eyes, tissues bundled in her fists.

The telephone rang.

"Would you get that, Evan?"

"There's been an explosion," he called as he walked to the desk. "Fire too. People hurt."

"I'm just getting my things."

He picked up the receiver. "Dr. Burwin's office."

"Well, well," said Paul, "how do you like it so far?"

Thirty

Evan dropped the receiver onto the cradle just as Addie hurried out of the back room, black bag in hand, Mrs. Dennis right behind her. "Addie," he said.

"Not now, Ev. Mrs. Winnry, would you mind locking up when you leave. Just close the door, thanks."

"Addie, it was Paul."

"Oh, lovely," said Mrs. Dennis. "Is he back then?"

Addie didn't stop, didn't pause, and she was on the sidewalk before he managed to grab her arm, just as another fire truck blared past them and the drizzle turned to rain.

"Damnit, didn't you hear what I said?"

"I'm not deaf, Evan."

"Then we've got to do something!"

She pulled her arm free, gently. "Evan, there are people hurt. I can't just leave." A slow shake of her head. "I want to go, really. You can't know how much. But I can't. Not now. Besides," she added with false brightness, "he can't hurt me with all those police and such around, now can he?"

And she was gone, trotting up the street, hair whipping her back, bag slapping against her leg.

Yes, damnit, he can, he thought angrily; he can damn well kill you.

He slapped his thigh in frustration, wanting to race after her and force her to go with him, the hell with the dying, the hell with the injured. The sight, then, of a panda car had him running across the street, blinking against the raindrops thrown at him by the wind. He pushed and dodged his way through the growing crowd. He didn't bother to look for Paul. Nor did he take more than a glance or two at the fire-hands reaching out of the fish 'n' chips shop toward the lowering clouds. But he did see that the stores on either side had had all their display windows blown in, and one of them was already burning fiercely at the roofline.

The stench was powerful, forcing him to cover his mouth and nose with one hand as his elbow jabbed him a way through to the other side.

By the time he stumbled through the police-station door, he was panting, and he collapsed against the counter. Several policemen were at their desks, answering the phones, scribbling messages, then passing what he assumed were instructions to Eisley, whose radio never stopped. Sergeant Ludden stood behind his own desk, on the telephone himself, loudly demanding reinforcements from an obviously reluctant counterpart in Salisbury. By the time he finished and had slammed the receiver down, his face was red, his eyes so narrow they were nearly closed.

"I've got four known dead and more than a dozen injured," he announced to the room in not much less than a bellow, "and do you think the bastards care? Half the town on fire, and do you think they care?"

Evan braced himself on his elbows, wiped his face with both hands, and looked up. "It was Paul Burwin."

No one else stopped.

A constable ran in, threw a paper on the counter, and ran out again.

Ludden glowered. "What's that?"

"Paul Burwin. He did it."

The telephone rang, and Eisley grabbed up the extension on his dispatch desk.

Sergeant Ludden took a deep breath. "I see. And how did he manage it, Mr. Kendal?"

"I don't know. I just know that he's responsible. And for Constable Purdy, too."

"You're daft."

"Damnit," Evan said, "I don't give a damn what you think of me, Sergeant, but I'm telling you that Paul Burwin is the cause of everything that's happened today!"

"For you," Eisley interrupted, pointing at the phone half-buried in the shambles on Ludden's desk.

The sergeant picked up the receiver and covered the mouthpiece with a palm. "The bus driver lost control, there was a gas leak. Tell me, Mr. Kendal, how Professor Burwin accomplished all that in a single day."

Evan knew he sounded crazy, but he couldn't shut himself up. "How the hell should I know? But if you had found him in time, instead of humoring us—"

"Get out!" Ludden yelled. "Get out of here, Kendal, before you're arrested."

Evan leaned over the counter. "Listen to me, Sergeant, please!"

"Out!"

Evan's fist slammed down. "God *damn* you, Ludden, if you'll just talk to Dr. Burwin, she'll—"

"Eisley!"

Evan watched the dispatcher push his chair back, saw the expression on Ludden's face. It was no use, he didn't blame them, and he ran out, took the steps down two at a time and sprinted back down the High Street. The pavement was slippery and he skidded several times, at one point careening off a hedge before regaining his di-

301

rection. The wind rose and drove the rain before it, pelting into the back of his neck like blunt needles. Traffic was backed up despite the best efforts of a constable trying to divert it into a side street. Despite the wind the smoke was thicker, the fire no longer visible, the acrid stench of burning wood and plastic wrinkling his nose as he reached the hundred or so onlookers who had been confined to the sidewalk by sawhorse barriers.

Get out, he told himself; get the hell out of here.

Not without Addie.

Shading his eyes against the rain, he kept to the fringe and searched for signs of Burwin, the hat, the coat, but had seen nothing by the time he broke through on the other side.

On his toes, he tried to see into the mass of firemen and police across the street, but he couldn't find her.

He edged off the curb, noted that barricades had also been set up across the tarmac, two constables serving as gatemen while the others made sure no one tried to break through.

A Greenfield ambulance nudged its way free of the vehicles scattered on the street, the barriers parted just enough, and it sped away. He couldn't tell if Addie was inside.

"Move along there!" a policeman called to him.

He backed away, still straining, willing her to come to him so they could return to the station and convince that mule, Ludden. And the moment he thought it, he dismissed it with a weary gesture, looked at his hand and saw the skin speckled with wet ash.

The rain increased.

He wiped his face.

The wind began to moan above the rooftops, and many of those watching began to scurry away.

Then he whirled and sprinted back for his car. If the

police wouldn't listen to him, most likely wouldn't listen to Addie, perhaps someone they respected would change their minds for him. And the only one he could think of at the moment was Rupert Flaunter. A long shot, probably worse, but it was better than racing from one shadow to another, waiting for Addie to take a turn thinking of herself for a change.

By the time he reached the church, fighting the wind that tried to slam him off the road, he was convinced that this would work; by the time he had parked in the driveway and had jumped into the rain, he was equally convinced that Ludden was right and he really was nuts after all.

No one answered the doorbell or responded to his heavy knocking on the rectory door. He stepped back, cupped his hands around his mouth and called out against the wind, squinting at the windows, called out again, then hurried across the grass toward the church.

He stopped when he reached the graveyard gate.

He could see the top of Flaunter's head above an ancient tombstone, the trees twisting, their branches snapping like angered geese. Several dead limbs had already fallen, a sodden leaf slapped him stingingly on the cheek. As he clawed it away, he pushed through the gate and held up an arm to shield him as he moved.

"Reverend Flaunter!"

The head stirred.

Unless it was the wind.

Darker now, the headstones growing, a dead-flower wreath spinning away across the grass.

Halfway there he saw the branch, a huge one, split open and lying across the grave where the minister sat. He tried to run, but the wet grass took his traction; he sprawled on his chest, took a taste of mud, and crawl-ran to the marker and hauled himself up, and looked over.

"Oh Jesus," he said. "Oh Jesus."

The wind sighed.

As he batted and tore his way through the tangle of twigs and smaller branches, most of them too wet now to snap away easily, he noted the raw pale wound where the limb had been torn from its trunk and had landed square across the minister's chest. A gouge in his cheek that ran blood and rain; one eye swollen, purple, bleeding lightly from under the lid; a gash across the top of his head; one hand pinned to the ground, the other to his stomach.

Evan tried to lift the branch, and failed, tried to break or bend away the rest that held the man down.

The wind soughed through the belfry.

"Doesn't matter."

He jumped at the voice, looked down and saw the minister looking back with one eye. "Have you out in a minute," he told him.

Flaunter winced and shook his head. "Doesn't matter, lad. Me and Lem are friends."

A cough; a bubble of foam the rain missed for a while.

Evan dropped to his knees in the mud and grass. "Your door's locked. Where do you keep your tools? I need a shovel, an ax."

Flaunter's one-eyed gaze traced the twigs, the little branches, made Even look at the man's chest and face. "I'm not that dim, Mr. Kendal. Not that dim."

Aw shit, he thought, and could think of nothing else to do but try to wipe the rain from the minister's face.

"I saw Professor Burwin."

Evan froze. "Where?" His voice was strained.

"Across the way, in the field. I tried to call him, but he couldn't hear me."

A cough; a whimper; the rain finally took the bubble. The eye closed.

In his helplessness, Evan felt like weeping.

"Lem and I."

The wind.

Evan leaned closer.

"God's will, Mr. Kendal."

He couldn't help it: "Your time, Reverend?"

A nod, a gasp of pain.

"There . . ."

"Don't," Evan cautioned, an automatic response.

Flaunter managed a one-sided smile. "You never argued with me, Mr. Kendal. Never argued, like the doctor."

An ambulance sirened by, and Evan tensed to leap to his feet, thinking that somehow he might be able to flag it down. The tension died; he sagged.

"Always a plan, you know. Always a plan."

The eye opened.

Evan smiled. "God's?"

"Who else, Mr. Kendal?" A smile there again, faint but true. "A hell of a time you picked to take me on."

The wind gusted, but the rain eased somewhat.

Harsh whisper: "You don't trust my word, Mr. Kendal?"

"It's not a matter of trust, Reverend. The proof, I guess."

"Ah. Well, I can't help you there." Flaunter swallowed, and choked, something faintly yellow slipped between his lips. "It's not proof you'd need, it's belief. All of it, Mr. Kendal, is a matter of belief."

Evan didn't know what to say.

Flaunter said it for him: "Oh Jesus, I'm frightened!"

Another branch crashed somewhere deep in the graveyard.

Evan wanted to tell him *not this time, Rupert, it's not God this time, your faith is intact*, but the eye closed again, and rain sluiced across their faces, and he touched the man's shoulder and said instead, "God speed."

Something touched his shoulder.

He whirled, still crouched, and angrily slapped away a portion of the branch shoved against him by the wind.

When he turned back he knew, and in knowing rose and left the graveyard.

The drive back was slow.

Rage at Paul made it nearly impossible to breathe; sadness, not quite grief, made his breathing hitch. He rolled down the window, not caring about the rain, he was already so drenched he might as well be naked, and took a series of deep breaths as he followed the road and the village grew and the High Street widened and there, standing on the sidewalk, Addie with her black bag, brown hair blackened, face smudged.

He pulled over.

She climbed in.

"Bad?"

"Not as bad as could be."

He sat there, not knowing where to go next. When a panda car pulled up alongside him, a policeman asking him to move off the main road, Evan told him about Rupert Flaunter. Addie gasped. The policeman nodded solemnly and asked him again to move on.

He did, and turned right at the first intersection, hissing through streets of brown brick rowhouses, their already dying gardens half-beaten to the ground. Cars at the curbing. No one on the sidewalks. A waste bin rolling around near a storm drain, rattling on the tarmac, drummed on by the rain.

They reached a small playing field, goalposts grey, no netting, and he followed the streets around it until they faced the center of town.

He parked.

"This is dumb," he said. "There's no way anyone will believe that it's all Paul's fault."

"Is it?"

"You know it is."

"How?"

He lifted an eyebrow. "Ludden already asked me that, and if I had a concrete answer, I'd tell you. But I don't know. I just know."

"So many people," she whispered.

He looked at the field, at the goalposts, and saw Paul. "Jesus."

He was out of the car before Addie could say a word. Running across the grass. Arms tucked to his sides.

Paul stood at the far side, head up, water dripping from his hat. He didn't move. He waited.

Evan felt the rage fold his hands into fists, narrow his eyes, draw his lips tight across his teeth. He didn't care if anyone could see them; he was going to strangle the man, kick him to death, tear out his goddamn heart if he had to.

Paul's head jerked slightly.

Evan slowed, looked back, saw Addie following. "No," he called, and waved her back. "Addie, no!"

Paul laughed, the high-pitched shrill of a madman, and slapped his knees in delight.

Evan stopped just six yards away. "I'm going to kill you."

"Oh, I wish you would," Paul said unconcernedly. "Truly, I wish you would. But as I believe I already told you, I'm not quite ready for that just yet. How are you, Addie? Practice doing well?"

Addie stopped level with Evan, though some distance away; three points of a triangle, Paul at its head.

Paul's face was jaundiced, even in the hat's shadow, and when the wind caught the brim and threatened to take it, the hand that clamped the crown was vein and bone. The other hand was still gloved.

"My god," Addie said, but she didn't move forward.

"How?" Evan demanded, a gesture toward the fire on the far side of all the housing.

Paul smiled. "Well, I suppose you could say I've cursed this place, Ev. Yes, I suppose you could say that."

Addie held her bag to her chest; the bag was open.

"I don't believe it." He took a step closer. "It's nonsense, Paul. All you have to do is think about it. Whatever you've got has made you crazy."

Paul shook his head. "Oh, you do believe it, Evan. I know you do. Perhaps I was exaggerating when I said 'cursed,' but the end's the same, wouldn't you say?" He winked. Slowly. "You believe it, my friend. You just don't want to."

Another step. "It's crazy."

"Paul?" Addie said. The bag was closed, at her side.

"You know, my dear, I had once hoped, long ago, that perhaps you'd give up that ridiculously sainted profession of yours and join me—join Evan and I, actually—in our ghoulish pursuit of history. It's much more rewarding, and exciting, than watching your patients die, wouldn't you think? Ours, as it were, are already dead."

Evan and Addie as one—another step.

Paul smiled.

"Look," Evan said evenly, "you told me you were going to kill us."

"But I am, aren't I?"

"What? How the hell do you figure that? You've just about killed everyone else but." He glanced at Addie, saw her left hand behind her back. Something there. A syringe. "So we're here now. So why don't you try it?"

"Evan," Paul chided, "it doesn't work that way. You know that. You've seen. You have."

Addie sprang for him, Evan a second later, a second too late as Paul clubbed her aside with his gloved hand, then used it to grab Evan's collar, the bare hand between them.

Evan smelled death.

But when he struggled, grabbing Paul's wrist in both hands, the gloved grip tightened, and the sight of that scabrous hand suddenly between their faces froze him. He couldn't not look at it, though he saw between the spread fingers the dead look in Paul's eyes.

Addie moaned.

"Ah no, Evan, not this way. Not this way at all." A smile, water spilling from the hat, the wind rising again. "Think about it, Ev. Think hard. I'm killing you, you fool, and you don't even know it."

He threw Evan aside as if he weighed nothing, dropped quickly beside Addie and said, "Listen to me, bitch, you'll be dead by week's end. Ask your lover. He knows." And he slapped her again, rolling her over, making her cry out.

Evan to his feet.

Paul holding out the bare hand and casually slipping on its glove.

"The taxi," Paul said. "I give you that free because you're too dim to remember."

As Evan vacillated between helping Addie and charging Burwin again, Paul backed away, nodding, waving his hand as if he were royalty dismissing a peasant. When he suddenly turned and ran, Evan ran a step toward him, cursed, and hurried to help Addie back to her feet.

"Take me home," she said shakily.

He looked at the rain falling where Paul had stood, had run. "I'll do better than that. Where's your passport?"

Thirty-one

Addie stared at him as he sped through the back streets, fishtailing around corners, leaning on his horn whenever someone got in his way. He knew she was watching, could feel her struggling for the right question. He didn't help. Couldn't. She had to know for herself why, because no amount of explanation would truly convince her.

Like Flaunter had said, it was a matter of belief.

A matter of faith.

Paul was right.

Evan believed now that if he stayed in Bettin Wells, sooner or later he would die. Murder it would be, though murder couldn't be proven. He would die as much of terror as of anything physical. Terror because he wouldn't be able to leave the house, ever, for fear of happening upon an accident in which he was the luckless victim. Like Purdy. Minding his own business and some drunk loses control of his car, or something falls from a ledge, or he slips, or . . .

The next thing would be locking himself in one room, then staying in bed or on a chair.

Slow death.

Scared to death.

Unless he got away from Paul.

"Evan?" A plea for understanding.

"Simple," he said, mauling the car around a turn that shot him onto the High Street just below the Cross and Sword. "You're staying at my place tonight, no arguments. First thing in the morning I'm pulling all my money from the bank and I'm taking the first flight out of Heathrow for the States."

"You can't."

"Of course I can. And you're going with me."

She shook her head. "That's impossible."

"So's dying," he told her, swerving into the fork. "At least for now." A thumb jerked over his shoulder. "It's easy, Addie—as long as we stay here, there are going to be accidents. Some of them as bad as the fish 'n' chips place. People are going to be hurt, they're going to die, because Paul wants us caught up in one of them. And it'll happen, sooner or later."

"I don't . . ." She shook her head again and stared out the window, didn't move when he braked into a turn and nearly slammed into the closed garage door.

He touched her arm. "C'mon."

And once inside he double-checked the windows, double-locked the doors, and brought her a large glass of whiskey.

They sat facing the window.

The wind had stopped; the rain fell harder.

"I've been thinking," she said, and said, "Don't," when he shifted to speak. "I've been trying to understand why."

"Why us, or why Paul?"

"Yes to both."

His expression told her he had no answer to the latter, and she ought to know, now, the answer to the first.

"You make plans," she said, talking to the window and the rain that snaked down it. "A nice little practice in

311

a nice little town. No riches, surely, but a comfortable life nonetheless. And then things happen and you wonder why you bother to make plans at all." She looked at him, looked back. "You've no control, you see. You've no control at all." Tears in her voice. "And when you try to get it back, that control you thought you had, it only gets worse, don't you see? It only gets worse, and you're deeper in than when you started."

He sipped his own drink, afraid to say anything because he sensed she had come to the same threshold as he—the threshold of belief in what Paul was doing out there, in the storm. If he nudged her, she'd shy away, and in shying away might try to contact Paul again.

They drank, and watched the rain.

She made one call—to a colleague, to cover her practice while she was gone.

"Why," she asked when she hung up, "doesn't he just kill us outright?"

"You heard him."

"Yes, but why?"

Evan massaged his brow with his fingertips. "Torment, Addie. Nothing more than torment. He's mad. Crazy mad, I mean."

Dark afternoon gave way to darker night.

He dozed after his second glass, maybe his third, he couldn't remember, and when he woke up she was standing at the window, a palm against the glass. Looking out. Head tilted. Free hand on a hip, massaging it lightly. When he stirred, she turned and he could see the faint glow of her teeth.

"He has some sort of power, doesn't he?" she said.

He rubbed his eyes, licked his lips. "I don't know. I mean, I'm not sure that it's really a power the way you mean it—to cause things to happen."

"A psi power," she said, not moving, the dark behind her. "He can make things happen."

A moment's thought: "Maybe. All things considered right now, it's as good an explanation as any, I suppose."

"No!" she snapped, nearly yelling. "It's not very good at all, damnit, Evan! It's insane. It's not possible."

His temper lurched. "Then *you* tell *me*, okay? Tell me why we're hiding here from your husband, Addie. Tell me why he's falling apart, literally falling apart." A disgusted wave shut her up. "No disease, Addie, you know that now. He's not sick the way your doctoring understands it." He reached for his glass, found it empty, held it anyway, turning it slowly in his hands. "And I don't particularly care if it's possible or not. I've seen it in action. And you have, too. Whatever it is, he's got it, and if we don't leave, we'll be trapped here, waiting, until he decides to use it against us."

She moved away from the window toward the door, turned from the door toward the stairs. "We're still soaked, you know. We'd better change clothes."

He watched her climb until the wall hid her, then clamped his teeth against a violent chill. Immediately, he set the glass down and stood, stripped, and went upstairs to his room. Addie was in the shower, steam curling around the edge of the not-quite-closed door. He stood in the bedroom, naked, and raked through his drawers until he found his passport and passbook. A check of the balance after turning on the dresser lamp told him there'd be plenty for their tickets, with not much more left over; he prayed that Addie had some money stashed away.

The shower stopped.

He grabbed up a pair of dry jeans and held it in front of him as he walked into the hall. When she came out, towel clasped to her chest, most of her legs exposed, they stared at each other, examined each other in the steam-fog that cloaked them before drifting to the ceiling.

"If I may say so," she said, moving aside to let him pass, "we look rather stupid."

"Silly," he told her. "There's a difference."

She dropped the towel. "Silly?"

He nodded. "Very, no offense."

She laughed and snatched the towel back from the floor. "I'm glad you said that, Evan. Not completely glad, but glad."

He saluted her, showered, and stood before the mirror as he dressed.

Sometimes, he told his reflection, you really do say the right things, you know what I mean?

His reflection stuck out its tongue.

Yeah, well, what the hell.

Addie cooked a late supper, and he was amazed at how hungry he was and how tasteless was the food. It was fuel, nothing more. Afterward, they sat in the front room, the radio playing softly, all the lights out. He told her about Port Richmond, the students he used to have, his uncle, his uncle's landlady, and the people renting his house who were going to be damned surprised when he showed up on their doorstep.

"Evan," she said, reaching across the couch to grasp his hand, "why there?" She wore one of his shirts, a pair of his jeans, her feet were bare. "Why America?"

"Why not just drive to another city, maybe Scotland, maybe the Continent?"

"Yes."

"Because it would be too easy for him to follow. To cross the Atlantic, however, is another matter entirely. Over there we can rest easy, take the time to think this out, think of a way to stop him, if we can."

"If he doesn't die first, you mean."

Ashamed, he nodded.

"That's all right." She released the hand and patted it. "I think you're right. I just wish—"

"Don't try so hard," he suggested gently. "Don't work at it so hard. It'll come."

"Like a nightmare."

"I'm afraid so."

She jerked her face toward the window. "I was thinking about poor Flaunter." Fingers wiped away a tear. "We never even got so far as to agree to disagree." Another tear, another wipe. "And I yelled at him when Pris died."

"And I argued with him when he did."

They said nothing after that, and when she pushed herself into his arms, her legs stretched along the cushions, he closed his eyes and told himself not to sleep too deeply.

He didn't.

Sometime during the night he heard a siren.

Sometime during the night he heard something moving on the back stoop.

The Plain, he thought; it's the Plain, nothing more.

When he woke, the rain had stopped but the clouds were still thick enough to smother the dawn. He snapped on all the lights to drive the shadows to their corners, ate only a slice of toast, drank some coffee, before he couldn't stand it anymore. A single bag packed and ready by eight, he was prowling by eight-thirty, and he yelped when the telephone rang at nine. He stared at it, fumbled the receiver into his hand, and looked to Addie as she hurried in from the kitchen where she'd been making sandwiches for the trip.

She mimed that he should answer.

"Two-nine-eight-eight," he said, and cleared his throat loudly.

"My heaven's, Evan," Paul said, "you sound as if you've caught a nasty cold."

He couldn't answer.

Addie covered her throat with one hand.

315

"I just wanted you to know there was a fairly serious do at the Royal John just after midnight. Seems a grandmother type took a tumble and broke her neck."

"You bastard."

"Not to worry, old son. She was French, no loss, didn't even speak a word of English."

Evan slammed the receiver down.

"Another accident?" she asked. "No, don't tell me."

The telephone rang immediately after.

"Very hasty," Paul said, chuckling. "And you didn't even wait for your message."

Evan felt a cramp grow along his jaw. "What message?"

"Eat, drink, and be merry, my friend, for today's the day you die."

The line went dead.

The lights went out.

Evan closed his eyes and said, "We're going. Now." His eyes opened and he moved. "If the bank's not open, we'll use a cash machine at Heathrow."

Addie ran into the kitchen, returned with her fodder wrapped in a tea towel. "My house, my passport," she said as they ran out the door.

He drove so cautiously he wanted to scream, came to a complete stop whenever he thought a pedestrian was about to cross the road, then sped up when a vehicle behind them shouted its horn. He'll drive me nuts, he thought; Christ, I won't even be able to breathe.

He saw the Gerry Twins standing in front of the bank when he got out, Addie sliding over to drive to her house for her things. Mrs. Dennis gave him a look, Mrs. Winnry smiled too broadly.

"Am I too early?" he said, squeezing past them to try the door. It opened easily. "Guess not," and went inside, thanking all his gods there was no queue, thanking them again when the teller asked no embarrassing questions about the amount he withdrew, in cash.

The old women were still outside.

He stood on the curb and tapped his foot.

"It takes a while, you know," Mrs. Dennis said.

"I'm sorry," he said, looking over his shoulder.

"To get to the doctor's house and back, she means," Mrs. Winnry told him. "Depends on what's she after."

"Ah."

Down the street he saw workmen replacing the broken glass in the shop windows. The fronts of at least half a dozen stores were blackened, and a handful of men trod the roof with caution.

"Eloping, are you?" Mrs. Dennis asked.

"Dulcie!"

"Well, they're not going on a picnic, are they? Not on a day like this."

Evan tapped his foot.

A panda car pulled up to the curb and Sergeant Ludden climbed out, his eyes bloodshot, his cheeks and jowls vaguely red, his uniform rumpled. "A word with you, Mr. Kendal?" he said, nodding to the two old women.

"Of course, Sergeant."

He checked the street for Addie, demanding she appear, now, don't waste time.

Ludden rested a hand against the top of the small car. "You were saying things yesterday, about Professor Burwin."

"I was," he agreed, still watching the traffic.

"He called this morning."

"Did he?"

"They're eloping," said Dulcie Dennis.

"Dulcie, hush!"

"Indeed, Mr. Kendal, and he suggested that perhaps

317

you and I have a chat. It seems the professor is rather worried about his reputation. And his wife."

Evan almost laughed at Paul's brilliant nerve, almost felt like applauding.

"I've nothing to say, Sergeant. It was all said yesterday, and, if I recall, you chose not to believe me."

The policeman cleared his throat. "Mr. Kendal, American citizen or not, I'm bound to ask you to come with me, if you will. To assist in some inquiries I'm making."

He saw his car two blocks away.

"Oh really? I'm a suspect in something?"

Several passersby looked at him oddly, and looked away when he grinned at them and nodded.

"I should lower my voice if I were you, Mr. Kendal," the sergeant said.

One block, and a car tried to make an illegal turn, effectively bottling up traffic.

Evan began to walk in that direction.

"Mr. Kendal," Ludden said.

"I'd love to talk, Sergeant," he answered, "but I'm afraid I'm in a hurry." He paused at the curb. "And when Professor Burwin calls you again, why don't you ask him about the woman at the Royal John?"

"Mr. Kendal!"

Evan ran, a matador in traffic, slapping a fender, dodging a bumper, ignoring the shouts behind him and the sudden whoop of the panda car's siren, the high-pitched shrill of Ludden's whistle. He had no intention of being detained, nor locked up when he couldn't tell them what they wanted to hear. Whatever the hell that was, he amended as he ran straight down the white line toward Addie, who waved frantically out the window.

As fast as I can, love, he told her.

"Kendal, stop!"

Up yours, he thought.

318

The illegal turn was made, the traffic broke as if racing, and he grabbed the passenger door handle just as the car behind rammed the rear bumper. The jerk nearly toppled him. The other driver immediately left his car, calling, "Sorry, mate, my foot slipped. I—"

"Don't worry, it's just a scratch," he called back, throwing himself into the car.

"Scratch, hell!"

"Go!" Evan ordered.

Addie wasted no time with questions. With a sharp twist of her hands, she pulled out of the lane and raced down the center of the street, forcing Ludden to throw himself to one side and shake his fist before she cut in front of a slow bus and darted into an empty side street.

Several minutes later, Evan still finding a decent breath, she returned to the High Street and put the accelerator to the floor. She took the right-hand fork without slowing, but Evan turned to look up the lane.

"Is he there?"

He started, then shook his head. "No. No, I didn't see him."

They crossed a low stone bridge, entered a grove that lasted nearly half a mile, and came out the other side into faint sunlight as the clouds began to split.

A car on the verge pulled in behind them.

"How long?" he said.

"Not long," she told him. "The traffic there will be murder, though."

"You have your passport?"

She nodded. "Not much money, though. Evan, I'm scared."

The car passed on a curve; Addie gave him a slow middle finger.

"Scared," she repeated.

"Join the club."

319

Ten minutes later they were on the motorway, two lanes in both directions, lorries and vans and a curious sense of isolation.

"I've never been to America, you know."

He watched the traffic, thinking that when he was a kid he used to count how many different license plates he saw, how many states he could mark before the end of the road. He didn't try it now; he hadn't yet been able to figure out the British system.

"Evan, are you listening to me?"

He straightened slowly.

"Evan?"

An army transport thundered past them in the fast lane.

"Faster, go faster," he said urgently.

She frowned. "Evan, the road's still wet. We'll—"

"That car," he told her, nodding to the one just in front. "That's the one that passed us back there."

"So? Lots of people are going in the same direction, in case you hadn't noticed."

"Lots of people don't wear Paul's hat."

Thirty-two

1

He barely had time to brace himself before she veered into the fast lane and pushed the accelerator to the floor. Brakes. A scolding horn. Addie staring directly ahead, into the rain. Her arms nearly straight, her chin tucked slightly toward her chest. Spray from a limousine in front of them blinded the windshield until the thumping wipers smeared them, cleared them, and Evan looked right as they passed the other car.

It wasn't Paul.

It was a woman, all tweed and scarf, cigarillo in her mouth, lips moving.

Relieved and further angered, he closed his eyes and muttered to himself, saying nothing, just wanting to hear his voice above the hiss of the traffic, the horn still angry behind them.

He felt them swerve sharply back into the slow lane, back into the fast. The car rocked, and his stomach began to rock with it.

"It's not him, we don't have to—"

"I know."

She didn't slow down.

"The police," he said, daring a look at the road ahead. "Addie, for crying out loud, they'll pull us over."

"I'm a doctor on an emergency call," she answered flatly.

It didn't reassure him, and he forced himself not to watch the dark shapes blurring, growing even, slipping behind as they sped on, whales and sharks; hunting. Finally thinking that maybe this was close to the dumbest thing he'd ever done in his life. If he had been thinking clearly, he should have stayed with Ludden, stuck with it, kept insisting, let the man do what he had to until, at last, Evan was believed.

About what?

He scowled, remembering Paul's last words, telling him to remember the taxi.

A touch?

Was it all due to a touch?

No. Something else. Something—Christ, he wished she wouldn't drive so damned fast.

They dove into a roundabout and shot out the other side, causing another chorus of enraged, disbelieving horns.

"Jesus, Addie."

"Evan," she said tightly, "I am running away from my husband, I am leaving my practice behind, I am about to leave my country against my will. Do *not* say anything unless you have something to say."

Despite a rush of sympathy, he didn't much like her at that moment. He understood—god, how he understood—but she wasn't the only one in flight. For the second time in a year he was abandoning a life, however tenuous this one had been, and this time it wasn't his fault. This time he'd only been standing up for himself and, like Port Richmond, had failed just as badly.

It made him angry, but the anger didn't displace the fear.

A hand touched his leg lightly. "I'm sorry."

"No need," he said.

Another few miles, and the rain eased to a drizzle, the sky lost its storm-dark, the traffic increased to the point where, if Burwin showed up now, they wouldn't be able to lose him. Nor would he be able to catch them.

Flashing blue lights on the verge—a tow truck, a pair of cars with smashed bumpers, a policeman in rain gear jotting something on a pad.

Paul? he wondered.

An army convoy slowing the inside, and a flower-painted van trying to wedge its way into the faster lane, forcing cars to veer dangerously close to the median.

Paul?

An overhead grumble that became a constant roaring. An airliner slipped out of the overcast, cloud shredding behind it, tipping side to side in the winds up there, lining up with a runway. Dropping. Swaying.

Evan's mouth dried, his throat filled with sand, and he cleared his throat a half-dozen times before he was able to swallow again.

"Will it be hard, do you think, to get tickets this time of year?"

He shrugged. "Do you believe in luck?"

"God's will," she answered with a bittersweet smile.

He reached into his denim jacket for the fifth or sixth time to be sure the packet of money was still there. All he had left. Change it here or over there? Change it at all? Save it in case he came back? Did he want to come back when all this was done?

Signs, arrows, white airplanes on blue backgrounds, the motorway forking and Addie sliding over to the left and visibly relaxing.

The faint smell of jet fuel.

"Fifteen, twenty minutes," she said. A motorcycle cut

in front of her. Her hand moved, but didn't touch the horn. "What about the car?"

"Do I have a choice? We'll have to leave it in the car park."

As they entered the Heathrow complex, he looked through the rear window.

A black taxi.

Damn you, Paul, are you there?

2

Greta watched her gym class trot around the track, the teacher on the grass exhorting them as if they were Olympic material. She should have been down there, but she didn't feel like it. "Period, bad," was what she told the woman, who believed her, the idiot, and let her sit in the stands.

A noise behind and below.

When she looked, not much caring, she saw Shane step out the back door. She closed one eye, grinned, and waved at him.

He smiled and came over, sat beside her. "Hi."

"Hi."

They watched the class take a second lap.

"Not working today?"

He shrugged. "The glorious Patriot Lodge can do without me for a change."

"Wow."

"Yeah."

They watched another lap.

"So?" he said.

You're nuts, she told herself.

"I've been thinking."

"Dangerous," he told her. "Look at all the crap it's gotten me into."

"How's about a little revenge?"

When he stared at her, she tried and failed to look away. It was as if he could see everything inside her, all the small things straining to get big.

"What do you have in mind?"

Sarra is going to kill me, Greta thought.

"You know those effects things you're always talking about?"

He nodded, warily.

"How'd you like some practice?"

3

The Luncheria was packed, the counter two deep, all the booths taken. The jukebox blared, but the music only blended with the noise, nobody was listening. In the back booth, beneath a cackling cardboard witch, a hissing cardboard black cat, Brian wedged himself into the corner and watched the others sourly. They'd been on his case all day, in the halls, in class, at lunch, at their lockers, waiting for his promise, unspoken or not. Mickie hadn't looked at him at all, but he could feel her question in the way she walked when she knew he was behind her, in the way she made sure he had more than one opportunity to study her profile from waist to brow.

"Look," Corky pleaded, "we gotta get organized here, guys, or nothing's gonna be done. Saturday, in case you've forgotten, is only a couple of days away."

"The man," said Rita, "proves again his genius for math."

"Shove it, Galiano."

"You wish," she said, and grinned at him.

Blue ate a french fry, picked up another and pointed it across the table at Brian. "There's no way you're gonna get caught, you know. I swear. No kidding."

"Right."

"Jesus," Corky muttered in exasperation. He leaned his elbows on the table and covered his face with his palms. "I am," he said behind his hands, "surrounded by chickens."

"Chicken has nothing to do with it," Brian said.

"You against the idea of stunts?" Corky asked, peeking out between his fingers.

"No."

"Especially this year?"

"Especially this year."

"Then?"

"He's weighing the odds of getting killed," Blue explained. "Death comes not easy to a man of his sensitivity."

Corky dropped his hands. "What? We talking about Linholm?"

"Mickie," Rita said, as her lips were touched with bile.

"Ah." Corky leaned back. His expression was thoughtful. "So, no big deal. We deal her in."

"Like hell," Blue said. "No offense, Brian, but she—"

"Yeah," he said.

She's not one of us.

And she wasn't. Never would be. And he wished Rita wouldn't keep looking at him. Sideways, as if she didn't want to look him straight in the eyes.

"All right," Corky said. "So look, all you have to do is give me the key—"

"No!"

Corky shrugged. "No sweat. You just let us in, right?

You don't even have to stick around, you don't want to. We're in, the place is redecorated, the picture taken, we're out in less than an hour. No lights. Who's to know?" He stared. "I don't get it, Oakland. You never punked out on us before."

He knew what they were thinking: Mickie had him square by the balls and wasn't letting go. Ring through the nose. Crook her little finger and he'd come running like a pet dog. Leash time. Promise him a treat if he does his little trick.

There was a hot dog on his plate; he poked it with a thumb.

Rita gripped his upper arm, gently. "You don't have to if you don't want to, you know. We can find another way in. Corky just doesn't want to work any harder than he has to."

He looked at the hand, then up into her eyes. Big eyes. Dark. Saying nothing at all that he could read. When he looked over to Blue, Blue quickly popped another fry into his mouth and whistled tunelessly around it.

"I'm getting suckered, right?"

Rita squeezed. "Right."

"You'll die first before telling."

"I swear," Corky declared, crossing his heart, and his eyes.

"Homework for the rest of the semester?"

"You're pushing it, Oakland," Blue said.

Brian feigned thoughtfulness, a finger tapping his cheek, humming low under his breath, staring at the ceiling, at the mob by the counter, twisting to look at the heads above the tops of the other booths.

Rita jammed a knuckle into his leg, just above the knee. "Hey!"

She stuck out her tongue, then grabbed her soda and

began to drink. But not before he saw the flare of red on her cheeks.

"Well," he said, "it seems to me that I ought to know more about the party of which I am to be a party of, *if* I'm going to join the party."

Corky chuckled and shook his head.

Blue, a french fry dangling like a cigarette from the corner of his mouth, leaned over. "Seems that our flunk-bound friend here—"

"Damnit, Cross, lay off!"

"—has managed to collect a few things that, he claims, belong to a certain bleach-head typist in the front office."

"True," Corky said solemnly.

"These certain items of, shall we say, an extremely personal nature, will be strategically placed about the environs of the school in order that a clean-up in the morning cannot be accomplished before the population of said school returns to its academic pursuits and receives the full impact of said exhibit. We do believe, because of the nature of these extremely personal items, that a certain dictator will achieve a new orbit in intrastudent relations."

Brian stared at him.

Corky rubbed his hands.

Rita leaned her head close to his and said, "Translation: Corky has some of McCarthy's underwear—it has her name on them, he won't say where he got them—and Linholm will shit a brick when he finds out everybody knows he's been screwing her."

Brian stared at her.

Corky laughed loudly.

Blue ate his last fry and nodded.

"Miss McCarthy?"

"Sure," Rita said. She leaned away from him in surprise. "Didn't you know?"

"He really is . . ." He waved his hands.

"Jesus, Brian," Corky said in disgust. "Where the hell have you been all your life?"

Brian inhaled slowly, exhaled quickly. "Damn." He shook his head. "Damn." He watched Rita nod, then looked up. "Oh damn."

Greta stood at the booth. June was right behind her. "Move over," she said to Corky, "there's no place to sit in this goddamn place."

Greta rolled her eyes and slid in next to Rita, complaining about the traffic on Tyler, hell because of a trailer truck that jackknifed on the edge of town.

"It's worth your life just to cross the street anymore," she said, reaching for Corky's drink.

Rita shifted again, and Brian did his best not to feel her leg against his, smell the powder, or look at Blue, who, he saw from the corner of his eye, was suddenly most interested in the cardboard witch and cat.

"What's up?" June said brightly.

"The stock market," Corky answered.

"Very funny. I forgot to laugh." She nodded to Rita, smiled at Brian. "So, you gonna marry Mickie or what?"

4

There were only two coach seats left on an evening flight to JFK. Not together. They'd arrive shortly after midnight, East Coast time. Evan bought them, and walked arm-in-arm with Addie through the crowded terminal. He didn't bother to check for Paul; there were too many people, too much noise, too much movement; it was difficult enough just maneuvering through all the luggage

329

carts and around outbound tourists laden with bags and children. Instead, he concentrated on the jitters playing in his stomach. A comfort he hadn't expected—it meant his worry about flying had already kicked in.

They ate and tasted nothing at a snack bar in the main concourse, browsed listlessly through a bookstore, the duty-free gift shop, sat on contoured plastic chairs and stared at the flags and banners hanging from the high ceiling, at the pilots and flight attendants rushing to and from their planes, at the occasional policeman strolling along the carpeted flooring.

They said little.

There was nothing left to say.

He walked again, to stretch his legs, changed some pounds to dollars, and paused by a coin-operated television bolted at an angle to a chair. The old man watching it muttered obscenities at it until he noticed Evan.

"Damn IRA," he said, nodding to the tiny screen.

Evan leaned over to see more clearly, automatically shaking his head at the smoking ruins of someone's house. The roof was gone in front, hoses and firemen trampling over the lawn and through the hedging.

Then he straightened.

The reporter, microphone in hand, pulled a constable into the picture for a comment.

It was Sergeant Ludden.

The ruined house was Evan's.

5

John sat in his rocking chair.

Beside it, on the floor on the right, bits of fur and bone.

He could smell nothing but the pine the breeze brought through the open window.

330

A station wagon pulled up at the curb, its color stolen by the twilight. A long-legged woman in tennis shorts slid out. As she hurried up the walk toward the porch, he recognized her, and sneered. Tressa Galiano, come to mooch another one of the old bitch's stupid recipes. The next thing you knew, the old bitch would open a restaurant and there'd be no peace left in the neighborhood. He shifted. Grunted. Had half a mind to go down there while Galiano was inside and *touch* that damned car. *Touch* it, follow it, and see what the hell would happen. But he didn't move. Only thought about it, and the thought made him smile, and rock.

Soon enough.

Soon enough.

He flexed his hands.

That redheaded piece of lard, Blue Cross, had been over earlier, shooting baskets with Brian. John had heard them talking, and hadn't felt so good since he'd gone hunting the night before.

A stunt. At the high school. Halloween night.

No. No sense *touching* that fat-assed Galiano's car when he could do so much more.

Kids, he thought.

Goddamn kids.

Then he reached down to his left and pulled the squealing rabbit up by its ears.

6

". . . flotation device under your seat . . ."

Evan paid no attention to the barely visible screen at the head of the cabin section, where a flight attendant smiled her way through the ways he couldn't possibly survive a crash in the North Atlantic. He never listened. He'd flown enough times to have memorized the speech, and had been through enough bouts of terrifying rough weather to realize, at last, that it didn't make any difference.

God's will.

Coincidental bad luck.

The result was the same.

Instead, he tried to settle himself for the nearly seven-hour flight. Addie had gotten a window seat four rows ahead of him; he, on the aisle, had nothing to lean his head against, and he knew he'd have one hell of a stiff neck by the time they arrived in New York.

The smell of plastic, jet fuel, the attendant's perfume when she walked by, checking to be sure all seatbelts were fastened, the fear from the woman sitting behind him, chattering nervously with her husband, sour milk from a baby who had just thrown up all over her father's suit.

The engines bellowed, whined, bellowed again.

When the airliner pulled away from its docking space, he stared at the back of Addie's head, trying to force her to look around so he could smile, wink, do something to let her know they were going to be all right. But she already had a pillow propped between her and the window.

The baby screamed.

The wife asked her husband how long the flight was.

The airliner turned toward the runway, and he stared at the terminal, at the windows glaring in the setting sun.

No waiting.

The airplane took off without missing a beat.

Evan closed his eyes and instantly fell asleep.

In his dream it was snowing, and coming toward him, a bloodstained wolf.

IX

IN THE
SHADOW
OF THE
WOLF

Thirty-three

"So this is America."

Evan, too bone-weary to answer, only shrugged as Addie turned from the motel window and pushed her hair away from her eyes with both hands. It was clearly an effort; she didn't smile. And when she sighed more like a groan, rubbed the back of her neck, she looked as if she hadn't slept for over a week. He had no doubt at all that he looked the same.

"I suppose," she added, "I ought to be counting my blessings."

The flight had been a horror: constant turbulence over the Atlantic only added to his dreams, finally waking him into a storm that brought on the "no smoking/fasten seat belt" signs, sending the airliner into steep dives and laboring climbs that threatened to wrench his stomach loose. Something crashed to the floor in one of the forward galleys. A child wept, another cried softly. The woman sitting behind him muttered prayers for an hour. The engines whined, roared, struggled for purchase, and during a sharp leftward bank, an overhead compartment snapped open, spilling briefcases and overcoats into the aisle.

He had stared out the window, seeing nothing but the night and half-expecting to see Paul there, prancing and laughing on the wing.

335

And afterward, when it was done, the praying and weeping over, the plane trembled the rest of the way to North America, where they had circled for nearly an hour just below Boston because of a thunderstorm that had stalled above Long Island. A vicious landing that should have crumpled the undercarriage. Two hours getting through customs, surly inspectors taking out their late shift, bad-weather blues on passengers too shaken to protest. Renting a car had taken another hour, and by the time they reached the Patriot Motor Lodge just outside Port Richmond, they had had quite enough of anything, and anyone, that moved.

Addie threw back the coverlet, the blanket, and sat with her back to him. "Do not touch me," she said. "I am not in the mood to be seduced."

He grunted.

An apologetic smile over her shoulder while she pulled off her shoes.

Not, he agreed silently, the most romantic place in the world.

The second-story room was small, and made smaller by two double beds, a long dresser, and a television set bolted to its own chrome stand which, in turn, was bolted to the floor.

The heating unit beneath the window grumbled.

The walls were papered a faintly fading red and white, the carpet was worn of its color, the draperies were a brilliant blue and white, three bland prints over the beds depicted General Washington moving his army through New Jersey during the early days of the Revolution.

Addie stood, stretched, and stripped to her underwear. "Do you know," she said, looking to the clock radio on the stand between the beds, "that it's damn near dawn?" She knelt on the mattress. "I feel dead."

"I think I am dead. I'm just too stupid to know it."

A look: *are we . . . will we be all right?*

He nodded: *how can we not be? He's not here, he's over there.*

Her head lowered, she slowly fell onto her side and dragged the covers over her. "Get some sleep," she muttered into the pillow. "But don't wake me until I wake up. Jet lag be damned, I've had it."

His shoes and socks already off, his belt undone, his shirt unbuttoned. He moved to the wall switch by the door and turned off the lights. Then he pulled the corner of the drape aside and looked out.

The Patriot was a courtyard motel, better days long gone, just busy enough not to get worse; the rooms ranged around a pool ringed by a stained concrete apron, second-floor access from a narrow concrete balcony. Parking was in the rear. Straight ahead he could see over the brick wall that fronted the highway, the door in its right-hand corner already bolted shut against the night. Light blurred as a mist dropped from unseen clouds. Traffic. A horn. Even in here the faint smell of gasoline and diesel fuel. Stores, gas stations, shabby offices, empty lots; and beyond them, just one block away, was the southern end of Port Richmond.

He was home, and he didn't feel like it.

Too much had happened too quickly. No time for thought, no time to figure out what he would do when he returned.

It was Friday.

Weekend in Port Richmond.

When Addie snored lightly, he realized he had never felt so lonely. So disconnected.

Exhaustion was part of it. The run, the flight, the hassles with bureaucracy just to get a simple car—his temper had gone the way of his patience the moment he'd stepped into the terminal. Too many emotions abruptly

337

severed at the base when he'd stumbled into the room and closed the door behind him.

And anxiety. Now that he was here, what was he going to do? He needed funds, he needed work, and he needed someplace to stay.

Christ, he wouldn't even be able to get back into his own house without wrangling.

He yawned and let the drapes fall to.

He felt his way across the room and got into bed.

"Good night, Addie," he said softly.

At least, he thought to her, we're safe, for a change.

Thirty-four

1

Brian had the dream again.

Glass; guns; knives; acid; chains and a razor-tipped whip.

Eric Linholm hadn't stood a chance.

Blood speckled the gymnasium walls, crawled in rivulets along the hardwood floor, ran in winding streams down the high windowpanes, stained his hands and dried under his nails, splattered onto his lips and he shivered when he licked them.

Screaming.

Begging.

All of it in silence while Shane Bishop looked on from his post at the iron door. Rusted iron. Blood rust.

When at last the nightmare ended, he sat up in his bed, panting with exertion.

And excitement.

This time he didn't make it to the bathroom before he threw up.

"I mean," he said later, sitting at the breakfast table in the kitchen, an untouched bowl of cereal before him, "I was actually having a good time, you know what I mean?" He shuddered and rubbed his arms.

"Not surprising," said Lyanna Gough, still wrapped in a Day-Glo dragon bathrobe and holding a cup of coffee. There was still an hour to go before any of them had to be at school. The furnace rumbled; fragments of morning frost on the window over the sink. "There are days when I wish I could do the same thing." A slip of ginger hair drooped over her forehead. She blew up; it fell back. "Not in dreams, though, I can tell you that."

"Lyanna," Shirley Atkins cautioned. She stood at the sink, slender in jeans and sweater, sweatband around her short hair, cheeks flushed from her run around the block.

"Hey, I don't care," the pudgy woman answered. Her voice was hoarse, almost masculine. "The kid thinks we all love the bastard?" She grinned. "Pardon my French."

Brian grinned back. "I won't tell, if that's what you're worried about."

Miss Atkins turned with a glass of water, leaned back against the stainless-steel sink. "That's not it at all," she said over the rim of the glass. Pale eyes serious; dark eyebrows lowered. "It's what we in the profession call an indiscretion."

"Bullshit," the art teacher muttered.

Miss Atkins grunted and drank, put the glass behind her without looking, and said, "It's like Brian here telling us what stunt his class is planning for tomorrow, you see."

"Hey," he said.

The history teacher held up a palm. "Now don't get

excited, Brian. I'm not going to pump you for information, and I'm certainly not going to tell you not to do it. I don't even want a hint. Because," she said, shaking her finger to make the point, "that would be an indiscretion. You see?"

"Bullshit," Miss Gough muttered again.

Brian didn't see. It was no secret that there were still a handful of teachers left who continued to fight the principal's autocratic changes every step of the way; it was also no secret that the fighting, which had resulted in faculty and staff purges three years in a row, had ultimately cost Mr. Kendal his job. But not before a long, loud, and very public battle which had, so far this year, sent Linholm's tactics underground.

Except for the stunt decree.

There were teachers you could talk to, and teachers you avoided. The two who stayed at Neeba's were still on probation.

On the other hand, Miss Gough had already cornered Blue's lust without knowing it; and Miss Atkins, in the morning no matter what she wore, always looked like a spring fawn—wide eyes, soft and cuddly, too cute and young to be a teacher. Which thoughts weren't getting him anywhere but close to trouble.

He ate.

"Your dream," Miss Gough reminded him a few seconds later, cup rattling now on her saucer. "Whatever *we* may think of the man—"

"Lyanna," the other woman warned a second time.

"—you obviously have reason to hate him. Or to think that you hate him. And it's obvious to everyone who has two eyes why you've included Shane this time, considering all that's happened to the poor dope so far this year. So why shouldn't you dream about doing the schmuck in?"

"But I liked it!" he protested, dropping his spoon to the table. "I've *never* had dreams like that. Never. I was having a good time, don't you get it?" He shook his head. "You should have been there!" He stared at the back door without seeing a thing. "Shane was."

She bowed her head for a moment, but not before he saw her smile. When she looked up again, she said, "It wouldn't do you any good, give you any satisfaction, if you didn't like it, now would it? It wouldn't help Shane, either."

He considered it, and shrugged. "I don't know. I guess not."

"Sure. So, in your dreams, you enjoy yourself, and you give Shane a bit of revenge. It is, Brian, only a dream."

"Yeah. I guess."

Miss Atkins walked over and put her hands on her friend's shoulders, leaned over her head, and said, "Brian, don't sweat it, okay? If you had truly liked it, had really gotten into it, it wouldn't have been a nightmare. Then, kid, you'd definitely have something serious to worry about."

Brian waited for the "bullshit."

But the art teacher only sighed. "You know," she said to him, "I hate people who are so damned clever and cheerful on school mornings. It isn't natural."

"It's Friday," Miss Atkins reminded her. "Two days of freedom dead ahead."

"It still ain't natural."

He laughed and pushed his chair back.

"I'll tell you what's not natural," countered Miss Atkins. "It's people who sleep until noon on Sundays, eat everything in the house while they read the papers, then go take a nap until supper."

Miss Gough reached over her head and slapped at her awkwardly.

Brian headed for the back door.

"Damnit, this is teacher abuse, Gough, and the kid is a witness."

He laughed again and slipped out to the back porch, let the hard autumn chill bring him the rest of the way awake. The night's rain blown into New York. A beautiful day left behind. White on the grass, his breath in puffs and clouds. Later, much later, he would think about his dream, and think about what the teachers had told him. Meanwhile, he'd better get the garbage cans out to the curb for collection before Neeba thought he was goofing off.

Down the steps, a right toward the garage, and he glanced up at his grandmother's bedroom window. The shade was still drawn. He frowned. A first—she never overslept, not even on Sundays when her boarders had to fend for themselves until dinner. He chewed thoughtfully on his lower lip, wondering if he should go up and knock on her door. Maybe she was sick. Maybe she was still upset about Mr. Naze.

Then Miss Gough laughed, startling a jay off the grass.

Brian decided to mind his business. Besides, he ought to be at school early, he and the others had final plans to make if things were going to work. Assignments, Corky called them, making it sound almost like a war.

The jay scolded, and he watched it dart low over the yard, swerve into an elm at the last second and vanish. For a minute he thought it was Soldier's doing. Then he remembered finding the cat in the street last night. What was left of him, that is. And he hurried.

3

"Miss Gough, why do we have to draw apples?"

Lyanna wiped a palm over her knee-length smock and used her best patient smile. "Because," she said, having said it a thousand times before, "round isn't as easy as it looks to give dimension to. You give dimension to round, you learn shading, you learn light, you learn passing." She grinned. "How simple can it get?"

Eighteen students, most of them unwilling, in a large room that still managed to be crowded, each facing an easel, each with a smock, glaring and squinting and studying and leaning away from eighteen shapes that might, given time, be transformed into apples.

Because, she wanted to add, *we only have fifteen minutes today because the Führer is probably going to wreck your Halloween with another goddamn speech about the difference between good citizens and not graduating.*

On the back wall, a series of oversize, cluttered pigeonholes for dumping texts and notebooks into while class was in session; low tables beneath the windows with paper cutters and jars of paste, bottles of paint and stacks of colored paper; on the left wall an exhibition of artwork, much of it mediocre, some of it fine.

"I hate apples," the student said.

Lyanna heard rebellious muttering spread, and grabbed a small yellow pad from her desk. She tapped it against her wrist once, then made her way to the back, stood behind the black-haired girl, and saw that indeed apples were not high on her list of favorite things.

"Miss Galiano, you're hopeless."

Rita shrugged. "My mother says I've got talent," in a tone that told her the kid didn't believe it either.

"Right." She scribbled Rita's name on the pad, tore off the top sheet, and handed it to her over her shoulder.

"What's this?"

"Freedom," Lyanna whispered. "Go to the girls' room and hide out until the assembly."

Rita hesitated, sensing envy in the others, then grabbed the pass gratefully, hastily unsnapped her smock and practically tore it off, turned around to thank the teacher, and her elbow bumped the easel. It rocked. She grabbed for it, saved it, and managed to kick the easel's forward leg. It toppled backward, smacking into her neighbor's back, who yelped in surprise, turned, and in turn knocked over a small table that held all her oils.

"Oh boy," Rita said.

"Out," Miss Gough told her. "Out of here, kid, before you murder someone."

Rita snatched her gear from its cubbyhole and escaped, slowed her rush to a walk midway down the hall when she decided just to wander. As long as she stayed away from the front office and didn't look too guilty, she didn't think she'd be caught.

Her elbow stung where it had caught the canvas's corner.

She rounded the corner and headed for the central corridor and its breezeway, orange lockers on her left, red lockers on her right, the pale tile beneath her heels gleaming like ice under the ceiling's recessed lights. Murmuring in classrooms. A burst of laughter. One darkened door and the sputtering whir of a projector.

Dom Pastori leaning against the wall beside a door, arms folded over his chest, heel kicking back. Exiled, no doubt, she figured, for causing trouble in class.

"Hey," he said as she passed him.

"Dom."

She was several yards by when he called, "So what're you doing tomorrow?"

She stopped, half-turned. "What?"

"Tomorrow," he said. "Saturday. What're you doing?"

She couldn't believe it. "You asking for a date?"

"Get real," he said, lip curled. "You know what I'm talking about. What do you got planned?"

She shook her head and tried a scowl, denying she had anything planned at all.

"Right," he said, in clear disbelief. A glance up and down the corridor. "But if you want to have real fun, give me a call, okay?" A teacher opened the door, told him to come back in. Dom took his time unfolding himself. "Call me," he said as Rita turned to move on. "It'll be a hell of a lot more fun."

She doubted it. She knew it. The only thing Dom would do for her was get her fifteen-to-life in Rahway. A hesitation in her step when she realized that he was planning a stunt too, and she decided Brian or Corky had better know. There was no way Pastori wouldn't target the school. Which meant big trouble unless they stayed out of each other's way.

God, she thought, I don't need this too.

June had intentionally avoided her all week, and the more she thought about it, tried to be reasonable about it, the angrier she became. The girl had had no right, *no right*, to hit her, or treat Brian the way she did. Christ, she had only been talking to him, not hanging all over him. And so what if she had been? What claim did the girl have anymore?

Her heels, louder.

She hugged her books tight to her chest.

So what if she had been?

Blindly, she swung into the next hall, and collided with Corky, who had been carrying a plate of pasta until the impact jarred it loose and shattered it on the floor.

"Jesus!"

"Oh god!"

"God, I'm sorry!"

"My fault, I wasn't looking."

"Sorry!"

"No sweat."

346

They knelt on the floor, tackling her books and papers first, then staring at the meat sauce and the noodles and the pieces of cafeteria china.

Corky shook his head. "It isn't my day, Galiano."

"God, I'm sorry."

He giggled. "We go through all that again, we'll be here until graduation." He made a move to wipe it up with his hands, drew back when a shard pricked his thumb, and stood instead. "The hell with it. I'll get a janitor. Miss Atkins can wait for her morning snack. Runners," he added, "are totally nuts, have you ever noticed?"

Rita didn't move.

He held out his hand, waggled it in front of her eyes until she saw it, then pulled her easily to her feet. "Does this mean I get to be on Spinner's major hit list?" he asked with mock concern, and smacked himself mentally when he saw her dark expression. "Sorry." But he wasn't, not really. Just one more nail in Rita's lovelorn coffin. He smiled gently, pushed her gently on her way, and scratched his head as he examined the mess spread at his feet.

Like a squirrel after a shotgun, he thought.

"Corky?"

It was Rita, stopped and looking nervous.

"Yeah?"

"I think Dom's going to do a stunt too."

He nodded. "Makes sense. He doesn't have anything better to do with his life."

She started to say something, changed her mind and hurried off.

He knew what she meant though—the guy was trouble. But who cared? Dom was a paint-and-shit guy, no imagination, and for damn sure no class. He'd probably

347

come to the school, but so what? Blue would be here, in case the jackass wanted trouble.

He grinned suddenly.

In fact, that might be a good thing. Maybe they could figure a way to blame it on Pastori. The perfect way to end the century's perfect stunt.

A check over his shoulder, then, to see if anyone had been nosy enough at the commotion to poke a head out of a classroom. A nod to himself as Rita ducked into the breezeway. Then he sucked the tiny cut thoughtfully, stepped over the debris, and marched down the corridor, passing the intersection Galiano had jumped out of, and headed for the back of the school. He'd tell Miss Atkins what had happened, she'd tell him to find the janitor, and if he worked it right, he'd be able to miss the whole assembly.

He grinned.

The Führer could, and probably would, the bastard, talk until he was red in the face about maturity and civic responsibility, but nothing in this world was going to stop tomorrow's celebration. Especially now. Yesterday afternoon, with Blue's help, he'd managed to liberate a mannequin from the Drama Arts storage closet. It hadn't been easy, but it was in his garage now. Waiting.

A quick laugh, a snap of his fingers.

Life, he thought, can be so goddamn *good*.

He kept close to the lockers, dragging his knuckles along them and humming to the hollow rattles, the clicks, the every-so-often knock he gave one to see if it would pop open. A week ago, he'd found a box of crackers; the week before that, a pack of cigarettes. Treasure. Nothing spectacular; he wasn't dumb enough to steal money. Treasure. Enough to keep life interesting.

Left turn.

Eyes straight.

Hard heels, arms swinging.

And a yelp and belated jump when a door swung open and the edge caught his forearm.

"Damn!" he said.

Brian looked at him, looked at the door, and said, "You okay?"

Corky rubbed the stinging. "Yeah, I guess so."

At a teacher's weary command from the room behind him, Brian closed the door and walked with Corky.

"Where you headed?" Ploughman asked.

"Office." Brian rolled his eyes. "Seems I was two minutes late today. Gonna get fried."

"Late? You were late?" Corky's eyes widened comically. "Oh my lord, Oakland, I'll never see you again." He grabbed Brian's hand and pumped it. "God, it's been good knowing you, though."

Brian looked woefully at the floor. "I know. Same here."

"Can I have your coat? You know, the green one with the tassels?"

Brian hit him, not easy, and Corky laughed as he pushed open a door at corridor's end. "How about Rita?" And was gone.

The urge to give chase was quickly suppressed. If there had been time, he might have tried a foot to the guy's rump, send him down the short flight to the outer door on his pointy head, but time was something he didn't have. And he didn't have an excuse. No note from Neeba explaining why he was late, and since he didn't take the bus, no excuse there either.

He had been late because Neeba had come down to the kitchen just as he was ready to leave. She looked horrible. Old. Incredibly tiny wrapped in a robe as drab as Miss Gough's was gaudy. And when he'd asked if she was all right, if she needed any help, she'd nearly

349

snapped his head off, swinging into a tirade about all the sacrifices she'd made, first for her husband, then for him, and what thanks did she get for working herself to death. He was stunned, could think of nothing to say, yet had to stand there until, as if she'd been slapped, she blinked fiercely and stared at him.

"Neeba?" he'd said.

"Go away," she'd told him flatly. "I didn't sleep very well. Just go to school."

He had, but on the way, he had promised himself that today he would find out what the hell had happened when she'd been in Mr. Naze's apartment.

Not to mention finding out where June got off slugging Rita the way she had.

He stopped.

He leaned against the wall, poked his head around the corner and stared at the front office wall—all glass, floor to ceiling, the secretaries at their desks, the dark door on the left that led to the lion's den. In front, Gunnar Weldmar, the grey-shirted, grey-haired head janitor with a wheeled bucket at his side, passed a dripping mop over the floor, a small warning sign placed at the rim of the area he was washing. Brian pulled back and blew out a slow breath. Take it easy, man. There was nothing to worry about. He had been late; big deal. Two lousy minutes. What would he get, a day's detention? An essay? Fifty lashes? Ten years? What's the big deal?

What could happen?

A hand touched his waist.

He spun away from it, hit the corner with his shoulder and felt his arm go numb. "Hey!"

Mickie, bosom fluffed in a bulky sweater, snug in a skirt a size too small and an inch too short, covered her mouth with one hand, her eyes bright with laughter.

He massaged his arm gingerly. Jeez, that hurt.

350

"You free or something?" she asked.

"Nope. Linholm calls. I was late."

She patted his cheek, kissed it, and said into his ear, "See you later, okay? We still have things to discuss."

She walked away, back down the hall, and he knew she knew he was watching—hips slow and easy side to side, tugging at the back of the sweater so he would imagine how it looked from the front, a hand briefly brushing across her buttocks.

He turned away quickly.

This was definitely getting out of hand. He wanted no part of whatever stunt she was planning; he had awakened wondering if he really wanted any part of her.

Why me?

He had no idea.

Nervously, he rubbed a thumb over his fingertips, took a condemned man's deep breath, and stepped into the front hall. Ahead, beyond the wide entrance foyer carpeted in dark red and lined with display cases for the school's suddenly growing list of trophies, he saw Shane swing into the lobby from the front door; at the same time, Blue staggered out of a room, lugging a stack of books.

Brian waved as he aimed for the office.

Shane waved back.

Blue called, "Wait up, Oakland," and tried to hurry.

Brian saw it before it happened and tried to head him off, but Blue, chin resting on the top of the stack to keep it steady, didn't see the warning sign, didn't see the wet floor.

He slid.

The janitor stood, cursing loudly as the sign clattered over the tiles, and caught Blue's weight, caught the shower of books, and was slammed into the glass wall.

Which shattered as Blue fell backward, Weldmar fell,

and icicles of glass fell into the man's chest, sliced the side of his neck.

A secretary screamed.

Shane ran up, slipped in the soapy water, and skidded on his buttocks to the office entrance.

Brian ran to Cross, who was on his knees now and staring at the red that turned the grey shirt dark.

"It was an accident," Blue said plaintively. His face, when he looked up, was streaked with dusty tears. "Jesus, it was an accident!"

Linholm came out of his office, snapped at a secretary to call the police and an ambulance, then grabbed Shane's shoulder and yanked him to his feet.

"Well, Mr. Bishop," he said, "you've really done it now."

Thirty-five

1

The motor lodge coffee shop was open twenty-four hours a day. Aside from the Patriot's guests, Evan judged from the menu and prices that it also served the truckers on their way south to the George Washington Bridge, salesmen, and those who couldn't afford the restaurants in Port Richmond itself.

The food was tasteless.

The service brash and friendly.

"Just like home," Addie said, grinning over a cup of coffee.

They sat in a window booth, traffic building toward evening rush hour, shadows reaching across the highway to flood the buildings opposite.

He was still a bit groggy, but now that his stomach was full, not quite as gloomy, definitely not as pessimistic as he'd been when he'd fallen asleep. The trees still held much of their autumn foliage, signs of Halloween were everywhere, the weather a deep-blue-and-cool-breeze that kept everything in sharp focus.

Now if he could only stop looking for Paul in window reflections, behind trees, driving cars.

353

"So," she said, "now what?"

"It's too late to go to the bank—I want to talk with someone, get the rest of this sterling changed over—so we'll have to stay here for another night."

"I shall not forget you for this, you know."

"And tomorrow, we'll check the real estate office, see what I can do about nullifying of my lease." He looked out, saw a child in a ghost sheet skip by with its mother. "It'd be nice to sleep in my own bed sometime soon."

"Will there be a problem?"

"Sure."

She waited.

He shrugged.

The waitress filled their cups again.

"And now?"

"Now," he said, leaning back and stretching to get a hand in his jeans pocket for money, "I'll take you on the royal tour."

He paid, and with her hands tucked around his arm, they crossed the road and walked into Port Richmond.

Houses with ears of maize tied to front doors, pumpkins on porches, witches on porch roofs, black cats on welcome mats, a scarecrow hanging from a limb; bare trees, lawns speckled with leaves, piles of leaves in gutters and stuffed into plastic bags, leaves in the streets dancing away from tires; a man wrapping his rose bushes in burlap, a woman on a porch screaming shrilly for her children; sounds sharp from heels to whispers; light slipping to dark, leaving motes like black gnats to blink away, ignore.

"Tyler Avenue," he said. "The main drag, named after a president without much of a reputation."

Shops in black and orange.

"I'll be damned, the King's Castle burned down."

A dead-end street, iron fencing, the river below, turning black.

"Supposedly you can fish there now. Myself, I wouldn't touch one."

He hadn't seen anyone he knew and, from time and distance, was mildly surprised at how large the town really was, how few of the adults he really knew, how many of the children.

The thought came to him to call Uncle John. No. Not yet. He wanted to be more alert. He'd surprise him tomorrow, just knock on his door and remember the look on the old man's face.

Sometime during the next hour the streetlamps flickered on, and the trees lost their color, the houses opened yellowed eyes.

Light and shadow, colder, breath smoking.

They walked.

He breathed deeply.

They faced a solid wall of forest.

"You know," she said, pulling until he turned around and faced her, "I have a feeling we've been doing a circle."

He shrugged with a half-smile.

She looked around. "Where is it?"

A pointing finger to the street just behind them.

"Well, then."

As they crossed over, entered the block, he said, "What if they've repainted it? God, I hope he didn't cut back the Rose of Sharon in front, it's a zillion years old and I like it sprawling the way it was. Maybe—"

"Evan, for heaven's sake."

"Right."

He stopped. "Over there. The Cape Cod."

She stood beside him, an arm around his waist. "It's lovely."

His look was skeptical.

"Really," she insisted. "It is. It's lovely."

He wasn't sure about that, but he was sure about one thing: "He didn't touch the Rose of Sharon."

355

No lights showed, no car in the drive. He frowned, tilted his head, and stepped off the curb. "C'mon." Puzzlement to concern as he hesitated at the foot of the driveway. "Y'know, Addie, I don't . . ." Slowly he moved up the blacktop to the spot where the front walk began. A glance around the neighborhood; there was no one watching, no one on the street.

"Is there something wrong?"

He shook his head; he didn't know.

Midway along the concrete walk—cracked during the winter, he noticed—he stepped onto the grass and walked to the living-room window, large and uncovered and reflecting like black ice. A row of angled bricks marked a narrow garden between the grass and the house; he stepped over the boundary and stood on tiptoe, saw nothing, gripped the shallow outside sill with his fingertips and pulled himself up. He was only able to stay there a few seconds, but it was long enough.

"I'll be damned."

"What?"

He didn't know whether to smile or be angry. "I think the bugger's gone."

2

The pool was supposed to be ten feet deep at this end when it was filled. Shane figured another two feet to make it twelve. He sat crosslegged on the edge beside the diving board stand, the board itself long since unbolted and placed in winter storage.

If he jumped, he might die; if he jumped, he might not.

If he jumped, he wouldn't be able to help Greta, but he

wasn't sure he wanted to. What good would it do? If he was caught, Linholm would expel him; if they were successful, no one would know except those they decided to tell. And if anyone talked . . .

Fisting his hands into his jacket pockets he stared at the bottom. Aquamarine paint chipped, faded, shabby without its water. A pile of leaves and papers he was supposed to sweep up before he left. The broom was down there too. All he had to do was jump down and use it.

Shadow down there as well.

The star-shaped amber lights beside each door were not strong enough to reach here; streetlamps made no inroads; the inset lights along the bottom were on, but only five of them worked, all at the shallow end.

They were going to blame him for the accident.

Brian had defended him against Linholm's accusations, but the principal had ignored him, ignored Blue's tears, only shoved Shane aside and ordered him to wait for the police. He had. So had Blue, and after Weldmar, moaning, bleeding, unable to hold his head still, had been taken away, the police took less than half an hour. A question about the water on the floor, about the scattered books, and they were satisfied. Brian had taken Blue away; Linholm had glared at him, accusing him anyway.

"Watch yourself," was all the man had said before returning to his office.

Shane left school immediately, not caring about permission, only wanting to get home. His mother was gone, off to visit her sister, she'd be back sometime tonight, supper was in the fridge. He took the gun into the bathroom, stood in the tub, and pulled the trigger until he'd stopped crying.

The sound of harsh brakes brought his head up, just in time to see the door in the wall open, two figures step through, holding on to each other and laughing quietly.

They couldn't see him. He was shadow. He was night. He watched them move toward the staircase in the middle of the motel's right-hand arm, stop at a soda machine while the man fumbled for change. The woman turned, and Shane tried to make himself small.

Her voice was clear: "How deep is that?"

An accent. He frowned. When the man answered above the clatter of a can rolling out of the machine, she walked toward the low iron fence and leaned against it.

She saw him.

"Hello," she said.

English. That's it, she's English.

"Addie," the man said.

She waved.

Shane waved back, surprised that he did, and watched them disappear into the stairwell, appear on the second level and walk down to the door just opposite his shoulder. When the door closed behind them, he looked back at the pool and was equally surprised to realize he was smiling.

Incredible.

Strange lady with an English accent says hello, and he acts like Linholm just bit the big one.

A sharp exhalation.

He'd better get finished. There was a lot of work to do before tomorrow night.

3

"So *this* is how it works," Corky said, standing aside to let the others see.

After a long moment, a stunned silence, Rita choked into laughter, Blue applauded and whistled, and Brian simply shook his head and grinned inanely. They were going to be killed, slaughtered, arrested, dragged through the streets behind a team of horses. No adult would ever speak to them again. Neeba would truly lock him in the basement and never let him see daylight again. If they pulled this off, only God would be able to save them from total destruction, and he doubted that God was paying much attention.

The automatic door to Corky's garage was closed behind them. There were no cars here; there was never room enough. The walls were paneled with pegboard, on which hung garden tools, carpentry tools, and automobile supplies; the floorspace was taken up by wheelbarrows, cartons, stacks of tied newspapers, stacks of magazines, a workbench on the left, another on the right. In the center of the floor two small spotlights were braced against cinder blocks, their beams converging on a spot on the back wall.

"We're dead," Blue said gleefully. "Oh my god, we are dead meat and already rotting."

The mannequin sat on a ladder-back chair, hands on the armrests, feet barely touching the floor. Blonde wig in tight curls; face heavily, ludicrously, made up; a long pink cigarette jammed into a mouth outlined by black lipstick; a peek-a-boo bra, black, filmy, edged with vivid scarlet lace; panties a screaming green; a rosebud-studded garter belt holding black fishnet stockings that glittered because of the rhinestones that described large diamonds on the thighs.

And between the thighs, a teddy bear dressed in a makeshift Redcoat football uniform.

Behind the chair, and making it seem like a beauty queen's throne, was a huge red and white valentine.

On the valentine, written in red sparkles: *Secretary of the Year.*

Corky stepped into the light. "I've got it all figured out. We put this on the Führer's desk, tape the valentine in the window beside it, pull up the blinds, and set the spotlights on the lawn. Then we cut off the usual night-lights, the ones that shine on the doors and all, so that no one will miss it. They walk by, they're going to want to see better, so they come up and . . . pow! Instant gratification."

Blue applauded again.

Brian, leaning back against the door, slipped his hands into his pockets. "It won't work."

"The hell it won't."

"Corky, no one goes down that street at night. You got the church, the school, the nearest houses are a block away. A long block. It doesn't go anywhere, not downtown, not out of town, nowhere. Who's going to see it?"

Corky grinned. "No sweat."

"Signs?" he said fearfully. "God, you gonna use signs?"

"Nope."

Rita folded her arms over her chest. "I am not making anonymous calls, Ploughman. Forget it. No way."

"No problem," Corky said. "Brian, hit the lights, okay?"

Brian pushed away from the door and switched on the overhead while Corky turned off the spotlights. A look to Rita told him they were thinking the same thing: Corky had screwed up again, and it was too late to do anything about it.

"Give me a hand, Blue," Corky said, and the two of them wrestled a pair of king-size sheets over the display. When they were done, Blue took the boy's shoulders and stared at him.

"The Goodyear blimp, right?"

Corky grinned. "You're making such a big deal over nothing."

"Nothing?" Brian pointed at the sheets. "You want me to get you into the school to set . . . this . . . up, no one's going to be able to see it anyway, we're going to be sent to prison for the rest of our lives because there's no way we're not gonna get caught, and you call that nothing?" His hand slapped against his thighs. "Ploughman, this is insane."

"Who cares, as long as it works?"

Rita made a strangling sound.

Corky punched the button to open the door, and once it had rolled up, waved them all outside. Then he led them around the side of the house to the front. Brian was miserable. He'd risked his job sneaking the keys from Weldmar's office, risked his whole damn life if this didn't work, and Corky was acting like they weren't doing anything worse than soaping a few windows.

If he had the guts, he'd back out, and the hell with what they thought of him.

"Very nice," Rita said, looking up and down the street. "Looks like my block."

"Classier, Galiano."

"The point, Corky," said Blue. "Get to the point."

Corky nodded. "Okay, okay." He nodded at the house across the street. "In there lives a kid named Howard Dimarco."

"I know," Brian said impatiently. "So what?"

"Well, Howie, he's a good kid. Helps his mother, rakes the lawn, babysits his kid sister who is a royal pain in the ass." He pointed at the night sky. "He also goes to church."

Rita sighed loudly, turned her back against a gust that slapped them with sharp-edged leaves.

"The Methodist church, Blue."

"Okay," Blue said. "So what. I—oh no."

Corky grinned. "Oh yes."

Rita took Brian's hand. "We're leaving now, you guys.

361

We don't think in code, I'm cold, and Brian's promised to do my homework for the rest of the year."

Blue grabbed Brian's other arm. "Methodist church, Oakland," he said. "Remember what I said the other night?"

Suddenly he did.

And wished he hadn't.

Half the school would show up there at one time or another, generally using it as an excuse to kick off a round of other, private, parties that lasted until parents threw everyone out.

But it wasn't the party Corky and Blue meant.

It was the people.

A couple hundred of them.

Right across from the high school.

"Kids by the trillions," Corky said. "Grownups by the quardrillions. All we have to do is make sure they know." He spread his arms. "Ladies and gentlemen, I rest my case."

4

"He doesn't talk to me anymore. I think he's mad."

"Who cares? You don't need him anyway."

"But I want to do a stunt or something, Dom."

"So do one with me."

"You're doing one?"

"Damn right."

"But I wanted to do something at the school."

"Mickie, get the cotton out, huh? What've I been telling you for the past ten minutes?"

"Brian will be pissed."

"Brian can go fuck."

"Oh no he can't."

Dom laughed, and let the swirling water float his arms to the surface. Damn, but this was fine.

Damn.

"So. You think you can do it?"

"Don't worry, okay? He'll do anything I want as long as I don't wear a bra."

5

Sitting at the window.

Rocking.

Watching the sky change colors, the light change texture.

Listening to a buzzing inside his head, words that weren't words, insistent without being demanding, blinding him to the changes he'd seen in his hands—the pain still gone, swelling still down, but the flesh beginning to dry, to peel away. It didn't matter. He couldn't see them now. The buzzing wouldn't let him. It didn't matter.

His head shook slightly, minor spasms every few seconds.

It didn't matter.

Today was Halloween.

Tonight they would be out there. Bothering people. Annoying people. Begging for candy, destroying people's property, ruining people's sleep, turning the entire town into hell and not caring at all. Laughing about it.

Taking over.

It didn't matter.
Tonight they would be out there.
He would be too.
The little bastards.
They want a monster, they were going to get one.
As soon as he finished with the old bitch in the house.

Thirty-six

1

The telephone rang.

2

"I'll get it!"

"Bri-an."

"Mickie? Hey, hi!"

"We still on for tonight?"

"What? Tonight? But . . . this is a little late, you know. You—"

"Honey, you know how busy I get. And my parents have been real pricks. But I haven't forgotten."

"Yeah, well . . ."

"So, you want to come over later?"

"Mickie, I can't. I've got a zillion things to do around the house, y'know?, before the party. My grandmother wants me to practically rebuild the place. And Miss Atkins thinks we have rats in the attic, for god's sake. Plus, I still have to put in some hours at the school now that Weldmar—"

"Oh, c'mon, Brian. Please?"

"Mickie—"

"If you hurry, we can use the tub. It's not that cold today, in case you hadn't noticed."

"Look, I—"

"They're not home, you know. They went to the city, some kind of stupid play."

"Mickie, it isn't—"

"Make it about two, okay? I have to get ready. Warmed up and stuff. I still remember the last time. This time it's my treat."

"Mickie—"

"All day, Bri. They'll be gone all day."

3

"Mrs. Bishop, can I talk to Shane?"

"Who is this?"

"Sorry, Greta. Greta Rourke."

"I think he's busy, Greta. He's been out in the garage working on something since before I got up."

"Really?"

"Sounds like he's making a tank or something. If you'll hang on a minute, I'll—"

"No! No, that's okay, Mrs. Bishop. Just tell him I called, okay? I don't want to bother him."

"Mom, I'm going to be a little late, okay?"

"Rita, where in heaven's name are you? I've been wondering about what to do for lunch. Your aunt—"

"Mom, please. I think I got another job."

"Pumping gas, no doubt."

"Very funny, Mother. No, at the Luncheria. I don't know. Mr. Gilder's coming in in an hour, I'm going to talk to him then. It won't be as many hours as the Castle, but it's better than nothing."

"Well—"

"So look, if Brian calls, will you tell him I'll call him later?"

"Dear, I have so much—"

"Just tell him, okay, Mom? It's important. It's about tonight. The party, I mean. Talk to you later."

"Rita?"

"Yes, Mom?"

"Good luck with the new job."

"I haven't gotten it yet, Mom, but thanks."

"And remember your posture, dear. It's very, very important. Good first impressions are very important."

"Sure, Mom. Thanks."

"Just don't slouch. And don't break any dishes."

"Listen, Reynolds, don't give me any shit, okay? It's a little late to be bitching now."

"This is crazy."

"Just do what I tell you, there won't be any problems. It's gonna work beautifully. A charm. No sweat. You'll be famous, I ain't shitting you. So be there about seven-thirty. I may already be inside."

"Wait a minute, how the hell you gonna pull that?"

"Part of the stunt, m'man, all part of the stunt."

"Pastori, I don't think I like this."

"Who gives a shit? It's better than sitting on your ass, telling people you're doing some kind of antistunt, for Christ's sake. What the hell kind of way is that to spend Halloween? God, you're—"

"Just don't bring that gun."

"Right."

"Beer and guns don't mix, Pastori."

"Jesus H, Reynolds, you turn into an old lady over-night or something? Just be there, okay? Jesus."

6

"Blue, I'm in deep shit here."

"You called to tell me that? You couldn't walk a couple of feet, knocked on my door? A beautiful day, the sun shining, and you had to call? Very sorry, Oakland, that's very sorry. You're turning into one of those potatoes, man, and that's not cool."

"Blue, Mickie called. She wants me over there. Just about now, as a matter of fact."

"So what? Don't go."

"In the hot tub, Blue."

"This is a bad thing?"

"Her parents are in New York."

"Jesus, and you ain't there yet?"

"Blue, c'mon."

"Okay, okay, but I should have your problems. Thing is, pal, you go there and she's gonna pull some kind of crap, you know that. I mean, like, that's like saying the sun's gonna set tonight, you know what I mean? And when she does, you aren't gonna show up tonight and Rita will be after your flabby buns. Not to mention Corky and me."

"Yeah, I figured."

"She's bad news, man. Bad news. Take a cold shower or something, and I'll see you later."

"I guess."

"Besides, I got troubles of my own."

"What?"

"Dreams. I had dreams last night."

"Oh. About Gunnar."

"Yeah. I mean, he's gonna be all right and all, I called the hospital just before, but these dreams, Brian. They're worse than the real thing. I never saw so much blood in my life. God."

"I know, Blue. Believe me, I know."

7

"Mr. Galiano, this is Anita Oakland."

"Mrs. Oakland, good to hear from you. How are you?"

"I've been better, to tell you the truth. I'm sorry to call on a Saturday, but I've just made a decision and I couldn't wait."

"Of course. Sure. So what can I do for you?"

"I'd like to make an appointment to see you next week."

"Well, sure! What's the problem?"

"Well . . . I'd rather talk to you in person, but you can answer me this maybe—how much trouble would I be in if I evicted someone before their lease runs out?"

"That depends on the reasons. And you're right, this is something we should discuss in my office. Tuesday morning? Ten?"

"Fine."

"I'll see you then. And don't forget the copies of your leases with . . . whoever."

"Yes. Of course."

"And say nothing, Mrs. Oakland. No sense stirring up hard feelings before the fact. Who knows? Things may work out."

"Oh no, Mr. Galiano. No, I don't think so."

8

John Naze didn't answer.

He had just been for a long walk.

Now he was hungry.

The telephone could wait.

Thirty-seven

1

The telephone rang.

2

With barely audible grunts and groans of small pleasures, Evan drew his arms from under the covers and stretched slowly, pressed his palms against the headboard and pushed, then rubbed his eyes with one hand while he scratched his chest with the other. Lord, he thought; oh lord, that feels good.

When the telephone rang again in the room behind his head, he closed his eyes and waited for someone to answer. The noise, though muffled and distant, intruded on the peace of mind he had discovered, and nurtured, since awakening what felt like at least an hour ago.

The ringing stopped.

He nodded once—*good riddance*—stretched again, and opened his eyes for the first time. He squinted across the room to the window. Stark slashes of light above and below. The sun was up, long past dawn. But he wasn't about to make the same move. It felt too good still in the twilight room, traffic muffled, a maid's bad-wheeled cart squeaking someplace down the line, Addie in the next bed muttering in her sleep. As his vision adjusted he could see her, little more than a mound of sheet, and there was no guilt. No guilt at all.

Finally, reluctantly, he let himself look at the clock radio, let his eyebrows lift at the time, an hour before noon. Last night he wouldn't have thought he could sleep this long. But last night he was too busy telling Addie stories about Port Richmond, the school, the kids, his uncle, too busy feeling himself believe that he was really home, nothing to fear, nothing to hide from.

In fact, he had almost gone out to speak to Shane, but changed his mind. The boy had been sweeping the pool clear of windblown debris, and hadn't exactly been one of his biggest fans. Not that it bothered him, but he wasn't about to announce his return to someone who probably wouldn't have given much of a damn.

By the time he'd looked again, Shane was gone.

And Addie hooting over American television shows.

I'll never sleep, he had thought; excitement, too much sleep already—it'll never happen.

Addie rolled over, the sheet held to her chin.

But if he wanted to get to the bank, get some money and start the changeover process, he'd better get moving. Then to the real-estate office to find out what had happened to his tenant. Then to Uncle John's.

He sat up, yawned mightily, swung his feet down to the floor.

A knuckle to clear his vision, and he picked up the

telephone receiver, to find out how long until checkout time.

There was no dial tone.

He read the instructions to get the front desk, pressed the button, and heard nothing.

He frowned.

"Hello?" he said cautiously.

Addie opened her eyes. "Hello yourself," she said.

"Very funny," he said, and said again, "Hello? Anyone there?"

"It doesn't work?"

"Nope."

"Tragedy."

He set it back on its cradle, picked it up again, and listened.

Nothing.

Addie moved to the far side of her bed and sat up, facing the window. He stared at her back, wrinkled by wrinkles in the sheets; he watched the way she stretched, gripped her waist and tipped side to side; he winked when she looked over her shoulder and gave him a mock-angry look.

"Is that an American thing?" she said. "You have to keep the phone on your ear five minutes every morning?"

He felt stupid and hung up. "I'm going to take a quick shower, then we have to go."

"Is there time for me?"

He almost suggested a communal affair, just to save a few minutes, but her expression told him this wasn't the time. "Sure."

"Then hurry."

He did, and waited impatiently at the door, outside the door, on each bed in turn, the TV on and off, changing his shirt once. Addie laughed once, once told him he was more like a father waiting for his first child, and finally ordered him into a chair before he drove her nuts.

It was too late for the bank.

The real estate agent, after a great deal of fussing, told him the tenant had skipped out two days ago, dropping the keys off with a thoroughly unsatisfactory and practically incoherent letter of explanation, he could see it later if he wanted; however, as far as she was concerned, Evan could move back immediately. Would he mind if they postponed whatever paperwork there was until Monday, however? She had to make sure her kids were ready for tonight.

He didn't mind.

Addie said nothing. Somewhere in there, papers shuffling and hands fluttering, the woman had called her Mrs. Kendal.

By three, they had done some quick shopping for food and extra clothing; by three-thirty, they had put everything away and opened the windows; by four, Evan had stopped searching the house for the bodies he figured had to be there, or the dope stash, or the press the tenant had used to make his counterfeit money.

"You won't believe it, will you?" Addie said, standing at the living-room window, a cup of coffee in hand.

"What?" He looked around the room yet again. Nothing had changed. The couch against the back wall, bookshelves around the fireplace still filled and overflowing to stacks on the floor, his records all there, the stereo working. "Believe what?"

A small smile. "Luck. You've had a bit of luck."

He shrugged. "Seems odd, though, doesn't it? We need a place to live, I want my house back, and . . ." He spread his arms. "We get it, no questions asked."

A sly smile this time. "You don't believe in coincidence, Evan? A prime ingredient of luck, you know."

374

He opened his mouth, closed it, joined her at the window. "Rupert didn't." Said softly.

"No, he didn't."

The shadow of the house had already reached the curb; a trio of half-size hobos ran through it, carrying plastic pumpkins by their handles.

"Not even dark and they're starting already," he said.

She touched his arm. "Evan, has it ever occurred to you that you think about things too much?"

"Yeah." He watched a crow stalk a gold leaf, peck at it, fly away. "Like right now, I'm thinking it's time you met Uncle John." He nodded, felt suddenly much better. Connections, he decided; first the house, now the people. He wouldn't truly be home otherwise.

On the table beside the couch, the telephone rang.

He jumped.

It rang again.

Addie nudged him. "Go on, it won't bite."

"But nobody knows I'm back," he said in exasperation, crossing the room, picking up the receiver.

A dial tone.

"Great," he muttered, slammed the receiver down.

He turned away, and the telephone rang.

"Clever," Addie said. "Can you do it again?"

"Right." He picked it up. "Hello?"

"Trick or treat," said Paul Burwin. "My trick, your treat."

X

STUNTS

Thirty-eight

1

The air knife-sharp, sharpening the shadows, carrying sounds of children shrieking and calling and ringing doorbells and pounding doors, carrying scents of cooking and leaves and wool scarves and leather jackets; the light fading to faintly gold while the sun grew red as it slipped below the trees; the wind waiting.

It wasn't that cold, but Evan shivered anyway every few paces, hunching his shoulders to drive the shivering away. His jacket, comfortably close to tattered, wool-lined, brown leather, made him larger than he was; Addie in denim, ponytail, cheeks flush from the exertion of keeping up with him as he walked.

"He knows your number," she said. "Evan, for heaven's sake, what did you think—that he thought you were running to Calcutta?"

"I know, I know," he said.

Breath in ghost puffs blowing back into his face.

"But he sounded so *close*."

"Which is exactly what you've told me a hundred times, when you've called."

"Yeah, I know, I know."

They swung around a corner, parted for a Freddy Krueger who was arguing with his date.

"Lovely," Addie said, a glance over her shoulder.

"Sign of the times," he told her. "Only they don't know the boogeyman is real."

She grabbed him, yanked him still. "Damnit, Evan, I won't have this!"

He glared. "Trick or treat, he said. The bastard actually said trick or treat."

"Right. And that was it!" She shook his arm. "You *know* how he is. And the way he is now. There's no way he could have come over. Even bundled like a mummy, they wouldn't have let him on the plane. He was too horrid. Too . . . horrid. He was calling from home, it's just that simple."

Reluctantly: "Yes. I suppose."

"Of course! Now forget it. Don't let it spoil things."

"He's your husband," he snapped, regretted it, winced.

"Was my husband, Evan," she answered stiffly. "Was. My Paul, the old Paul, was gone long ago." Her hand dropped away. "How much farther?"

"A couple of blocks. You really still hungry? You wouldn't want to see John first?"

She waited.

"You're a tough woman, Adelaide," he finally said with a smile.

She didn't smile back. "That's right, you great clot, and don't you forget it."

He put a finger to his temple, inscribing the instructions indelibly on his brain, and thought she would slap him, relaxed when she finally sighed, smiled, and told him that meeting his famous uncle on an empty stomach was not her way. Besides, she admitted as they moved on, she needed a little more time to calm down.

380

He agreed.

And suggested Gilder's Luncheria as their stop of choice. A decent place, he explained, for a quick meal, reasonably cheap, and a good place to kill time. Eavesdropping, not eating, was the primary reason for its existence, an opportunity to find out what was going on in town tonight. Places to avoid.

"Stunts," she said.

"Exactly," he answered. "They'll happen, no question about it. Linholm's edict guaranteed that."

"Nice man."

"No gentleman, for sure. He took credit for whipping the school back into shape, and, god help me, he deserves that much. But the price . . ." He cleared his throat; it sounded like a growl. "There are ways to keep kids in line without destroying their spirit. If he'd concentrated on getting rid of the dead wood on the faculty, brought in people who cared, he would have accomplished the same thing with a lot less bloodshed."

"Yours."

"Mine. For one."

Tyler Avenue. A haze around the streetlamps, around the shop lights, traffic moving slowly.

The Luncheria was nearly empty. No one at the counter save a patrolman having coffee, only two of the booths taken. Evan chose the front one, in order to watch the street. Addie sat beside him, not opposite him.

"You're English," the waitress said in pleasant surprise.

"I am. It's the second revolution. We're taking over."

"Your lips to god's ears," the woman said. "It can't get any worse."

Addie laughed. "I like her."

Evan hadn't recognized her. And even if he had known her, he wouldn't have recognized her, he thought, mentally slapping himself several times to each cheek; he had been too busy sorting through memories, the reasons why he'd left, feeling dormant resentments and possible hatreds vying for position to steamroller his emotions. It wouldn't work. It hadn't before, it wouldn't now, what's done is done and let's get on with the world. It almost sounded right. And he wouldn't have been this way if it hadn't been for damned Paul, calling across an ocean just to make sure he didn't forget.

Bastard.

"If you think about him one more time," Addie not quite whispered, "if I see his name in your eyes just once more tonight, I am moving back to the motel."

He looked at her closely. A promise there? A reckoning?

She smiled softly. "Evan Kendal, you are truly dense, aren't you?"

He made to deny it, puffed his cheeks instead. "Damn right."

"And proud of it?"

"Damn right."

"Well, not to worry. Accommodations will be made."

"Yeah," he said. "I think that's what I'm afraid of."

When their food arrived, she ordered him to eat slowly, for which he was grateful. It allowed him more time to allow Port Richmond to return to him in easy stages, every so often pointing out a hurrying pedestrian he recognized, a car he thought he did, while simultaneously skipping through a dozen stories, none of which he finished unless she ordered him to before he drove her crazy.

The sun set.

Addie demanded dessert.

Tyler Avenue emptied, even though it was Saturday night.

He walked her by the Galaxy, grinning at the costumed

382

line for the triple horror program. Most of the customers were adults, most of them ignoring the little kids and their pillow sacks making their way back from the ticket office, knowing there'd be no candy, hoping for money instead.

At the corner, a teenage girl wearing a yellow-dyed mop wig and coveralls, her face covered with huge green freckles, collided with them as she yelled at a car from which several sarcastic whistles came.

"Hey," Evan said, catching her shoulders, turning her around. "Take it easy."

"Sorry," she blurted, and ran on.

"Lovely," Addie said.

"You think that's good, wait'll you see Uncle John."

2

Sarra Marlow stopped running.

She turned around.

Oh my god, she thought; oh my god, that's Mr. Kendal!

3

"Well," Brian said, "what do you think?"

His grandmother looked up from the kitchen table, blinked several times very slowly, and said, "For this I came all the way from the Bronx?"

"Easy, ma'am," he said in a drawl. "Got itchy trigger fingers here."

She smiled.

He couldn't believe it.

She actually smiled.

"Where did you get that thing?"

He stepped away from the table and performed a model's turn, making sure she saw it all, in all its glory—the snug black cowboy shirt with pearl buttons, glittering studs, silver fringe on the sleeves and across the bottom of the yoke; tight black pants with studs along the seams, tucked into black boots that had a coiled snake tooled in green running from the pointed toe to the top; and a gunbelt with mock bullets, silver six-guns, and fringe on each holster.

The hat was black as well, with a white feather in the beaded band that encircled the crown.

A shame Miss Gough wouldn't see it; she was in New York, some party of her own. Miss Atkins, however, had already promised to be at the church.

"MaryBeth Cross," he said.

"I'll have a word with her."

He laughed, tipped his hat, looked at the clock. "Gotta run."

"Not too late," she called as he headed for the front door. "There's a thing coming tonight. One of those cold fronts. They say lots of wind."

He nearly fell when his left ankle turned. "Damn boots," he said.

"Brian!"

"Sorry."

"Remember what I said—not too late."

"Promise," he called back, paused at the table she'd set by the door and grabbed a handful on tiny chocolate bars.

"And leave the candy alone!" she yelled. "That's for the kids!"

He left, chuckling, almost skipping, wondering what

had changed in the last twenty-four hours that had brought her back to herself. No growls, no snapping, no sitting in the darkened living room by herself. The old Neeba, and he almost turned around, went back in to find out.

"Hey, Tex, c'mon!"

Blue waited on the sidewalk, in his old football uniform minus the helmet; in its stead he wore a seaman's wool cap.

"Coming already, coming."

Boots and cleats on the sidewalk.

The sky grey in moonlight, stars gone in patches as thin clouds sailed over, the moon itself gone and back as the clouds tried to hide it.

"I feel like a jerk," Blue complained on the second block, after yet another group of small children whistled at them and laughed.

"Not my idea," Brian reminded him.

"Yeah." Blue rubbed his nose. "Corky will pay for this, whether the stunt works or not."

"Oh, I don't know. I kind of like it." He drew one gun, blew a pair of ghosts off a lawn. "Besides, we've got to blend in with the party, right? And you can't go to the party without some kind of costume."

Blue rolled his eyes. "Tex, I do believe you done never grown up."

Brian twirled the gun perfectly, dropped it into its holster.

"Exactly what I mean," Blue said.

Another block, shadows of bare trees like skeletons on the street. Laughter, doorbells, *trick or treat* on the breeze that carried apples and pumpkins and cooking cookies as well.

"Did Mickie call?"

"No."

"Good."

He said nothing. Most of the afternoon had been spent with MaryBeth as she finished the costume, made him model it several times before pronouncing herself done. Lucky. Had he stayed home, had he had the time to think, he knew he would have gone over to Palisade Row, knew he would have gotten into that tub, knew . . . he blew, blew again, and decided that he and Mickie Farwood were undoubtedly history. And he couldn't believe he didn't feel worse than he did.

Rita was already on the porch when they arrived, and he held back when Blue trotted up the walk.

He swallowed.

Rita? he thought.

Blue said something to her, and she slapped his cheek, not gently.

Rita?

He supposed she was supposed to be some kind of peasant or gypsy woman, with a bright red, tattered full skirt that almost reached the ground, her hair pulled back with a red scarf, her face begrimed. Around her shoulders she wore an equally tattered dark shawl, but before she gripped it closed across her chest, he saw that her baggy white blouse had a neckline that was raggedly low, saw a shadow that marked the gap between her breasts. When she grinned at him, three teeth had been blacked out, and someone had painted two white scars on her cheeks.

She was beautiful.

"You too can get slugged, Oakland, if you keep staring like that."

He didn't know what to do, what to say, so turned and began walking, forcing the others to catch up.

"Where's Mickie?" she asked.

"I don't know," he said.

386

"Oh."

"A wise man hath been born this eve," Blue proclaimed loudly.

"Shove it, Cross," he said.

She took his arm, made a show of feeling his muscles. "You going to protect me tonight, Tex?" she said. "Keep them bad old bad guys from insulting my virtue?"

Blue giggled.

Brian glared at him, looked down at Rita and reminded himself she was a friend, nothing more. Rita Galiano. Nothing more.

He tugged his hat lower over his eyes.

Rita nudged him with a hip.

They crossed Tyler, and began meeting others on their way to the party. He endured the jokes, had a quick showdown with another cowboy, which he won by what seemed like hours, and prayed that Corky was on time for a change. The guy seemed never to be concerned with time, as if that concept belonged to a universe he only read about in all his science-fiction books. If it weren't for his favorite television shows, he probably wouldn't even know what day it was.

He thought of Mickie when a busty cheerleader ran by, chased by two football players and a corpse. Neeba hadn't said that she'd called, so he assumed she hadn't. Which meant she was either royally pissed and wouldn't talk to him, or she was thoroughly pissed and would chew him in front of the entire room. Which meant, he figured, that June would be there to compete for Best Snotty Remark.

Suddenly he wasn't sure he wanted to go.

"All right, folks, all right," Blue said quietly as they rounded another corner and found themselves on Coolidge Street. "Step right up, the show's about to begin." He tapped Brian's shoulder. "You got the keys, right?"

Brian patted his back pocket. "Yeah."

"Know the plan?"

How could he not? Corky had called the Cross house at least a hundred times with changes, suggestions for changes, and demands that he and Blue repeat the latest change. He stopped when Blue hung up on him twice.

"I forgot my watch," Blue said then. "Damn!"

"Don't worry," Rita said. "I've got one. I'll let you know when it's eight."

At which time they were to leave the party as unobtrusively as possible, lie if they had to, and make their way around to the back of the school, where Brian would open the door and let them in. Corky swore he would have all the props ready, nothing left to chance. They would be in and out in less than half an hour, just about the time the first party guests would be leaving for other places. Back to the party, then, and a few words here and there to spark curiosity. A call, too, to the local newspaper Corky also swore he would make.

"What can it hurt?" he'd asked when Rita had objected. "They send someone, they don't, no big deal."

Linholm they hadn't decided upon, and had finally decided to leave it to the last minute, a spur of the moment call or not at all.

Corky waited on the sidewalk in front of the parish hall.

"Damnit, Ploughman, you just can't help screwing up, can you?" Blue said. "In case you forgot, you were supposed to have a costume!"

Corky wore a three-piece suit, a club tie, and a folded topcoat slung over one shoulder. "I am," he said. "I'm going as a lawyer."

"Well, it's for sure no one will recognize you in that

getup," Brian said. He looked across the wide lawn to the well-lighted building, looked over his shoulder at the school across the street. His stomach jumped. His throat dried. "Hell," he said, "let's get it done."

4

Greta, her coat on, her hair covered by a tartan beret, stared in disbelief at the wall over the telephone.

"What do you mean, you're grounded?"

Shane sounded as if he were calling up to her from the bottom of an empty well. "She found the gun in my room."

"The gun?"

"Yeah."

"Damnit, Shane, what gun?"

"Hey, don't shout, okay? I'll tell you about it later."

"Damn right you will," she said. "I'm coming over."

"No!"

She hung up, kicked the air, punched the wall, and left the house without saying goodbye to anyone.

A gun.

Wonderful.

Everything ruined because Shane—

What was he, crazy? What the hell was he doing with a gun?

5

John stood in front of the bathroom mirror and buttoned his coat for the second time that day. His reflection was distorted, fractured, and though he tried to remember how the glass had broken, he couldn't. It looked as if something had hit it square in the middle, something thrown, maybe a fist.

He looked at one hand, flexed it, saw bone and vein beneath the milky skin.

Nothing there. No cuts or scratches.

The other hand was the same.

It didn't matter.

He picked his hat up from the counter and put it on, brushed hair and pale flecks from his shoulders, and smiled at his face smiling crookedly back.

First the afternoon walk, now the evening reward.

Someone knocked on the door.

Goddamn kids.

Trick or treat.

He strode into the front room, kicked bits of bone and fur aside as he crossed the red-stiff carpet.

Another knock.

He pulled the door open.

Neeba Oakland on the landing, fist up to knock again.

"What the hell do you want?"

Her jaw trembled and she backed away.

"Well?"

He snorted and stepped outside, closed his eyes against the gentle cold, the sharp night, opened them again and leaned forward, sweeping off his hat because the old bitch was, after all, a goddamn lady.

"What the hell do you want?"

Neeba turned to run, and he slapped her shoulder, watched without moving when she spun, caught the back railing, flailed to grab something and grabbed his bare hand.

She screamed hoarsely.

He released her with a push he didn't feel.

When she fell, not a sound, not a cry, he turned

around and closed the door, kicked it because he wanted to, and made his way down the stairs. At the bottom he looked over his shoulder and saw her on the grass. A dark mound in darker shadow. It wouldn't do. Not at all. He rolled her under the stairs and behind the garbage cans with virtually no effort at all. When he returned to the driveway, he couldn't see her, not a sign.

He sniffed, and smelled blood.

He licked his lips.

He decided to run; it would cover more ground.

6

Standing at the end of Forest Road, Evan felt suddenly nervous, and was glad that he sensed the same in Addie. It was silly, of course. It wasn't as if they were looking for a blessing or approval; they were simply going to meet the only family he had left, and perhaps a few of his friends, if anyone was home.

Silly.

He took her hand and crossed the street.

"I feel like a schoolgirl," she said.

"I know. And it's only Uncle John."

"That's the problem. If it were your parents, I'd know that this was the way I should feel. But you've spoken so often about him that I'm beginning to think he's your father."

He nodded understanding, squeezed her hand quickly, and hesitated when they reached the house. The lights were on, at least one on every floor. Two houses up, a gaggle of children poured from a station wagon and ran up a walk; across the street and down, several pirates and a princess rooted through their bags. Rock music from a stereo. An airhorn on the distant highway.

He pointed at the garage; the windows were dark.

"That's where John lives, but let's check Neeba first. She'd be insulted, probably cut my heart out."

Addie said, "It's your show," and followed him as he turned into the driveway, staring at the house and wondering why he had expected it to look so different. It hadn't been that long, less than a year, yet it was as if no time at all had passed. An afternoon. No more than a week. But something ought to have changed. Even if it was something small.

Crazy, he thought, and took the steps to the porch, rang the bell, and waited.

"A lovely house," Addie said.

"Yes. She keeps it up. A fanatic sometimes, you know?"

Addie nodded.

He rang again. "Damn, I wonder if she's out?"

"Could be."

He looked up, leaned over and tried to look in the window. "Well, hell." A disappointed shrug before he led her back to the walk, over to the garage where he shook his head at the dark light over the door. "Must've burned out. She always keeps that thing on, John's always bitching that it shines in his bedroom, keeps him from sleeping."

"Does it?"

He started up the stairs. "His bedroom's in the back. He just likes to complain." A look toward the backyard. "He likes to play the part of being an old man, you know what I mean? I think it's the thrill of watching other people wonder if he's gone senile or something."

He knocked.

Addie leaned back against the railing, staring at the sky.

392

He knocked again. "John?"

"Evan."

"Damn," he said. "Hey, John, open up!"

Addie stood beside him, held his arm. "Evan, do you smell something?"

"What?" His fist against the wood, frustrated. "John, it's Evan!"

Addie grabbed his wrist. "Evan, try the door."

He would have argued but for the tension in her voice and, as he tried to read her expression in the moonlit dark, a smell that made his nostrils flare.

The door was unlocked.

"God!" he said even as he stepped across the threshold. "Jesus, what the hell?"

Decay. Rot. And over it all, blood fresh and blood old.

His right hand flicked the wall switch up, and a lamp in the far corner sputtered on, remained dim.

"Oh, Evan," Addie said quietly.

Dried blood on the walls, handprints and blotches; an overturned table, the rocking chair by the window, the two-cushion couch pulled away from the baseboard, its back torn, stuffing spilling; on the floor, all over the floor, scattered and in piles, decomposing bodies of small animals, dark and stiff strips of fur, bones, tiny teeth, half a skull. Beside the rocking chair, the head and tail of a red squirrel connected by a naked spine.

Holding his hand over his mouth, Evan stumbled into the bedroom and gasped at more of the same, except that the bed was perfectly clean and made. In the bathroom the mirror had been shattered, the tub half-filled with brown water, in the basin and on the counter clumps of hair and pieces of dead skin.

Paul, he thought, and swallowed panic, choked on bile.

Finally he could stand it no longer and used the walls to propel him out to the landing. He leaned over, waiting

393

to vomit, swallowing air, gulping air, while Addie took several steps down and sat heavily, rubbing her arms.

"He ate them," she said to the street. "Dear god, Evan, he ate them."

"It's not. . . ?"

"Not that I can tell, no. It's not his blood, it's theirs."

"Hey, Mister, trick or treat?" a skeleton called from the sidewalk.

"Sorry, just visiting," he called back, amazed that he could do it without screaming. Then he pushed himself down the stairs. "The house," he said, and ran across the lawn to the back porch, knocked only once before trying the door.

It was open.

"Neeba," he called, nearly falling into the kitchen. "Brian! Shirley!" A breath. "Lyanna, are you here?"

No one answered.

"Upstairs," Addie said, pushing him from behind. "I'll do down here."

He nodded and ran, stairs two at a time, hurtling into rooms, slamming open closed doors. But he found no one, and nothing of the macabre scene he'd discovered at John's. By the time he returned downstairs, Addie had just finished looking through the basement. The house was empty.

"I don't get it," he said, standing in the middle of the living room. "Damn, I don't get it." He looked at her, praying for an answer. "It was like . . . in his bathroom, it was like Paul had been there."

"No," she said.

He brushed past her and flung open the front door, let it bang against the wall. "Where is he?" he demanded. "Damnit, Addie, where is he, what's going on?"

Brakes harsh and loud, followed almost immediately by the slow sound of a crash had him off the stoop and running, Addie only a step behind. At the corner they turned right, toward a woman kneeling on the sidewalk, a child clutched in her embrace, while an automobile steamed and hissed, lifted off the ground against a tree, its hood up, front wheels still spinning. Beyond, in the middle of the street, two men struggled until one of them abruptly sat down and held his head.

To the woman Addie said, "I'm a doctor, is she all right?"

The woman nodded shakily; the little girl, face damp with tears, stared over her mother's shoulder at the damaged car.

Evan walked into the street. "What happened?"

Doors opened, people murmuring.

The first man glared at the one still seated, now clutching his head. "Drunk as a goddamn skunk," he said. "Son of a bitch damn near hit my daughter."

"Didn't," the driver said drunkenly. "Hit the tree."

The father raised a fist, dropped it. "The hell with it. He ain't worth it."

"Guy ran out in front of me," the driver said, looking up, a nasty cut bleeding from his forehead.

"Right," the first man said, looking up and down the street. "What guy?"

"I don't know. Some guy. Coat and hat. Ran out in front of me. Made me hit the tree."

Evan walked away and stood at the curb with hands in his jacket pockets. Addie had the little girl giggling shyly, the mother smiling, then straightening when a siren and blue flashing lights pulled onto the block. She backed away down the sidewalk. Evan joined her, took her arm.

"Did you hear?" he asked.

"He was yelling. Of course I heard."

Checking the shadows, peering ahead, moving so fast he was almost at a trot.

"Evan."

"It's the same."

"For heaven's sake, Ev, it was an accident. A drunk."

"And a man in a hat and coat who runs out of nowhere on an empty street." He kicked at a shadow. "A million dollars says he touched the car."

"Stop it, Evan, you're scaring me."

Noise rose and fell behind them as an ambulance joined the patrol car. No one called after them; they had already been forgotten. Evan looked and saw the drunk still sitting in the street, the little girl's father standing over him, gesturing angrily as a cop tried to calm him.

The second block was empty, no trick-or-treaters, no cars, no one in doors or windows.

"Halloween," he said as they entered the third block, ducking under a low branch, batting aside another. "Lord, Addie, kids all over the damn place. Teenagers in cars, little kids running around . . . my god."

"Evan!"

He couldn't help it. She hadn't spent time with Paul as he had; she hadn't talked with him as he had; she hadn't smelled him, seen his disintegration physical and mental. She may believe Paul had some power, else why had she run, but she didn't really know what it was like to see it firsthand, and see Paul.

Paul. Who was in England.

And Uncle John, who was here.

He shook his head; it wasn't right, it couldn't be right, there couldn't be two of them prowling at the same time, two of them touched by the shadow of the wolf.

There couldn't be.

Accidents happen, something told him.

Sure they do.

People die.

Sure they do.

Two of them?

He turned to Addie, to tell her she had to say something before he drove himself crazy. He didn't. Her eyes were filled with tears.

"Addie."

She lifted her chin. "Look."

On the sidewalk, just beyond the pale fall of a light fifty yards away, stood a dark figure in topcoat and hat. Watching them.

He thought *Paul*, and then thought *Uncle John*, and then told himself to knock it off before they came to take him away.

He kept walking; Addie stopped.

Closer, and the streetlight picked up highlights on the figure's coat, whitened the shoulders, cast a shadow over the face.

"John?" he said, voice slightly high and disbelieving.

"Be damned," the figure answered. "Be damned, it is you. I thought it was."

Evan picked up speed, his stomach hollow. "Jesus, Uncle John, I thought—"

"What the hell you doing home?"

"Nice to see you too, Uncle."

The light shifted as John raised his head, let the shadow fall away.

Evan stopped, nearly falling sideways as he did.

It was Paul. It was John. The only difference, in the eyes.

"Never called," John said, turning slowly, moving back. "What the hell's so great over there you never call?"

"Uncle John—"

"Damn woman is driving me nuts, Evan, is what I wanted to tell you, but you never bothered to call. You didn't give a damn. Wants to marry me, y'know, same as

397

killing me. I hate her. Always following me around, trying to suck me dry, make me weak, put me in some miserable home where I can watch the old men die. Hate her, Evan. Damn, I hate that bitch."

Evan couldn't move.

He had heard this all before.

"Sitting all alone at my place, y'know, minding my own business. Sitting all alone until them goddamn kids come along, I hate them too, I never did like that Brian, he was always too damn good, always helping that old bitch like he was sucking up to her, like she sucks up to me."

Fading into the dark between the falls of light.

"Night's not too bad these days, you understand me, nephew? Not all that bad. I like to walk daytimes too. Did. Today. Pretty day, lots of sun. But tonight is better. Tonight I look like them. What a hell of a thing, don't you think? All these years, I end up looking like them. Sunny today, cloudy tonight. Sometimes, you know, you can have fun just watching. I think so. Gonna try. Damn bitch. You never called. Damn me, nephew, but you never called."

Evan felt himself weeping, and didn't try to stop.

"Damn kids," John said, a little louder. And a laugh. "Trick or treat, Evan. God damn, they're gonna pay."

He ran.

Automatically, Evan started after him, but the air wouldn't fill his lungs, his legs wouldn't move the way they were supposed to, and the old man vanished around a corner long before Evan reached it.

The street was empty.

Too many shadows.

Fists pressed to the side of his head as he forced calm to return, forced himself to think, forced himself not to scream when Addie's arm slipped around his waist.

"You won't believe it," he said dully.

"I saw."

"Nightmares are supposed to end."

"Yes," she said, "and right now you're thinking that we have to do something before someone really gets hurt."

He nodded.

"And what will be different this time, Evan, if we try? Use your head, love. Who will believe us here when they didn't believe us back home?"

No one.

Sergeant Ludden lived all over the world.

All right, then. All right.

"C'mon," he said, taking her arm, turning her around.

"What? Where?"

"Home. To get the car. Then to find Uncle John."

"And?"

He looked at her, hard, and wasn't pleased to see her look away.

7

Patrick Reynolds slapped Pastori's shoulder so hard he turned the boy around. "What the *fuck* are you doing with that?" he demanded in a furious whisper.

Dom looked innocently at the gun case in his hand. "This?"

Patrick groaned. "You are an asshole."

The back of the school was dark. Dom had already taken care of the three lights that kept the rear wall lit for cruisers on their patrol.

"And where the hell is Mickie?"

"Y'know," Dom said, settling himself on the ground, "for a rich guy, you really are stupid, you know that? She'll be here, don't sweat it."

"Right."

"Pass me a beer."

"I didn't bring any," Patrick said, then reached into his knapsack and pulled out a bottle. "It was supposed to be for a celebration."

Dom grabbed it, held it up to the moonlight. "All right! Champagne! Reynolds, you are a genius."

"You just said I was stupid."

"Only sometimes. You got glasses?"

Patrick looked at him in disgust.

Dom shrugged. "What the hell, we'll slum."

Then he popped the cork and drank until he couldn't swallow anymore, handed the bottle to his friend, and cradled the rifle to his chest.

A firecracker exploded somewhere in the dark.

Thirty-nine

1

Brian leaned against the wall near the entrance, arms folded across his chest, hat low over his eyes. He felt like a jerk. Blue was out there somewhere, and Rita had decided to get something to drink from one of the six long tables of food ranged against the far wall. He figured more than a hundred people in here right now, and more coming in all the time. Miss Atkins, looking like she was a hundred years old in a black cape and witch's hat, sat by the door, accepting donations. To his right, at the other end of the room at least fifty feet on a side, a low platform doubled as a stage for a rock band who had evidently been ordered to keep the volume down to deafening; to his left, two dozen or so round tables for the adults to use when they tired of trying to keep tabs on their children.

Dozens of them.

Running around, playing tag, ducking in and out of the dancers, raiding the refreshments, only occasionally obeying orders to keep it all to a dull roar.

Orange and black streamers; Halloween clichés taped to the brick walls; orange and black balloons; beyond the tables, bobbing for apples and pin-the-tail-on-the-don-key; chatter, music, laughter, the scrape of chairs, lifting to the bare iron-rafter ceiling but not escaping through the windows that cranked inward to admit the night air. The dancing was relatively sedate, for the parents, though those nearest the bandstand were mostly hidden, and having the most fun.

The costumes were diverse, some elaborate, most simple, the masks more often than not worn up over the brow instead of the eyes.

It was warm, and he knew it would be hot before the evening had ended.

But at least June wouldn't be here; Blue had found out that much soon after they came in.

Corky eased up to him, topcoat still on his shoulder. "On my way," he said, not bothering to whisper. "Five minutes, okay?"

Brian nodded.

Corky patted his back and moved away, toward the band, toward the red exit sign glowing in the corner, behind a speaker almost as tall as he.

Five minutes.

He wiped his palms on his pants.

Five minutes.

He touched his back pocket to be sure the keys were there.

Rita returned with a paper cup filled with red punch. He drank it all in a gulp, and grimaced.

"You said it," she agreed.

"Corky said five minutes."

She nodded. "Blue's already gone."

"What?" He looked around. "I didn't see him."

"That's the whole idea, dope."

A scarecrow bumped into her, and Brian grabbed her waist to stop her from falling.

"My hero," she said, clamping a hand to one of his to keep it where it was.

402

"Nothing to it."

They listened to the music, watched the minister—in a devil's costume—laughingly stalk the dancers with a rubber pitchfork, and finally headed for Corky's exit. It was easy. All they had to do was dance in that direction, not bothering to stay together as long as they kept moving. He lost her midway there; when he spotted another cowboy in hot pink and brilliant blue, he didn't feel quite so bad; when a harem girl gave him a gentle hip and a wink and definite look at her gauzy cleavage, he felt even better.

When a soft hand snaked around from behind and rested against his stomach, he turned with a smile, lost it and said, "Jesus, Mickie!"

She wore a Daisy Mae costume, the shorts high, the ragged blouse low, her midriff gleaming with perspiration. Her hair had been tightly curled, freckles painted on her cheeks, and in her teeth a long weed stalk she flicked at his nose.

"You didn't come," she pouted, not letting him go.

"Couldn't. I told you. Sorry."

"That's okay." Closer still. "Did you bring them?"

"Jeez, Mickie, c'mon, huh?"

Her hand brushed across his buttocks, and suddenly she grinned. "You did!" Kissed him. Hard. He felt her tongue and froze, eyes trying not to widen when she pulled away and winked. "What're you waiting for?"

"Mickie, look, I've got something to tell—"

She grabbed his hand. "It's okay, okay? Don't worry." She winked again.

He wished then he had worn something else, something less conspicuous—a hobo, a clown, something that would have matched a dozen other people; he just knew everyone was watching, following them and smirking as they threaded around and through couples and groups, stood for a moment by the speaker, wincing at the blare, then ducked around it and through the door.

The night was colder than he remembered.

"Brian," she said.

There were shrubs here, the trees, and he decided there was nothing he could do. Too late. She would have to come, and swear to keep her mouth shut.

They hurried without running, keeping as much as they could to the shadows, waiting near the end of a hedgewall until a van unloaded noisily, a sickly sweet smell released to the dark until the breeze took it away.

He checked the school nervously; the front lights were out, the lawn dark, the building darker.

With a series of gestures he told her to follow him, do nothing else, and put his arm around her waist and started walking down the street. She nestled her head against his arm, her own hand on the small of his back. Rubbing. Pinching lightly. Until he suddenly broke into a run, grabbing her hand to pull her along, crossing the street, squeezing through a narrow gap between the evergreens and the fence.

He didn't think about being spotted.

He only ran.

Until the school was alongside him, drawing him into its shadow.

Then he walked to the corner and made the turn.

"Brian," she whispered.

"Hang on," he said.

He could see Corky, Blue, and Rita waiting at the far door. At least he hoped it was them and not a police squad waiting to take him away. Or worse—the Führer and some teachers. He'd rather go to jail.

"Brian!"

"Be quiet," he snapped, and yanked her hand, trotted up to the others and nearly pushed Mickie at them. He said nothing, only gave them all a look that dared them to challenge, then took out the keys. "I was the last one out this morning," he said. "There's no chain, unless someone came in this afternoon."

No one said a word until Blue said, "Alarms?"

"No," Brian told him. The damn key wouldn't fit. "You should read the paper, learn . . . damn! . . . about budgets. Damn, this goddamn—"

The door opened.

"Outstanding," Corky said, relief and nerves giving a quaver to his voice. He and Blue hefted a large and clumsy bundle wrapped in a tarp and slipped inside. "Twenty minutes," he called softly back. "Let's go, c'mon."

"Linholm," Brian said.

"No sweat," Corky said. "Pay phone in the parish hall." He grinned. "God loves me."

Rita groaned and went in.

Brian followed, held the door open, but Mickie didn't move. "C'mon!" he said. Sweat ran along his sides. He felt one of his knees giving way.

Mickie shook her head. "I changed my mind. I'm . . . I'm scared."

"Oh, for Christ's sake!"

"Go ahead," she said, stepping to him, scratching him quickly behind the ear. "I'll be your guard."

"Brian!" It was Rita.

He heard the hall door open at the top of the stairs, the squeal of the hinges loud enough to wake the dead.

Mickie kissed him on the cheek. "Hurry, Bri," she whispered, and pushed at the door until he backed away, saw her fade to shadow, and swore as he turned and ran to catch up with the others.

Rita waited for him, matched him stride for stride as he stormed toward the front office.

405

"Bitch," he said, teeth clenched. "Goddamn bitch's gonna get us all fried."

"I'll kill her if you want."

He looked at her, barely saw her, and realized that he'd forgotten to bring a flashlight. "Tell you the truth, I don't care."

"I know," she said, grabbed a fistful of shirt and yanked his face down so she could kiss him.

It took him no longer than to taste her before he kissed her back, holding her, his hat slipping and falling, rolling into the dark.

"Wow," she said when they parted.

"Stunt," he said.

She punched him in the chest.

"Jesus!"

And took his hand, yanked, practically dragged him the rest of the way to the front hall.

He didn't have to ask how Corky planned to get into Linholm's office—the cardboard taped across the shattered plate glass had been peeled away, and the inner door already unlocked. The dim glow from the street made him duck instinctively behind the counter, Rita crouching beside him. A thin beam of light in Linholm's office, and Blue cursing, a chair scraping loudly.

Brian rose, peeked over the top.

The blinds here were halfway up, and he could see people moving toward the parish hall, a few standing on the lawn, a few more already leaving. Black ghosts. No faces. All the doors were open now, all the high windows, and all he could hear of the music was the steady rhythm of the drums.

"Hey!" Corky whispered from the doorway, and Brian dropped so hard he clipped his chin on the counter. Tasted blood. Saw stars and a bright red light. Came to his feet in a rush, his hands out for Ploughman's throat.

406

Rita stopped him, Corky laughed and backed away. "C'mon, Oakland, help that idiot set up the lights."

He didn't think after that, simply did what Blue told him while Rita stayed in the outer office and kept watch over the street.

No sound then but their grunting, the scrape of the desk, the thud of a chair against the wall; no light but the penlight, propped on a bookshelf and aimed diagonally across the room; no smell but his own sweat, and wood polish, and something else, something dead, he couldn't identify it and didn't want to.

A chair heaved to the desktop.

The mannequin fell over twice until Blue rummaged through the desk, found some oversize rubber bands and used them to tie her down.

The worst part, the most dangerous, was nailing tall plywood posts to the sides of the desk; they would hold a crosspiece to which the valentine had been taped. If it worked. Otherwise, they would have to tape it to the window.

Corky took two hammers and some nails from the unrolled tarp. "We gotta do this fast, guys," he said, taking several deep breaths. "It doesn't have to be perfect, just right. Brian, go tell Rita not to shit when she hears the noise."

"I can hear it already," she said, poking her head in. "You guys would make lousy spies. Hurry up. They're starting to leave."

Oh shit, Brian thought.

Blue took a hammer, some nails, stood by the desk.

"Just a few whacks," Corky said. "Just as long as it stays up."

"Hurry up!" Rita said.

It was deafening, and Brian cringed as he helped Blue hold the thin post up, keeping it straight, standing back, moving over to help Corky. When it was done, he jumped onto the desk and maneuvered the crosspiece into place, straightened the crown Corky had made for Miss McCarthy, then suddenly grinned and kissed her wooden cheek.

"Come *on*!" Rita urged.

Corky snatched the penlight and shined it on his watch. "So far so good, boys and girls. Now we test the lights."

"Jesus, Corky!" Blue protested.

Brian raised his fists, shook them, let them fall.

"No choice," Corky explained. "Just a quick on and off. Okay, get over there, Blue. When I turn them on, let me know." He frowned. "No, someone has to go outside."

"Crap," Brian said.

"Guys!" Rita warned.

"All right, all right." Corky appealed to them, arms wide. "It's the only way, right? We don't raise the blinds, we just open them a little, a quick flick and it's done." He jerked his thumb. "Get moving, Blue."

"Me? Why the hell me?"

"Because you can run faster, that's why. Move! You only got a couple of minutes."

"Aw shit," Blue muttered, but he ran anyway.

"Brian," Corky said gleefully, "we are about to make history."

2

"Bang!" Greta said when Shane showed her the gun. "You freaking asshole."

"Yeah," he said glumly. "I guess she thought I was going to kill myself or something."

Shivering in her too-thin sweater, she nodded toward the garage. "Well . . . I don't suppose . . ."

He shook his head. "No way. It's too late."

She didn't look back. "How long?"

"Couple of hours."

"That's still before midnight."

"Yeah, but everybody'll be gone."

Shit, she thought.

When she did look back, he had the barrel aimed at his temple.

"Bang," he said, smiling sadly. "Bishop's screwed up again."

3

Dom loved it on the roof. It was like being in some incredible steel jungle, ducts and housings all shapes, all sizes, larger in the dark, silent now that the building was empty. One of the first things he had done as a freshman was find out how the repairmen got up here. And once that had been learned—up a retractable ladder in a storeroom at the school's back—he tried to get here once a week. On weekends he used a ladder, when a Redcoat team wasn't playing at home.

Though the houses down the block, the church across the way, were all taller, he still felt bigger. More powerful. The secret of invisibility—nobody's up here because nobody thinks there will be. They don't look, they don't see, and Dominic Pastori is the Invisible Man.

He sat crosslegged in the middle of the central roof, rifle at his side, wire and pliers and a screwdriver before him. Off to the left, near the auditorium, Reynolds

409

should be just about finished placing the last speaker, if he doesn't screw up again. There were six of them—one at either corner, one each in the center front and rear. The wires were black and kept low, commonly attached at the cassette player he was ready to lower into the rearmost air-conditioning duct.

Mickie squatted awkwardly beside him, exaggerating her shivering, moaning under her breath.

Music from the parish hall kept him humming to himself.

The moon crept behind a thin cloud.

The breeze kicked up.

The temperature began to drop.

"I'm cold," she complained.

"Then you should've brought a coat, dope."

"I didn't think I was going to have to climb mountains. Why the hell didn't you bring a ladder?" She rubbed a scrape on her right arm. "I could've killed myself getting through that little hole."

"You didn't have to come," he said calmly. No sense in getting mad at her. She had saved him the trouble of doing just that—bringing a ladder that would have to be left behind, and possibly traceable. Nothing else was. Reynolds had driven them down to the Paramus Mall, the Garden State Mall, and out to the Willowbrook Mall two days ago. There, they'd purchased the wire, the bookshelf-size speakers, and the player. None of them were in any store at the same time. Dom wore his suit, Reynolds was in leather, Mickie had frumped herself up with fake glasses and a dress only someone like Greta Rourke would dare wear in public.

Tonight, he and Reynolds wore gloves.

Mickie hadn't touched a thing.

"I don't see how it's going to work," she said, easing closer, less than an inch away.

It would, he promised her silently.

And in keeping that promise, knew that he wasn't going to let her renege on hers. An evening in the hot tub. Alone. With her. No holds barred, and nothing less than champagne. She'd done it because dork Oakland had chickened out on a stunt. Until tonight. But that didn't matter. He didn't care what they were doing down there. Whatever it was, if Ploughman was involved, it would be something less than spectacular. But Mickie had done her part—she had caught the door before it had closed and locked.

In. Up. Half an hour, tops, to set everything straight.

A footfall, barely heard above the music.

Reynolds dropped beside him. "Done."

Dom grinned, slapped once, silently. "All right. All right! Now it begins."

From his jacket's breast pocket he pulled a cassette, slipped it into the player. Using Patrick's penlight, he made sure the speaker connections were still solid. A nod. He sniffed, rubbed his nose with a sleeve.

Mickie was right; it was goddamn cold up here.

"There's a five-minute blank lead," he said, uncrossing his legs and lifting to a crouch. "That means—"

"I know what it means," Patrick said. "But I still want to know what you're gonna do with that gun."

Dom grinned, showing his teeth. "We have to get their attention, right?" He handed the player to Mickie, picked up the rifle and held it against his chest. "This will do it."

Patrick snapped a finger against the scope screwed onto the top. "If you're only going to shoot a few blanks into the air, why do you need this?"

"Jesus, Reynolds, it's just part of the equipment."

"Dom?"

He looked at the girl, telling himself that patience was a valuable asset right now. "What now?"

"How do we get down? You closed the trapdoor."

"Jump," said Patrick.

Her eyes widened. "You didn't tell me that!"

"Don't worry, I'll catch you."

"Dom, he can't do that."

She shivered violently.

A look to Reynolds, who only shrugged—*she wasn't my idea, pal*—and he stripped off his jacket, caped it around her shoulders. "Don't worry," he told her. "It isn't like you're falling off a cliff. You just hang onto the side, push off a little, and let go. Patrick will catch you, and you guys run like hell."

"What about you?"

"Me?" He drew back as if insulted. "Hey, you're talking major-league fullback here, lady. I do my thing and I'm gone off the other side. I'll meet you back at Patrick's place." A slow leering wink. "Then we'll have a party."

"The rifle," Patrick said.

Dom's face hardened. "You just do what you have to, buddy, and don't worry about it."

"Right." Sourly.

Slowly they moved to the rear of the building, Mickie guiding the wires to keep them from snagging. At the chosen duct, a gooseneck, Dom removed the mesh covering and concealed it between two bulky housings a few feet away. He tied a rope to the player's handle, tied the other end around the duct's base.

"My friends," he said then, "we are about to make history."

Patrick cheered silently; Mickie smiled, but her eyes were doubtful.

"We are about to commit the first ever high-school hijacking, all thanks to the miracle of electronics, and a few measly hundred of Mr. Reynolds' hard-earned dollars."

Patrick bowed, and giggled.

412

Mickie licked her lips.

Dom hefted the player. And hesitated.

He wasn't worried that it wouldn't drive the speakers; he had tested the rig a dozen times.

He wasn't concerned about the tape; he and Patrick had recorded over two dozen of them, disguising their voices, using a stopwatch to time the gaps, the messages, and the announcement at the end—should the stunt last that long—that Port Richmond could relax, their precious school was safe, happy Halloween, trick or treat, fuck you, Eric Linholm.

Everything was cool.

Barring a miracle—Linholm descending upon them from an invisible helicopter—it would work like a charm.

But what if one of them was caught?

He had a good feeling about Mickie—not nearly as dumb as she sometimes made herself out to be; he knew he could pull it off, just play the confused but arrogant teen who also happened to be a Redcoat football star; but Patrick was something else. A puzzle. A friend for what seemed like forever, and the cruelest bastard he'd ever met in his life. His problem was that he thought too damn much, kept looking for snags and catches. Thinking, now, would get them in trouble. And if the cops got him, Dom didn't know which would be more important—he and Mickie, or the precious Reynolds name.

"My leg's going to sleep," Patrick said.

Dom glared.

Patrick gave him a sharp Nazi salute.

"Five minutes," Dom reminded them.

A deep breath. A second one.

Mickie suddenly leaned over and kissed him solidly on the cheek, blew warmly into his ear, pinched his thigh.

Right, he said, and lowered the player inside, nodding when it stopped just beyond the bend. Then he reached in, grunted, and found the "on" button, scored with a file so he could recognize it by touch.

"Ready?"

"Go, man," Patrick whispered.

He pushed it.

They ran.

He watched them for a second, reached down and felt the player, felt the faint vibration that told him it was working. Then he sprinted to the front and grabbed up the rifle, lay down so that he could just see over the low brick lip.

He chambered a round.

He fit his eye against the scope.

4

A sigh of disgust and defeat, and Evan pulled over to the curb, stopped, let his forehead rest against the steering-wheel rim. He felt Addie stir beside him, felt the car tremble slightly at a gust that sprayed the hood with leaves. He didn't bother to check his watch, or the clock in the dashboard. It didn't matter. Whatever time it was, it was too late, and had been the moment he'd seen his uncle's face.

Paul's face.

His hands became fists in his lap. They pressed down, hard.

"Crazy," he muttered. "This is crazy."

Port Richmond. Easily ten times the population of Bettin Wells, easily four times the physical size. How the hell did he expect to find one lousy man in all these shadows when the man was virtually a shadow himself.

Where did he look? Where did he begin? Driving around blindly as he had been only exacerbated his frustration until his jaw ached from being clenched so tightly, his stomach stabbed from bubbling up so much acid, his eyes watered from staring at everything that moved, everything that didn't.

"Tell me again," Addie said quietly.

"I—"

"Tell me, Evan."

He did. Every word he could remember that John said to him, seeing the old man, a ghost in the windshield, and knowing on the verge of faith that there was something else. Not in the words. In the presence. In the deeds. Something he had figured wrong when he'd tried to figure Paul.

"He went out today," she said thoughtfully.

He sat back and nodded.

"If he went out . . ."

"I know. But it's a big town, in case you hadn't noticed." And smiled at her when she smiled at the echo of her own words spoken so many years ago.

"He hates the kids."

"He never did."

"He did something. Paul and the cab, remember?"

His mouth opened.

A car drove at them, past them, headlamps momentarily blinding him. White light. Too bright.

"Dear Jesus," he whispered. Prayed. "Dear Jesus."

"What? Are you all right?"

He released the parking brake and made a swift U-turn that squealed the tires and bumped them over the other curb, just missing a tree.

"I was wrong," he said, a hand over his face to wipe away cold sweat. "Paul told me to think about the cab. I

415

did. I wondered why . . . I wondered why he wanted to kill that poor woman, the one crushed in the accident."

He ran through a stop sign.

"I thought he wanted to prove he could kill me whenever he wanted to. An object lesson. I thought he wanted to teach me that I couldn't escape, no matter how I tried."

Addie was puzzled, said so. "And?"

He shot across Tyler Avenue and turned right at the next corner. "He wasn't trying to kill that woman, Addie. Not that woman in particular."

Her frown deepened. "Evan, I'm sorry, but—"

He inhaled, held it, let the breath go. "Rupert Flaunter."

"Evan, please! What's the point?"

He felt cold. Very cold.

"That is the point, Addie. The whole point is that there is none. No point. No direction. No focus." He hummed a few bars of the Loch Mairen ballad. "You were right all along, Rupert was wrong. Paul, and John, are the hunters in that damnable song. But not the way we think of a hunter. Not someone who deliberately goes out to kill something. Someone. The poor guy who saw the wolf wasn't a hunter when his village began to die. He was just there. He didn't have to touch anything to cause harm. He was just . . . there."

Her hands clasped tightly in her lap.

"A pebble that creates a ripple," he said. "A shadow that disrupts the sun." His eyes closed, opened. "They don't have to do anything. They just have to *be*."

A large dog ran out in front of them, barking furiously as the car missed it by several feet.

"Slow down, Evan."

"I can't. John was out today. Why? Because one of the biggest town parties of the year is tonight. The Methodist Church hall. Kids. Most every kid in town will show up for at least a few minutes."

416

"And he's going to kill them?"

"He already has."

Coolidge Street; the curbs began to fill with parked cars. Evan grabbed the first space he saw, was out of the car before the engine stopped its ticking. He grabbed Addie's hand and began running toward the church, still two blocks away.

He could feel her fear because it matched his own, could sense her confusion because he hadn't been able to articulate what he knew. On faith. Like Rupert, who believed that all was as God had planned. Like Addie, who believed nothing was planned at all.

They were both wrong.

Every accident was stirred by the presence of the hunter, brought to life, a Frankenstein monster in manifold disguise.

The victims were unimportant.

There was no reason why this one lived and this one was injured and that one died.

No reason at all.

No point.

They just did.

No reason.

It was all on a whim, the whim of the hunter.

In gasps, between pants, he told her this, tried to tell her, and saw the fear turn to horror, the horror to disbelief, the disbelief lingering while the horror returned.

A block away he had to slow down to a brisk walk, his face running sweat, back, chest, between his legs. Colder than the night.

"Then there's nothing we can do to save them," she said without emotion.

"No. All we can do is help the victims."

She started to protest, caught a sob, brushed a hair

from her brow. A short bitter laugh. "A whim. My god, Evan, you have a way with words."

He heard the music, and realized he had already been aware of it for some time; he just hadn't been listening. And saw the sidewalk in front of the church, the lawn, and all the people. Most of them kids. Costumed and playing, ducking in and out of the brightly lit hall over whose entrance was a huge grinning pumpkin. The pagans and the Christians, he thought as he took a short-cut across the grass, through the oddly spaced apple trees; he wondered if the minister was wearing a costume too.

"You didn't take it far enough," she said then, not thirty feet from the entrance.

"Probably not."

"If you can't stop it now, you can stop it later."

"Yes." He didn't want to hear it.

"To stop the whim, you stop the hunter."

"Yes." Impatiently.

"Evan."

He stopped, turned to face her. "Damnit, Addie, what the hell do you want me to do?"

"What do *you* think?"

That was easy.

Kill the hunter.

A girl's voice then: "Mr. Kendal!"

A quick turn, and he saw the yellow mop wig he'd seen earlier, on their walk. The girl wearing it ran toward him, grinning foolishly, skidding to a halt just before they collided.

"God, Mr. Kendal! I thought it was you!"

Evan felt the struggle to put a smile to his lips. "This," he said to Addie, "is a travesty among women, though she's a pretty nice kid without that disease on her face."

"Mr. Kendal!"

"Sarra, this is Dr. Burwin. A friend from England."

418

Sarra flashed a smile, made to reach for Evan's hand, then pulled back, acutely embarrassed. Her questions—when did you get back? where are you staying?—came too fast for answers, and before he knew it, his smile was real and he struggled not to laugh. She did take his arm then and, with a glance at the door, pulled him away, beneath one of the trees.

"What?" he said. Then he made himself tall, deepened his voice. "A stunt."

She nodded, the wig slipping. "But you can't tell anyone, okay? Corky would kill me."

"Oh lord, not Corky."

"It's okay, really," she said. A look at Addie, and Evan assured her Dr. Burwin knew all about stunts, and how, he understood, they had been banned this year.

"Oh big deal," Sarra said scornfully. A pointed look at the school. "I'm waiting for the signal."

Evan felt the cold return. "Sarra, what are they going to do?"

"Mr. Kendal, you know I can't tell."

He took her shoulders, looked to Addie. "It's important, Sarra. It's very important. Are they in there now?"

"Oh, Mr. Kendal."

The disappointment in her expression, in his name, made him release her and rub his hands nervously against his jacket. "Sarra, look, it's not what—"

She ran away, darting into the hall before he could stop her. Several heads turned in his direction. The music stopped. The noise of the crowd inside drifted through the door.

"Evan."

"Maybe," he said, "I could say there was a fire. Electrical or something. We could get them to file out, nobody would be hurt."

"Evan."

419

"The school." He turned and started toward it. "I'll—"
The low fieldstone wall.
Port Richmond in gold letters.
John Naze to one side, hands at his sides, and watching.

5

"It isn't loaded."
"I know," Greta said, looking down the barrel. The grip was cold. The gun was heavy. She had fired one before, with her father, on the range. "I heard."
Shane's laugh was rueful.
A footstep on the driveway.
She looked over and saw a man. Not quite tall.
"You've got a visitor," she said, holding the gun behind her.
Shane pushed off the steps. "Who are you? My mother's not home."
"That's quite all right, young man," the man said. "I'm just passing through."
He turned and walked away.
Shane and Greta exchanged puzzled glances, then moved over to watch him.
He was gone.
The drive was empty.
Greta aimed the gun at the place he should have been. "Bang," she said.
Shane chuckled.
She aimed it at her forehead. "Life is not worth living, O Hamlet person. Not even a ghost wants our company this foul night."
He laughed.
She pulled the trigger.

Forty

Evan ran.

Addie tried to stop him, but he shook off her grip with a snarled curse.

And ran.

A black convertible stripped with silver lightning raced by as he sprang between two parked cars, and he threw himself against one, rolled, and ran on.

A flash of light beyond the fieldstone, almost too quick to register, and he couldn't be sure but someone stood on the school's lawn.

John didn't move.

Another car, honking wildly, laughter trailing, music blaring.

The band in the hall started up again.

Addie screamed his name.

John began to move sideways.

Evan dared him with a look to run away again, cold and heat, his arms heavy, his legs disconnected, gliding through the night and hearing only the wind that gusted a cloud of leaves out of the gutter and into his face. He batted them away with both hands, and was pummeled by another gust, more powerful, smelling of smoke, that shoved him into the low wall, his hip cracking against it and sending him to his knees.

"John!"

John smiled, yellow teeth, blood-red lips, eyes so hollowed they looked infinitely black.

Evan used one hand to push and pull himself to his feet, took a step and cried out, took another as the pain became its own anesthetic. "John!"

Someone vaulted the low evergreen border and slammed into him, spun him around as he grabbed at him for balance and toppled them both to the sidewalk.

John moved on.

Evan shoved the figure away, swearing, suddenly recognizing the boy and, as he got to his feet, grabbing the boy's coat and yanking him up as well. "Reynolds," he said, "where is Brian?"

Patrick gaped at him; his nose was bleeding, there was a nasty scrape across one cheek.

Evan shook him. "Damnit, Reynolds!"

Patrick pointed.

Corky yanked the blinds up.

Brian called, "Showtime!"

Blue switched on the lights, and they all ran like hell.

Dom rubbed his eyes hastily to clear them, set the rifle to his shoulder, and used the scope to watch the hall, the people, follow with puzzled amusement a wild man running toward the street, ducking between the parked cars and nearly getting himself hit. Running again, then losing him when the wind kicked and shook the weapon.

Shit, he thought, and rubbed his eyes again.

The man was gone. No, there he was, standing up on the other side of the wall.

If everything worked to schedule, Patrick should be in the hall right now, passing the word to a few select people. It was the idiot's idea, a last-minute one coupled with a threat to make an anonymous call to the cops. No more panic than necessary, he'd insisted. Nobody gets hurt.

Dom had had no choice.

What the hell, no kid would tell a grownup anyway. Not right away.

The little prick.

The son of a "Bitch!" he said aloud when Patrick tried to jump over the border and collided with the running man.

"Damn!"

The speakers hissed.

A few people looked his way.

"Damn!"

He aimed at Reynolds, saw the man pick him up, saw them turn, and he pulled away from the scope as if he could see them more clearly on his own.

Son of a bitch, it's Kendal.

He grinned.

Resettled.

The speakers stopped their hissing.

"Out out out! Go! Go! Out!" Brian yelled, not caring if anyone heard him, only wanting to be clear of the building before the first alarm was sounded.

Corky slammed through the back door and held it open for Rita, who barely held it long enough for him before vanishing into the wind. Brian couldn't tell which way they went, but Corky hadn't planned for anything beyond turning on the lights. Just get back to the hall. Let people know there's something odd outside. But make sure they think you'd heard it somewhere else.

By the time he reached the corner of the building, he was already out of breath, less from the swerving sprint on the goddamn stupid boots that were going to break his neck than from a sudden and powerful urge to burst into laughter. It made him stumble, and he careened off the wall, slipped, recovered, and saw the others near the front. When he caught up with them, he saw they had already succumbed—Rita's face was streaked with tears, Corky had the hiccups, Blue was thumping his chest and giggling as if he were a thoroughly stoned Tarzan.

They embraced each other.

They tried to make themselves sober and only made the laughter worse.

"Can't stay here," Corky warned them, stumbling backward, finally falling. "Damn, I forgot my coat."

Blue brayed hysterically.

Rita grabbed Brian's hand and said, "We've got to run."

He nodded.

Corky was on his back, kicking his feet in the air.

"Blue, get him," he said.

Blue gasped, wiped his eyes with the backs of his hands, and picked Ploughman up, slung him easily over one shoulder.

"One, two, three, go?" Rita asked.

"Why not?" he said.

"Go!" shouted Blue, and left the safety of the building, angling sharply toward the fence on the right, keeping in the shadows.

"You're a hell of a date, Oakland," Rita told him.

Brian grinned like an idiot.

And ran.

A sudden deafening shriek of sirens exploded over the street.

Evan shoved Reynolds away and stared at the school, looked back quickly and saw those on the parish lawn frozen, a few with hands over their ears. Addie was at the curb between two cars, her mouth open, one palm to her chest. When he looked back, the sirens stopped, and the hissing he had heard before started again.

Tapes, he thought.

And a deep voice with a hint of echo:

No one move! No one call the police! There are guns all around you! Stay where you are! Port Richmond High School is in our hands and—I said, no one move!

The gunfire began.

Too startled to think, Evan ran for Addie and pulled her down between the cars, pushing her head into his chest, hunching his shoulders.

Someone screamed.

A car started up.

No one move! The next one who moves will be shot where he stands!

"Tape," he said to Addie, feeling her tremble, feeling himself shake. "Listen. It's only a goddamn tape."

The car whined, roared, as it pulled out into the street.

Someone screamed again.

The rock music blared.

Gunfire.

A look over his shoulder, and he saw people rushing into the hall, pushing frantically against those trying to get out. The screaming became contagious, and louder when the car's driver, startled by the sound of the gun, slammed into a van, ricocheted off it and jumped the curb. The rear tires smoked. It caromed off a small tree and slammed into the side exit. The metal door dropped from its hinges.

"Tape," Evan said again, pulling Addie with him to the grass between curb and sidewalk.

The windshield of the nearest car blew in.

"Jesus!" he yelled, and threw himself on the ground, one arm over her back.

The first car exploded.

The music stopped.

No one move!

425

There was screaming.

The dense cloud of smoke from the explosion, white and black and noxious, never made it to the sky. The wind collected it, pushed it down, turned it into a fog as something inside the hall blew up. And something else.

As Evan lay there, eyes tearing, trying to sort the tape from the real, he could see sparks fly from the high windows, something aflame flutter after them.

And the people.

No one move!

Streaming through the door. Some carrying children, others knocking little ones aside.

A tire blew out, and Addie jumped and whimpered.

"C'mon," he said, and pushed up to his knees. To his feet. Taking her with him. "Over there." Pointing with his chin to the spot where he'd last seen his Uncle John. "C'mon, Addie. Let's go."

She made it as far as the second tree before she shook herself hard and sagged against the bole. Her hair streaked over her face like cracks in soiled porcelain, and her eyes were wide and unseeing, or seeing something he couldn't see himself.

"Addie?"

She blinked.

"Addie."

Shouts behind him.

The gunfire.

He saw someone racing across the grass with something clinging to his back. Three steps into the moonlight, and he recognized a football player, and a man in a suit.

The wind gusted, steadied, and he had to shade his eyes, blink them, until he saw, almost directly ahead of him, a cowboy and a gypsy running toward him awkwardly, bending low.

Gunfire.

No one move!

A glaring light in one of the school's windows, and though he realized something was spotlighted there, he couldn't make it out.

The cowboy fell.

The gypsy dropped to her knees beside him and shook him, slapped his hat off, and dragged him back to his feet.

The wail of sirens.

Jesus, he thought angrily, don't they know—

The sirens were real.

The football player tripped when he blundered into the plants, his burden pitching over his shoulder onto the pavement. Evan ran over immediately, grabbed the man in the suit and dragged him to the grass, cursing, and cursing louder when he realized the man was laughing. He knelt and stared. It wasn't a man at all.

"Damnit, Corky! Damn you, this isn't—"

Someone grabbed his hand before he realized he had it raised in a trembling fist. He looked up, saw Blue, and yanked his hand away.

"Not us," Blue pleaded. "Jesus, it wasn't us."

Gunfire.

The wind.

Light flickering gold, flickering orange, flickering red, accentuating all the black; blue lights spinning, staining trees and faces, as a fire truck wheeled into the street behind a patrol car, their sirens clashing, people trotting beside them, shouting, pointing, until the patrol car finally stopped and two policemen leapt out, revolvers drawn. The firemen immediately swarmed from their perches, dragging hose, dragging equipment, and were joined by a second truck headed in from the other direction.

Gunfire.

The police instantly dropped behind their vehicle, one scrambling inside where Evan saw him grab for his mike to radio for help.

Oh Christ, he thought, oh Jesus, oh Christ.

"I swear to god," Blue said, grabbing for his shoulder. "I swear to god, Mr. Kendal, this isn't us."

"Then who the hell is it?"

They turned when they heard a cry and saw the black and silver cowboy trying to lift the gypsy to her feet. She had hold of an ankle, and he was none to steady on his boots.

"Shit, Oakland!" Blue yelled, and sprang to his feet.

Sarra grabbed a tiny fairy princess away from the mob still shoving at the door. She ran, felt her wig slip off, felt the little girl sobbing against her breast.

Someone bumped into her.

She yelped and whirled away, her arm abruptly hurting, her mouth opening in a gasping scream when a man stumbled on, his hair and clothes afire.

A man in shirtsleeves ran out of the dark onto the church lawn, arms up, eyes wide in disbelief.

"Jesus Christ!" Eric Linholm yelled, face dark with rage. "Jesus, what the hell's going on here?"

Gunfire.

He whirled at a muffled explosion in the hall behind him, whirled again and staggered toward the curb when he saw his school through the smoke, saw the light in his office window.

"Goddamnit," he yelled, "if this is some kind of joke . . ."

Dom slapped the roof and whooped.

One more shot, he thought; just one more, then I'm gone.

The wind blinded him.

He waited.

No one move!

He couldn't see shit from apples through all the smoke, and would have probably been out of here long ago if he hadn't seen the driver of that car crawl away on her hands and knees long before it blew up.

Perfect.

People screaming and yelling, no one hurt, and I'm gonna be a fucking legend.

One more shot.

A hand scrubbed his eyes clear, and he saw the man on the curb, yelling, waving his arms, stumbling into the middle of the street.

Oh god, he thought with an hysterical laugh.

Linholm.

Fucking Linholm!

The police car pulled in.

He stood, eyes tearing in the rolling smoke, and braced himself against the wind. It punched him. The rifle wavered. He fired once before running as fast as he could toward the back wall.

Mickie would be waiting.

Jesus, I love it!

Brian had no idea when the laughs became panic, when panic became confusion, when confusion returned to fear.

He had been running, that's all he knew, thinking that this stunt would be the one the others had to measure up to, no question about it. Even if Neeba found out, it would be worth it, all worth it.

Then the unnatural booming voice had stopped him and Rita, turned them around, had them stare at each other, still gasping, laughter dying.

"What?" she asked.

429

"Beats me."

When the shooting began they froze in indecision, started back for the school, changed their minds and ran for the street, the hell with not being seen, get to the wall and hide behind it, that's all they thought.

He fell.

She grabbed him up.

She kicked one of the not quite underground sprinklers and fell, and swore in a scream when he tried to pick her up.

"My foot's broken!" she yelled.

"It is not," he yelled back over the shooting and the sirens, coughing suddenly when the smoke blew into his face. "Get up! I can't carry you!"

She did, and they ran again, hobbling, leaning against each other, and he grinned broadly when a gust parted the smoke and he saw the people on the sidewalk. Blue had jumped the border, was heading toward them; Reynolds was against a tree, holding a hand to his face; Corky was kneeling, his face streaked with dirt; and hot damn, there was Mr. Kendal!

The wind pushed him sideways.

His grip slipped; Rita was gone.

Oh damn, there's Linholm!

The wind pushed him again.

Stupid boots.

And he fell.

Evan ran.

"I didn't know," Shane said.

He couldn't stop crying.

"I didn't know."

A policeman took his arm. "Let's go, son. There's nothing you can do."

On the way to the police car, Shane looked over his shoulder.

"It's so small," he said, childlike, surprised. "The hole is so small."

Blue stumbled when the wind hit him, and Evan reached Brian first, ready to take him by the shoulders, carry him if he had to.

There was blood on the black shirt.

"Addie!"

A drop of blood, quivering at the corner of Brian's mouth.

"Addie!"

Rita stared at him, obviously still trying to believe it was really him.

Addie came, not running.

"Addie!" Anguish so clear it made Rita cry.

When Addie knelt, saw the blood, she said, "Oh damn, poor thing," and he said to Blue, "Get those cops to call another ambulance." Without waiting for a reply he spun into a run that had him on the sidewalk and down the street before anyone could stop him.

There were others running with him.

The first panic had given way to another, and his progress was slowed, making him shoulder around some, push between others, until he moaned in exasperation and darted into the street. Several steps later the gunfire was cut off, the dark abruptly too silent even with the fire, the screaming, the footsteps that matched his as he ran. Into light. Into dark. Forcing one car to swerve out of his way, sideswiping a parked sedan. Slapping around another when it persisted in coming at him. Into dark. Into light. Easy steps now, easy strides, smelling smoke on his clothing, feeling a myriad of small burns on the back of his neck, the backs of his hands, listening to his breathing, hard, pushing, listening to the curses that lined up to be howled.

Swinging left toward Tyler Avenue he remembered the car.

He didn't falter.

He ran on.

A small boy in a cowboy suit sat in a driveway, his bicycle lying beside him, slow-spinning its wheel. He wasn't crying, but there was a cowboy hat on the sidewalk, and his hand was on his stomach.

Evan ran an invisible white line until he reached the main street, paused, checked both directions, wiped his brow with the crook of his arm. Pedestrians stared at him. Many walked quickly in the direction he'd just taken, staring at the sky which, when he looked, had taken an orange glow.

Halloween.

He ran again.

Everything was automatic now—arms, legs, the working of his mouth while he rehearsed the righteous speech he'd give before he murdered his uncle.

Ahead.

There he was, straight ahead.

He slowed and felt the pain.

The man wasn't moving away; he was moving toward him, walking in the street, brushing against parked cars, ignoring a horn, a shout to get the hell on the sidewalk.

"John!"

The man looked up.

Oh Jesus, he thought, and stepped into the street himself.

"How did you get here, Paul?"

Burwin stopped, swayed, leaned against a pickup, finally draped an arm over the bed wall to hold himself up.

The wind took off his hat.

There was nothing left of his face.

He flapped his free arm. "God save British Air, old son," he croaked. "Sunglasses and bandages. Your idea, you know. Claude Rains and all that."

Behind them, a fire truck split the road with its lights as it crossed from black to black.

"I'm going to kill you," Evan said.

"No need," Paul answered. "I'm already dead."

"So are they, you bastard!" and pointed over his shoulder, half-turning him, seeing a cruiser follow the fire truck, seeing a bus pull in at its corner stop. Hissing. Its insides dark.

A noise turned him back.

Paul was slumped, coat open. What was left of his mouth was moving, but Evan could hear nothing but sounds, meaningless sounds. Until Burwin lurched upright.

"On the slopes of Loch Mairen," he sang. Again. Over again. "Do you remember what happened to that poor sod in the village, Evan? Do you remember what happened to the hunter?"

"Who the hell gives a damn?"

He stepped forward.

Paul staggered back, nearly fell until his arm looped through the truck's open driver's window.

Evan glanced into the bed, saw a tire iron and grabbed it. Held it. Felt the cold metal turn hot.

Paul giggled, and something hard and white fell to the street. "He dies."

"Damn right," Evan said.

"Dies of old age in less than a month." He hummed. Giggled. Swayed and reached for the door's handle but his fingers wouldn't take hold. "Oh Christ, Evan."

The first bus passed them, its backwash shoving Evan gently, tips of light like mica glinting on its chrome sides.

"Oh Christ," Paul said again, and stepped in front of the second one.

Evan heard a shout, heard the impact much too soft for something human meeting something so damn large, and when the bus finally halted twice its length later, there was a coat on the street, twisted and torn.

Nothing more.

When the wind finally nudged it, a dead leaf crawled away.

A siren.

Evan walked. Across the street at an angle that took him past the bus. Its driver came toward him, hat pushed back, riders peering out of hastily open windows.

"Scrap it," Evan said as they passed each other, and hit the bus with the iron.

The man yelled, but he kept on walking. No need to hurry, he knew how it would end.

"Hey, lady," a cop said, "you mind moving away?"

"I'm a doctor," Addie told him.

Rita and Blue were in each other's arms.

The cop looked at Brian. "I'll get one of those am—"

"No need," she said. "Find someone who needs it."

Mickie heard him yell, heard him fall.

She wasn't about to run to the stupid hall; she wasn't that dumb. When trouble finally arrived, it was inevitable that it would, she had planned to take a shortcut, past the stands and across the field to the backyards on the other side.

But the noise held her.

It was great; it was exciting; it closed her eyes and let her imagine what Dom would be like. In the hot tub. Tomorrow night.

Then it stopped as if someone had pulled the plug, there was a yell, and a thud.

She watched him lie there for several minutes, leaning toward the end of the building in case she had to call a doctor.

The jackass, she figured, had tripped over the wires.

When he groaned, she relaxed, ran her hands through her hair; when he screamed something about a broken leg, she smiled to herself. They'll find him. He'll be all right. And when she slammed a leg into the edge of one iron support, she cursed, called herself clumsy, and took it slowly, all the way home.

Evan stepped out of the trees, the iron in one hand.

Nothing, he thought, had changed, nothing at all.

The station house was still small, still of dark brick and peaked roof. There were no lights—maybe there never had been—in the high windows arched and pointed at the top, no lights in the parking lot that stood empty behind it. When the wind blew and pushed his collar hard against his neck, the platform roof shifted, and the handful of naked bulbs burning alongside the beams scarcely cast a shadow, barely lit the air beneath them.

He climbed the steps slowly, as if his joints were not working.

The doors to the waiting room were locked.

Shutters had been closed over the barred ticket window, secured by a hook and eye that rattled on occasion.

"John?" Said softly. Almost sadly.

Over the main platform, under the roof and hanging by two thin chains, the Port Richmond sign twisted away from another gust, and succeeded only in swinging, creaking, short bursts of harsh sound that were brittle and without echo.

He saw the chair, saw his uncle, and moved toward him, his heels deliberately loud on the boards, the iron smacking each post once as he passed them. There were no lights left where John Naze sat. He was glad. He had seen enough.

The old man cleared his throat, spat onto the rails.

Evan started, stopped, gripped the iron more tightly.

"Don't bother," said John at last, a shadow nodding toward the weapon.

"I know," he answered. Cautiously, he let himself down to sit on the platform's edge. "You killed some good people, Uncle John."

"Something did." The laugh was a tired wheezing.

Evan rubbed his chin against his shoulder. "John, do you have any idea what's going on?"

Silence.

A cat yowled in the dark.

"Kind of, but I don't have to." A long pause. "It happened." Another pause. "Do you know?"

Evan shrugged. "I think . . . probably."

"Then I guess you know it isn't going to stop when I die. Maybe here, maybe. For a while." John cleared his throat, spat, choked. "Other places . . ."

A long grey cat stepped into the moonlight.

"Hate that son of a bitch," John said.

Evan threw the iron at it, deliberately missing.

The cat jumped to one side, hissed, and ran away.

"Damn," said John softly.

Evan climbed to his feet, zipped his jacket closed. He hated the old man; he loved the old man; he could smell death and dying and wanted to kill the old man.

He turned and walked away.

"You never called, you know," John said to his back.

He didn't look around.

"I wasn't alone, nephew! Damn me, I wasn't alone!"

He almost stopped. Almost.

"We're never going to be alone again!"

He closed his eyes. Didn't stop.

"Goddamn son of a bitch, you never called!"

As he crossed the parking lot, he heard the laughter, the gagging, the laughter rise and fall.

On his way over, he had convinced himself that he had known how it would end. He would sit with John and watch him die, bury him, grieve, then grieve for all the others, with Addie to give him strength. If she would have him. If she had any strength left to give.

But he couldn't stay.

John wasn't going anywhere. Not anymore.

He found the neglected road that would take him back to town, hesitated before stepping on it, then moved as quickly as he could.

He didn't care about having an accident.

Either he would, or he wouldn't.

Later, perhaps, he would renew caution, protect himself, learn to duck again, bob and weave and watch where he was going.

For now, however, for now it didn't matter.

A car jounced toward him, headlights blinding him, but he didn't turn away. He walked on, and the car passed him, turned around and stopped beside him.

It was Addie.

He sat huddled against the door, hunched deep within his jacket.

"I'm sorry about the boy, Ev," she said, her voice barely steady.

He grunted.

She drove.

"I love you, you know," he said when they left the forest behind.

"Thank you," she answered. "I'd love you for that alone."

Then he told her that he needed her, and though she

didn't ask, he told her why. And told her about Paul, what had happened in the street.

Paul and John. More than one. More than one hunter at a time. Could there be three? Four? Were there hundreds out there now, and were those hundreds growing?

"We'll live," she said. "I don't see we have much choice."

He agreed, and held her hand.

People would die whether he was careful or not, whether he tried to warn them or not.

Accidents would happen whether he avoided them or not.

The shadow of the wolf would linger, and move on, and there was nothing he could do about it, not even with the knowing.

Oh Jesus, he thought, and finally felt the real horror.

"Evan? Are you all right? You're trembling, poor thing."

People would die—in plane crashes, in car crashes, in bathtubs, in boats, crossing the street, walking the dog, walking along the sidewalk when a brick or stone falls from a building.

Oh Jesus, they would die.

For no reason at all.